PRAISE FOR **REMNANTS OF A SCARLET FLAME**

"Sell is a new voice that raises the stakes for dragon age fantasy. Remnants *delivers everything I want in a modern day epic: vivid world-building that feels fantastically real, tense political maneuvering, and tender character connections. Simply addictive and hard to forget. I can't wait to see what's next." —M.J. Lindsey*

"Sell's vibrant, epic world sucks you in and never lets go. Alar stole my heart the moment I met him." —Sarah Emmer

"Fantasy at its best. The world and characters of Remnants of a Scarlet Flame *are captivating and complex. This is a binge-worthy read that will take your imagination on an incredible ride." —K.A. Herdt*

"The world-building and in-depth magic system found in Remnants *are awe-inspiring. Sell created an immersive, captivating realm that had me devouring the pages. A true epic fantasy." —E. Rosemary*

"Remnants of a Scarlet Flame *is as enthralling as it is immersive. The intricate world-building, diverse cast of uniquely memorable characters, and heart-pounding stakes are complex and fresh in all the best ways. Sell's debut is epic fantasy at its very best."—Tia Cantrell*

Remnants of a Scarlet Flame

The Last Draegion Saga
Book One

Cindy L. Sell

Aether and Ash Press

Book Cover by Maria Spada

Edited by Emma O'Connell, Ellie Owen, and Erynn Snel

ISBN (paperback): 978-1-963768-02-2

ISBN (hardback): 978-1-963768-01-5

ISBN (ebook): 978-1-963768-00-8

1st edition, September 2024

AUTHOR'S NOTE

The Last Draegion Saga explores dark themes and situations that some readers may find unsettling, including fantasy battle sequences, trauma and abuse, and persecution of a fictional race. While I'm a firm believer in happy endings, those may be hard-won in these books. Please take care of yourself first and foremost.

For content advisories, please visit my website: www.thelastdraegion.com

CONTINENT OF EIDOSINIA
EIDOSINIAN CAPITAL
EIDOSINIAN CITY
ALLIAANSI CITY
NEUTRAL CITY
RUIN
THAUM
YORIGEN'S BLUFF
WURS
Iceborn Territories
MAUTOR
Jaiu River
In'Jasuu
Taaru'Kallii
BRYNN
NORTHLANDS
Mt. Eisekii
ON'IN
STARLIGHT
RU'ISKAAR
AESIN
PENRITH
LIOS'AMA
ZEO'TAARON
Natsa'Kallii
Innixwood
EIGAARE
GIFEVAAR
Marduu
Ru'Natha
KUMA'KIIR
WILLOWMARSH
RAVENSPORT
BLACKRIDGE
FAWN'S BREATH
TRIVVIX
SARTON
Sunrise Creek
Palisadic Mountains
Tinturus River
SUNRISE
EIDOSINIA
Emerald River
CLYSTERNA
BELDEN
Brogrenti
Highlands
Illucidine Tributary
DOVER'S CLIFF
Cintoshi River
Faeflight Mountains
CINTOSH
West
FERID
WATERSGATE
Denorian
Aivenosian
DENORIA
Feridian Bay
RIVERMARSH
Desert
Sea
NOHR
Nohri River
Narisett Bay
RYOST
Falcon River
ORTHOVIA
BRIGHTON
W
E
KEILLIAND
AARILON
S
SAHA
IDANIS
DUERWIST
Kjaltemore
Sea
DUERGUARD
0
100
KJESWUER
LEAGUES
MURENE

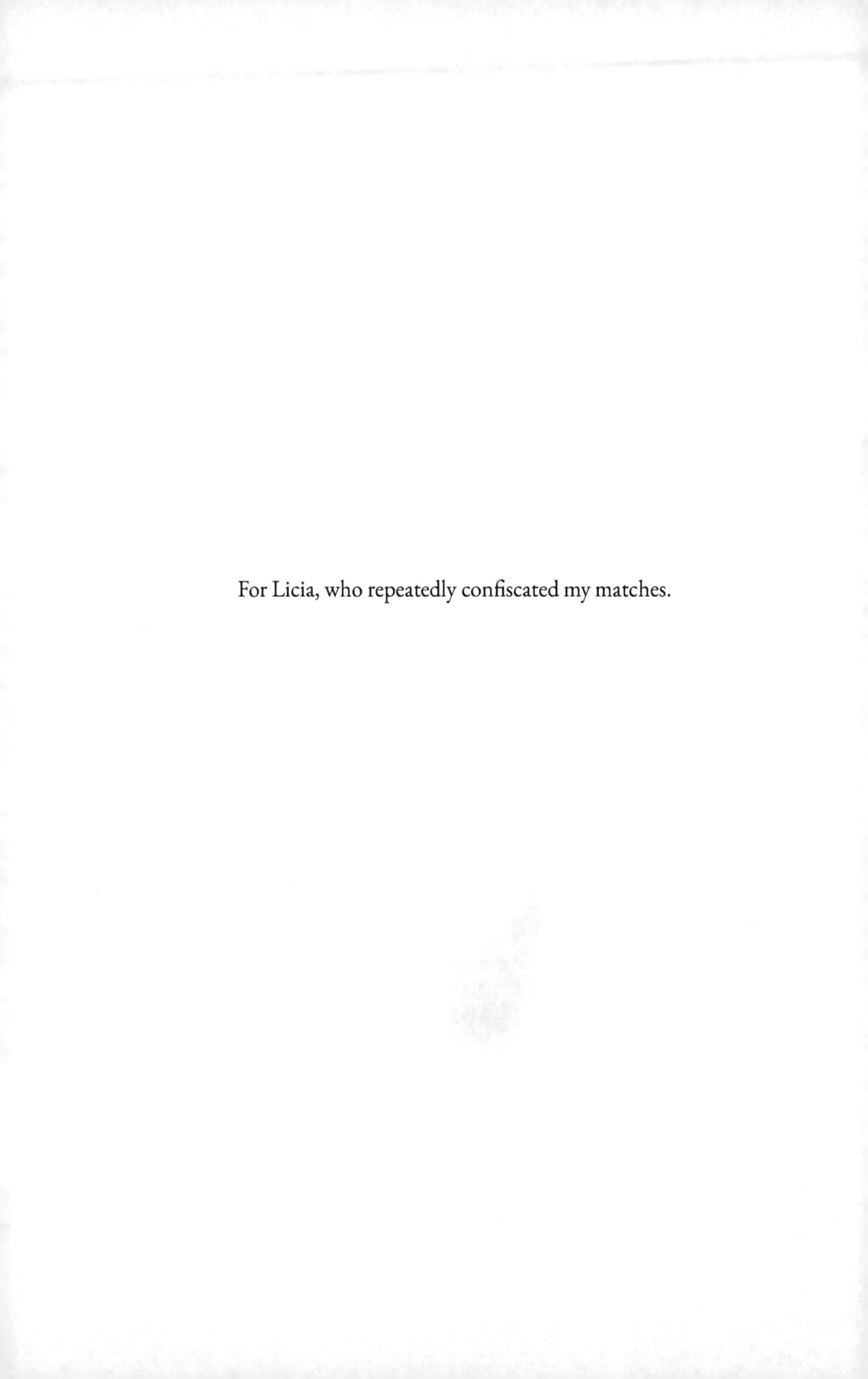

For Licia, who repeatedly confiscated my matches.

SIXTEEN YEARS AGO

NERIMORIA

Nerimoria stumbled through the undergrowth, clutching the baby to her chest.

Roots gnarled the ground with duplicitous intent, pushing her to the limits of her endurance. Thorny clusters bit into the trailing end of the blanket and made prickly nests in her frost-white hair. She dared not slow to pick them out.

Weak morning light filtered through the canopy, though the sky was still overcast from last night's rain. Nerimoria cursed the muddy ground for its treachery; the signs of her passage were stamped clearly in the forest behind her. She tried to step only on rocks, roots, or the rare patch of dry dirt, but there were often long stretches of sodden terrain that left her no choice but to leave a trail. At least the rain masked her scent. She hadn't heard the dogs in over an hour.

Her clothes clung to her lavender skin and chafed at her wounds as if the fabric were made of sand. Removing even one of the damp layers would let the inner ones dry, but if she stopped, she risked losing what little lead she had.

No, she had to keep going. For her daughter's sake, she had to get away.

As she picked her way over roots and rocks, she reached down to check the pouch at her hip. The wardstone was still warm. Good. As long as its magic held, neither the sorcerers' Aethersight nor the Light Paladins' aura tracing could find them.

The baby stirred, letting out a cry.

Nerimoria gritted her teeth. The cry was barely more than a whimper, but it was enough to carry in the cold, quiet air. She swallowed the lump in her throat.

"Shh. It's alright."

Her voice cracked like brittle glass against the lie. Of course it wasn't alright. None of this had been right for years. Not since the Saphyrum War, when greed consumed the sorcerers' leadership, and masterminds took over Syljia, and *everything* went wrong.

Her eyes swept the trees for signs of movement. When she turned back, she stumbled again, the toe of her boot snagging on a stone.

It should have been easy, recovering from that misstep, but her body was too weak from giving birth only a few days before. She fell in a heap, twisting to avoid landing on the baby. Her shoulder took the brunt of the impact, and another rock sliced a jagged trail across her right arm.

The baby screamed, cutting short her own yelp of pain.

Scrambling to sit up in the mud, Nerimoria tore open her tunic and undershirt to press her daughter's mouth against her breast. Her lacerated hand cupped the back of the girl's head, painting a scarlet smear across her tiny crown of white hair.

"Please, *ru'enniia.* It's alright," she repeated. "Everything's going to be alright."

As the newborn rooted, still whimpering, Nerimoria winced and readjusted her daughter's mouth against her nipple. When the frantic little grunts finally settled into desperate suckling, she did another hasty sweep of the trees. No sign of her pursuers. Yet.

So much for staying on the move. The thought might have drawn a bitter laugh from her if she hadn't been so tired.

"You had other plans, didn't you?" she rasped, looking down at the girl.

She shrugged out of her tunic and wrapped it around her waist. After struggling to tie the sleeves in a knot and balance her daughter on her arm, she drew her legs up around the child as if she could protect her from the world. Bowing her head, she prayed to Shavaan for the strength to stand again.

Wetness seeped through the seat of her trousers. Nerimoria shivered. The smell of blood was thick in the air. She shifted just enough to spot the streaks of red between her thighs. Her breath hitched. It wouldn't be long before the dogs caught wind of *that*.

She lifted herself off the cold patch of mud and onto a dry area between two thick roots. Her back came to rest on a tree several times wider than she was. Its enormous trunk curved inward on this side, as if a giant had kicked it hard enough to cave it in. While the baby nursed, she checked the other pouch at her hip.

"Baosanni take me." She only had five beads left. Her body would demand far more before her journey was through. Five beads would get her a few dozen leagues, perhaps, but only if she stayed ahead of the sorcerers. Only if she could avoid casting spells.

As if she *could* cast spells. She felt sicker now than she had moments ago. Sweat slicked her skin and rolled into dozens of stinging cuts. Her empty stomach twisted, threatening to turn itself out on the ground. The world spun, and her ears rang—

No.

Focus.

She took stock of her symptoms, something her brother would have done if he were here. Fever. Dizziness. Nausea. Between rationing her saphyrum beads and casting from them as heavily as she had last night, it was a wonder she hadn't collapsed already. The early signs of Mage's Folly were upon her.

Giving in was not an option. Not yet. She blinked a dozen times and clenched her shaking hands to stay them. Breathing deeply of the cool spring air, she ignored the copper tang of blood and let the scents of wet soil, green moss, and woody decay ground her.

Off in the distance, a dog howled.

Her heart leaped into her throat. The sound came from behind her tree, perhaps a league to the west. They'd found her trail. She cast a furtive glance down at her daughter.

The baby had fallen asleep, thank Mira. Tiny pink fingers rested against Nerimoria's chest; she tucked them beneath the blanket and wrenched her shirt closed. With a hand on the root beside her, she forced herself upright and leaned against the trunk until her legs stopped trembling.

It took three tries to shove herself off the tree, and the effort triggered a violent wave of nausea. Her stomach cramped and blood trickled down her thighs. She stumbled along the forest floor, mud sucking at her boots like it meant to swallow her whole. Truthfully, that would be a better end than the sorcerers had planned for her.

More ancient trees stood around her like sentinels keeping vigil. Some of their great limbs were already thick with leaves, while others bore large white flowers whose fragrant petals littered the ground like snow. She was careful not to disturb them, silently praying to Caelyn that the heady aroma might disguise her passage. Even better, that she might come upon a stream she could use to break the trail.

Would that I could Rift Bend at a time like this.

The clouds broke open and light poured through the canopy, revealing a gap in the brush ahead. She shuffled toward it. The howling was closer now, but she still had a chance. She could move faster over terrain that wasn't riddled with roots and weeds. Ignoring the accompanying thought that the dogs could do the same, she let her world narrow to that gap in the trees.

Her knees struck the ground when she finally reached it, lungs heaving, her body drenched in fever sweat. She kept one arm locked around the baby, using her other hand to keep herself from collapsing. It was all she could do to lift her head.

The gap opened onto a modest plot of farmland stretched over a sloping valley. A shallow brook cut through the land from northeast to southwest. A wooden bridge arched over the banks, some fifty spans from a one-story farmhouse, and an old stable stood up the rise, its weather-worn door open to the morning air.

Tears sprang to her eyes at the sight of the brook, but a wide-open patch of freshly turned mud lay in front of her. It would be slow going, even more so than her trek through the forest. Worse, smoke twirled out of the farmhouse chimney, and if anyone unfriendly toward Syljians spotted her, she was as good as dead.

She surveyed the rest of the valley. The forest stood close on every side. Spindly trees and evergreen bushes marched into the pasture as if in staunch defiance of the farmer's attempts to tame the land. The overgrowth could provide some cover, and if she circled around to the place where the brook emerged from the forest, she could travel upstream before returning east.

Alternatively, she could traverse the southern perimeter. It was a shorter path to the water, but the stream likely drained into the Falcon River. Following it for any amount of time would take her back toward the capital and the Sorcerers' Guild. No, it was best not to turn south again until she was well away from Ryost.

She attempted to rise, but the trees spun around her so fast that she dropped back to her knees. More wetness flowed from between her legs. Only the weight of the infant on her arm steadied her. That little face. The shock of white-blonde hair. Thin white eyebrows. Pink cheeks, not lavender. Perfectly rounded ears, like her father's.

Get up. Get up!

Nerimoria was on her feet and moving, but she couldn't remember standing. North. She went north, then east, around the clearing—

The sound of a dog barking shattered the quiet forest.

She cried out and threw herself to the ground, covering the infant as the shaggy beast burst from the trees. *Stupid*. Why hadn't she run?

As she curled around the baby and braced for the rending bite of vicious teeth, something warm and wet slopped along the side of her cheek. Raspy, eager panting filled her ears. She dared to turn her head to the side, and the dog's tongue lolled out, slavering all over her mouth and nose.

A shaggy dog. Red fur, flecked with brown. Not one of the Guild's sleek, black tracking hounds. Still huddled in a heap on the ground, Nerimoria did her best to muffle a cry that was equal parts relief and hysteria.

The dog's excitable circling didn't disguise the approach of footsteps. "Here, now! Here! Will, leave off now!"

Mira's mercy. She kept her head down, curling tighter into a ball while the dog danced around her, sniffing, not at all mindful of its master's summons. She couldn't reach the pouch with her saphyrum, but she could reach the star pendant with its single bead around her neck. Her fingers closed on it as she readied to defend herself.

"Give her some space, ye damnable mutt. Here!" The man spoke so fast, she could barely identify the language as Eidosinian.

Finally, the dog leaped away, and footfalls shook the ground. Nerimoria's hand tightened on the pendant, her heart racing. She tried to channel its power, tried to summon Aether, but couldn't. Mage's Folly held her firmly in its grasp. The baby beneath her began to cry.

"Well, ye're the biggest rabbit ol' Will's ever flushed. Are ye alright, lass?" A hand brushed her shoulder, trying to coax her out of her crouch.

Her breath came in labored gasps. Darkness crept into her vision. Her world spun again, and she was suddenly blinking up at a clear patch of morning sky. The young man looked down at her, then toward the baby, his bushy red eyebrows pinched with concern.

Concern.

Gods be good.

He hadn't shied from her, despite the obvious. Her lavender skin, her white hair, her tapered ears. He didn't seem frightened of her at all.

Yes, because I'm so terrifying right now.

Nerimoria tried to move her arms, then her legs, but they refused to obey. The baby still cried, and her heart lurched.

"Please," she attempted in her clearest Eidosinian. "My daughter."

"Aye, the little lass looks hungry." The man's green eyes were set in a friendly, square face and framed by a windswept tangle of red curls. He set his bearded jaw. "But ye don't look like ye've had much to eat yerself. Ye'll come back to the farm with me." As if expecting her to protest, he lifted a string of rabbit carcasses. "We've got plenty to go around. My Ali—she won't mind."

He slung the rabbits over his shoulder and reached down to gather the baby. She looked so small in his enormous hands. He placed the child on Nerimoria's chest and helped cross her arms over the blanket. Then he looked down at the rest of her with a wince. "Ye been runnin' a while, haven't ye?"

"They were nearly on top of us last night." She had nothing left to lose by telling him the truth. If the Guild discovered him aiding her, he'd be strung up right beside her. "I don't want to bring you trouble."

He scoffed, reaching down to scoop an arm under her shoulders. His other arm slid beneath her knees. "Don't worry about that. Best save yer strength, ye *kinnich.*"

As he hoisted her up, more howling carried toward them on the wind. He stiffened, and she followed his gaze to the west. They were close. Too close. Her heart fluttered. She should go on. Draw them off. Then she could circle back—

"I'm Angus, by the way."

"Neri."

Angus started for the farm. "Ye're a long way from the border, Neri."

She tried to snort, but the sound came out more like a sniffle. She'd been thrown so far off-course. "I know."

"Ach, nothing for it, I suppose. We'll take good care of ye and the little one. There's plenty of room for ye until ye feel well again."

Nerimoria stilled in Angus's arms, a calm, dreamlike sensation settling over her. Her heartbeat slowed. She might have drifted off.

Angus was still chatting away, his tone growing wistful. "Ali and me, we just lost one of our own a few days past..."

There was something she needed to tell him. The child. Something about the child. She blinked, trying to remember.

He sniffled. "I reckon she can help with the feedin' if—"

Reaching up an ashen hand, Nerimoria touched his lips. "She is special."

"Well, I—" Angus paused, brow wrinkling.

She pressed harder with her fingertips. "He'll be coming for her. She must be ready."

"Ready for what, lass?" His bewilderment didn't abate. "Who's coming?"

She breathed in, then out. Her hand fell like an autumn leaf onto the baby's back. Focusing on the warmth of her daughter's body, the tiny heart beating in her chest, Nerimoria let her eyes close. That dreamlike state claimed her once more.

"Chaos."

Chapter One

Alar

Alar ducked into the shadow of an alcove, the hastily scrawled message crumpled in his hand.

Tension knotted his shoulder blades, and his teeth clenched to stifle a groan. Other students shuffled along the corridor, paying no mind to him, but the one person he needed to avoid most sat a dozen paces away, absently twisting a white-blonde curl around her finger.

Daeya McVen lounged on a sofa made for straight spines, dusty boots kicked up on a low table. She seemed distracted enough by the tattered book in her lap, but if Alar's mentor caught him sneaking across the second-floor landing and away from his first class, she would have questions. While he often enjoyed their verbal sparring matches, today was not the day for one.

His body itched for motion. The spymaster would only wait so long. Roughly fifty paces separated Alar from the gold-inlaid staircase; he could make it in the span of a dozen breaths.

Stuffing the note in his pocket, he sidled into the stream of blue-and-gray-robed students, his own gray robe snapping at his ankles. The fresh assassin's clay disguising his tapered ears weighed with every step. He swung wide of the sitting area and clung to the mural-bedecked walls, skin tingling as if he could sense Daeya watching him. A ridiculous thought, of course; his psionic skill set didn't include such perception.

Six paces to the stairs. Four, then two. He reached for the handrail, at last allowing the tension in his back to ease—

"Hey Faustus, wait up!"

Cursed Wastelands.

His fingers wilted against the railing. No matter how urgent Val's summons was, Alar couldn't compromise his alias. Initiate Faustus Crex was a Guild-loyal magic adept who adored Daeya, despite her problematic views on authority. He would have never bolted down the stairs and out the front entrance before she could reach him. As tempting as the idea was, Faustus was the linchpin for Alar's mission, and thousands of people depended on his continued success.

Limbs heavy with resignation, he turned and forced a smile. She closed her book, gathered her pack, and rushed to join him.

"Good morning, Daeya."

"Morning." Light filtered through the stairwell's enormous stained-glass windows, painting her pale cheeks in shades of lavender and blue. It was hard to cling to his annoyance faced with those mirthful green eyes. "You going to commissary?"

Alar shook himself. She was a senior acolyte in the Sorcerers' Guild, not his friend. "I am," he said, taking the easy explanation in stride.

"Great. Me too."

He sincerely doubted that—she never met him before class on Mirasdays—but pointing out the novelty meant prolonging their encounter. Whatever she was up to would have to wait. Alar started down the stairs, saying nothing.

Daeya nudged him with her shoulder, that irritating, endearing, ever-present bounce in her step. "So, did you hear the news?"

He suppressed a sigh. "What news?"

She lowered her voice as a pair of senior acolytes passed them on the stairs. "There's going to be an execution tomorrow."

Alar glanced at her, brows tensing. He'd spent the last eleven months familiarizing himself with the capital, with eight of those months enrolled in the School of High Sorcery. Still, there were nuances of Ryost's city culture he wasn't well-versed in. "Is that unusual?"

Daeya's nose wrinkled. "Have you been blanked? Of course it's unusual." She rummaged around in her blue, black-trimmed robe and pulled out two oranges. "Want one?"

What he wanted was to extract himself from this conversation and get to Morgan's Inn and back before his first class started. "Sure."

They reached the ground floor, and Daeya's gaze darted around the sun-speckled rotunda as if searching for eavesdroppers. Alar quenched his irritation with a slow, deliberate breath. How and where Daeya got her intel was often suspect, but it was almost always good.

The rotunda was relatively quiet this morning. Its great expanse nestled in the middle of the three Sorcerers' Towers and served as the nexus for the eastern administrative wing, the west wing housing the School of High Sorcery, and the north wing with its libraries and dormitories. Mosaic floors, gem-encrusted tapestries, and gleaming stone arches bespoke the Guild's opulent wealth. All five stories and a dozen curving staircases were visible from balconies encircling the foyer.

The space still made his gut twist. How easy it was for them to bask in such luxury while his people scraped out an existence in the frigid Northlands.

Daeya ripped the skin off her orange, nodded politely to a passing instructor, and dropped the peel into a nearby vase. "There hasn't been an execution like this since I was twelve." With another nudge, she steered Alar toward the east wing and the commissary. "Rumor has it, it's an aethermancer."

His wide eyes snapped back to her. "An aethermancer? In Ryost?" Was that why Val's message had been so urgent?

"And not just any aethermancer." She leaned in conspiratorially. "I heard it's Cheralach himself."

"That's—" *Impossible*. A stone lodged in his chest. Alar floundered, trying to think of something Faustus would say. "That is big news. Where did you hear such a thing?" And what was Cheralach doing outside of Starlight?

One white eyebrow lifted. "I have my sources." She shook her head and laughed. "It's crazy, isn't it? To be that legendary, only to wind up at the end of a rope. It's almost sacrilege."

They entered the sunny east wing corridor. Another group of students passed by, carrying sacks of saphyrum and wearing the solid blue robes of junior acolytes. Alar usually noted the way they glared at Daeya—who was easily four years their junior and yet a rank higher—but if something had happened to Cheralach, he couldn't concern himself with the politics of Guild rank right now. He needed to get to Val.

The commissary was right around the corner, past the switchback staircase. He should stock up on saphyrum after all, just in case. In the meantime, Daeya continued the conversation without him in her usual rambling way.

"Do you think the Alliaansi are as scary as the Guild makes them seem?"

Alar stopped walking. *That* was not a normal thing for a sorceress to say.

She paused too and spun to face him, a familiar air of mischief about her—the same mischief that had nearly gotten her expelled from the School at least once before. If not for Councilor Gregory, Daeya would have faced over a dozen disciplinary actions in the last eight months alone. The last thing Alar needed—the last thing *Faustus* needed—was to be drawn into one of her schemes.

He leveled his sternest expression on her. "Daeya, it's not our place to question the Guild."

Her eyes glittered. "Isn't it?"

"The Alliaansi are made up of cutthroats, deserters, and Syljians." Alar poured all the incredulity he could muster into the words. "You don't want to get mixed up with them."

More students and a few instructors trickled past as they stood there, staring each other down. Sunlight cast her features in stark relief, lending a physical edge to the remark poised on her lips. But a real friendship was rare for the Guild's child prodigy, and she was more likely to sheathe her cutting wit than slice Faustus open with it.

Still, his argument didn't entirely sway her. As she resumed course, she muttered, "I'm going to meet one someday."

Alar couldn't help but smirk. "I wouldn't advise it."

The tension between them broke, and Daeya grinned again. "And what better opportunity than—"

A sorcerer stepped out of the stairwell. His black robe billowed behind him like a cloud of ill omens, and he stopped so abruptly in front of Daeya that she ran into him.

"Bleeding Aether, Normos! Watch where you're going." Under her breath, she added, "Gods-damned creep."

There was a time when Alar would have feigned surprise at his mentor's disrespect toward mages of higher rank. That time had passed. Still, he braced himself.

Normos was in his mid-twenties, not much older than Alar, with the sleek and deadly grace of a viper and a temperament to match. Watching him spar with the other sorcerers, it was no wonder he had become Councilor Gregory's right hand. However, his place at Gregory's side was tenuous at best. Once Daeya earned her black robe—the next step for her in the Guild hierarchy—there were rumors Normos would be replaced.

The sorcerer stepped in close, forcing Daeya to crane her neck to meet his icy stare. Slick blond hair accentuated prominent cheekbones and a cleanly shaven jaw. Though Normos appeared calm, Alar's aura-sense picked up the deep-seated rage shimmering around him like heat from sunbaked stone.

Curiosity piqued, Alar lamented the wards protecting Normos from deeper psionic probing. For most mages, such wards were exceedingly dangerous to construct, but all of Gregory's strongest sorcerers possessed them. There were techniques Alar could use to break a psionic ward, but such a move might reveal him, and exposure wasn't an option.

"Senior Acolyte McVen," Normos said, his voice dripping sickly sweet honey, "the Councilor wants to see you."

Daeya stiffened. Out of habit, Alar searched for her aura, but his ability to read her was, as always, nonexistent. In addition to her unnatural skill, she somehow resisted his mental touch without discernible wards. Her immunity extended far beyond that of any other psionics-resistant mages, whose auras were at least visible to him. Despite the long days and nights spent with her, he hadn't figured out why.

"Tell him I'll be right there." Daeya drew herself up, all seriousness now. She turned, opening her mouth to excuse herself.

Normos gripped her shoulder with one manicured hand. "Now, McVen."

A dark look stole across her face, and she shrugged him off. "Don't bleeding touch me."

Alar didn't have time for this. He stepped between them and offered Daeya a dismissive nod. "I'll see you later."

Then inspiration struck. Having Daeya's saphyrum on hand would be useful if Val had to bring in other aethermancers to deal with Cheralach. She would never notice if a few beads went missing. "Would you like me to collect your saphyrum for you?"

After a wary look in Normos's direction, Daeya slipped a hand into her robe. "Please." When she pressed her commissary coin into his palm, a spark of her prior humor flared. "By the way, you might stay away from Transmutations today. It seems someone released Master Terschill's experiment last night, and it made a mess all over the lab."

Normos bristled.

Alar could hold back his laughter, but he couldn't help the tightening in his cheeks. "How unfortunate."

Daeya started for the stairs, white-blonde brows pinched with exaggerated disapproval. "I can't imagine who would do such a thing."

Normos fell in behind her, scowling. Alar stepped into the space he left to watch them go. Daeya turned at the switchback and winked at him. Then she bounded up to the second floor and disappeared.

He stood there a moment, drumming fingers against his satchel strap. Had their circumstances been different, Alar liked to think they could have been friends. Perhaps if she'd been born in the north, where the Alliaansi had a stronger foothold. Perhaps if her talent hadn't been discovered by the Guild so soon.

He lingered on what she'd said, the spark of rebellion in her eyes, but it was only a fool's hope. Her willingness to challenge the reigning authority in Eidosinia was just a product of her youth. If he presented her with the opportunity, she wouldn't take it.

And if she learned what he was, she was duty-bound to kill him.

Alar joined the short line at commissary and glanced down at the orange Daeya had given him. His stomach grumbled, and with the slightest upturning of his lips, he began to peel it.

Having something in his hands staved off a fraction of his anxiety. Val would forgive the delay for extra saphyrum; they couldn't afford to snub a chance to pilfer more of the arcane metal. Fortunately, the line moved swiftly, and Alar dropped half the orange in his pocket when the stout Cintoshi attendant waved him forward.

Two gold teeth glinted beneath Linnar's braided mustache. "Good morning, Faustus."

"Good morning, Linnar." Alar placed a copper commissary coin on the polished marble.

Linnar claimed the coin in a meaty palm. "Just saphyrum today?" His lips moved as if they worked hard to hold up his enormous brown beard.

"Just saphyrum."

Linnar spun in his seat and reached for the wall full of pre-portioned bags, his short legs swinging into space. "How are your classes treating you, boy? Getting along better?"

"Yes, much better, thank you." In the beginning, Alar had opted to lower the instructors' expectations of him by shooting for just under average. But when Daeya insisted they begin nightly tutoring sessions to address his weaknesses, he'd been forced to show more initiative. Though others might disagree, he'd found her to be a remarkable mentor. If he'd really been an arcanist, capable of casting spells or manipulating elements, he would have excelled under her guidance. "Though Divinations is still giving me trouble."

A gray bag thumped against the counter. "You have Master Ulrich?"

"I do."

Those gold teeth flashed again. "Well, that explains everything. Don't worry, lad. Her exams still inspire nightmares in the lot of us."

Alar didn't have to feign his pained expression. Divination should have been an easy subject for a psionist—or a mastermind-in-training, as Val liked to joke.

He could influence others' thoughts and accurately predict events, but Ulrich emphasized the details of spellcasting over results. His psionic illusions and facsimiles of spells could only go so far.

"I failed the first two," Alar admitted, "but my tutor has been helping me." He made a show of starting and dug out Daeya's silver coin. "Speaking of, she asked me if I could pick up her saphyrum, too."

"Sure." Linnar hesitated. "I just need to see an instructor's permission slip."

Alar let himself shrink and fumbled with his pack strap before pouring a healthy dose of sheepish innocence into his voice. "I don't have one."

The displeasure on Linnar's face took a full three seconds to coalesce amidst all his deep wrinkles. He lifted one bushy eyebrow. "Now, I know you're still fresh blood around here, boy, but Daeya knows better than that."

It might have slipped Daeya's mind, but it hadn't slipped Alar's. Lower-ranking students couldn't turn in higher ranks' commissary coins without prior approval. It was one of many measures put in place to keep students from illegally selling saphyrum. But with the right pressure applied in the right place, Linnar would let it slide. "She was going to pick it up herself, but Sorcerer Beck called her away to meet with her Councilor."

"What did she do this time?"

Alar shrugged, the itch along his spine not entirely feigned. "I'm not sure."

Someone huffed an exasperated sigh behind him. "She's going to get herself expelled."

Junior Instructor Rizzy Tallion's frown was so well-practiced, it left permanent lines flanking his mouth. The skinny, wild-haired human was the last remaining in the commissary line, and he stood holding the strap of a straining pack over one shoulder. He didn't look like much beneath his gold robe, but the Illusions instructor was fast-tracked to take his father Freddick Tallion's seat on the Sorcerers' Council in a few years.

Linnar huffed his agreement. "After that stunt she pulled in Master Keph's lecture hall, I was sure they'd toss her out."

Alar attempted his best impression of a rabbit caught in a trap. He'd heard about the djinni Daeya supposedly summoned during Master Keph's lecture on the theoretical existence of Aetherial beings. Keph's reaction to the harmless prank revealed how cowardly he was in front of over two hundred students.

Rather than keeping a level head and seeing through the illusion, he'd panicked and nearly trampled two of his junior instructors on his way off the stage.

Indeed, the prank almost cost Daeya her place in the School. According to the more reliable cafeteria gossip, Councilor Gregory had transferred Master Keph to a satellite school in Orthovia to keep his prized student close.

"That wasn't even the worst of them this year." Rizzy tipped his chin toward Alar. "Do yourself a favor, Initiate. Ask for a mentorship transfer as soon as you can."

Reaching for his bag of saphyrum, Alar nodded. "I'll keep that in mind, Instructor."

He spared another look at Daeya's silver coin on the counter. With Councilor Tallion's son breathing down their necks, convincing Linnar to break the rules would be harder, but Alar was willing to gamble. His people depended on saphyrum for their very survival, and the Guild consumed it like a child left alone with Aivenosian hard candy.

Besides, not only was Linnar impressionable, but Rizzy also had a secret soft spot for Daeya. More than once, Alar had found her in Rizzy's lecture hall after class, sitting cross-legged on a desk while he explained an advanced spellcasting concept.

Alar held his dispirited look and shifted his gaze to Linnar.

The Cintoshi leaned back in his chair. "Now, lad..." he began, glancing furtively at Rizzy.

Using his aura-sense, Alar studied the instructor in his periphery. Unease flickered about Rizzy's body like a guttering candle flame. Alar reached out to him with his mind, stroking the man's consciousness with a feather-light touch. In lieu of wards, many mages underwent specialized training to recognize and resist psionics, but Rizzy either wasn't one of them, or he was especially bad at it. He didn't notice Alar's subtle intrusion.

As if dipping his feet into a fast-moving stream, it took Alar a moment to find his balance in the flow of the sorcerer's thoughts. He kept Rizzy in his line of sight all the while, alert for signs of discomfort. The jumble of Rizzy's mind was an abstraction right now, but given enough time and practice, Alar would be able to decipher and manipulate it as well as any mastermind. For now, he had to settle for implanting thoughts of his own in Rizzy's head.

He pressed gently into the stream and whispered telepathically, *Faustus is a trustworthy sort.*

Rizzy's aura quieted to little more than a ripple in a pond. His furrowed brows smoothed over, and the thin line of tension in his lips receded.

Keeping his psionic pressure steady, Alar projected his own self-confidence into Rizzy. *He'll make certain McVen doesn't have an excuse for missing another exam.*

Straight-backed as a Councilor, Rizzy stepped forward and slid Daeya's coin toward Linnar. He placed his own gold coin next to it. "Saphyrum for myself and my student, please."

Eyes narrowing in triumph, Alar dipped his chin to disguise the look as gratitude.

Linnar's face sagged with relief as he exchanged both coins. This time, the bags he placed on the counter were larger than Alar's—one blue, one gold.

Rizzy turned to Alar. "I know you are a trustworthy sort, Initiate Crex. Deliver this to Senior Acolyte McVen, please."

"Of course, Instructor." Alar accepted the bag and bowed dutifully. "Thank you."

Rizzy didn't bother to smile back. "She has an exam in my class tomorrow. I expect her to be prepared. No excuses."

"I'll make certain she gets the message."

He bade Rizzy and Linnar farewell and hurried off toward his first class.

Once he was out of sight, he circled back to a side entrance and slipped out the door. After scanning the alley for stray eyes, he stripped off his Guild robe to reveal the commoner's attire beneath it. He shoved the robe in his pack atop the two bags of saphyrum, checked the alley again, and started toward the cobbled street.

Brown leggings and a beige tunic allowed him to blend in with the foot traffic. Early autumn air hung thick with the smells of freshly baked goods, dozens of perfumes, tanned leather, and the musky scent of livestock. Carts of all kinds rumbled through the cobbled market streets. Carriages, too, crowded the roadway, bedecked with velvet curtains and metal scrollwork, their teams of horses driven by coachmen in expertly tailored suits. Every now and then, a young pickpocket moved like a specter through the crowds.

Alar scoffed to himself. Ryost might be the largest and wealthiest city in Eidosinia, but even the shiniest copper had its share of blemishes.

Over a dozen of Laerin's crew—the ragtag group of smugglers Val enlisted to run their saphyrum caches—loitered about the trade district today. Their attention slid off Alar like oiled pigskin. One of them signed in a secret code to another, who signaled to a third farther down the road. Their silent message traveled swiftly, and it would soon alert Val he was coming.

It was odd to see so many thieves clustered near Guild Center. Normally, Laerin cast a wider net. Prickling unease skittered across Alar's skin as he reached out with his mind toward a boy in a steward's uniform, then a red-haired woman, and a middle-aged man at a fruit stand.

His breath caught. Something *had* happened.

Evidence of Daeya's news saturated their auras. Those flickering distortions of the surrounding air somehow made the situation more real. The collective hum of anxiety rattled straight to his bones. And if the smugglers were worried, they should all be worried.

Alar forced himself to maintain a steady pace. Sprinting through the city like a wounded deer would only draw attention. Out of the trade district, past the lofty steeples of the Church of the Enlightened, far from the high-born mansions of the Noblemen's Court, and across the Falcon River Bridge he went.

All the while, an icy hand of dread threatened to close around his heart.

Chapter Two

Ravlok

By the time Ravlok finished reading the last page of Grandulli Bornen's philosophical dissertation, *The Theory of Arcane Appropriation*, the morning sun was filtering into the restricted archives of the School's library. He leaned back in his chair, muscles stiff from sitting all night, and stretched his arms above his head. Pops echoed through the empty room, and relief flooded him. The nagging pain along his spine settled to a dull, ignorable ache.

His thick-knuckled hands sifted through ear-length black hair. There was something to be said for Bornen; he knew how to make the mysteries of the arcane duller than a blunted butter knife. Yet Ravlok could see why the Guild censored his work. The Cintoshi professor had written over twenty papers about non-adepts and their connection to magic. Bornen believed all beings possessed some ability to harness the gift of the gods—the Aether, as some called it—whether it was through the use of saphyrum or some other means yet to be discovered. With enough practice and patience, Bornen proposed it was possible to strengthen that ability, like conditioning the body's muscles, to rival the skills of Guild initiates and possibly even acolytes.

If that were true, then it was possible to restore the balance of power between the Sorcerers' Guild and the people it had once promised to serve.

Bornen's assertions also vilified the Council's prohibition of formal teaching of the arcane outside Guild establishments and the Church. Though the Guild backed the decree with a sound argument of safety for those dabbling in dangerous arts, the penalties for violating the decree were much too steep: imprisonment, or even death.

It was just one of a dozen decrees that had made Ravlok nervous recently.

As a member of the Monastic Order of Ordeolas, Ravlok strived to embody the teachings of his deity, but he often found himself at odds with the elders on their interpretations of Ordeolas's will. They all clung to the Book of Order and meditated on the importance of attaining Balance, but they no longer tried to maintain order when things actually fell out of balance in the rest of the world.

With the growing strength of the Guild, its chokehold on all things arcane, and an acute state of fear and unrest among the populace, things had certainly fallen out of balance. This was what brought Ravlok here to the Guild library, rather than the reflection pool. The lackadaisical way his mentor, Yonfé, brushed aside his concerns troubled him. Yonfé didn't tell him to seek fulfillment by performing a kind deed for a stranger. He didn't suggest Ravlok ease his mind by reading to the children in the orphanage. He didn't even hint at discussing his concerns with someone more equipped to address them. His only advice was that he stop running around with Guild acolytes and remain in the monastery where he belonged.

At least here, he had a shot at finding answers.

He looked around the sunlit rows of dusty old texts, idly fingering the key Master Riddleston had entrusted to him. The Guild's librarian had gotten so used to Ravlok's late-night study sessions that he'd provided him with twenty-four-hour access just so he could get some sleep. Riddle's only request was that Ravlok lock up when he left—and, of course, that he stay out of the restricted archives. The last was only a formality, however. Wise old Master Riddle didn't really expect him to heed that directive. How could he, with such a vast wealth of censored knowledge behind an easily defeated lock on an alluring wooden door?

With the ache in his back nearly gone, Ravlok winced at the telling pain in his stomach. He pulled out the orange his study partner had left for him and peeled it. Daeya had helped him track down four of the Bornen essays last night. Even if she didn't have any interest in the subject, the senior acolyte enjoyed poking through the restricted texts with him, mostly for the sake of breaking rules.

A door opened somewhere off in the stacks, jolting Ravlok from his thoughts. He listened closely as he slipped the orange peel into his pocket. It must be Riddle coming in a little early to prepare for the last-minute crammers that wrecked the space before midterms.

He rose from his chair, carefully lifting it so the feet didn't squeal on the floor. The librarian's desk was sheltered from view in several places throughout the library. If he could reach one of those places, he could pretend to study a more mundane text for a while before departing.

As he replaced the chair and gathered the essays from the table, the echo of footsteps carried into the room.

Odes of Ordeolas. It wasn't Riddle's shuffled gait interspersed with the tap-tapping of a walking cane. Whoever it was strode purposefully across the library's polished tile.

And they were heading right for him.

The penalty for unauthorized access to the restricted archives was normally a temporary ban from the Guild library, but Ravlok had a history of causing trouble. If the wrong person found him here, he could just as well be imprisoned, and he had no intention of going back to jail.

There was a second entrance to this room, up the narrow stairs to his left. The door at the top led to a hallway in the north wing, between the restricted archives and several little-used mages' rooms. Ten-to-one odds it was locked, but the alcove beside it was dark enough that if he couldn't pick the lock, he would at least find shelter in the shadows. He started that way, only to freeze at the sound of keys rattling against the knob from the outside.

Damn.

No one ever used that entrance. And this time, Daeya wasn't here to save him. With the essays bundled in his arms, he darted down the nearest aisle and pressed himself against the end cap.

Both doors swung open within seconds of each other. From his vantage point, he could see neither entrance, nor the figures passing through them.

"Have you made any progress?" came a male voice. The deep, rolling 'r's, aspirated consonants, and gently emphasized vowels made Ravlok stiffen. Lucius Gregory's Duerwisti accent was unmistakable. Daeya's mentor was the last person Ravlok wanted to encounter here.

The second voice rang with frustration. "We've gotten nothing out of him, Councilor. It's like his will is made of steel."

"He's spent years with the blanker filth," Gregory said. "He's undoubtedly learned some of their tricks."

Ravlok glanced around the corner, trying to glimpse the second speaker. Too many scrolls and stacks of parchment were piled up between them. He leaned over to peer through a gap, only to have that view blocked by the corner of another aisle. Leaning farther still, he caught sight of a deep brown cloak just as the middle pages of the essays in his hands slipped. With a jolt of panic, he made a grab for them, gritting his teeth.

He froze, his grip death-white on the wayward stack of paper. Too much noise. Way too much noise. This was no time to be juggling censored parchment. Ravlok's heart hammered in his throat.

"Well, what should we do?"

The men's conversation continued. Neither gave any sign they had heard him. With a centering, meditative breath, Ravlok pressed his back against the end cap once more and contented himself with examining the wall in front of him.

"I suspect he will bend if we break someone he loves," Gregory mused. "Torture the others, one by one, until you find one that makes an impression on him. Once he tells us what we need, kill them all."

Ravlok's eyes widened. The Guild Council had outlawed torture years ago, and an execution without trial violated the most basic of citizens' rights. Turning one ear toward the men, he strained to hear the second man's reply.

"Don't you want to execute them publicly, Councilor?"

"No. They will have allies coming for them. We cannot risk an escape, no matter how unlikely they are to succeed."

"Yes, Councilor."

"Tighten your security at the bridge gate and prepare your men. I suspect the Alliaansi's rescue attempt will be underway by mid-afternoon."

"Understood."

The anxiety in the second man's voice was tangible. Apparently, the thought of facing a team of angry aethermancers and Syljians could put the fear of Chaos in even Gregory's men. The man's steps quickened as he attempted to flee the room.

"And Nicolas?"

The footsteps stopped. "Y-yes, Councilor?"

Gregory spoke softly, but the threat behind his words was plain. "I know you enjoy your duties, but there can be no mistakes this time."

"Of course, Councilor. On my honor."

Ravlok took a risk and peered around the other side of the end cap. Another flash of that brown cloak, oil-slicked black hair, sickly pale skin, and then the man named Nicolas departed. The door creaked closed behind him.

Silence filled the dusty air. Ravlok waited for signs of the Councilor's departure for an eternity. He dared not move, focusing instead on calming his mind, envisioning himself seated at the reflection pool, not in what felt like genuine danger. It was a foolish feeling, surely. It wasn't as if his life were being threatened. After taking a few deep, silent breaths, he finally heard Gregory start for the stairs.

He was just commending himself for keeping his head during the entire ordeal when the Councilor stopped.

For several seconds, Ravlok stared at the wall in front of him, urging himself not to look. However, resisting temptation was one of many devotional exercises he struggled with, and today was not the day to make any progress on his path to Balance. He peered around the end cap and through a gap between books on the neighboring shelf. Gregory stood at the table, examining the spot where Ravlok had been sitting minutes ago.

Puzzled, Ravlok tried to reposition himself to see around the tall, white-robed figure, fearing he might have left some of his research behind. He found a space between two leather-bound tomes with a clear view of the table and relaxed. Any evidence of his nightly endeavor was tucked safely under his arm.

Gregory reached out and swiped at something on the lacquered surface. His finger glistened in the morning light.

The orange peel in Ravlok's pocket turned to lead.

The Councilor surveyed the room. His full head of wavy gray hair was swept back from his forehead, lending to the severity of his sharp nose, square jaw, and close-set eyes. He might have been handsome in his youth, before time had added so many lines to his beardless face.

"You may come out now."

A chill swept down Ravlok's spine. Still, he didn't move. If he waited him out, Gregory might think whoever had been here was already gone. Through the gap in the shelves, Ravlok saw the old man rub his finger and thumb together.

Gregory's expression darkened. "What are you? A ghost?" A flash of violet lit the sorcerer's eyes. "I said, 'Come out.'"

The words carried the weight of powerful enchantment. The seeking spell struck Ravlok like a physical blow, staggering him. A terrifying instant later, the control over his body slipped away like sand through his fingers. It moved of its own accord, obeying Gregory's command.

There were techniques he practiced to combat arcane possessions like this, and he scrambled to remember them, but the damage was already done. Ravlok fought Gregory's dominion even while his bare, callused feet squealed their protests against the polished stone floor. The Councilor turned toward the sound and smiled with cool, collected detachment. By the time Ravlok could work through the mental exercise to break free of Gregory's control, he had traversed the entire length of the aisle down which he'd hidden. He adjusted his grip on the parchment and stared directly into the old sorcerer's face.

"We reserve this room for mages and instructors." Gregory's wintry smile morphed into a sneer as his magic left him. His eyes returned to their natural brown. "But you already knew that."

Outraged by the sorcerer's violation of both his body and the Guild's own constitution, Ravlok struggled to keep his composure. Balance was what he needed. Logic. Sound reasoning. He squared his shoulders and drew himself up to his full height, though he was still shorter than Gregory by several fingerspans.

"Has there been a new decree abolishing the restriction of magic use on non-adepts, Councilor?" He pulled out the gold medallion of Ordeolas he wore around his neck. "Because last I heard, what you just did is a hanging offense."

Ravlok hoped his station would at least give Gregory pause. All monks who practiced in the Orders of Saolanni, Baosanni, and Ordeolas were non-adepts, or else they had so little arcane talent as to be nearly so. Gregory wouldn't dare cross any of the Monastic Orders by possessing or harming him further.

His reaction, however, was not what Ravlok expected.

The Councilor barked a laugh and shook his head. "As if anyone is going to believe you. Tell me, servant of Ordeolas, what is it you seek to learn in my archives?"

"Secrets," Ravlok said, ignoring the cold stone in his belly.

Gregory reached out to take the essays still clutched in Ravlok's hands. Ravlok allowed him to do so; it was pointless to resist. "*The Theory of Arcane Appropriation*, is it? Trying to awaken your own talent?"

"You could say that." It had certainly crossed his mind.

Gregory placed the stack of parchment on the table. "Bornen was a heretic, spreading falsities and rumors with no proof his postulations carried practical merit. You should have been reading Balziver or Criiosh if you wished to learn anything of value."

Ravlok frowned. He turned the two names over in his mind. Both were ancient Duerwisti philosophers, if his memory served him. They were championed throughout Dessos for the creation of arcanology, Duerguard's leading field of study.

"I'll keep that in mind." He wasn't sure what else to say. "Thank you."

The wrinkles on Gregory's forehead deepened. "I wouldn't thank me yet. We still have the matter of your trespassing to settle."

Ravlok smirked, despite the knot of tension between his shoulder blades. "If you don't tell, I won't tell."

"I'm afraid it is not that simple."

"You've condoned the use of torture on multiple prisoners. You've also used magic on me. I think we can both agree my presence here is a nonissue."

Somewhere in the back of his mind, Ravlok knew he should stop talking. But this was exactly the sort of abuse of power happening all throughout Eidosinia. Sorcerers like Gregory, who thought they could bully compliance out of the common people, sat at the heart of the Guild's rotten core. If he let him get away with this, Ravlok would only contribute to the problem.

Gregory sighed, examining the floor between them. When he returned his attention to Ravlok, he clasped his hands before him. "These are perilous times in which we live. Every avenue we have available to us must be exploited if we are to protect our people from the blankers." His eyes hardened. "I expect you will remember nothing of our conversation here."

With his surprise victory in hand, Ravlok shrugged. "What conversation?"

The Councilor continued to regard him a moment more, the stern set of his brow betraying none of the anger he surely felt. There was nothing a man like Gregory detested more than being bested by a commoner.

When Gregory inclined his head and turned for the stairs, Ravlok turned as well. His legs still shook from the encounter, but his heart was no longer trying to break his ribs. He was halfway to the door to the public stacks when the sorcerer spoke again.

"On second thought—"

Some primal sense of self-preservation urged Ravlok to spin back around. He drew his dagger, but there was nothing cold steel could do against magic. The Councilor's eyes flashed violet, followed by the single-word incantation that sealed his fate.

"*Caesahd*."

Ravlok fell to his knees. Crippling pain lanced through his body, causing his stomach to reject the orange. Only vaguely aware of the vomit, he doubled over in his own bile. His dagger slipped from his fingers as he clutched at his torso to keep it from being torn apart.

Gregory strolled toward him and crouched down. "You have a history of being troublesome, young monk. Too full of questions to be left to your own whims."

Around his swollen tongue, Ravlok managed to gather enough frothy saliva to spit in the Councilor's face.

Gregory jerked backward, snarling. He swiped at his chin with his pristine white sleeve and seized a fistful of Ravlok's black hair, wrenching his head upward.

"I hope you enjoyed the sunrise this morning. It will be the last one you ever see."

Chapter Three

Daeya

"Let's go, Normos," Daeya called over her shoulder. She forced herself to smirk, despite the anxiety fermenting in her stomach. Gods, what did Gregory want this time? "You shouldn't keep him waiting."

When she reached the top of the stairs, she sped up, intent upon putting as much distance between them as possible. The wide hallway stretched in front of her, doors and arch-paned windows lined up like soldiers in perfect rows flanking her path. Her robe trailed behind her and her boots snapped against polished tile, pounding out an angry cadence that cleared the way of other students. Daeya ignored their side-eyed glances and focused on the bend at the end of the hall.

She hated when Gregory sent Normos to fetch her. He always had to make a spectacle of it, as if he thought embarrassing her would somehow make up for his own failings in their Councilor's eyes.

Once, Normos had been like a brother to her, but their days of working side-by-side in the Guild nursery and bonding over lavender tea and strawberry pastries were long past. Their contemptuous rivalry had raged for four years now.

Apparently, it was bad form for a newly promoted mage to have his arse handed to him by an acolyte in a training duel. Normos had only grown more embittered as she neared magehood. He'd even physically assaulted her twice, prompting Daeya to enroll in unarmed combat training with Ravlok at the monastery.

Despite her best efforts, Normos caught up to her easily with his long-legged stride. Daeya stiffened beside him, but he didn't reach for her elbow this time. That was just as well. She might have broken his bleeding fingers if he touched her again.

A bitter taste coated her tongue. She looked up at him. "Why did he send you, anyway? Where's Cam?"

Gregory normally sent Cameron Vika when he needed her. Cam at least had the sense not to bark orders at her or tear out of stairwells like a Nohri blood wraith intent upon its next meal. Daeya preferred Cam's company to that of most others, especially since she was one of her only friends in the Guild. At least, when Cam's brothers weren't around.

"She's busy," Normos snapped.

"What's this about, then?"

His jaw clenched. "You'll find out soon enough."

She didn't have to fake the smirk this time. "He didn't tell you, did he?"

Normos set his teeth, but for once he didn't fire back a retort. Daeya's eyes narrowed. He never turned down a chance to spar with her, verbally or otherwise.

"Or, if he did, it must be good news. For me, anyway." She tilted her head. The increased tension along his brow and the way he kept flexing his hands bespoke a tome's worth of information, but she couldn't decipher any of it. She prodded a little harder. "Maybe that's why you look like the milk soured in your oats this morning."

Still, Normos said nothing. But beneath that poor excuse for a calm façade, a tempest brewed.

Daeya rolled her eyes. Fine. She returned her attention to the meeting ahead. Without an argument to distract her, each step closer to their destination made the void in her gut worse. Whatever this was about, it couldn't be that bad if Normos was so incensed. She fingered the casting bracelet around her wrist. Its warm band and blue-green saphyrum beads provided some comfort.

They reached Gregory's office, only to find it empty. A bottle of wine sat uncorked beside a glass adorned with gold filigree. His inkwell had been left open as well. Its pungent scent nearly masked the peppermint and cedar blend of his cologne. The slightest breeze blew in from a wide window and disturbed the red curtains; their tasseled ends knocked against a bookshelf filled with tomes.

As the door between them and the antechamber swung closed, Daeya swallowed the bile rising in her throat. Rather than let apprehension show, she threw Normos a glare. "Must not have been that important."

"Have a seat," he ground out, nodding to the two finely upholstered red chairs in front of Gregory's desk.

How she loathed that desk.

"I'd rather stand, thanks."

Normos stepped toward her. "That was not a request."

She stood her ground, determined not to be intimidated, even by one of the most adept mages in Ryost. It helped knowing that Normos adhered strictly to the Guild's rules. He wouldn't use magic on her outside of the sparring ring. "If you've a mind to scare me, you're going to have to try harder."

His expression darkened, blue eyes like jagged shards of ice. "You forget your place, Daeya."

"That's alright." She smiled prettily. "I'll have yours soon enough."

Not that she wanted it—gods knew she'd rather not be chained to Gregory's side like Normos was—but she'd never waste a chance to score a perfect blow to his ego. Daeya began to turn, to distance herself again.

Normos's hand locked around her throat.

A sharp yelp escaped her. Her fingers closed around his wrist, waves of frigid panic seizing her muscles as he threw her off-balance.

Bleeding—

He pulled her toward him, his brows and nose pinched with disgust. His breath blew hot against her face. "No. You won't."

Rage thawed her frozen limbs. She remembered her training, got her feet back under her, and shot both fists into his elbow—a move meant to send a painful shockwave up his arm. He flinched backward with a snarl, providing the perfect opening for her to side-sweep his knee and wrap her arm around his neck. Before she could throw him to the ground, Normos recovered from the blow, twisted out of her chokehold, and shoved her across the room.

Daeya struck the corner of Gregory's desk. White-hot splinters of pain lanced up her lower back, prompting a snarl of her own.

She taunted him through bared teeth, one hand on the polished wood to steady herself. "Come on, Normos. You fight like a graceless fawn."

Normos didn't rise to the bait. Instead, he feinted left and slipped inside her guard, delivering a solid uppercut to her jaw. She bit her tongue with the blow and blood welled in her mouth. Her ears were still ringing when he lunged. Both hands closed around her neck this time. He sent her sprawling into the stack of spell books and stationery on top of the desk.

Terror took root inside her. She clawed at his fingers, but still they tightened, closing off her airway. This was no ordinary assault. Even at his most incensed, Normos was never this aggressive.

He was actually trying to kill her.

The thought pierced the fog around her mind. She brought her left leg up, planted her foot on the wood, and thrust to the right, sending them both off the desk, into the pair of chairs.

Gravity was already working against them when Normos released her to slow his fall. Daeya's momentum carried them into a second roll. Both chairs tipped backward. Wood splintered and crashed to the ground. They rolled away from the wreckage and came to a stop on the plush white rug. She sat astride him, and he tensed to buck her off. Rather than counter it, she wrapped her arm around her shoulder and let him throw her forward. Daeya fell, dropping all her weight into her elbow, and slammed it into his nose.

Normos yelped; blood gushed from the crushed tissue. While he reeled from the blow, Daeya tore away from him and took to her feet. She settled into the balanced, open-handed fighting stance Ravlok had taught her, readying for another round.

The door to Gregory's office swung open.

The Councilor paused in the doorway, lips parting for only a moment before his eyes pinned Daeya to the floor. His unsettling mask of neutrality slid into place.

"Councilor," she choked out, letting her fighting stance crumble into a subservient bow.

She could scarcely find the words to explain before Gregory's attention shifted from her to Normos, and then to the wreckage in his room. Daeya followed his gaze, taking in the scattered books, torn letters, spilled ink, and broken chairs. She swallowed hard and scraped together enough courage to open her mouth again.

"Councilor, this isn't—"

"Silence." The word held an edge that could have cut diamonds. His attention returned to Normos. "You are bleeding on my carpet."

The mage—who shoved himself into a seated position and was using his black sleeve to staunch the blood from his broken nose—looked down at the red droplets soaking into the white fibers. "My apologies—"

"Go tend to your face."

Normos wasted no time accepting the invitation. "Yes, Councilor." The nasal sound of his voice might have been comical if not for their current predicament. He pushed himself to his feet, bowed to Gregory, and left the room.

Daeya had never been more jealous of him. She clutched her hands together to stop them from shaking, cursing herself for her body's stupid reaction. Showing fear in any form was unacceptable, and it would come with dire consequences if she didn't get herself under control.

Gregory waited for the door to close. When he turned back to her, his eyes flickered violet. He spoke a single-word incantation, and the bolt lock slammed home.

Daeya flinched.

Such an insignificant reaction, but the way his chin lowered drove a hot spike between her shoulder blades. He knew. He always knew when her fear threatened to overwhelm her. She held fast against her desire to shrink away from him, keeping her shoulders straight and head high.

He nodded toward the wreckage, his tone calm. "Sit."

She would have rather leaped into the Aether itself. "Please. He attacked me—"

"I know," he said. "Sit."

Slowly, sighing to herself, Daeya turned. She could have attempted to sit on one of the broken chairs, but that wasn't what he wanted. To help her master her fear, he would place her in the most uncomfortable position he could, and that gods-damned desk had been the source of all her nightmares for as long as she could remember. Nearly a year had passed since he'd strapped her to it, but ten years of torture were not easily forgotten with the tapestry of reminders carved into her skin.

She stepped forward. Almost a year. There was no reason to believe he would start again today.

Well, perhaps there was. He still didn't know about the half-dozen runes on her hip she'd flayed off. Daeya shuddered at the memory. She'd risked his wrath by stealing that dagger, and if he uncovered her sabotage, it might very well begin her torture anew.

Her hands grew clammy, and the thought threatened to paralyze her where she stood. It was stupid to think she could get away with destroying his work, no matter how sluggish and insensible it made her feel. He would surely punish her for undermining him. He would—

Enough. She swallowed hard and clenched her teeth. Any further down that spiral would lead to ruin. *You have to move.*

He was watching her.

Waiting.

In three quick strides, she reached the ruddy brown surface. The color of old blood. Gods knew enough of it soaked its surface through the years. After pushing aside some stacks of parchment, she turned to haul herself up.

Gregory shrugged out of his white robe. Gooseflesh exploded across Daeya's body in hair-raising waves, like a barn cat doubling its size to ward off a feral dog. Another bad sign. He still wore his white and gold tunic. If he removed the outermost layer to expose the darker one beneath, she would know for sure.

Perched atop the desk, bracing herself on her hands, the memories came back in a rush. Scents of leather, blood, and magic. Hazy images of the mandalas painted on the ceiling. Cold-burning agony searing through muscle and bone.

Gregory smirked. "Your unarmed technique is improving." He gestured to the wreckage on the floor. "I am certain Normos won't be so eager the next time I challenge him to kill you."

"You challenged him—" Her brows furrowed. "This was a test, then?"

"Of course. You have shown you can defend yourself without magic." He draped the robe over one arm and stroked her cheek with his free hand. Icy fingers teased a lock of hair behind her ear. "And as always, my sweet, you have proven yourself worthy of my gift."

A test and a gift. Bleeding Aether, she was sick of his games. She knew better than to express her anger, though. She simply waited.

"But first," he said, making to round the desk—to reach his unbroken chair, she assumed. When he reached for something on the short side of the desk, however, her fear redoubled. Something *clicked* inside the wood. Her eyes fluttered closed against the wave of nausea threatening to douse all coherent thought.

Gregory sighed. "Oh, Daeya. We should be past this by now."

She didn't have to see them to know what the secret catches exposed. There were four eyelets—one on each corner. Whether he was still toying with her or not, it took everything she had not to leap off the desk and run. But the door was locked, and she couldn't open it without his permission.

"My intrepid warrior, undone by a piece of furniture." His disappointment sent blistering trails of shame down her spine. "What is it you fear, hm?"

"Pain, Councilor."

"Hm." He raised an eyebrow. "Try again."

There was no denying it. She swallowed once more. "You, Councilor."

Gregory smiled. "Closer."

Aether take him. "What you'll do to me."

He tossed the robe over his chair and opened the nearest drawer. Daeya fought back against the sting in her eyes. Crying was not an option. It never was.

"And what is it you think I will do?"

This was an exercise. Vocalizing her fears was supposed to help her move past them. He would expect her to be thorough, and any parts left out, she risked being reminded of.

Firsthand.

"You'll bind my hands to the desk," she began. That was where it always began.

Gregory took out the pair of leather cuffs and set them on the desk. She stared at them for a long moment, flexing her fingers against the phantom pressure.

"Then you'll choose which part of me to cut." Even the ghostly memory of his hand sliding across her skin felt like a violation.

He took out his cloth-wrapped dagger and placed it next to the cuffs. When he threw back the fabric, the sight of that shining black blade nearly shattered her resolve. Her heart hammered up her throat, blocking her airway and darkening her vision.

"Go on," Gregory prompted.

The bastard was enjoying this. Some of her fear burned into anger, and she blinked furiously. "You always take your time casting the enchantment."

He picked up the dagger and returned to the front of the desk. Daeya fought to keep her nerves steady. Thank the gods for Ravlok and his lessons on meditative breathing.

Gregory stopped before her, so close she could feel the warmth of his body against her shins. He spoke the incantation she knew by heart, holding her gaze. A hair-thin, black-violet glow sprang to life along the blade's edge. "And then?"

"Then you make your cuts." Daeya surprised herself by the growing strength in her voice. "Slowly and deliberately, so there is no error in the runes."

"Very good."

He lifted the blade to her throat. Daeya didn't pull away. Instead, she bit the inside of her lip—the same reflexive bite she always used to stay silent while he worked. She held completely still. Breathing in. And out.

He traced the veins in her neck with the dagger point, perfectly controlling the amount of pressure. His touch with the steel was so light, the blade could have been a feather against her skin.

"And why do I do this?"

Looking him full in the face, she exhaled slowly through her nose, her fear eroded away by quiet fury. She kept biting until her teeth broke through that heavily scarred layer of tissue and she tasted blood. For years, he had done this to her. For years, he had mutilated her body for the sake of wards and spells that should have been beyond even a veteran mage's limits. But he never gave her anything she couldn't handle. He always stopped just shy of the moment she would break. There was always something methodical to his malevolence.

"To make me strong."

"Yes. And what else?"

Her jaw clenched. "To make me fearless."

"My intrepid warrior." This time, his smile exuded genuine pleasure. "Now you are ready." He moved the blade away.

Daeya relaxed, dizzy with relief. As Gregory returned the items to his drawer, she asked, "Ready for what?"

He closed that drawer and opened another. From it, he withdrew a black drawstring bag.

Daeya's eyes widened. "Is that—"

Fatherly pride brightened his expression as he placed the bag in her hands. "Open it."

With numb fingertips, she worked the drawstring loose. Inside were several dozen gold commissary coins. Mage's coins.

She gazed at them for a long moment, disbelieving. Drawing one out, she turned it over and examined the mages' flame-and-orb symbol on one side. The Guild's open hands were stamped on the other. Daeya looked back up at Gregory, slack-jawed. "I'm being promoted?"

"Congratulations, Sorceress."

While she worked through her stupefaction, he crossed the room to a wardrobe. She replaced the coin in the bag, scarcely daring to hope this wasn't a dream. Her breath caught at the sight of the black mage's robe he pulled from the ornate cabinet.

"Remove your acolyte's colors."

Blue and black fabric rasped against her tunic and pooled around her on his desk. The movements felt sluggish, as if she were underwater.

He held out the new robe. "Come."

The immense honor he bestowed upon her rendered her speechless. Even though she had completed all the requirements to obtain the rank several months ago, she had done it a full ten years ahead of the Guild's usual schedule. That left the Council divided on whether to grant her the rank or make her wait a few more years.

Their final decision had just made her the youngest mage in Guild history.

Careful not to ruin the moment by tripping over the broken chairs, she maneuvered her way toward him. There was something surreal about slipping her arms inside that new, silk-lined cloth. Lighter by far than her bulky acolyte blue, it was tailored exactly to her small frame—so exactly, in fact, that she found it fit every subtle curve of her torso. The robe flared at the hip to allow her legs the greatest freedom of movement. The sleeves widened from biceps to forearms—perfect for hiding spell components or small weapons—and were cuffed at the wrists for unarmed combat, should she ever encounter a hostile non-adept. Her only true loss was the ample space the old robe had for storing oranges.

Gregory took her by the shoulders and turned her to face him. He straightened the lapels, smoothed her collar, and cupped her cheek. "Beautiful."

"Thank you." Warmth touched her face. "It's so much more perfect than I imagined."

"You have earned it." Gregory's fingers lingered a moment more. "I know you will not disappoint me."

Once, that statement might have frightened her. Remnants of the emotion flitted about her stomach before she squashed them with a dutiful nod. "My will is yours, Councilor."

"As it should be." Gregory stepped past her and made for the chair behind his desk. Once he seated himself, all traces of warmth in his brown eyes dissolved. "Now, I would have your report on the Crex boy before we discuss your new assignment."

Daeya trailed him back to the desk and stood before it, hands clasped in front of her. "Faustus took the news with surprise, as anyone would expect. He didn't show interest in finding the aethermancer. He also made certain I knew it was inappropriate to question the Guild."

"And you found him sincere?"

Daeya was careful not to hesitate. Her doubts were small and insignificant, and she truly liked Faustus. If she mentioned even the most miniscule of his idiosyncrasies, he would pay the price. "Yes, Councilor."

"Good. Well done. His instructors tell me your mentorship has been successful. You are henceforth relieved of that duty."

"He may still need some guidance." Gods knew the young man had no skill at all with divination or transmutation. "Some of his spellcasting concepts are weaker than I would like."

"I will find a suitable replacement for him after you depart." He laced his fingers together on top of the desk. "As to your mission, there are rumors of an Aetherian using magic on non-adepts in Orthovia. He calls himself Vortanis. I want you to find him and take him to the embassy for questioning."

"An Aetherian?" Daeya's brows tightened. If there were any true Aetherians left in the world, the last place they would practice magic was here in Eidosinia. Ever since the Schism and the founding of the Sorcerers' Guild two hundred years ago, neither Aetherians nor aethermancers were welcome inside its borders.

"Self-proclaimed, I understand," Gregory said with the same level of skepticism. "You will sail out of Keilliad this evening."

A spark jolted her. She had waited for her promotion, dreamed of it, for as long as she could remember. Her first mission. An opportunity to be on her own, out from under the Guild's watchful eyes. While her new rank came with the responsibility of protecting Eidosinia's people, it also came with freedom from her jealous peers and a chance to see the realm beyond Ryost's walls.

"Sorceress Vika and her brothers will accompany you."

The statement struck her like a stone.

Blood pulsed through her ears, drowning out the silence that followed. Daeya could scarcely draw breath as a writhing snake of rage twisted around her lungs. Her scowl tensed every muscle in her face. When she finally forced a response, it came out of her bared teeth like a snarl rather than a coherent word. "Why?"

Gregory sat silently, one finger tapping against his desk.

For once, she didn't back down from that dangerous stare. Her fury only mounted. "No other mages have escorts."

"No other mages are sixteen years old," Gregory said. "In order for the Council to grant your rank, this was the concession I had to make."

Daeya trembled, horrified by the implication that her promotion was contingent upon her every move being watched and reported to the Council. "So, you're saying you traded my freedom for my rank?"

His patience was wearing thin. She could see it in his rigid spine and the tight set of his jaw. "Their observation is only temporary. A few months, perhaps half a year, and then I will have the Council reassess the need for them."

Half a *year*? She might welcome Cameron's company, but any amount of time with Joss or Toby Vika was too much. Daeya clenched her hands into fists. "I don't need bleeding babysitters."

That did it.

Faster than any old man should be capable of moving, Gregory shot to his feet and backhanded her across her cheek. The sting hadn't blossomed fully before he grabbed her chin and forced her to look him in the eyes. "Swear at me again," he hissed, "and I will reacquaint you with the end of a switch." He thrust her away with a flick of his wrist.

Daeya stumbled backward, stunned out of her fury by the smarting blow. More blood welled in her mouth. Gods, had she lost her mind? She knew better than this. "Forgive me, Councilor." Her voice trembled. "It won't happen again."

"For your sake, I should hope not."

The air between them grew as thick as wool. His gaze held hers briefly before he turned away, upper lip curling. He waved a hand toward the door, uttered a word, and the bolt lock snapped open.

"Get out."

That rejection was so much worse than any physical blow he could deliver. Daeya knew how much he hated swearing. She was usually so careful around him. After all he had done for her in securing her new rank, this loss of control in his presence was unacceptable.

"I'm sorry, Councilor," she said in a rush, knowing her forwardness could earn another blow if her contrition wasn't convincing enough. "I know I shouldn't question you. I'll respect the Council's decision. You do me a great honor by granting me this title, and I can't thank you enough."

Gregory's intensity lessened only as much as torrential rain after a hailstorm. He stalked around his desk and looked down at her for five harrowing seconds. When at last his scowl faded, he caressed the spot where the ache from his knuckles still lingered. "You know I cannot stay mad at you, my sweet," he purred. "But you must not provoke me so."

"Forgive me."

"All is forgiven."

She leaned into his touch, relishing the feeling of his mercy made manifest. To be scorned by her peers was part of her day-to-day life. But to be scorned by this man—the one man in the Guild who stood up for her, challenged her, believed in her—was something she couldn't bear. Even if she often lamented his attention, even if his demands of her sometimes seemed insatiable, should she lose his support, she would lose everything.

"I will make you proud," she promised.

Gregory stroked her hair with such gentle fondness that it sent shivers down her spine. "I know you will."

Chapter Four

Alar

On the west side of the Falcon River, the suited coachmen driving carriages vanished and crusty old men in bedraggled traveler's clothes replaced them. Polished scrollwork gave way to worn wood and rusted metal. Beautifully dyed drapery became heavy brown canvas. Sounds became harsher. Smells grew sour. It was as if the Guild had a radius of wealth that could extend only so far before the true state of its populace was revealed.

Morgan's Inn rose over the short, slate rooftops. Alar approached the three-story building; its dark green awning rippled in the breeze as he mounted the steps. A sign bearing Morgan's wheatgrass-wrapped, horse-and-carriage crest squeaked overhead. Through the wall-length front window, he found Val sitting alone with a plate of food in front of him.

The spymaster was a year older than Alar, but his youthful features made him look much younger. He couldn't grow a beard to save his life, and his light skin was smooth and unmarked by scars. A black blindfold wrapped around his head, and a carved walking staff leaned against the table beside him.

Playing the part of a blind tradesman came easily to him, even though he wasn't blind. While most arcanists experienced a temporary change in their eye pigmentation after saphyrum use, some half-Syljians like Val were cursed with permanent violet coloring. That Val had managed to keep his ancestry hidden for the last year was nothing short of miraculous.

A waitress shuffled over to refill Val's glass. She placed it in his hand and patted his wrist. Val smiled into space and nodded. He took a sip from the glass, skimmed the table for a napkin, and wiped the corners of his mouth.

The message had been delivered. Val knew he was here. Alar drew a breath and reached for the brass door handle.

Conversation filled the bottom floor of Morgan's Inn and spilled out onto the porch as Alar stepped inside. Threading his way through the tightly packed tables, he listened to talk of the merchants, artisans, and farmers while the scents of spiced sausage, meadberry muffins, and warm bread wafted through the air. Local gossip traveled much faster than the Guild's daily periodicals, and it was by far less susceptible to censoring and manipulation.

Subjects varied from staple goods and shipping delays to bumper crops and heavy taxes. No one mentioned an aethermancer, much less an impending execution. Alar dared to hope that was a good sign.

He sat down at the bar two rows from Val's booth and flagged down the bartender. Early in their assignment, they had agreed never to be seen in a public space together, and today would be no exception. They would go about their business using Alar's telepathy to communicate. Having ordered an ale and a plate of eggs and sausage, he reached out to touch his friend's mind.

Unlike reading another's thoughts at will, telepathy required a willing recipient to establish the connection. Val let him in immediately, the door to his mind flying open as if caught in the wind. "*We have a problem.*"

By now, Alar knew Val's mind almost as intimately as his own. Their mothers had been close, so they'd often played together as children. Growing up in the mountains near Trivvix, Val had been one of the first friends Alar had ever made, and was one of the few he had left.

"*Cheralach?*" Alar asked.

Val's surprise sparked across their telepathic link and ignited an ember of curiosity. "*How did you know?*"

Val often teased him relentlessly with brazen and preposterous questions about Daeya—how she fared, when Alar would introduce them, what date they'd chosen for their wedding—so Alar left her name out of this. It was true he found her interesting, but he would rather stick to the matter at hand.

"*Lucky guess.*" The barkeeper thumped a mug of ale down in front of him, and Alar took a sip from the frosty glass. Condensation slicked his grip. "*What in the Wastelands is he doing down here on a supply run?*"

Val fingered the smooth surface of his staff, keeping his eyes forward in the booth. "*I couldn't tell you, but it gets worse. We lost all the saphyrum, the supplies, and six soldiers during the fight. Seven more were taken prisoner. Magnus, Orowen, and Kendi among them.*"

The news tightened the frigid hand of dread around Alar's heart, and pressure mounted in his chest. Magnus's presence was expected—Cheralach's first officer followed the old man everywhere. But the high priestess and the commander, too? If Alar didn't believe there must be more to this calamity than he could see, their carelessness would have made him furious.

He replaced his mug on the polished bar top with a noisy clatter, his hand trembling. Four barrels of saphyrum and a dozen crates of supplies painstakingly gathered over the last two months. Gone. He rubbed his temples, pinching his eyes closed behind his palm. Those supplies had been meant to buy them time. Now, with six fighters dead and four high-profile Alliaansi members captured, they were about to cost so much more.

Val adjusted the blindfold around his mess of tangled black hair, tightening the knot at the back of his head. "*I didn't want to drag you into this, but our closest allies are two days out. We may not have time to wait for them.*"

Daeya's incidental warning replayed in Alar's mind. No, if Cheralach was slated for execution tomorrow, they certainly didn't have time.

He lowered his hand and busied himself with observing the rest of the room. Rammie Riverdale, Laerin's younger sister, was flitting through the breakfast crowd with an enormous tray piled high with food. She didn't normally work on Mirasdays, and she especially didn't work mornings. Val must have enlisted her help as well. Not only was Rammie a Syljian sympathizer, but she was the single biggest contributor to their success in gathering supplies for the Alliaansi.

Alar shot a glance at Val. "*I assume you know where they're being held.*" The lack of gossip suggested it was not the city jail. Foreboding weighed on his shoulders like a heavy cloak.

"*Jack tracked them through the city late last night. He said they were taken into the eastern tower on Old River Bridge. There's a trapdoor hidden there, but he couldn't get inside to see where it led.*"

"*Under the city and that close to the Towers?*" Alar gritted his teeth, trying hard not to pound the bar top with his fist. "*The Guild likely has another dungeon down there.*"

Rammie deposited her tray on a vacant table laden with dirty dishes and edged closer to Alar. Her chin-length curly hair mimicked the color of autumn leaves, and a dusting of freckles across her cheeks and nose highlighted steel-sharp blue eyes. She glanced between them, but an urgent wave from a nearby customer stymied her attempt to sidle in on their discussion.

Val's remorse was a subtle eddy in the river of his thoughts. "*You know I wouldn't have asked you here if I had any other options. If they kill Cheralach, we lose our loudest voice of reason on the council.*"

It was true. Cheralach had long opposed Koraani and Nemaala in their desire to go to war with the Guild. The Deserter's annoying habit of shying from violence normally rankled Alar, but he agreed with him in this case. There were over ten thousand Syljians to care for, and more refugees arrived in Starlight every day. Without enough saphyrum to support them all, many would die before they could ever rally their forces.

Still, Alar hesitated. Going after Cheralach and the others likely meant burning his Guild alias. If anyone recognized him as Faustus, there would be no reintegrating himself into the School's ranks.

"*This is the most consistent stream of saphyrum we've had since the mine in Beigaare went dry.*" The barkeeper placed a heaping plate of eggs and sausage in front of him. Alar slid a pair of silvers across the bar in thanks. "*You heard Magnus's last report. Starlight's supply is nearly exhausted. Aon'In and Kuma'Kiir won't be far behind.*"

"*You think the trade-off isn't worth it?*" Val's incredulity buffeted Alar's senses. "*We can always find more saphyrum,* amii. *We can even hit the Ferid mine if we have to, but we can't replace our people.*"

A fair point. Kendi and Orowen were just as valuable as Cheralach. The pair had served as the backbone of the Syljian resistance for the last century. It would be a mighty blow to Alliaansi morale if the Guild executed them, too.

Alar looked around for silverware before waving the bartender down again. "*Say we get them out. What then? We can't just parade them through the city.*"

"*Rammie's supposed to be working on that.*" Val lifted his glass into the air and held it there. Rammie excused herself from a table full of farmers and hurried toward him, grabbing a sweating pewter carafe along the way.

"More water for ye, milord?" She took the glass from his fingers and poured from the carafe without waiting for his answer.

Val lowered his arm, turning his head in her direction. "Thank you, Rammie dear."

"Of course." Rammie placed the glass in his hand and took his plate from the table. "Can I get ye anything else? I see ye didn't touch yer biscuits. Did that old *napher gought* overbake them again?"

A chuckle escaped Val as he shook his head. Even Alar smirked. Rammie's Brogrenti slur was the equivalent of calling her employer a boil-faced sow. "No, no, Morgan did just fine, but I'd take a bowl of soup, if you don't mind. I've got a frightful pain in my tooth, and chewing's just miserable."

Val's request was a cue at which Rammie brightened. "I have just the thing. I'll be right back."

She slipped behind the bar and disappeared into the kitchen, coming back moments later with a steaming bowl of soup. Rammie placed it down in front of Val. "My uncle Cevlor says this recipe has been handed down through six generations. It took eight tries for me to get it right. Turns out the secret is in the three carrots."

Alar disassembled the code for its true meaning while Val sniffed at the bowl's contents and stirred it with his spoon. Cevlor—an anagram for Clover. Number codes were always delivered backwards. Six, eight, and three would amount to three and eighty-six.

An address: Clover 386. He tried to picture the building, then grinned to himself. She had already described it.

Karats. Not carrots. The old jeweler's shop.

"*Did you get that?*" Val asked him.

A safe house. It was a start, at least. They could go to ground for a while and make their way north once the excitement wore off. Alar's unease lingered, but he trusted her. If anyone could get his people out of the city, it was Rammie. "*Yes.*"

Rammie waited for Val to take a bite and voice his approval—his signal that they understood. He tipped his head back, lips parting. "Oh, this is marvelous." He rummaged in his pocket and drew out a few coins. "Here you are, dear. Keep the change."

Rammie smoothed a hand over Val's shoulder. "Oh, ye're too generous, milord."

The performance drew the attention of a couple one table over and earned the younger Riverdale sister two more sales of her signature recipe. She scurried off to fill the order with a promise to check on Val again soon.

Alar stabbed at his eggs with his fork. "*What do we know about their defenses?*"

Val spooned soup into his mouth, never once looking down into his bowl. "*Jack is doing recon work as we speak. So far, we know they're redirecting security all over the city to bolster Old River Bridge. At least five mages are stationed in the area. On his last count, there were twenty soldiers.*"

This was a suicide mission.

Alar violently speared a bite of sausage. Neither Val nor his accomplice, Jack, were arcanists. Alar could fall back on his psionics, but until they freed their companions, they would have no real defense against the mages. The soldiers alone were skilled enough with swords and shields to be dangerous.

"*They're planning for a rescue attempt.*" Alar chewed and swallowed. "*You realize that, right?*"

Of course he did. Val wasn't a fool.

Alar's oldest friend was quiet for a long time. Once he'd polished off his bowl of soup, he straightened and dabbed at his lips with a napkin. Defiance suffused his every word. "*I understand. I could really use your help on this, but I* do *understand.*"

Even without their telepathic link, Alar would have sensed the words Val wasn't saying. This was a cause he believed in. One he was willing to die for if necessary. He would attempt the rescue with or without Alar, and without him, he would surely fail.

With a last bite of eggs, Alar groaned and shoved his half-eaten breakfast away. "*Alright, fine. Someone has to watch your back, you damned lunatic.*"

Val broke character and grinned. He hid the look behind his napkin, but his amusement rippled through their link. "*I knew I could count on you.*"

Alar resisted the urge to hurl a coin at the bastard's head. His own grin tightened the corners of his mouth. "*We'll need a distraction. Something to draw the soldiers away.*"

Lessening the Guild's numbers in that area would be key. They needed to draw them off long enough to slip into the tower. Getting out, however, was another problem. Cheralach and Magnus were both powerful aethermancers, easily worth several average Guild sorcerers each, but even then the odds would not be in their favor.

Taking his staff in hand, Val rose from the booth. With slow, even passes, he tested the path in front of him and started for the door.

"*Leave that to me. I'll meet you there in an hour.*"

Chapter Five

Orowen

"What was he thinking, anyway?"

Orowen sighed, wincing at the dagger of pain that sliced through her lower ribs. Her chains rattled as she prodded the spot with her fingertips. The weight of the spellbinders on her wrists made her investigation awkward and sluggish. Nothing felt broken, but the swelling was worse, and she was certain an enormous bruise had formed beneath her white dress.

Outside her cell, further down the torch-lit corridor, Anwic continued his lamentations. "He shouldn't have sent us all to the drop point. We made too much noise—"

"Stop," Varkendios snapped at his second-in-command. His stern rebuke echoed off the stone walls and floor. Though he was usually slow to anger, the unfortunate circumstances of their captivity had stretched her old friend's temper to its breaking point. "There is nothing to be done about it now."

Shifting to derive some comfort from her little mound of damp straw, Orowen settled her manacled hands into her lap. The heavy chains were cold against her thighs. Rough gray stone pressed in on her from all sides. Orange firelight threw the barred shadows of her cell door across the floor, and a sickly blend of stale urine and feces choked the air. Somewhere off in the dungeon, one of their other companions—Sam or Jessie, perhaps—fell into a coughing fit. Rylan's low voice carried as the archer murmured unintelligibly once the fit subsided.

Orowen closed her eyes and envisioned the temple garden back home. Pathways burgeoning with pink and purple phlox. Clematis and morning glories tumbling over archways and stone walls, bursting with shades of tangerine and sapphire. Scents of winter lilac, honeysuckle, and pine floating on the breeze. A carpet of frost-hardy clover caressing her bare toes. Fingertips whispering over silky petals of dianthus and rose.

"Have faith, *neime*," she told Anwic. "Saolanni's light still shines on us."

Anwic snorted. "A piss-poor light, if you ask me. I can barely see the other side of my cage."

Orowen remained calm despite his blasphemy. "One needs only a single candle to light the way in the dark."

"How you stay so positive when we're all about to die is either remarkably sage or incredibly stupid."

A sharp scrape of metal against stone sounded from the direction of Kendi's cell. "You will not speak to her like that again."

"It was with all due respect, *Amaa.*"

Another sigh escaped her. Orowen rested her head against the wall. The two of them had done nothing but bicker for the last few hours, and there was little she wouldn't have given for a few minutes of silence.

"Have you lost all social grace as well as your ability to handle a sword?" Kendi's scathing accusation prompted a growl from Anwic's cell. "Apologize to her. Now."

Several seconds passed before Anwic grumbled his obedience. "My apologies, Devoted."

Kendi's chivalry often annoyed her, but Orowen welcomed it today. Fatigue and soreness made for poor cellmates, and the hazy film of saphyrum sickness only worsened with each passing hour. "Accepted, of course."

She couldn't be cross with the boy, truly. Anwic had witnessed the deaths of some of his closest friends last night. Half of their squad had fallen to the Guild mages, and her own grief turned her heart to lead.

Why the rest of them had been spared remained a mystery. It was more than a desire to set an example for others who dared defy the Guild; they had been led across the city and taken underground without so much as a public spectacle. That alone was enough to set Orowen on edge.

Cheralach knew something. He hadn't made that bad call at the river out of negligence. It hadn't surprised him when the sorcerers stopped killing and started taking prisoners. He seemed to have expected it, as if it was part of the vision driving him on this reckless flight south.

Just how much of this did you see, neime*? And why didn't you tell me?*

Questions burned for answers but only received enough kindling to keep them alight. The sorcerers had taken Cheralach away hours ago. Despite her prayers for his safe return, a sickening disquiet wriggled its way under her skin.

He had told her some of what he had seen—just enough for her to interpret the timing and location of a catastrophic event he believed would change the course of history. All the signs had brought them here, to the capital, but there were too many variables she still didn't understand. The scarlet flames, for one. Those kept recurring through every one of his visions, along with the image of a young woman. Orowen kept her eyes closed, letting her hair buffer her shoulders and upper back from the chilly stone.

Somewhere else in the dungeon, a cell door screeched open. The sound of Magnus's swearing soon followed. "Take your scabbing hands off me."

"Move, dog."

"You'll get nothing from—"

The dull sound of something striking flesh cut off Magnus's defiance. "Shut up!"

A scuffle ensued, and more voices rallied against the sorcerers.

"Let him go!" Jessie shrieked.

Orowen started as metal rang against metal. Samara's snarl of fury came with it.

"Chaos-sworn animals!"

Though she couldn't see Kendi's youngest recruit from her position, Orowen stared out the barred door into the hallway.

"Sam, don't—" Rylan's baritone accompanied Sam's sharp yelp and another weighty thump. The sound made Orowen bristle.

"Blanker-loving trash." Malice dripped from the guard's voice. "Take him. I bet this one will get him to talk."

Orowen shuddered. As a healer, she was no stranger to victims of Guild torture. Her fists curled in her lap as the sounds of Magnus's struggle faded into the bowels of the dungeon.

"What are we going to do?" Anwic asked, breaking the silence that ensued.

"For now, we wait." Kendi had reclaimed control of his poise. "Valaxes oversees our network here in Ryost. He'll have heard the pickup went awry and send someone to investigate."

"As if anyone could find us down here."

"An opportunity to escape will present itself." Not even a single word rang with doubt. It was one of many things Orowen loved about him. No matter how badly things went, Kendi always stayed positive for those under his command. "We will get out of here. We just have to be patient."

A door screamed on its hinges; voices speaking Eidosinian carried from the main entrance. Kendi fell silent as footsteps approached their side of the dungeon. Shadows crept along the wall before the mages appeared. Orowen straightened, frowning. Dragging an unconscious man between them, they stopped outside a cell half a dozen paces down the hallway.

The man was human, as far as she could tell—in his mid-twenties with sun-kissed skin, short black hair, and well-toned shoulders and arms. His tawny vest and trousers fit loosely and bore dark, wet streaks down the front. The mages searched him, removing several small items from his pockets. A flash of metal caught her eyes as one removed an amulet from around the man's neck. A monk?

One mage shouldered the man's weight while the other unlocked the cell. The prisoner didn't make a sound as they dragged him inside and out of Orowen's view.

"We chaining this one?" one sorcerer asked.

"Nah, he's a non." There was a sharp intake of air, then a heavy thud and a muffled groan. Both mages laughed. "Ain't gonna hurt nobody."

Orowen seethed. She addressed them in Syljian, both to annoy them and flout their superior position. "Does it make you feel powerful, hurting a man who can't fight back?"

Both men paused. The shorter one, with the wide nose and tangled nest of a beard, stepped back into the light. He sauntered toward her cell and rested his hands on the cross brace. An ugly, nasal quality accented his Syljian, and he butchered the emphasis on half the words he spoke. "Careful with that little mouth, blanker, or I'll make better use of it."

Orowen's lips twitched upward. "Your threats of violence and assault are highly unoriginal." She tilted her head. "Might I give you some advice?"

Even silhouetted against the torchlight, it was clear she'd caught the sorcerer off-guard. He leaned against the bars, staring at her, until he snorted a laugh and gestured with a wave.

"Alright, sure, I'll bite." Derision saturated his tone. He lifted his chin. "Enlighten me."

Orowen gave him a languid smile. "Only open your mouth when it does not create a deficit in the wealth of mortal knowledge."

Silence greeted her as the mage puzzled out the implication behind her words. His companion approached her cell after locking the one behind him. He side-eyed her through the bars and slid his attention back to his baffled friend. "Come on. You can play with the blanker later."

The mage ignored him. He pressed his face closer and peered in at Orowen. "You calling me stupid?"

She kept her hands neatly folded in her lap and did her best to sound affronted, though her smile remained. "I would never do such a thing."

A growled curse escaped him. He reached for the lock on her door. "Bleeding bitch. I oughtta cut off those pointy ears—"

"Lux," his companion warned. "Don't open it. She's getting in your head."

Orowen's smile broadened. She didn't possess psionics, but if it kept them from harming the young prisoner further, she would happily play on their fears. Adopting a smooth, authoritative tone, she said, "Yes, Lux, I'm in your head. Now you will open the door and release me."

Both sorcerers backed away from her cell, their complexions drained of color. The taller mage grabbed Lux's arm, his eyes wide. "Come on. We don't have time for this."

They hurried down the corridor and out of sight. Seconds later, the main door scraped open and shut with a resounding *clang*.

When the echoing report finally tapered off, Kendi exhaled. "I wish you wouldn't do that. You put yourself at risk."

His concern made her smile in earnest. "You can't always be my fearsome protector."

"That doesn't stop me from trying, does it?"

A hint of amusement betrayed Kendi's own smile. She clung to the thought of that lopsided grin and savored the warmth it brought.

Anwic only groaned.

Forcing aside the pull of exhaustion, Orowen crawled to the front of her cell. Her chains dragged behind her, scattering her pallet of straw across the floor. Movement made her dizzy, and she placed her hand on the bars to steady herself.

"Hello?" She formed the word in Eidosinian. "Young man, can you hear me?"

Torchlight illuminated one of the man's bare feet. He didn't so much as twitch in response.

"Why even bother?" Anwic asked. "It's not like he's in any better position to help us."

Orowen's hands tightened on the bars. "It isn't about getting help." It was about giving it if she could.

Kendi—Saolanni bless him—heard every word she didn't say. "There's nothing you can do for him, Devoted."

Orowen switched to a lower dialect—one she knew the Brogrenti commoners favored. "Hello?"

She tried one last time before sitting back on her heels, brows tightening with concern. Kendi was right; there was little she could do for him without her magic or healing herbs. She couldn't even examine him for concussion or broken bones at this distance. Bowing her head, she spoke a prayer to Shavaan for the man's well-being. Then, with a huff of frustration, she crawled back to her pallet and tried to push the wet straw back into a pile. By the time she settled atop the mound again, her arms ached from lugging the chains and the cell swam in a cloudy haze of orange and gray.

Orowen sagged against the wall, squeezing her eyes shut against the spinning room. She struggled to rake in enough air. Her body tingled, screaming for saphyrum to slake her need. A day or two more without it, and she would be too weak to move.

"I overcast last night," she informed her companions. "I may not be much help in the escape."

"*If* we escape," Anwic corrected her.

Though she was too tired to laugh outright, Orowen still managed a chuckle. "Your positivity is contagious, *neime*."

"Get some rest." Kendi's command was gentle but firm. "We'll address that when we know more about their plans for us."

Anwic scoffed. Chains clinked and straw rustled. "I'm surprised they haven't killed us already."

Kendi made a soft sound in his throat. It was the same noise he made on the battlefield when presented with troubling news. "They want something from us. Secrets, perhaps."

Orowen tried to recall something Cheralach had said weeks ago. It had come during one of his episodes of delirium, shortly after the visions first started. The thought—the name—was elusive. No matter how she tried to reach for it, it slipped through her fingers. "Not just secrets. They're after something specific. Something Cheralach knows."

"You mean something in his visions?" Kendi asked.

They all knew about the old aethermancer's condition. This wasn't the first time Cheralach had suffered from such hallucinations. Some of his earliest visions, he claimed, had led to his defection from the Guild and the founding of Starlight.

Before she could answer, more rustling and clinking came from Anwic's cell. "Then why in Baosanni's name did we bring him here?"

Orowen's answer came easily. "To find the girl."

Every time Cheralach spoke of his visions, he circled back to the girl—to rescuing her. There was no deterring him from it. He believed the visions came from Tiior herself, and if he ignored them, the consequences would be unfathomable.

But when Orowen asked what he believed the stakes were, he changed the subject. *"I have to do this, Devoted,"* he said. Each time, the sadness in his green eyes multiplied. *"For our people's sake, I will do what must be done. And when the time comes, you must do the same."*

"I don't see any girls. Do you?" Anwic's grating drawl sent prickles down her spine. "Whoever she is, we're not going to find her in here."

"Maybe not." Kendi took a deep breath. "In any case, she can't be our priority until we find a way out. We can't do that if we're too exhausted to stand. Get some rest, both of you. We'll revisit this later."

He was right, as he so often was, especially when Orowen didn't want to admit it. She had fought, and healed, and prayed up to this point. Now, there was nothing left to do but wait.

Her efforts to stay awake became insurmountable, and sleep beckoned to her like fae song. As her eyelids drooped, she slid down the wall to huddle on the pallet of straw, resting her head on folded arms.

Minutes or perhaps hours later, while she drifted between slumber and wakefulness, the first of Magnus's screams wrenched her awareness back into her body. Orowen sat bolt upright, wide-eyed and breathless.

Her stomach turned, and she clapped a hand over her mouth to stifle a sob. She'd known Magnus ever since he was a young man, headstrong yet courageous, always willing to put others before himself. Like his mentor, Cheralach, he loathed violence, and he never raised his voice or spoke unkindly to anyone. To think of what those animals were doing to him—

His next wail of agony pierced her like a dagger to the heart.

Chapter Six

Ravlok

Ravlok awoke to the sound of screaming.

He rolled over on the cold floor, bits of straw sticking to his body, the stench of vomit still clinging to his clothing. Three walls of solid stone surrounded him. A barred door broke the last wall near the middle. Staring through the bars at a single torch outside the cell, Ravlok rubbed his eyes. He wasn't in the city jail. The stale air, the dank smell, the hollow way sound carried—

He was underground.

The screams echoed down a corridor to his left. Their muffled quality suggested that at least one door stood between him and their source—a man's voice, made hoarse by whatever manner of torture afflicted him.

As the sound went on unabated, it stirred something visceral inside Ravlok. With nothing left in his stomach to expel, he spent the next several minutes alternating between dry-heaving and cursing every deep, intermittent breath he drew. The stench of excrement, urine, and sweat raked into his lungs. When he finally regained control of himself, the gut-wrenching cries of the suffering man had stopped. Ravlok slumped onto the floor.

An airy female voice called down the corridor. “Rip a few shreds of cloth from your trousers. Wet them and stuff them in your ears.”

Her soothing tone astonished him. It took several seconds to form a response. “That’s good advice.” His voice echoed in the dismal space. “Thank you.”

While his body still suffered a phantom ache from the spell Gregory had cast on him, Ravlok found it in himself to crawl the short distance to the barred door. Outside, three more torches cast trembling shadows on the walls of a long corridor. Above five spans to his right, on the opposite side of the passage, another cell door stood bolted into the stone. The torchlight was too weak to dispel the darkness for more than a few handspans inside that cell, but a smattering of dirty straw littered the floor.

To his left, the corridor stretched ten spans or so before turning away from him. He gripped the bars of the cell door and gave them an experimental tug. The door didn’t so much as shift on its hinges. He looked toward the other cell. “Do you know where we are?”

“Beneath the Towers, I think.” Though she didn’t come into the light, the woman’s voice came from that cell.

“Beneath the Sorcerers’ Towers?”

“Yes.”

Mingled anger and disbelief heated his blood. How in Tiior’s name had the Guild concealed this from the public? Surely, in all his years living on the streets of Ryost, he would have heard rumors of a dungeon right beneath his feet.

Unless no one held captive here ever left.

More bile seared his throat, and he tried not to think about what that meant for him. “How long have you—”

Another scream shredded the air. Ravlok clapped his hands over his ears. For several long seconds, the cries continued, until the man’s voice gave out and all that carried down the corridor were broken whimpers interspersed with eerie moments of silence.

Ravlok took the woman’s advice and reached down to tear a shred of fabric from his trousers. A single sob issued from the other cell, halting his movement.

Guilt crept over him, and his fingers relaxed on the tattered hem. How could he even think about making himself more comfortable while others suffered?

"Do you know him?" he asked her, abandoning his previous question.

"Yes."

Ravlok waited, expecting her to say more, but only the rattle of chains and a sniffle followed. He needed to say something. Anything. "I'm sorry."

"Thank you," came her choked response.

There was no anger in her tone, only gratitude. What a strange emotion to feel at a time like this. If he were in her position, he wouldn't be able to concentrate on anything except escaping and exacting vengeance. But she seemed resigned, as if she had given up on the possibility of freedom.

As if she was simply waiting for her turn to die.

"This isn't the end for us. We're going to get out of here." Ravlok ripped a strip off his trousers. Whatever rage the woman didn't feel quickly mounted inside him. The Guild couldn't get away with this. "And we'll make them pay for what they've done."

"'Evil is no cure for evil.'"

Ravlok paused. It was a proverb from the Book of Life—the doctrine used by the Monastic Order of Saolanni. The monks of Ordeolas used a similar tome, the Book of Order, in their teachings. But while Ordeolas's monks made their home here in the capital, Saolanni's order was over two hundred leagues northeast of Ryost in the Healer's City, or Ferid, as the Eidosinians called it.

Perhaps she was from Ferid. But there was a Guild embassy in Orthovia, halfway between the Healer's City and the capital, that could have handled whatever crimes she'd committed. How had she ended up in Ryost?

"'Should the scale of balance tip toward evil's favor, one must counter it with good.'" Ravlok recited the passage from the Book of Order. "In this case, I would argue removing the source of evil *is* an act of good."

The woman sniffled.

"You quote the goddess of life," Ravlok said. "Are you a monk of Saolanni?"

"No."

Then who are you?

He wanted to ask, but Ravlok was aware her short, simple answers probably bespoke her desire to be left alone. Instead, partly to stifle himself from asking more questions, he ripped his strip of fabric in half and stuffed both pieces into his mouth. As he moved them about with lips and tongue, saturating them with saliva, he leaned back against the wall beside his cell door. If the woman came into the light—assuming her chains would permit her—he would see her easily through the bars. He took the pieces out of his mouth and balled one between his fingers and thumb. As he raised his hand to cram the ball into his ear, the woman finally offered something of her own accord.

"I serve her as a priestess."

A healer. Of course.

And not just any healer. The priests and priestesses of Saolanni were said to be the greatest miracle-workers in the world. While Ravlok had witnessed exhaustive, hours-long rituals performed by the priests of Shavaan, the lesser goddess of healing, it was rumored that healers blessed by Saolanni could reknit flesh wounds in a matter of seconds. Some even claimed they could restore lost limbs within minutes, but Ravlok had never found a credible source to confirm such a thing.

He could think of only a few reasons a priestess of Saolanni would be locked in a secret underground dungeon. Either she had practiced arcane medicine on a non-adept, or she'd taught others how to use magic outside of a Guild school. Both preposterous charges to have warranted this sort of barbaric punishment.

"Why are you here?"

She sighed. "It's a—"

A howl of inexorable rage cut off her response. Expecting more tortured screams to follow it, Ravlok quickly stuffed the cloth into his ears. Through the stone at his back came a sudden reverberation, like that of a door slamming shut. Shouted curses and a stream of orders followed.

Ravlok missed the first part of the orders as he pulled out one of his ear plugs. "—your mouths shut. Let me do the talking." It was Nicolas, the man from the archives.

"I told you it was too much!" exclaimed another.

A third snapped, "How was I supposed to know—"

"Shut up! The lot of you," Nicolas ordered.

Footsteps traveled toward Ravlok's cell. He turned to peer out of the bars, but he couldn't see around the bend. A door opened and closed on angry hinges, and when Nicolas spoke again, his words were muffled.

"Stay here and keep watch. If anything gets past you, I'll make what happened to the blanker-lovers look like Tiiorsday morning tea."

A chorus of acquiescence echoed down the corridor, and then their voices faded.

The silence didn't last long. An unfamiliar voice bearing the same airy northern intonations as the priestess's carried from beyond her cell. This one was equally soft and free of anger, but it was distinctly male. And it was speaking Syljian.

Ravlok was still wrapping his mind around this discovery when the priestess responded in kind. He knew some Syljian from books, but had only heard it spoken a handful of times. Even though it was a cousin of Aivenosian and a direct descendant of Ancient Dessian—both of which he knew well—the two spoke so fluently he couldn't parse out individual words.

But he didn't need to. Understanding dawned.

"You're with the Alliaansi," Ravlok breathed. He leaned against the bars, trying to spot the cell where the woman's companion was held. "You're Syljians."

They both paused. Ravlok simply waited. If they were already imprisoned inside a Guild dungeon, they had nothing left to lose by revealing themselves.

Perhaps having reached the same conclusion, the man finally responded. His words held both pride and a note of challenge. "We are."

Ravlok sat back on his haunches, letting his hands go slack on the bars. He'd heard all the stories of the Syljians. It was said they could manipulate, or 'blank,' the minds of others, thus forcing their will upon them. They had once demonstrated this ability to catastrophic effect at the Coup of Vale's Hollow nearly two centuries ago. By taking control of the minds of four Guild generals, they'd delivered over twelve thousand soldiers to their deaths in the infamous valley pass. Vale's Hollow was still spoken of today as a warning for anyone who dared entrust themselves to a Syljian.

Unease wormed its way under his skin. "Do you all have psionics?"

"No, none of us." The woman's tone was gentle, placating.

"Very few Syljians do," the man added. "That's been a misconception since the Saphyrum War."

Another male voice, even farther down the corridor, hissed something at the first. Ravlok didn't need to understand the words to identify both surprise and derision in his tone. The first man snapped something equally biting, drawing a grumble of obedience from the second.

Ravlok tried to recall what he knew of the Saphyrum War. Most texts claimed it had started after the Syljians killed a group of Guild ambassadors seeking to open trade with Syljia, which hoarded the greatest stockpile of saphyrum in the world. But the truth, Ravlok had extrapolated from cross-referencing several manuscripts and scrolls, was that some time around the year 11, the newly established Sorcerers' Guild had formally invited Syljia to assimilate its people into the larger realm of Eidosinia as a federated state. One clause in the drafted agreement demanded a state must submit its saphyrum stores to Guild regulation. The Syljians had refused, and by the year 37, the Crystal Towers of their capital, Astenpor, fell to the Guild's might.

It didn't take a skilled tactician to puzzle out what had really happened.

Ravlok must have been lost in his thoughts for too long. The second man muttered something under his breath, and the first man scolded him again. There was a louder rattling and scraping of chains. Ravlok looked toward the woman's cell to find her kneeling on the stone, gazing out at him.

Torchlight illuminated her dirty lavender skin. Her long, pointed ears stuck out from elbow-length white hair. The filthy remnants of her clothing might have been a white dress once, or perhaps a form-fitting blouse with flowing skirts. White runes etched along her temples accentuated feminine features. She held herself with poise and grace despite her condition. Her violet eyes betrayed her exhaustion, but they were no less striking in their intensity.

"We have no quarrel with the monks, if that is what you are. Perhaps we can work together to escape this place."

And just like that, she turned his prior assessment of her hopelessness on its head. Straightening, he nodded once. "That seems wise. I am Ravlok, servant of Ordeolas."

"Well met, Ravlok. My name is Orowen. Your next-door neighbor is Kendi, and the loud-mouth at the end of the hall is Anwic. There are more of us spread throughout the dungeon. Eight in all."

Surprise bloomed in his chest. So many of them. "Are you all Syljians?"

"Only we three. The other five are human like yourself."

That would at least make blending into the city a little easier. Masking only three purple-skinned outlanders when they reached the surface seemed less impossible, somehow.

"Since our presence here is obvious enough," Orowen tilted her head, "might I ask what a monk could do to earn such stellar lodgings?"

He snorted. "I was caught reading. And I suppose I threatened a Guild Councilor."

She studied him a moment before throwing a glance toward Kendi's cell. "You speak truly?"

"He used magic on me." Ravlok shrugged. "I didn't appreciate it much."

Orowen nodded. "Threatening a Councilor," she mused. "So, you're either crazy, or you're in good company."

He allowed himself a smirk. Some of the finest scholars in history were often accused of madness. "'A little touch of insanity makes life grand,'" he said, quoting one of his favorite Cintoshi philosophers.

For the first time, the ghost of a smile formed on her lips. "Spoken like Hanmuth Blackburr himself."

"You know his work?"

"Oh, yes." Orowen chuckled. "Though if you'd ever seen the man play tiffleball, you would believe him truly mad."

Imagining the late Hanmuth Blackburr engaging in such a barbaric and reckless sport didn't align with Ravlok's lofty impression of the scholarly old professor. If Orowen had known the Cintoshi in his earlier years, she was much older than Ravlok had thought.

"I would like to hear more about him." Indeed, there was much he could learn from this woman. "After we address our current predicament."

"Of course."

With this budding sense of camaraderie between them, Ravlok turned his attention to the subject of their escape. There was no telling how long the Guild would keep them alive down here, and he didn't plan to stay and find out. He drummed his fingers against the bars, considering. "Do you have friends on the outside who might help us?"

An organization as big as the Alliaansi would likely have operatives inside the capital. Unless these *were* the operatives.

Orowen's face fell. "We don't know. Our group was ambushed outside the city. Everyone the mages didn't kill ended up here."

"There should have been a scout watching the drop point," Kendi said. His Eidosinian was thick, with rounded vowels and loosely articulated consonants. "If he tracked us to the bridge, there is a chance for rescue."

Ravlok frowned. They couldn't count on a so-called 'chance' for rescue, but knowing their terrain and whom they were up against would help. He'd fallen unconscious shortly after Gregory's attack, and he had no idea how he'd arrived here. He didn't even know what time of day it was now. "You saw the way you came in?"

"Yes," Kendi said. "They took us upriver and through a trapdoor inside a bridge tower. The mages forced us down a ladder, then through a long corridor snaking off to the northeast. We passed four checkpoints and a guard room. There were two soldiers at each checkpoint and probably ten more on watch."

Eighteen soldiers. Ravlok could handle at least a few at a time, provided his new allies had any proficiency in combat. It was the spellcasters that concerned him. "How many mages?"

"Twelve. Plus the man in the brown cloak. I didn't see him use magic, but I think it's safe to assume."

As the weight of that knowledge settled in, the man named Anwic grumbled in Syljian.

Orowen sighed. "*Ciir*, Anwic. *Ros aaken*."

"What did he say?" Ravlok asked.

Before she could answer, Anwic spoke again, this time in perfect Eidosinian. "There are only five arcanists among us. Even if they had saphyrum to cast spells, we would still be outnumbered three to one."

"Then what would you suggest?" Ravlok didn't bother to hide his annoyance. "Because I certainly don't plan to die in this cell."

"You would rather burn in mage's fire than starve to death in the comfort of these stone walls?" Anwic's tone dripped with condescension. "Perhaps you would prefer steel in your belly instead?"

Ravlok's hands tightened on the bars. He took a slow, centering breath before responding, allowing his irritation to subside. Scornful jests would not help them, but neither would his own poor reaction to such things. He could give Anwic a little quarter; no doubt the Syljian's ill temper was a product of his circumstances.

"I would rather die fighting for my freedom than languish in the arms of my enemy." Surely a Syljian could agree with that.

Anwic seemed unmoved. "Pretty words, *bashiin*. We'll see how you fare after you get past the lock on your door."

Ravlok didn't know what a *bashiin* was, but it certainly sounded like an insult. Orowen's scowl in Anwic's direction confirmed it. She barked a few words in Syljian, to which Anwic responded grudgingly and fell silent.

"Please forgive Anwic," Orowen said to Ravlok. "He has a knack for being insufferable. I'm afraid it's a product of his youth."

"Hm." Though Ravlok was loath to admit it, Anwic had a point. No amount of planning would do them any good if they couldn't get outside their cells. He examined the steel framework holding the door in place, gave the bars another tug, and turned his attention to the locking mechanism—a slotted wing welded to a thick bolt and fitted over an eyelet on the door. The bolt slid into a mounting plate seated into the stonework. It was held in place by a padlock roughly the size of his fist.

He reached through the bars to examine the padlock, then patted his pockets, searching for the lock pick he always carried. One could argue such a device was more suited for a thief than a monk, but old habits were hard to break. Ravlok found himself in places he didn't belong often enough that to go without one for propriety's sake would have made him a fool. Even so, the lock pick—as well as his library key, tinderbox, pens, and ink—was nowhere to be found.

He sighed. It was only a temporary setback. If he couldn't pick the lock, perhaps he could break it. Though, as he fingered the heavy steel piece again, he suspected doing so without the help of a tool was unlikely.

Fine. If not the lock, then a part of the lock's surroundings. After all, the world's most unbeatable lock was only as strong as the object to which it was fastened. He examined what should be one of the weakest points: the slotted wing. To his disappointment, the craftsmanship was excellent. There was no sign of rust, porosity, or warping at that joint. The eyelet, however—

Ravlok squinted in the dim light, turning the padlock this way and that, trying to deflect enough light off its steel casing to get a good look at the eyelet. It was on the underside that he finally found something that could help him: a small stress fracture in the metalwork's curvature. It had been oxidizing for long enough, sheltered in the snug fit of the padlock, that a significant amount of rust had taken hold. If he could hit that point hard enough, he could break the eyelet clean off the door.

He would need something to act as a hammer. Turning back to examine his cell, he took only a few seconds to determine that the mound of straw in one corner and the rusty bucket beside him wouldn't be of much help. He could maybe crush the bucket into a metal roll small enough to fit through the bars, but as he reached down to test the bucket's thickness, he scrapped that idea. No amount of mundane strength he possessed was going to bend that metal.

Outside his cell came the clinking of chains again.

It was as much a sign from the gods as Ravlok had ever experienced. When he turned to look, he found Orowen watching him, her brows furrowed with interest. Her manacled hands rested on the crossbeam below the lock on her door.

Glancing around his cell again, he found a similar set of chains and manacles wrapped with morbid care over a large metal hoop driven into the stone.

"Orowen." Ravlok eyed the heavy irons on his wall. "How far do your manacles reach?"

"Far enough, I suppose."

He turned back to her. "Show me."

Orowen obliged him, reaching out of her cell. The chain went taut at the bar just past her elbow. "What are you thinking?"

Ravlok rose to his feet. It was a long shot, but it would have to be good enough. "I have an idea."

CHAPTER SEVEN

DAEYA

Daeya scrubbed her skin until it was red and raw. When that didn't help, she gripped her mother's saphyrum pendant and shot a hand outside the stream of water, toward the coals beneath the washbasin. Magic coursed hot through her veins.

"*Vuurmas.*"

Fire shot from her fingertips. The coals burned white-hot for an instant, and the bottom of the metal basin glowed red. It took several seconds for the water to reach her through the bathhouse's amalgamation of pumps and twisting pipes, but when it did, she nearly recoiled from the scalding heat. Steam filled the shower stall. After steadying herself against the tiled wall, she scrubbed harder, willing the combination of soap and searing pain to make her feel clean.

Still, the memory of Gregory's icy hands remained.

Each time, she vowed their meeting would be different. Each time, she promised herself she wouldn't allow him to twist her around his fingers. And each time, no matter how hard she fought it, she wound up exactly as he wanted her:

clamoring for his affection like a wounded animal, fearing what would become of her without it. The person she was in his presence made her want to climb inside that washbasin, slip beneath the water's surface, and never come up again.

It was by defiance alone that she hadn't fallen prey to those thoughts, for the person she was apart from him reviled every aspect of their relationship. In the past six years, she'd tried everything in her power to escape him. She'd requested mentorship transfers, filed complaints, engaged in delinquent behavior, and pulled pranks on nearly every instructor in the Guild. Nothing had worked. Gregory was always several steps ahead of her, placating the Council and blocking her expulsion at every turn.

Daeya had even run away once. She'd sworn off magic, sold her saphyrum, and made it all the way to Belden last year before a terrible illness left her bedridden in the town abbey, where Cameron Vika caught up to her. After Gregory's expert tracker returned her to Ryost, he'd made certain Daeya understood the consequences of making that mistake a second time. For her father's sake, she would never run again.

She dropped the sponge at her feet and pressed both hands to the wall, letting the water scald her neck and shoulders. Her skin glowed red between hundreds of ghost-white scars on her arms, torso, and legs. She squeezed her eyes shut against those cursed runes and stood there a few moments more, contemplating whether an extensive network of burn scars might rid her of them more easily and less painfully than flaying them had.

No. They would just grow back. Unless she got hold of his enchanted dagger again, they always would.

Gregory claimed his work made her strong. He claimed the runes focused her excessive power and allowed her to harness the Aether more successfully. Sometimes, she even believed him. But he also demanded she keep them hidden because not doing so would invite others to question the purity of her human bloodline. Only Syljians possessed such runic markings naturally. If anyone should discover them—anyone other than Cameron, who was sworn to secrecy as well—Gregory had assured her no amount of weight his rank carried would stop the Council from condemning her to death.

Because she wasn't certain whether he was being truthful—or perhaps because she suspected he would throw her under the wagon before owning up to the runes' creation in front of the Council—Daeya kept them to herself. Their secret alone had shaped her life within the Guild more irrevocably than even Gregory's favoritism. It had been years since she'd showered in this room with another person. Everything she wore was long-sleeved and oppressively modest, even in the heat of summer. Daeya had never worn a dress to the Midsummer Ball, or gone swimming, or even jumped off the rope swing into Opal Creek. She'd certainly never been intimate with anyone.

Her scars, just like her rapid advancement through the Guild ranks, were Gregory's way of keeping her isolated and yearning for meaningful connections of any kind. Deep down, she understood this, but there was little she could do about it. So she'd obeyed him, more or less, and bided her time, believing her promotion to mage would eventually free her from him.

Gods, had she been wrong.

By assigning her an escort, Gregory had foiled even that small mercy. She would be as much a prisoner outside Ryost's walls as within them. The Vikas were loyal to him, and the two brothers hated her almost as much as Normos did. There was no doubt in her mind that Joss and Toby would take every opportunity to make her life miserable.

As the water returned to a reasonable temperature, she lifted her face toward the stream and let out a sigh. Their assignment was only temporary, Gregory had said. Should she dare to hope he'd spoken truly, she risked being disappointed again—he made a habit of changing the terms of their agreements—but there was nothing for it. Her only option was to endure their presence, perform her best work, and give Gregory's minions nothing of value to report.

"Hey!" Sharp pounding at the bathhouse door jolted her out of her thoughts.

"Bleeding—" Daeya reached for the spigot to shut off the water. She had lingered here too long. Fortunately, she was an expert at this diversion. "The door must be stuck again. Just a moment!"

The pounding stopped. She toweled off, donned her casting bracelet, and dressed quickly to the sound of inarticulate grumbling from outside the room. When she finished, she threw her black robe over her arm and whispered the words to reverse the Seal she had placed on the door.

The combination of constant humidity in the bathhouse and archaic construction techniques was, in fact, known to make the old wooden door stick in its frame. She vocalized the difficulty of opening it with a series of grunts and expletives. When she felt hands pushing from the other side, she finally moved her foot from in front of the door to the small lip at the bottom and lifted with her toes. The top scraped against the frame and popped free, sending Tom Bennick sprawling into the room.

Daeya caught her former study partner before he fell, hissing when his hand closed around her arm. The soft fabric of her undershirt rubbed painfully against her burned skin.

Tom released her with a wince. "Sorry, Day-a."

"No harm done." She salvaged a smile for the older boy and resisted the urge to correct him. He'd always mispronounced her name, despite how many times she explained the Brogrenti *ae* was pronounced like 'aye.' "You'd think maintenance would finally fix this bleeding door."

Tom returned the smile as he righted himself, straightening his stack of clothes and toiletries. "That would be the day." His attention strayed to the black robe over her arm, and his eyes widened. "You got promoted! When did that happen?"

"This morning." She looked down at the robe. "It was sort of a shock to me, too."

"Well, congratulations. Or condolences, as it were." The junior acolyte's smile faltered. He gestured to the sunlit hallway outside the room. "Now you'll have to leave all this shining splendor behind you and find love among the commoners."

Daeya fought the urge to snort. With Bennick's noble blood, his worst nightmare was probably a trip to a village without pump-fed water. "I'm certain I'll get along with them well enough."

"Of course, you were a commoner too, weren't you?" He wrinkled his nose and eyed the robe again. "Fancy your luck."

There was an inkling of jealousy in his tone that signaled the luck he referred to had nothing to do with her dodging the life of a commoner. Her modest roots had been his favorite way to tease her in the brief time they shared rank, but they'd become a knife once she got promoted to senior acolyte. Tom had failed the advancement exams twice since then, and with each failure, he grew more embittered.

She sobered and cleared her throat. "Yes, fancy my luck." Before the awkwardness between them could get any worse, she dipped her chin. "Good day, Tom."

He nodded, friendliness dissolved. No longer an inkling, his envy blackened his expression. "Same to you, Sorceress."

With nothing left to say, she backpedaled out of the room and let the door close between them. The hallway was deserted this late in the morning, so she could afford some time to gather her wits. She pressed her blistered back against the cool stone wall and clutched the robe to her chest, drawing several lungfuls of air to steady herself.

Her promotion was beginning to feel more like a curse. Not only had Gregory thwarted her attempts to escape him yet again, he had also ensured she was both too young to fit in among the mages and too skilled to find friendship among her peers. Tom's reaction would be much the same as any other student's.

Except, maybe, for one.

Faustus would be happy for her. The twenty-year-old initiate could always cheer her up. Whether it was his small-town sensibilities or the fact that they were both very different from others of their ranks, Faustus was never jealous or disparaging of her, and he never bought into the rumors his classmates spread. He'd even defended her from them a few times.

She checked the clock on the wall and turned south for the rotunda. His Divinations class ended in a few minutes. She owed it to him to explain her promotion and his reassignment personally.

And, truthfully, she was going to miss him while she was gone.

Moths flitted about Daeya's stomach as the students funneled out of Master Ulrich's classroom. Her sigh was half a growl at being made to wait, and she tried one last time to groom her wet hair into some semblance of presentability.

It didn't matter, though. The last students departed, and Faustus wasn't among them.

Brows tensing, Daeya approached the door and peered inside. Her eyes swept the six sets of tables equipped with scrying mirrors, crystal balls, and various handouts detailing the basic incantations and sigils. The chairs were in slight disarray, but all of them sat empty. At the far end of the room, she spotted Master Ulrich.

Like most Cintoshi, Ulrich was an enormous presence in a stout little body. The crown of her head barely reached Daeya's elbows. Her arms and legs were nearly equal in length and as thick around as any blacksmith's apprentice. Lily-white patron's beads—the purest and most potent of all saphyrum—were woven neatly into her beard with fine gold thread. She wore the crimson robe of a master instructor, tailored impeccably to match her compact frame; the color perfectly complemented the ribbons tied into her long golden braids, which coiled at the nape of her neck before spilling down to her waist.

She stood on a small ladder, erasing a set of runes from the chalkboard. Loose white dust clouded the air. "Daeya McVen," she said without turning. "To what do I owe this honor?"

It was out of habit that Daeya straightened when the old master addressed her. She'd finished the last of her Divinations requirements a year before, but Mardis Ulrich made a lasting impression on her students.

"Good morning, Master." Daeya stepped carefully into the room. "I'm looking for Initiate Crex."

"Mr. Crex wasn't in class today." Ulrich finished wiping her chalkboard and climbed down.

"He wasn't?"

"No."

Daeya's jaw worked for a moment. It wasn't like Faustus to skip class. "Did he send an excusal?"

Ulrich turned to her, expression impassive. "He did not."

Maybe he'd taken ill after she left him this morning. Daeya thought back to their last conversation, trying to recall his appearance. He'd been a little harried coming down from his quarters. He'd paled at hearing Gregory's rumor, but who wouldn't at the thought of Cheralach the Deserter inside their city walls? His color had returned to normal as soon as he started scolding her for implying they should try to meet the infamous Alliaansi leader.

"He is certainly one of the last students who should be missing my class," Ulrich said, bringing Daeya back to the present.

She cringed at the disapproval in Ulrich's voice. "I apologize for him, Master. I'm sure something just held him up."

As she spoke, she tried to stave off the sinking feeling in her gut. Maybe Gregory's suspicions about Faustus were correct. If his absence was because of her fake news about Cheralach, it would confirm that he was not who he claimed. Ever since his enrollment, Gregory had been distrustful. He believed Faustus's hometown, Sarton, was too close to the border with Alliaansi territory to discount its influence on the people there. But Daeya had observed Faustus for months, and no part of his demeanor ever seemed concerning or unusual to her, aside from his continued use of the proper term for Syljians. She had never once heard him utter the word 'blanker.' Still, that didn't make him an Alliaansi spy.

No, there must be a better explanation for his absence. Students missed class all the time.

Ulrich smoothed the front of her robe and regarded Daeya with unnerving shrewdness. She gestured with one ring-smothered hand. "Miss McVen, is that what I think it is?"

Having almost forgotten its existence, Daeya looked down at her black robe. "It is."

Her old instructor's face lit up. "Well, put it on. Let me see you."

Heat flooded Daeya's cheeks. She bowed her head before moving to obey. "Of course." The robe settled around her shoulders, feeling just as perfect, if not better, than it had in Gregory's office.

Ulrich walked a full circle around her, humming appreciatively. "It suits you. An honor well-deserved."

The heat in Daeya's face redoubled, and pleasure rushed all the way down to her toes. That was high and unexpected praise, coming from Mardis Ulrich. "Thank you, Master."

"Where is Gregory sending you first?"

As quickly as it had come, the flood of pride receded. She sucked in a silent breath before answering. "Orthovia."

One neatly braided eyebrow lifted. "You are not pleased by that assignment."

It was not a question. Daeya couldn't hide from the Divinations instructor any more than she could lie to her. "It's not the assignment, Master. The Council requested Gregory send an escort along with me."

"Whatever for?"

"Something about my age. He said the Vikas will accompany me on my missions for the first few months."

Ulrich scowled. "That's preposterous. I've seen your grades in Diplomacy. You are much more capable than those knuckleheads. I will speak to the Council on your behalf."

A phantom ripple of Daeya's earlier panic stuttered through her. She had promised Gregory she would accept the Council's decision. If Ulrich went to them and argued in her favor, it would surely upset him. "Please, there's no need. It's only temporary."

Ulrich regarded her with silent skepticism. Truly, her ability to speak without words was remarkable.

Daeya balled one hand at her side and shielded it in the folds of her robe. "It's frustrating." She lowered her gaze to avoid that penetrating stare, focusing on the sharp bite of fingernails into her palm. "But it's something I agreed to accept."

After another moment of silence, Ulrich mercifully relented. "Very well. I wish you good fortune on your journey." She spun on her heel and returned to her chalkboard. "You should visit your father before you go." Picking up a nub of chalk from the ledge, she added, "I'm sure he'll be pleased by your promotion as well."

Daeya's fingers relaxed. The thought of her da made her smile. The braggart would surely have half the city aware of her promotion by day's end. "I will. Thank you."

Ulrich reached for her ladder and began to climb. "No thanks needed, Miss McVen. Now be off with you. I have work to do."

Daeya clasped her hands and bowed again. It made little sense, considering that the instructor was facing away from her. However, anyone who had taken classes with Ulrich would have done the same. It was largely out of respect, but partly out of caution. To this day, Daeya still wasn't sure Ulrich didn't have eyes in the back of her head.

"Farewell, Master Ulrich."

As she left the classroom, a knot twisted inside Daeya's abdomen. There had to be a reasonable explanation for why Faustus wasn't in class. She would try to find him in all his usual places, as well as the infirmary. If he didn't turn up in any of those, she could go to the Administrator's Office. Maybe there was an excusal request he'd submitted late just waiting to be filed. If there wasn't, she would have no choice but to report his disappearance—and her mistake—to Gregory.

That, of course, was the last thing she wanted to do.

Chapter Eight

Alar

The twin towers of Old River Bridge jutted proudly into the early afternoon sky. Moss and ivy covered the structure, and a fine mist slicked its worn surface. Carriages crowded the narrow roadway, and heavy foot traffic filled any gaps. Shouts and curses from men and women on the ground echoed across the water, accompanied by those of frustrated coachmen guiding their horses through the melee. Soldiers in green and gold livery struggled to control the traffic. Alar likened the chaos more to a Solstice Festival than a typical Mirasday afternoon.

It was a manufactured chaos, thanks to Val. With a series of well-timed mishaps involving a mason's cart, a wagon, and several large pieces of forge equipment, he'd forced the city guard to redirect much of the Falcon River Bridge traffic so the damaged stonework could be repaired.

In all the confusion, it was easy for Alar to slip through the crowd. None of the mages looked his way. None of the soldiers questioned him. But when he pushed open the door to the eastern bridge tower and stepped inside, he froze.

Val knelt at the feet of a black-robed mage, head bowed.

An icy spear of panic lanced through Alar. He summoned a volley of crushing psionic energy, readying to strike out at the mage's mind—

Val lobbed a grin over his shoulder and pulled off his blindfold. "Welcome to the party," he said, pushing his unruly black curls out of his face. His violet eyes danced with excitement in the thin stream of light filtering in from a window high overhead.

Alar's shoulders sagged, the tension unspooling from him like a weaver's thread.

Using the sleeve of his stolen mage's robe, seventeen-year-old Jack Orrin wiped blood off his dagger. "If a hopeless dungeon rescue is your version of a party, then I chose the wrong employer."

Val laughed and returned to searching the trio of bodies at Jack's feet. "Say what you will." He tossed the first soldier's coin purse toward the thief; Jack caught it smoothly in his free hand. "At least I keep food in your belly."

"It's no consolation if I'm dead," Jack grumbled, pocketing the purse.

"No one's dying today." Alar turned back to the entryway and found a thick wooden bar mounted on a swivel attached to the door. He slid it into place with ease, grateful for the few extra moments it might afford them. "We get in, we get out, and we hole up until the excitement wears off."

Val started stripping the soldier of his green and gold uniform. "See? I told you Alar had a plan."

Jack's morose expression didn't change. "Great." His brown eyes rolled skyward. "I feel so much better now."

"Good. Now make yourself useful and help me with these clothes."

"You'll want to wear the robe, Val," Alar suggested, watching him pull boots off the dead man. He crossed the small room and nodded toward the trapdoor between the bodies. "Anyone down there should just assume you recently cast a spell."

Jack was already taking the black robe off. "Be my guest." He held the robe between his index finger and thumb, as if he couldn't bear it touching him any longer. Alar couldn't blame him. It was the mages whose 'questioning' had killed Jack's father when he was a child. He was one of many orphans the Guild sorcerers had created to keep the secrets of magic to themselves.

Val finished stripping the guard and traded the uniform for the robe. They quickly dressed and transferred all their belongings while Alar stripped the second guard. As Alar pulled the soldier's chain mail and uniform on, Val stepped toward the trapdoor and loaded his hand crossbow.

Alar fidgeted in the heavy chain. "Do we have any idea what's down there?"

This time when the spymaster grinned, it was with the air of a madman. "Not a clue." Val nodded toward the bodies. "Three fewer, now, though."

Jack's tan skin lightened several shades. His eyebrows shot toward his cap of close-cropped black hair. "I thought you said—"

"Ready weapons," Val broke in, kneeling down next to the door.

With a sigh, Jack knelt on the door's opposite side and drew his own hand crossbow.

Val threw a glance at Alar. "At your leisure."

With a silent nod, Alar focused his mind on the thick metal ring and willed it upward. The ring stood on end easily, but just as if he'd lifted the door with his hands, he met resistance trying to pry the heavy wood out of its frame. He focused harder, visualizing exactly what he wanted from his telekinetic hold, and a few seconds later, the door swung up.

As soon as there was enough light pouring into the opening to see, Val and Jack moved as one, taking aim at whomever might be lingering at the bottom of the hole. Alar stayed back and let the two work, minding how quietly he settled the door against the floor.

The two men stayed frozen, their weapons balanced unwaveringly on their knees. Val relaxed a moment later, and Alar spoke in his mind. "*Walk in like you own the place. We'll cover you.*"

"*You'd better.*"

Knowing Alar could only create one telepathic link at a time, Val used a series of hand signals to relay his messages to Jack. Some of Alar's trepidation lifted as he observed them. Much as Jack bemoaned his employment, the two worked well together. They just might have a chance.

Val's hand crossbow disappeared up his sleeve, and he started down the metal ladder under the floor. Alar and Jack followed. A long, narrow corridor greeted them at the bottom. From the relative depth of their descent and the dank stench of mildew, they must have passed below the riverbed.

A series of torches set in sconces lit their path to the east. Fire bathed the wet stone and cast ominous shadows along the walls. Stale water lingered in puddles that reflected firelight like dozens of mirrors strewn about the floor. Up ahead, the corridor turned a tight corner to the north. There were no guards along this first stretch, as far as Alar could see.

Val strode forward with a confidence that could very well have been real. Even though the mage's robe was too long for him, it swept over the floor as if it had its own part to play in their deception. Alar envied him for the simple garment as he adjusted his noisy chain mail again. Still, it would be foolish to go into this battle without it. If the mages down here could resist psionics, he'd likely need the dagger in his boot, too.

The thought of having to get up close to kill someone didn't sit well. Alar preferred to stay far away from the action and keep his hands clean. But he had a reputation for doing whatever was necessary to get a job done; a little blood and dirt would not deter him.

As they approached the blind corner, Val spoke in his mind. "*Guards around the bend.*" He motioned the same message to Jack.

"*How many?*" Alar didn't hear anything, but he had learned in all his years of friendship with Val not to ask how he knew things. His answers to such questions were often nonsensical, anyway.

Val held up two fingers and glanced over his shoulder. Wicked mischief gilded his expression. "*Maybe they could use a little Syljian suggestion. On my mark.*"

Alar nodded once and readied his mind for the work of a psionic suggestion. Once he saw his targets, he could seize their auras and force a brief window of suppressed emotion, making them more likely to agree to any course of action Val might propose to them.

Val gestured again to Jack, who fell behind Alar and came around his other side, pressing his back to the stone beside the corner. He disappeared into the shadow thrown by the closest wall sconce.

Without breaking stride, Val swept around the bend, Alar only a half-step behind him. Sure enough, five paces down the corridor, two armed guards stepped out of a pair of alcoves flanking the path. Projecting his aura-sense, Alar saw into their emotional states as easily as he saw the gleam of their raised swords in the torchlight. Both men's auras extended beyond their normal limits, suggesting alertness. They also shimmered steadily, denoting caution.

"Password, Sorcerer," the guard on their left said. His deep voice carried eerily in the stone tomb.

Val gave Alar a mental nudge. "*Now.*"

Alar reached out with his mind. Much as he had envisioned the rising trapdoor a few moments ago, he envisioned the soldiers' auras shrinking back toward their bodies. He *squeezed* with all his might, and within two heartbeats, both men went glassy-eyed and lowered their weapons.

"Your shift's over, boys. Go have a drink." Val flipped a silver coin toward the man on the left.

The guard fumbled to catch the coin, stared at it in his hand, and looked at his companion. With their emotions subdued, their personal desires should subvert any greater sense of fear or duty they possessed. Alar couldn't force their thoughts toward a specific feeling in his state, though. It took all his mental focus to suppress their auras.

Four seconds passed.

Like the beginnings of an avalanche, Alar's hold on them slipped. The two still didn't move. That was the problem with psionic suggestion; the psychic hold on a living being's aura met with fierce resistance and degraded rapidly, making it extremely demanding for anyone but a mastermind to maintain for long. He clenched his fists, struggling to stall the cascade a second or two longer.

Val used the borrowed time to gesture toward the men and sidestep away from Alar, allowing enough room in the corridor for the soldiers to pass between them. "I don't have all day," he snapped.

No doubt, the sight of his bright violet eyes contributed to the performance. As Alar's mental dam crumbled, a sudden burst of fear flooded the soldiers' auras. Both men paled. They clamored over each other to retreat through the gap Val had made.

"Yes, sir."

"Good day to you, Sorcerer."

They hurried past them and disappeared around the corner. Val turned back, looking smug. "*That went well.*"

Alar breathed a quiet sigh, shoulders sagging with fatigue. He allowed himself to relax and pulled out a bead. His fingers closed around the saphyrum, light seeped through his skin, and a wave of cool, restorative energy surged through his limbs.

The retreating footsteps down the adjacent corridor stopped. "Hey, wait a minute—"

Snick—thock.

"What—"

Snick—thock.

Two crossbow bolts fired in quick succession found their targets. Bodies dropped with the implacable weight of death. A gurgling hiss followed.

More sounds issued from around the corner—grunting and rasping, then two more thuds. Jack rounded the bend moments later. His expression, unlike Val's, was all business, and he wiped at a bloodstain on his sleeve. "At least they had the courtesy to die quietly."

"The bodies?" Val asked.

Jack rewound his crossbow and placed a bolt along the tiller. "Taken care of."

Val nodded and looked north, tilting his head as if listening for something. Alar tucked his bead away and followed the spymaster's gaze. For another few hundred spans, the path was clear and straight before turning east again. The tunnel floor was drier this way, but the smell of damp stone lingered. Dripping water and the crackle of torches filled the silence.

From deeper underground came footsteps.

Alar stiffened, and Val's good humor dissipated like smoke on the wind. They shared a look; it was much too soon for them to be discovered, but no alarm had been raised yet. Perhaps they could play this off.

"*The alcoves.*"

Val nodded. He gestured the message to Jack, who wasted no time slipping into the right-hand gap in the stone. As the footsteps drew closer, Val turned his ear toward the sound and held up three fingers. "*The soldiers usually travel in pairs. Could be mages. Follow my lead.*" He pulled up his hood, and his features disappeared into shadow.

Once Alar settled into the alcove on the left, Val spun toward him, upper lip curled. "And if I ever catch you sleeping on the job again, I will make certain it is the last time."

Alar took his cue in stride. "Beggin' yer pardon, Sorcerer," he stammered, injecting a healthy dose of fear into his interpretation of a Ryostian commoner. "I swear on me mum, it won't happen again."

Their enemies must have turned the corner at the end of the hall. Louder footsteps carried down the passageway, coupled with the distinct rattle of sword and chain. At least one soldier. Possibly two, but not three. That meant at least one mage was with them. He and Val were taking a tremendous risk with this charade. If the sorcerers assigned to this place were a close-knit group, this one would recognize right away that Val didn't belong.

He relayed his concerns to Val, whose only acknowledgment was to lean deeper into the shadows; the hood disguised the vast majority of his face.

"See that it does not," he snapped.

"What's going on here?" said a smooth, pompous voice. The sound made Alar's skin crawl.

Val turned to the newcomers and gestured at Alar. "Caught this useless sack of meat sleeping on his watch. If I'd been a filthy blanker, I'd have strolled right past him." Dry amusement passed through their telepathic connection. "*Two soldiers. One mage. A seasoned one, by the looks of him. Thin little bastard. Ten gold says I could snap him like kindling.*"

"In his defense, the shift change is long overdue." The mage seemed unconcerned by Val's identity. "But you are right; we cannot afford to make mistakes."

He stepped into Alar's view. His black robe clung to his body like a burial shroud. There was no mistaking his air of contempt. From his straight-backed, aristocratic posture to his cruel blue eyes and gangly limbs, he was built to intimidate, not to fight.

"*Provided he doesn't set you on fire first.*" Alar kept his eyes downcast, letting his posture slump further, as if the attention from a second mage so thoroughly unnerved him that he might piss himself.

"You are relieved, soldier," the mage said. "Report to Captain Sangrin immediately."

"O-of course, Sorcerer," Alar stuttered. "Right away, sir."

As he slipped out of the alcove and around the mage, it occurred to him that he didn't know which way this Captain Sangrin might be. If he was stationed further underground, the mage would expect him to turn north, back down the way he and his retinue had come. If the captain's office was among those of other military officers, he should turn south for the bridge tower and the surface. Reasonable arguments could be made for both possibilities, but Alar didn't have time to ponder them. He went south, toward the exit and greater probability. He could double back when the mage was gone.

"Soldier," the mage barked.

Alar gritted his teeth. Apparently, he'd chosen incorrectly. "Y-yes, sir?"

Though he kept a white-knuckled grip on the fear in his tone, he was already puzzling out how to get them out of this mess. From the cursory glance he'd stolen in their direction, he knew the two helmed soldiers flanked the mage a full step behind him, and Val was only a half-step to his right. Without actually looking at the mage himself, Alar couldn't target him with a psychic blast. He also hadn't gotten an opportunity to check him for psionic wards.

He eyed the four torches on the walls in front of him.

"Captain Sangrin is that—"

"*Duck*," Alar commanded Val, *seizing* the torches with his mind. All four tore out of their sconces and flew over Alar's shoulders.

Alar spun as the molten cloud of embers exploded against the two soldiers. Jack moved as well, firing two shots in their direction. One bolt missed its target and rang off the closer soldier's helm. The other struck the second soldier in the hand as he tried to shield himself from the torches.

Jack swore as the soldier screamed. He slipped out of the alcove, drew his dagger, and lunged forward to silence his target.

Val threw himself into the mage's legs, sending them both sprawling into the eastern alcove. The mage spat out a breathless incantation, and fire erupted. Alar dashed forward to assist Val, but the uninjured guard intercepted him. The man smashed his gauntleted fist into the side of Alar's head. Pain exploded. He bounced off the wall and hit the ground.

Stars swam in his vision, but the sound of a sword rasping out of its sheath was warning enough. He rolled to the side as the guard's rapier skewered the stone beside him. Alar kicked outward and the soldier's leg buckled, sending him crashing to one knee. As his sight returned, Alar *seized* the guard's sword; the weapon flew out of his grip, right into Alar's outstretched hand. He shot to his feet and chopped the blade down into the man's neck. It was too unwieldy a weapon in Alar's unpracticed hand to do much more than slice the skin, but it bought him enough time to draw the weapon back and pierce the side of the man's throat. The guard died gushing blood all over his green and gold uniform.

The second soldier slumped in Jack's arms, his mewling cries silenced by the hand clamped firmly around his mouth and nose. Drawing his dagger in one smooth stroke across the man's neck, Jack shoved the body away and started for the alcove. Alar reached the gap in the stone at the same time.

The sight before them was not at all what Alar had expected. Val sat atop the mage in the torch-lit space, desperately scrabbling to break the sorcerer's hold on his neck. His dagger lay discarded above the mage's head, and Val had disarmed the mage of his saphyrum, which lay scattered about the small space like glittering gems. Their lack of weapons had reduced the two to fighting like savages, the sorcerer choking Val, while Val alternated between attempts to claw out his strangler's eyes and break his fingers.

Despite Val's superior position, the mage's longer reach awarded him the upper hand. Alar focused on his face, reaching out to the mage's mind.

The instant he made contact, the sorcerer's eyes snapped toward him. "Blanker swine!"

"Wastelands." This one, at least, had trained to recognize a psionic touch.

"Alliaansi!" The sorcerer's voice carried alarmingly well down the corridor. "Alliaansi dogs under the—"

Jack strode into the alcove and shot the mage in the throat.

Val gasped, raking in gulps of air as the mage's hands fell away. He slumped to one side.

Jack caught him under one arm. "Easy there, boss. I've got you." He hauled Val to his feet and supported the spymaster's weight with his own.

Somewhere further under the city, the shouts of men and running footsteps stole Alar's attention. He stared down the corridor to the north, fists clenched at his sides. There was no way to know how much farther they had to go, but they surely weren't close enough. It was best for them to keep picking off guards a few at a time, but the mage's alert would likely bring the entire garrison down on them.

"Alar," Val rasped.

Alar's gaze leveled on him as Jack helped him into a seated position against the wall. Val's hood had been thrown back during his struggle with the mage. The bluish tint to his face was fading, but the bruises on his neck already looked gruesome. He held out his curled fingers to Alar with the smallest tremor in his arm.

"We'll hold them here." Val pressed a set of keys, likely taken off the mage, into Alar's palm. "You can fake your way in."

Alar was shaking his head before his friend finished speaking. Even if he could fake the role of a disheveled soldier running back for reinforcements, the likelihood of succeeding and getting past any more mages was too slim to risk going in alone. He would, if he must, leave his companions behind, but he was certain the time for that was not yet upon them.

"You have to." Val's expression grew pained. "Tell Finn I love her."

"You'll tell her yourself," Alar said firmly. His lips twitched into a thin smile at the thought of Val's hot-tempered wife. "Besides, she'd never forgive me if I let something happen to you."

Val's chuckle was just as much agreement as wry amusement.

Alar turned back down the passageway; pounding reverberations of the advancing troops echoed toward them. The alcoves could protect them from a ranged assault, but the sorcerers would quickly overrun them here in close quarters. He would need some kind of deterrent to hold the soldiers back. Or at the very least, make them hesitate.

On the wall, perhaps a hundred paces in front of them, he could see the shadows of the soldiers thrown by the firelight around the corner. He looked again at the torches aligned in a double row all the way down the tunnel.

"Load your crossbows." Alar wrapped his mind around the four torches closest to them. He pulled them gently out of their sconces this time. They drifted slowly down the corridor, allowing darkness to creep in from behind and fill the alcoves. "We're going to need them."

Chapter Nine

Ravlok

Ravlok's attempts to break the rusty eyelet off his cell door weren't going well.

He'd tried wrapping the chain around the lock and pulling with all his might to pry some movement out of the cracked metal. He'd also tried slamming a manacle into the eyelet. Sparks had flown a few times, but it wasn't enough to break it. Apparently, the oxidation was more superficial than he'd thought.

His work on the door had an unintended benefit, however. The noise eventually drew a mage to investigate. While Ravlok wouldn't ordinarily consider that a boon, the moment he saw a set of keys and a bag of saphyrum carelessly swinging from the mage's belt, he knew exactly what to do.

Ravlok had spent the last eight years in the monastery serving Ordeolas, but before that, he'd grown up on the streets and picked pockets for a living. When he joined the Order at sixteen, Yonfé told him theft would not be tolerated among his students. Uninterested in angering the only source of free lodging and food he'd had since Madame had kicked him out of her courtesy house, Ravlok swore an oath not to steal so long as he walked the path to Balance. However, borrowing wasn't forbidden. Ravlok promised himself he would return the items when he was finished.

But first, he had to acquire them. Initially, the sorcerer kept enough distance to make that impossible as he snarled threats through the cell door. When he returned the second time, though, Ravlok was ready.

"I thought I told you to knock it off," the mage said as he approached the bars. Though he was of human ancestry, his overgrown eyebrows and massive beard would have better suited one with a Cintoshi heritage. He was shorter than average, yet the looming shadow he cast over the cell door was tall enough to look menacing. He brandished a quarterstaff as if to make good on his threat to beat Ravlok with it after all.

Ravlok knelt on the stone floor with the manacle still clutched in one hand, wrist resting against the crossbeam beside the lock. His other arm hung up to his elbow outside the cell, level with the sorcerer's belt. "Well, I'm *trying*," he said, exaggerating his exasperation. "But it's not as easy as it looks."

"You know what I mean. Stop making that racket."

Ravlok snorted. "I'm sorry. I don't take orders from acolytes."

It took a moment for the mage to process the insult. He drew back the end of his staff. "Insolent little shit."

"*Daale!*"

The mage paused. Across the corridor, Orowen stood at her cell door. She lifted her chin and rattled off something in Syljian. The mage lowered his staff, turned toward her, and barked a reply in the same language.

Of course he would know Syljian. Though Ravlok's own ignorance annoyed him, it made sense the sorcerer would have learned it. He *did* work in a dungeon meant to harbor Syljians.

While Orowen occupied him with a contemptuous tirade, Ravlok eyed the items tied to the sorcerer's belt. He squinted through the torchlight at the easily slipped highwayman's knots holding them in place.

A rookie mistake, or perhaps a choice made from overconfidence and too little time spent among the city markets. Even though most thieves wouldn't chance a tangle with a mage for a simple coin purse, a poorly secured bag of saphyrum was almost always worth the risk for a veteran pickpocket.

Steadying himself with a slow breath, Ravlok reached for the bag. His fingertips closed on the string, eyes flicking up to ensure the mage's distraction. Heart quickening, he pulled the knot with expert precision. Silken fibers glided against one another without a sound. He contained his excitement as the bag came away, careful not to move too fast and disturb its contents. Once through the bars, he set his prize beside him, out of sight around the wall. Another breath settled the prickling in his limbs; it seemed he hadn't lost his touch in eight years of retirement.

The sorcerer didn't notice. Orowen spat something else that provoked him enough to hiss several long-winded phrases. Ravlok admired her ability to rattle him. But as he went back for the keys, only fingerspans from untying the knot, the mage stalked toward her cell, his tone a mercurial combination of anger and malevolence. Ravlok jerked his hand back to avoid caressing the man's hip as he passed.

Orowen's expression shifted as the mage continued. Fear and uncertainty flickered across her face, at which the man laughed. His amusement sobered her, and she glared at him with a fervor that might have set the entire corridor alight.

"*Ithe'ruh caezo.*"

That was a phrase Ravlok recognized. It translated to 'Eat shit.' Aivenosian had an almost identical pronunciation for the same insult.

Now he liked this woman even more.

The mage switched back to Eidosinian. "I'm going to enjoy watching you die."

He thrust the end of his staff into Orowen's chest. She didn't cry out, but she still collapsed in a heap of limbs and rattling chains.

Ravlok started against the bars, hoping he'd imagined the sound of snapping bone. She was such a tiny thing, and she looked even smaller curled against the stone.

The mage turned back to him. "Now, where were we?"

He reclaimed his spot in front of Ravlok's cell for only a moment before the door to the dungeon screeched open and another shout echoed down the hallway. "Lux! Where are you, man? We've got company!"

Ravlok nodded toward the sound of that voice. "Yeah, Lux. Better run along and stop assaulting unarmed prisoners."

Lux ignored his companion, reached into Ravlok's cell, and grabbed the front of his tunic. Hardly believing his luck, Ravlok allowed the mage to pull him close. With his face jammed against the cold metal bars, pain smarting along his cheekbones, he made one last attempt for the keys. It was a risk he had to take.

"Do you want to know what we did to the last mouthy prisoner we had down here?" Lux's hot breath slithered across Ravlok's ear.

"No, but I don't suppose you'll keep it to yourself." Ravlok kept his eyes on Lux's face, hand searching, careful not to touch the mage directly.

Lux thrust him back a few handspans and wrenched him in close again. "Took out the man's eye. Burned it right out of his skull."

At last, Ravlok's palm grazed iron. He laughed to mask the sound of his last three fingers closing around the keys, using his first finger and thumb to clamp the end of the knot. "That doesn't make any sense. Why would you remove his eye if his tongue was the problem?"

"You think you're smart. I can tell," Lux sneered as Ravlok slipped the knot and tucked the keys up his tunic sleeve. "But let's not forget you're the one in a cage."

"How kind of you to notice." Ravlok shook his head as much as the bars would let him. "I envy your talent for observation."

Lux shoved him away from the cell door. "We're not finished here." A slow smile split his face. "Don't go anywhere while I'm gone."

With the keys to the dungeon pressed reassuringly against his wrist and inner forearm, Ravlok returned his smug grin. "Don't take too long. I have places to be."

Lux turned and started down the hallway. Seconds after he disappeared around the corner, the dungeon door opened and closed.

"Do you think he was telling the truth?" Kendi asked.

Unsure what he meant, Ravlok regarded Orowen, who stared after the mage with one hand over her chest. She managed to sit up, but pain suffused her expression with every breath.

"I hope not." Her focus shifted to Ravlok. "Tell me it was worth it."

He slipped the keys out of his sleeve and held them up. "I think so."

Orowen blinked. "*Saonis miraar*," she breathed. "You did it."

Farther down the hallway, Kendi and Anwic both exclaimed with surprise.

"Well, what are you waiting for?" Anwic asked. "Let us out."

Examining the keys, Ravlok chose the largest of the three and tried it in the padlock. When it didn't budge, he tried the next largest. It slid into the lock and turned easily, popping the hasp with a satisfying *click*. He slipped the padlock off, pocketing the heavy metal piece just in case, and removed the wing from the eyelet. The bolt was harder to move from the inside of the cell, but he eventually pulled it free of the stone and pushed his door open.

He grabbed the bag of saphyrum and left his cell to open Orowen's. She struggled to her feet as he approached, using the crossbeams for support. Ravlok passed the bag to her through the door, and she shook her head in amazement. When she looked up at him, tears streaked her pale purple cheeks. He reached for the padlock, and she touched his face.

"Our meeting is a blessing from the gods. There is a place for you among us, should you need one."

Ravlok paused before sliding the key into the lock. Would he need such a haven after this? Most likely. Though leaving with Orowen's people also meant leaving Daeya. His closest friend would never know what had happened to him; she might think he abandoned her. But even if he returned to the monastery and refrained from ever setting foot in the Towers again, word would eventually reach Gregory that he'd survived the Guild's special prison. It was too dangerous for him to stay.

Daeya would understand, especially if he could get a letter to her later, once he was safely out of Eidosinia. He pulled the padlock free and opened Orowen's door. "That seems wise."

She smiled—a motherly sort of smile that felt out of place in a dungeon, yet stirred up a rare feeling of warmth all the same—and quoted a portion of a famous line from the Book of Order. "'And so does the gods' path unfold before us.'"

"'In equal parts, light and dark, for all must bear both sun and storm.'" Ravlok turned his attention to the locks securing her manacles, his lips turning up at the corners. "A funny way of saying everything happens for a reason."

"Would you disagree, servant of Ordeolas?" Her tone bordered on playful.

"No." After all, everything he had ever done in his life had led him to this moment. He tried the smallest key, and the first manacle sprang open. He moved to the second one. "I don't make a habit of disagreeing with the gods."

"If you two are finished," Anwic grumbled, "I'm sure whatever drew that bastard away won't distract him for long."

"Could it be your rescue party?" Ravlok took Orowen's arm to help steady her.

"Possibly." She winced, rubbing an ashen palm over her battered chest. Head bowed, she allowed him to escort her a few paces down the corridor. Her body flagged before they reached Kendi's cell. Cold sweat beaded on her forehead, her complexion already several shades lighter than it was moments ago. "I just need a minute." She sagged against the wall and reached into the bag of saphyrum.

Alarm lanced through him. "What's wrong?"

"She suffers from saphyrum sickness," Kendi answered for her. As Ravlok looked toward his cell, he added, "We all do."

Ravlok grimaced. Saphyrum sickness was a deadly condition brought about when Syljians couldn't obtain enough of the arcane metal to meet their daily needs. Though the Guild claimed the condition was only a fae tale, many censored accounts confirmed that saphyrum was just as important to Syljians as food or water. Without it, they could wither and die in a matter of days. "What can be done?"

"The beads will help." Kendi's expression softened. "She should be fine in a few moments."

Even as his stomach clenched, Ravlok nodded. Assuring himself she stood firmly enough against the stonework, he stepped away to unlock Kendi's cell.

Though Kendi was sturdier of frame than Orowen, Ravlok could still see over the top of his head while standing flat-footed. Dark stains marred the older man's leggings, and his leather jerkin hung open at the collar, revealing a blood-spattered shirt beneath it. A long, white braid fell to his waist. In the dim light, his eyes appeared lavender, rather than violet like Orowen's, but there was no mistaking the same discerning quality behind them. This was a man who bore the burdens of others.

When the door swung open and the manacles fell away, Kendi placed a hand on Ravlok's shoulder. "We owe you our lives, *amii*."

Friend. Glancing around at their surroundings, Ravlok shook his head. "I wouldn't say that. We're not out of trouble yet."

Kendi's lips twitched. "I suppose you're right, though our condition is much improved, thanks to you. Go and fetch Anwic. I'll see to Orowen."

Anwic's cell was the last one on the left, several paces down from Kendi's. Unlike his companions, Anwic's skin was darker, more supple, and free of the lines of age. Unusually tall for a Syljian, he stood even with Ravlok, and he was just as muscular through the shoulders. Short white hair and stern violet eyes enhanced his severe expression.

He said nothing to Ravlok as he unlocked the cell door. When there were no longer bars between them, Anwic pushed up his tattered sleeves and offered his wrists.

The irons fell to the floor, and Anwic gave him an enormous grin. He stepped out of the cell and pounded Ravlok once on the back. "Welcome to the Alliaansi, *bashiin*."

Though Anwic's tone was free of scorn, that word still rankled. Ravlok's jaw tensed as he trailed after him, wondering if he couldn't have left this one in his cell a little longer.

After checking on Orowen, Kendi pulled two beads from the bag and passed one to Anwic. Both men clutched the beads, and a white-violet glow shone through their fists, casting soft rays against the walls and floor. The pallid lavender of Kendi's skin grew richer, as if the influx of saphyrum was an infusion of life itself. Anwic's color darkened further, and his entire body relaxed, as though he had been holding his breath for too long. When they opened their hands again, the saphyrum turned to dust.

Orowen, however, still hadn't moved. The light from her pair of beads was little more than a candle in comparison. Though the white runes on her temples glowed softly, the sickly pallor of her skin lingered. Again, worry constricted Ravlok's chest.

His concern must have been evident; Kendi gave him another reassuring look. "She just exhausted herself fighting the mages last night. You need not worry."

Seems like a fine reason to worry to me.

Anwic spared a glance for the priestess and shrugged. "The sickness is always worst for arcanists." He turned to Kendi. "We need weapons."

"I'm sure there will be something of use in the interrogation room."

Anwic nodded and stalked down the corridor to peer around the corner. Kendi waited a moment more for Orowen. With the slightest brush of his fingers against her forehead, he said, "Come back to us, Devoted. We haven't much time."

The runes framing her face brightened at his touch. When they faded, Orowen blinked open her eyes as if woken from sleep. Both saphyrum beads she'd taken from the bag crumbled to dust. She didn't look any better off to Ravlok.

"You're right." The priestess sighed, returning her hands to her sides. "That will have to be good enough for now."

"Sounds of battle from beyond the main door," Anwic called back to them.

Orowen and Kendi shared a look.

"It could be Val," Orowen said. "His scouts run the drop points down here."

"Let's get the rest of our people out. Then we'll join him."

The older man studied Ravlok, either for his overall fitness or his usefulness in combat, or both. Whichever the case, Ravlok smirked. There was little to do in his free time at the monastery other than read books or practice his forms. Sometimes he spent several hours a day on the mat fighting with Yonfé, training the other monks, or even teaching Daeya when she could sneak away from her studies.

"I can hold my own," he promised.

"Good." Kendi's eyes strayed back to Orowen. This time, Ravlok caught the apprehension that flickered across his face. "Are you ready?"

"*Ciïr.*" She took her first steps away from the wall like a sailor regaining her sea legs after months at port. She stumbled, and Ravlok reached for her elbow to steady her.

Kendi put up a hand to stop him. He shook his head as Orowen righted herself, using the wall for support.

When she was far enough down the corridor, Kendi lowered his voice and leaned toward Ravlok. "Let's see how she does on her own. Should her condition worsen, it's best if we catch it before we engage the enemy."

"That makes sense," Ravlok admitted, still watching her make slow progress toward Anwic. After all, collapsing here on the dungeon floor was better than collapsing into the swing of a Guild sword.

Foreboding settled like a stone between his shoulder blades. He vowed to himself that he would not stray far from her side during the battle to come. Ordeolas knew the world could not afford to lose a priestess of Saolanni.

Chapter Ten

Daeya

It was an hour past noon by the time Daeya finished scouring the Towers and the surrounding courtyards for her missing charge. None of Faustus's instructors had reported seeing him. He hadn't filed an excusal, and she hadn't found him in his quarters, the library, the infirmary, or the mess hall. She'd even checked the nearby markets and the city jailhouse, but there was no sign of him there either.

Finally, she was forced to admit that her nagging suspicion had merit. It wasn't like Faustus to go missing. Even more damning was that he should disappear less than an hour after she'd delivered Gregory's fake rumor about Cheralach. There was only one old man in the city jailhouse, and he was no more a legendary aethermancer than she was a blanker herself.

Daeya prayed to whichever gods might listen that she'd simply missed Faustus in her search, and there was a reasonable explanation for his absence. Still, her sense of dread was unabated. It demanded she consider the possibility that his good-naturedness and endearing charm had blinded her to what Gregory had suspected all along.

Either way, his fate was in his own hands. Having exhausted all other options, she crept back to the Councilor's office to make her report.

She stopped twice during her trek to breathe through several moments of gut-churning panic. Though she'd been punished for misbehavior many times before, this was different. This was failure—inarguable, inescapable failure—and that was the only thing Gregory disliked more than swearing. It took every ounce of courage she possessed to reach his door.

For once, it seemed the gods were on her side. Gregory was absent when she arrived.

Reeling from her poorly restrained terror-turned-relief, she left a note with his receptionist and scurried out the door like a mouse fleeing for its life. With any luck, she would be halfway to Keilliad by the time he received the message.

Yes, you're certainly fearless. She winced. *Like a newborn lamb.*

Back in her room, she stuffed what few belongings she needed in her satchel, slung the strap over her shoulder, and left her quarters. The boat departed at fifth bell, right before dinner, so there were a few hours to spare before making her way to the docks. She stopped by the monastery to bid farewell to Ravlok, but her friend was also absent his routine. With too little time to search for him, she decided to take Master Ulrich's advice and visit her father, after all.

McVen's Smithy was down the road from the fishmongers' stands in Southgate, one of the farthest places from the Towers she could go inside Ryost's walls. Daeya usually enjoyed the journey, but today, something about it felt off. It could have been her lingering anger at herself, or the discomfort from the morning's exploits. It could also have been the nagging pain in her blistered back.

Whatever the case, more than a few people on the street sidled away from her, as if they could sense how out of sorts she was. It surely didn't help she'd been scowling to herself this entire time, and she did her best to soften her expression.

It must not have been convincing. When she neared her father's smithy, she found it difficult to elicit the usual cheerful smiles and greetings from the neighboring shopkeepers and market vendors. Her studies only allowed visits a few times a year, but most of the neighborhood knew her, thanks to her father's prideful boasting. Still, even Arien the barrel maker—who would normally regale her with stories of his youth for hours on end—spared only a cursory word or two for her today. That was probably for the best, though, if she wanted to spend any amount of time with her father before she had to leave.

Despite it all, she strode down the waterfront, letting some of the weight lift from her shoulders. On her right, the Falcon River sparkled in the midday sun. The city wall and its five arches loomed tall in front of her, spanning the wide river. Two of the five portcullises were raised this afternoon to allow boats to pass beneath the wall. The other three were sunk far below the surface and into the riverbed. Eddies swirled as the thick metal grates diced up the fast-moving current.

Between the wet cobbles underfoot and the smell of mud, fish, and hot iron in the air, Southgate was a vastly different world from the city's center. Near the Towers, rich tapestries, banners, and livery in every shade of red, green, gold, and blue bombarded one's senses. Elegance, refinement, and pretension engulfed everyone and everything. Here, the colors were muted, the markets less ostentatious, and the people far rougher, dirtier, and simpler. Nobles like Tom Bennick would have balked at such surroundings and retched at the smell.

To Daeya, this was coming home.

She side-stepped a group of men hauling a net full of fish onto the boardwalk and smiled to herself as the hammer-and-horseshoe sign above McVen's Smithy came into view. Nestled within a row of tightly packed shops facing the riverfront, the squat stone building bore a blackened chimney, a slate roof, and small, poorly glazed windows. She mounted the creaky wooden steps to the sun-weathered landing, yanked the bell string three times, and pushed open the door.

Inside, the place was sweltering. Only the slightest breeze blew in from the open windows facing the alley. The hot iron smell from the road was strongest here. It mingled with the pungent tinge of sulfur, coal dust, and various solvents needed for the craft. Along the left and right walls hung an arrangement of new swords, shields, plate, and chain, all commissioned for the Guild soldiers who protected the city streets. Hammers and tools covered the back wall, and at the room's center sat the great forge.

The shop was much roomier than it appeared from the street. It had to be, or the great bear of a man standing with his back to her at the forge would have never fit. Angus McVen bore all the stereotypical features of a Brogrenti clansman, from his curly red hair and thick, well-muscled shoulders to his strong, *aeyak*-wrapped legs.

His skirt-like *aeyak* was longer than the traditional Brogrenti garb, nearly brushing his boots, to protect him as he worked. Its long leather strips lay atop each other like a carapace, backed by flame-colored fabric. He stood a full head taller than Daeya, and he was over twice as broad through his torso.

"No need to be breaking my damned bleeding bell, ye *kinnich*!"

Angus's Brogrenti accent was as thick as his red beard. Instead of pausing to see who had entered his shop, he pulled a glowing blade out of the fire with a set of tongs and turned to the anvil beside him.

Daeya dropped her pack on the floor and crossed her arms. "If you answered the door like a proper shopkeep, I wouldn't have to ring it so hard."

At the sound of her voice, the sword bounced off the anvil and clattered onto the bricks surrounding the forge.

"Daeya," Angus breathed. He turned fully this time, and his soot-covered face lit up with the happiest smile she had seen in months. "Is that me wee lass?"

Fighting back the sting of joyful tears, she struggled to force a greeting past the lump in her throat. There was truly nothing like coming home. "Hi, Da."

Angus rushed to pull off his gloves and slip the tie on his leather apron, letting the grimy garments fall beside the forgotten sword. In four long strides, he crossed the space between them and swept her into his arms. "C'mere, ye scrawny thing."

Daeya ignored the pain of her fresh burns and hugged him around his neck, her booted feet dangling off the floor. Closing her eyes, she breathed in the scent of the forge on his skin and in his hair. It had only been four months since her last visit, but it felt like an eternity.

"I've missed you," she said into his ear, squeezing him tighter.

"Not as much as I've missed ye, lass."

He placed her feet back on the ground, holding her at arm's length to look her over. His eyes widened at the sight of her robe.

"And ye're a mage, now!" Both callused hands cupped the sides of her face. His beard tickled her nose as he kissed her forehead. "My, what fine news ye bring yer old man. When did this happen?"

Daeya's cheeks flushed. "Just this morning."

He pulled her into another embrace, this one hard enough that Daeya winced. Fortunately, her reaction went unnoticed. When he released her the second time, he steered her toward a small table and a long bench full of supplies, which he unceremoniously dumped onto the floor to make room for them both to sit.

"I always said that old boy Gregory'd take good care of ye. Why, ye've done us both right proud, ye *kinnich*?"

Her stomach flipped at the mention of Gregory. "Yes, I know."

She avoided his eyes by adjusting the folds of her robe. Angus had always liked Gregory. He'd facilitated Angus and Ali McVen's adoption of her, after all. Not only that, but he had secured Angus's livelihood with the Guild's armor and weapons commission, and pulled strings to allow Daeya more than the yearly visit after Ali died six years ago. Truthfully, the Councilor had been so good to her family, she never could find the heart to tell her father about any of her concerns. There wasn't much Angus could do for her, anyway.

"Ye just keep up yer good work, lass. He'll have ye sitting the Council before long." His green eyes went misty as he gazed at her. "Why, yer ma'd be so proud of ye."

Daeya did her best to hide her unease by thinking of Ali. If anyone could have been more vocal about her accomplishments than Angus, it was his wife. Ali had lost her only natural child shortly before Daeya came to them, but she'd always loved her as if she were her own.

"Ye seem distracted, lass." Her father's expression grew serious. "Ain't no lads or lasses been vying for yer affections without asking yer da first, have they?"

The tension inside her gave way like an over-tightened lute string. She laughed at the absurdity of his concern. "No, Da. Gregory keeps me too busy for all that."

"And well he should. He's a smart man," Angus said with a satisfied nod. He took hold of her chin and gave her a gentle shake. "Ye're a real *breigh* lass. Anyone'd be lucky to catch yer fancy. But don't let 'em deter ye from yer dreams."

She let out a sigh and pulled away, grinning. "I know. You say that every time I come home."

"Aye, 'cause ye need reminding. Ye're destined for greatness, Daeya." He tapped his temple with a callused finger. "I *kinnich*."

Her smile faded. She shook her head as if to brush off Angus's fatherly prophesizing and tried to change the subject. "How's Murtagh?"

Angus's face soured. "Ach! The wee lout's been worse than useless in the shop." He waved a dismissive hand. "He's had his head in the clouds ever since he started courtin' the potter's daughter."

Daeya didn't know who the potter's daughter was, but surprise fluttered through her just the same. Her cousin Murtagh had moved in with Angus and Ali when Daeya was two. Though her parents enrolled her at the School only a few years later, she and Murtagh still fought like siblings whenever she returned home. The thought of the scruffy lad pursuing a woman was exactly the sort of distraction she needed. "Tell me everything."

Angus rose to his feet. "How much time have ye got, lass? He's prob'ly down at Davy's right now. I'm sure he'd love to see ye."

"I can spare another hour or two. I leave for Orthovia at fifth bell."

Her father nodded and extended his hand to help her up. "I s'pose I'll take what I can get." Once she stood, he looked her over one last time and tousled her hair. "I'll buy ye lunch, too. Someone's got to put some meat on yer bones."

The man who owned the establishment known as Davy's Tavern wasn't actually named Davy, nor did he have any other relation who bore the name. He was a Rillanese native with the longest, most convoluted name Daeya had ever heard, but he insisted everyone call him Po for short.

She'd once asked him why he hadn't named it Po's Tavern. His answer had been a testament to his wisdom: "Keep asking questions, Magelet, and Po rename shithole after you."

Davy's was packed when they arrived. The four hours between fourth and fifth bell marked the time of day between lunch and dinner where many working-class men and women were either relaxing after a long morning in the field, or having drinks before a long evening on the docks.

Several rugged-looking patrons eyed Daeya with a mixture of unease and suspicion. Fortunately, most of them seemed to know her father. They relaxed as soon as Angus ducked through the entryway and placed a hand on her shoulder.

"This way, lass." He steered her toward the back of the room.

They waded through a dozen tables ringed by an assortment of mismatched chairs, their boots squelching through piles of sawdust on the ale-drenched floor. Scents of sweat, fish, and potatoes all mingled in the close quarters. Wax candles overflowed their sconces and pooled on the heavily scarred woodwork. The only natural light in the hazy tavern poured through a long line of cracked windows overlooking the river.

When they neared the bar, Daeya caught sight of a tall young man with striking red curls seated next to a portly woman with a friendly smile and round, rosy cheeks. Murtagh must have been regaling the woman with one of his outlandish stories, because she looked thoroughly enraptured. Neither noticed Daeya and Angus's approach.

Daeya gave her father a mischievous grin, and he winked back. She left him to circle around the bar and come at the pair from behind. She didn't have to creep up on them; the general din of the tavern masked any noise she could have made.

When she was close enough to reach out and grab her cousin's shoulder, she spun him around on the bar stool, slammed a hand against his chest, and gave him her most intimidating scowl.

"Murtagh McVen, ye two-timin' bastard!" Daeya let her Brogrenti accent shine through, planting one hand on her hip and jabbing at him with the other. "I shoulda known ye were sneaking around."

Her sudden declaration drew startled looks from both of them, but the woman proved to be a quick study. She recovered instantly, and her attention snapped back to Murtagh. His horrified expression nearly made Daeya burst into giggles; she had to bite down on her tongue to hold them back.

"I—wait. Daeya? Ye—"

As he stumbled over his shock, the woman's friendliness dissolved. Her green eyes darted toward Daeya. "Who is this, Murtagh?"

"A-Annie, no, this is my little sister." Murtagh tried to placate her with a wave of both arms. He flinched away from Annie's lethal stare. "Daeya, for the gods' sake, are ye tryin' to get me killed?"

"Only a little." Daeya shrugged, letting her Brogrenti lilt fall away.

Behind them, Angus burst into laughter.

As realization dawned in Murtagh's pale blue eyes, Daeya smiled. She extended a hand toward Annie. "We're cousins, actually, but we grew up together. I'm Daeya McVen."

Annie took her hand and gave it a cautious shake. "Annie Maissier."

"Ye're as much a sister as ye are a pain in the arse," Murtagh grumbled. He spun back around on his stool and glared at Angus. "Put her up to this, did ye, Uncle?"

"Ach, I did no such thing!" Angus was still laughing as he leaned over the bar and called to the short, leather-skinned man at the other end. "Po! Four mugs of ale, and a plate o' ham 'n' hash."

While Po set about getting the mugs, Angus took a seat at the bar on the longer side adjacent to Murtagh and Annie. He patted the seat next to him and looked meaningfully at Daeya.

She took the invitation, climbed up on the stool, and smiled again at Murtagh. "Da told me you'd met someone. I figured I should see for myself."

Murtagh looked at Annie with no small amount of trepidation, as if he expected her to still be angry.

Annie, however, was transfixed by Daeya, her expression somewhere between disbelief and awe. "You didn't tell me there were mages in your family." There was an odd tone in her voice, and a furrow of uncertainty lined her brow.

"Daeya's one of the good ones, lass." Angus pounded Daeya on the back—hard. Daeya exhaled sharply, and her teeth closed on the inside of her lip to stifle a whimper.

Murtagh frowned. "I wasn't aware ye'd been promoted yet. Does this mean ye'll be leaving Ryost?"

Daeya nodded, trying to hide her pain as Po shuffled over and thumped four mugs of ale down on the sticky bar top. She used the momentary distraction to recollect her wits. Wrapping her fingers around the mug's dirty handle, she took a long, slow drink to wash down the blood in her mouth.

Once she trusted her voice not to break, she lowered her mug. "Yes. I leave today, actually."

Murtagh studied her for a few more seconds. For once, the look on his face was unreadable. Finally, he shook his head. "I'd say I'm happy to see ye." He tipped his glass toward her. "But truth to tell, it's been right peaceful round here since ye've been gone."

He spoke with a straight face, but the corners of his mouth turned upward as he gulped his ale. When he put it down, the glass was half empty, and he was grinning.

Daeya glowered at him. "You're an arse."

Murtagh laughed and rose from his stool. "And ye're a clodpie." He wrapped his arms around her. Daeya followed suit, chuckling as she gripped the rough-hewn fabric of his cloak.

Annie relaxed while Murtagh and Daeya caught up. At some point, Po waddled back with a plate of ham and potatoes, which Daeya ate with gusto. There was something about sharing drinks and a simple meal in a seedy tavern that could bring any two people together, and soon enough, Annie seemed to forgive her for her harmless prank.

Angus ordered three more rounds of ale for all of them, and they drank until Daeya swayed like a leaf in the breeze.

"I wish ye had more time with us, Daeya," Murtagh lamented. "Annie here's a real *braugh* tiffle player. Stomped me right in the dirt last week."

Annie gave him a dubious look. "You went easy on me."

Daeya's words slurred a little as she spoke. "Murtagh doesn't have it in him to lose on purpose. He wins so little as it is."

Murtagh lifted one bushy red eyebrow. "Maybe against ye. Ye're a damned cheat, using yer magic."

Though it was true she often tweaked the path of the ball, Daeya feigned offense. "You're just jealous I can play more angles."

Murtagh's eyes narrowed. "Prob'ly not as well as ye used to. It's not like ye can practice at the School. I bet ye're rustier than a scrap of iron."

Angus guffawed and leaned in toward Daeya, sloshing ale onto the bar top. "That's a challenge if I've ever heard one. Ye ought to put that boy in his place, lass."

The more sensible part of her tried to reason that she didn't have time for a full nine rounds of tiffleball, but that sort of logic was buried four drinks deep now. If she played only two or three rounds, that wouldn't hurt.

Well, that wasn't true. It was going to hurt worse than a switching, but it would be worth every minute she got to spend with her family. Daeya stared down at the new mug of ale in front of her, considering. When she looked back up at Murtagh, she caught the playful, knowing gleam in his eyes.

Her lips twitched upward. "I suppose I have time for a few rounds."

Annie slid off her stool and made her way around the corner of the bar. She placed a hand on Daeya's shoulder and locked eyes with Murtagh. "I call the sorceress."

Chapter Eleven

Alar

The first torch exploded upward and twisted into a great, fanged beast with rippling orange claws. It leaped at the nearest soldier, engulfing the man in flames. As the infernal image savaged him, his three companions stumbled over each other, trying to retreat. With the second torch, Alar created a fiery whirlwind and knocked the next man prone. He *pushed* the third and fourth torches into the backs of the other two soldiers, setting them ablaze in a shower of embers.

Shouted orders echoed down the passageway, blending with the cries of burning men. Using the wall as his guide, Alar fell back into the alcove. He had no intention of staying out in the open when the mages started casting spells.

His trick with the torches had deterred the soldiers' advance. Without crossbowmen or archers among them, they held position around the corner, unwilling to venture into the black space that sheltered Alar and his companions.

A pair of fire bolts shot down the corridor. The fleeting orange glow of the sorcerers' attacks illuminated Val and Jack, who were poised like statues across from Alar. Val knelt on the stone, crossbow on his upraised knee, while Jack stood above him, steadying his aim on Val's shoulder. Their shadows swung against the south wall of the alcove, and then the fire struck the turn in the corridor behind them.

Alar stole a glance around the corner, but the thick, orange-gray haze beyond their cover of darkness didn't stir at all. He waited, watching the space for signs of movement.

Val turned one ear toward the enemy. "*At least six around the bend. More on the way,*" came the spymaster's voice in Alar's mind.

Up ahead, a flash of violet and a blast of frigid air sent smoke, dust, and debris barreling down the passageway. Alar ducked, shielding his face, his hair whipping around his ears. The remaining torches and the flaming pile of corpses guttered.

The entire corridor went black.

Wastelands.

"*They've leveled the stakes,*" Val said, echoing his thoughts. "*We can't stay here.*"

He was right. Alar was reluctant to leave the shelter of the alcove, but they didn't have a choice. Word of their presence would have reached the surface by now. All the sorcerers had to do was wait for reinforcements. They would outnumber him and his companions in a matter of minutes.

"*Okay, new plan,*" Alar said. "*Got a flare?*"

Without a visual on his target, his psionic skills were limited. Val and Jack were equally limited with their crossbows. But if they could light the way just enough, Alar could use one of the corpses as a shield to get them down the passageway.

Fabric rustled across the hall. "*Ready.*"

"*Throw it north on my mark. Be ready to move.*" Centering his eyes on the space outside the alcove where the dead mage should be, Alar took a slow, deep breath. "*Now.*"

Val struck the saphyric flare in a blaze of red-violet light. Alar *seized* the black silhouette on the floor. As he blinked his vision clear, surprised shouts rang out right on top of them. Jack accompanied the sounds with a string of savage curses. He fired his crossbow twice. More screams punctuated each bolt. Val threw the flare, and Alar spun out of his alcove in time to see two of the four backlit figures collapse with crossbow bolts sticking out of their eyes.

He lifted the mage's body with his mind. Fire bolts hammered into the corpse's back, wracking Alar's psionic hold like physical blows to his head. Forcing the pain aside, he gritted his teeth and tightened his telekinetic grip.

The remaining two sorcerers raised glowing hands before them and wove sigils. Alar braced himself for the spells, but it was the crossbow bolt whispering past his ear that made him stiffen. One mage went down. The other snarled in outrage. A white-violet sphere of lightning formed between the mage's fingertips, casting his bearded features in stark relief. Alar spun to the right, and the lightning shot past him.

Light erupted, and Jack screamed.

With a spark of fury, Alar swung the smoking corpse around and hurled it into their attacker. The man ricocheted off the wall and fell to his knees. Val spun to Alar's left and punched a knife into the mage's throat.

Alar reclaimed the corpse of the first sorcerer and lifted it to shield them both from another volley of fire bolts. The blows strained his psionic link as the body jerked and swayed. While he struggled to maintain his hold, he stepped toward the other alcove, keeping the body in front of him.

Val pressed close, his back to Alar's, making himself as small a target as possible. When they were close enough for Val to reach Jack, the spymaster hauled the boy to his feet. Throwing Jack's arm around his shoulders, Val turned back to Alar. "Go! *We're right behind you.*"

Alar pressed forward, *pushing* the body before them. The blasts intensified, honing in on their position as Val's flare burned out, and the only light in the corridor came from the smoldering robes hanging like tattered drapery from their manmade shield.

Dizzy with the effort, blood pounding in his temples, Alar made it within a dozen paces of the turn in the corridor before his legs turned to lead. He stumbled, and something heavy fell to the ground in front of him. Singed hair and charred meat filled his nostrils. Blackness threatened to engulf him, and searing pain erupted in his left shoulder.

"Alar, get up."

Jack. There was a hand under his arm, and another pounding at an odd, orange light on his shoulder. Cold stone bit into his hands.

"Get up, or we're all dead men."

The sound of swords clashing snapped Alar back to his senses. He recoiled as the orange light near his face came into focus. He'd taken a fire bolt, and his uniform was burning. Jack smothered the flames with a shred of black cloth. A sorcerer's robe?

"Saphyrum." Alar felt about for the bead he kept close to his chest.

Jack pressed another one into his palm. "Hurry up."

The hand under Alar's arm vanished. Jack's liveried green-and-gold form disappeared beyond the burning remains of their corpse shield.

Staring through the fire ruined his night vision, so Alar settled for closing his eyes and willing the saphyrum to recenter his mind and restore his strength. Within seconds he was moving again, shoving himself to his feet, drawing his dagger and staggering toward the sounds of battle.

Chaos greeted him around the bend. There were still torches burning further down the hallway, but the light suffusing their immediate surroundings came only from mage's fire. One downed soldier provided a significant obstacle for three more. Val engaged two mages, staying in close quarters to interrupt their spellcasting. Jack got off a shot at one soldier, and the iron bolt took her in the throat, sending her sprawling into her nearest companion. Both went down in a heap, clearing Alar's line of sight as two more guards came into view at the end of the passageway.

While Jack slipped forward to engage a soldier, Alar focused his mind on the new pair. Readying his psionic suggestion, he *squeezed* their auras, and shouted, "We have this under control. Get back to your posts!"

Without looking to see if they heeded his command, he leaped into the fray.

Hand-to-hand combat was not something Alar excelled at, and his opponent reminded him why he avoided such brawls as soon as he smashed him in the mouth with a meaty fist. He took another blow to the jaw before Jack slit the soldier's throat. Alar hadn't even wet his dagger. Still, he charged the nearest mage as soon as the soldier fell. The sorcerer rewarded him with a blast of white-violet frost that froze the upper half of his chain mail and seared his skin all the way through his clothing.

Cursing his ill luck, unable to move his arms, Alar lashed out on impulse with his mind. The psychic blow shattered the sorcerer's stream of thought and he screamed, clutching the sides of his head. A crossbow bolt sprouted from his mouth a beat later.

Jack dispatched the last soldier while Alar turned his attention to the other mage.

"Hey, easy." The sorcerer backpedaled right into Val's dagger point and raised his hands in surrender. "Look, maybe I can help you—"

Alar repeated the barrage of psychic energy, dropping the man to his knees between them.

"Please!" The man pressed the heels of his hands to his temples. "Gods, have mercy!"

"As if you would do the same." Alar's voice was as cold as his frozen chain mail. His eyes met Val's. A subtle nod, and the sorcerer died.

"Relieve them of their saphyrum." Alar motioned to Jack, flexing and pulling at his armor to break up the ice. He rolled his left shoulder, wincing at his burns. On his lips, he tasted blood.

Val wiped his dagger on the mage's robe. "Nice work on that diversion."

"The soldiers came from the north." Alar looked down at the two sorcerers. "That means there's either another exit, or still more troops down here."

"Or both." Jack poked at the gruesome burn on the side of his neck before bending to collect both black bags and a pair of casting bracelets from the nearest mages. He offered them to Alar.

"Your eyes are violet," Val pointed out as Alar tucked the bags and one bracelet away. "You should grab a robe."

Alar considered that as he slipped the other bracelet on. "You're right."

He'd been pulling all his energy directly from the beads like an arcanist. It was no surprise his eyes had changed color. It would be easier to pass himself off as a mage rather than a mundane soldier, so he set about stripping the taller of the two sorcerers.

"Let's make some noise going in." He shoved his hands through the black robe and let it settle on his shoulders. He considered pulling up the hood to hide his swelling lip, but thought better of it. A Guild sorcerer was not likely to conceal his wounds, and it was dark enough down here that it might not stand out, anyway.

Jack tucked away a soldier's coin purse. "That seems like a bad idea."

Val glanced over his shoulder at him. "All the sorcerers look the same to you, right? You think the soldiers share that sentiment?"

Jack attempted a shrug. "Probably."

"Then we use that to our advantage. If we were sneaking around, it would be suspicious."

Alar took a moment to examine Jack's burn. Pink fluid saturated the left side of his uniform. The wound would need treatment soon. "We need to find Orowen."

"She's down here." Val paused, listening. Far off in the distance, the echo of a door closing carried down the passageway. "*Eight more inbound*," he said in Alar's mind, gesturing the same message to Jack.

Alar tucked the dagger up his sleeve and strode forward, taking point as Val and Jack trailed behind him. He moved with purpose, as if he belonged down here, allowing the sound of his footfalls to travel. They passed a second alcove—this one empty—and journeyed down the corridor before turning north. There, they found a shorter hallway and another vacant alcove. As he turned the corner again, eight figures came into view. The two in front were mages, followed by another six soldiers.

Beyond them was a solid ironclad door.

Alar threw a glance at Val. "How many blankers did you say there were?" he asked, letting his voice carry toward the men.

"At least five." Val didn't miss a beat. He curled his upper lip. "Maybe ten blanker-lovers with them."

Alar scoffed. "And already running for the surface, the cowards." Looking the reinforcements over, he pulled out the ring of keys Val had stolen. "You lot have the easy job."

The short Cintoshi-looking mage on the left snickered. "You'll be cleaning up Nick's mess, I take it?"

Val sighed, exasperated, as the eight newcomers filled the space between them and the door. "Obviously. The little shit is incapable of doing it himself."

Ugly-Cintoshi bared his teeth. "What do you think ol' Greg will do to him this time?"

"Not enough." Alar chose a key from the ring. He made to step around the mages, feigning disinterest. Of course Gregory would be involved. "Just deal with the blankers, will you? And hurry up. I have a report due at fifth bell."

The sorcerers nodded, responding to Alar's authoritative tone. "With pleasure."

The troops passed by and turned the corner, leaving Alar, Val, and Jack to approach the door unhindered.

"*I can't believe that worked,*" Val marveled as he watched them go. "*Who's Nick?*"

"*I don't know.*" Unease crept up Alar's spine. He stared at the door for a moment, listening. There was activity in the room beyond, but there were too many possibilities to guess at exactly what awaited them on the other side. They had encountered fewer sorcerers with psionics-resistance than he'd expected. The worst case was a room full of such enemies behind that door.

"*Val?*"

The spymaster took up a similar position at the door, eyebrows pinched. "*Six? No. Eight.*"

"*Can you tell what they are?*"

"*They aren't moving around much.*" Val listened for a few more moments. "*At least three soldiers.*"

Alar's jaw tensed. "*So maybe five mages.*" He closed his eyes and forced a smile. "*We've faced worse odds, I suppose.*"

Val snickered. "*That's the spirit.*"

"*If we get the drop on them, we can take them out quickly.*" Alar placed his hand on the door's curved iron handle.

Surprise rippled through their connection. "*You want to go in swinging?*"

Alar hesitated. He supposed they could try talking their way past a second time. Apparently, even the mages weren't familiar with every face they might see down here. The majority seemed hopelessly dimwitted. Maybe it was worth the gamble.

His hand fell away from the handle, and he beckoned to Val. "After you."

Val's grin could have outshone the sun. He made a few quick gestures to convey their intentions to Jack, then reached for the handle. "This should be fun," he said aloud.

For once, Alar agreed with Jack, who muttered obscenities under his breath.

Firelight spilled over them as Val yanked open the door. Eyes watering, Alar squinted into a large chamber lit with dozens of braziers and sconces. Racks of weaponry and armor lined the wall to their right. There were empty holding cells in the far-right corner, and to their left was a crude spiral staircase leading up. Four tables with bench-style seating were arranged in a square at the center of the room. Spread out among them sat eight Guild soldiers. To Alar's surprise, there were no mages present at all.

He eyed the staircase, masking his scrutiny by placing himself behind Val.

A soldier dressed in formal gold livery leveled discerning eyes on them. He was older, gray-haired, and balding, but with a full mustache perfectly trimmed above thin, pursed lips. He sat atop a table on the left, drawing from a pipe and resting one elbow on his knee. His booted feet rested on the bench. Alar recognized the captain's bars on the man's lapel.

"*Captain Sangrin*," Alar guessed.

Val lifted his chin toward the man as he strode forward. "Captain," he said in greeting.

Sangrin's eyes narrowed. Smoke billowed from his nose and mouth as he spoke. "Who the fuck are you? And what in the gods' names is happening out there?"

"Bunch of blankers came in through the tower." Val didn't bother to stop on his way to the only other door. He approached the space between two tables. "The situation is under control."

Behind the captain, Alar spotted the two soldiers he'd sent away with his psionic suggestion. They both regarded him with uncertainty. Alar avoided staring directly at them as he trailed behind Val, but with his aura-sense, he saw the spark of recognition flare in the younger one.

"Captain—"

"Quiet," Sangrin barked. He peered beyond Val and Alar at Jack, and his aura pulled taut as a bowstring. "You're not one of mine."

"Nope." Jack didn't waste another breath. He spun away from Alar and Val, drawing his hand crossbow.

"So much for tact," Val grumbled, drawing his own weapon.

Alar sighed and rolled his eyes as the room exploded with movement.

Jack got off two shots at the captain before the closest soldier charged him. Sangrin leaped off the table, the bolts passing harmlessly to one side. The other soldier collided with Jack, knocking him to the floor. She straddled his chest and smashed her gauntleted fist into his face twice before Val buried a crossbow bolt between her shoulders.

Another soldier leaped onto Val's back, wrapping an arm around his throat. Alar reached out with his mind and ransacked the soldier's thoughts until his grip on Val loosened. The spymaster spun and slammed him against the edge of the nearest table. The man slumped to the stonework, gasping in pain.

Sangrin barked orders to his other five soldiers. Two more made a grab for Val while Jack rolled the dead woman off and staggered to his feet. Bleeding and breathing hard, he pulled her Guild-issued rapier from its scabbard to hold another advancing soldier at bay. The last two guards and Sangrin himself moved toward Alar.

Sangrin drew his sword. "Bleeding blanker trash."

"Now, that's not very nice," Alar scolded, backing away. His eyes darted toward the rack of weaponry to his right. "Do you sing Enlightened praises with that mouth?"

Sangrin roared, and the two soldiers flanking him charged.

Alar *seized* every piece of metal he could grasp on the rack and sent it flying. A shield cracked into the rightmost soldier's skull, dropping him like fruit from a tree. The soldier on the left had enough sense to throw her arms over her head to block a loose armor plate that would have fractured her jaw. Swords and daggers pummeled Sangrin's armored torso. The gleaming blades sliced his uniform and cut him open at neck and face. He snarled again, clutching one gloved hand against the wounds, and swung his sword at Alar's left side.

Alar spun away, but the blow still sent him sprawling. Its lethal edge glanced off his chain mail and pummeled his left kidney like a cudgel. If any air had remained in his lungs when he hit the floor, he would have cursed the captain in every language he knew. Instead, he rolled out of reach as Sangrin's sword came down again. Steel sparked against the stonework. Before the captain could draw back a third time, Alar drew his dagger from his sleeve and threw it at Sangrin's face. The blade glanced harmlessly off one upturned bracer, but in Sangrin's distraction, Alar picked himself up and ran.

The brief respite allowed him to leap onto the nearest tabletop and survey the room again. Jack was dueling viciously with one of the Guild's better swordsmen. Two soldiers had wrestled Val to the ground between the tables. One sat atop him, holding Val's wrists, while the other knelt and made to open his throat. With a flash of horror, Alar *seized* the closest item available—a metal brazier—and sent it flying, spilling hot coals over all three men on the floor. He cringed at the sound of Val's screams, but both soldiers scrambled away from his friend.

The duelist died on the end of Jack's sword. Whipping his black hair from his eyes, Jack reclaimed his hand crossbow and began loading it, sharing a brief look with Alar before turning his attention to Sangrin and the remaining female guard.

Alar leaped between the tables, hauled Val to his feet, and swiped off a few coals that threatened to set Val's robe ablaze. "Are we having fun yet?"

"Definitely not." Val rubbed at his wrists. He looked askance at the two burned soldiers, who now guarded the path to the east door with both sword and shield. The first soldier Val had body-slammed was back on his feet. His breathing was still labored, but he completed the trap between the tables just the same.

Val turned and pressed his back against Alar's, facing the single soldier. "Tell me you have a brilliant plan to get us out of this mess."

"I'm thinking." Alar struggled to calm his mind as he stared at the two guards in front of the door, honing in on their auras. The younger, freckle-faced soldier bore a trembling silhouette of anxiety as he gazed back at Alar. If he could gain a few moments—

Behind him, Sangrin barked a laugh. "I admit you're a gutsy lot." He strode forward, throwing a sneer at Jack. "Put your crossbow down, boy. You must know when you've lost."

"*Stall them,*" Alar told Val.

His surroundings faded from Alar's awareness as he dipped into the young soldier's stream of thought.

Your shield is useless against a mastermind, he whispered into the stream.

The youngest soldier paled.

From the boy's most recent memories, Alar deciphered his name among the jumble of increasingly panicked thoughts. *Your companions will die, but you, Hadley, may yet be useful.*

Hadley's sword hand went as slack as his jaw.

Alar smiled at him. *Your thoughts are mine now.*

Both shield and sword slipped from the boy's grasp. Metal rang against the floor, and Hadley screamed. "He's in my *head*!"

The rest of the battle was over in seconds. When the soldier next to Hadley recoiled from the boy, startled, Alar tore out of Hadley's mind and into his. He released a wave of psychic energy so powerful that the man's nose and eyes gushed red.

As Hadley scrambled away from the horrific sight and the older soldier crumpled dead, Val struck. A distinct crunch of bone and another scream preceded an armored body hitting the floor. The hiss of Jack's crossbow sounded twice. When Alar turned to look, Sangrin's hand had closed around the pair of bolts in his neck. The captain opened his mouth, but only a burbling sound issued from his throat. He collapsed, glassy-eyed, and went still.

Val and Jack swept in to dispatch the last female guard. Alar turned back to the quivering soldier trying to round the tables and flee. The last blast of psychic power had left him feeling dizzy, but he steeled himself for one more and hammered his will into Hadley's mind.

Down, Alar commanded.

Hadley dropped with a cry, clutching his head, drawing his knees up to his elbows. Deep, hiccupping sobs wracked his body.

Alar knelt beside the boy, more to steady himself than anything, and gripped the front of Hadley's uniform. "What's up those stairs?"

Hadley's brown eyes darted toward the spiral staircase. His voice trembled. "Th-the catacombs. Under th-the School. Please, don't hurt me."

"Is there another entrance to this dungeon up there?"

"I-I—" Hadley's face was eclipsed by shadow as Val came to stand over them. "Please—"

"Answer him." Val's voice rumbled low and dangerous.

"I-I don't know! The mages never let us go up there. Said it was off-limits."

"He can't help us," Jack said from somewhere behind them.

Alar narrowed his eyes. "I think he can."

"Please, I don't know anything!"

Alar returned to the nagging feeling of unease he'd had in the corridor. "We know the Guild has sorcerers who are warded against psionics. Where are they?"

There was the slightest hesitation in Hadley's response. He blinked a few times, looking between Alar and Val. "I don't know what you mean."

"Liar," Val snapped.

Alar relaxed his hold on the soldier's uniform and took a moment to smooth its lapels. Hadley cringed and looked away, as if bracing for a blow.

"Listen." Alar's tone softened. "I have no interest in killing you. If you tell me where the Guild has stationed the rest of their mages, you will walk out of this room alive."

Hadley began to weep with relief, but Alar held up a hand to silence him. "But if you lie to me again, my friend here will open your belly like a fish and leave you to die tucking your entrails back into your body. Do you want that, Hadley?"

The boy shook his head, his red-rimmed eyes going wide again. "No, sir."

"There's a good man." Alar patted his knee. "Now, I'm going to ask you again. This time, in here." He pressed a finger to Hadley's temple. "All you have to do is think your answer. I will know if you're lying. Do you understand?"

Sobering, Hadley took a shaky breath and nodded.

Alar broke his telepathic link with Val to form one with the boy. His head throbbed from the strain, and he pulled energy from the casting bracelet to ward off the dark haze in his periphery. "*Where are the sorcerers who resist psionics?*"

Hadley swallowed. "*They were guarding the aethermancers. But they left maybe half an hour ago.*"

Alar weighed each word, paying careful attention to the way Hadley's stream of thought coursed through his mind. He found no ripples of deception. "*Why?*"

Hadley threw a glance toward the east door. "*Something happened to one of the prisoners.*"

Fighting to keep his expression neutral, Alar said, "*Tell me what you know.*"

"*Not much.*" The boy glanced over Alar's shoulder again and—perhaps finding something in Val's expression that encouraged him—began to elaborate. "*After Nicolas and his sorcerers left, one of the other mages went to check on them. He found the old man dead.*"

The old man. Alar turned the words over, his brows knitting together. Only one member of their captured party matched that description.

Bile rose in his throat; anger flared white-hot in his chest. He stood abruptly and turned away, pulling more from the bracelet to stave off the intense pounding in his head. The cool wave of arcane relief did little to temper his fury.

This was exactly what he had feared. With the Guild and the Alliaansi so precariously balanced on the brink of war, this would tip them over the edge. As much confidence as he had in his people, between the shortage of saphyrum and thousands of Syljian refugees to support, it was a war the Alliaansi could not win.

"Alar?" Val asked.

Alar forced down his simmering rage and turned back to his companions. Val still stood over Hadley, watching him with a grim, guarded expression. Jack stood at a nearby table, wiping off the crossbow bolts he'd harvested from the dead. He paid no mind to Hadley's interrogation until Alar spoke again.

"Thank you, Hadley. You may go."

Jack's eyes flicked upward. No doubt the young spy caught the darkness in Alar's tone.

Hadley threw a wary look at Val before attempting to rise to his feet. He moved slowly at first, as if he expected a trap. To offer encouragement, Alar slid his attention to the west door and *pulled* it open. Hadley stared at the door for a long moment, and then took off running.

When the boy's feet struck the stone outside the room, Alar looked at Jack. "Kill him."

No sooner had he spoken the words than the thief shot Hadley off his feet. Alar let the door between them swing closed. Unperturbed, Jack went back to cleaning his weapons. Val, however, approached Alar and put a hand on his shoulder.

"What did he say, Alar?"

Alar gazed back at him. "Cheralach is dead."

Chapter Twelve

Magnus

Blood ran into Magnus's remaining eye. He tried to blink it clear, but it did little to dispel the cloudy splotches from his vision. The left side of his face pulsed with searing heat. What blistered flesh remained had swollen near to bursting. That agony had voided his stomach four times, making all the other burns and lacerations pale in comparison.

Good morning, Magnus. My name is Nicolas. I'm hoping you can help me.

He tried to adjust his arms against the chains that held him. One shoulder protested his efforts, rewarding him with a fresh stab of pain. A weak moan issued from his throat, provoking more pain from vocal cords made raw from screaming.

You see, your commander has been less than forthcoming with the information I need. But if you ask him nicely, perhaps he will be more willing to cooperate.

Rough stone dug into his bloodied knees. Time had stretched to infinity during the interrogation, and there was no telling how long he'd knelt there. He'd lost consciousness more than once. Eventually, he had given Nicolas what he wanted. Cheralach, however, had remained steadfast, even when Magnus resorted to begging.

I do apologize for this, my friend. If he would simply tell me how to find Draeconis, then your torment could end.

Who or what Draeconis was, Magnus didn't know, but it was obviously important. He could tell Cheralach knew something, but he'd never shared it with him. That was probably for the best. If he had known any of the information Nicolas sought, Magnus would have given it freely.

It's obvious he does not have your best interests at heart. Perhaps he never truly cared for you at all.

That wasn't true. Cheralach had deflected many times, taunting Nicolas, trying to pull his attention away from Magnus. It worked in brief spurts, as if getting him to talk at all was the goal. Cheralach had endured the worst of their torturer's maliciousness when he lied, having several bones broken and half a dozen fingers and toes removed over countless hours of questioning. But Nicolas had always returned to Magnus after he tired of Cheralach's games.

You know the worst part of all of this? You are suffering in vain. They all talk in the end.

Each wound Nicolas had inflicted was worse than the last. The worst one of all—the swollen mass of burned tissue that had once been Magnus's left eye—still did not move Cheralach to speak truthfully on his behalf. Magnus might have hated the old aethermancer as Nicolas heated the dagger over the brazier. His pleading with Cheralach to say something, anything, had only caused his mentor to squeeze his eyes shut and turn away.

He has forsaken you, Magnus. See how you have become unworthy? He cannot even bear to look at you.

A broken sob wracked his body, eliciting more suffering.

The sight of his mentor's revulsion had spurred its own agony. The Guild sorcerers overseeing their torture had pried open Cheralach's eyes, forcing him to watch Nicolas approaching with that glowing hot dagger.

But not to worry, my friend. I will be here for you.

He tried to retreat from the memory of what came next, but to no avail. Long after his eye had burst and his flesh burned away, long after he'd passed out and woken up alone in the same, dimly lit room, he could still hear Nicolas whispering in his ear. No matter how hard he tried, Magnus could not escape the voice inside his head.

I will be with you for the rest of your life.

"What took you so long?"

Ravlok studied the young woman standing at the first cell door on the far side of the prison. She watched him in turn, placing both scabbed hands on the bars in front of her. Her blonde hair hung limply against her shoulders, and her sleeveless black shirt and gray trousers were almost as filthy as her face.

Anwic snorted. "Our new friend had to stop and chat with one of the guards first." He jerked a thumb over his shoulder toward Ravlok.

Kendi beckoned Ravlok forward, sparing a sour look at Anwic. "We needed a little help getting out," he said. "Sam, this is Ravlok. Ravlok," he gestured toward the bedraggled woman, "Sam."

Ravlok stepped around Anwic, brandishing the ring of keys. "A pleasure," he said to her, slipping the key into the lock.

Sam's eyebrows pinched together around a sizable bruise. She gave him an appraising look, and her split lips twitched into a smile. "I'll say."

A hot flush swept up Ravlok's neck. He made quick work of the spellbinders around her wrists, careful not to encourage any undue attention.

When Sam stepped out of the cell, she took both of his hands and squeezed them. "Thank you."

He squeezed back, surprised by the strength in her callused palms. "You're welcome."

A soft gasp drew Sam's attention back the way they'd come. Ravlok followed her gaze to find Orowen leaning against the wall. The Syljian woman was staring at the floor, one hand on her chest, the other bracing her body against the rough stone.

"Oh gods," Sam whispered. She started toward the priestess.

Kendi stopped her with an upraised hand. "Where are the others?"

"Here," called a deep male voice from farther down the corridor. "Jessie is hurt."

"I'm fine," groaned a second female voice. "Nothing a few shots of whiskey won't cure."

Kendi lowered his hand and looked back at Orowen.

Her condition was getting worse. Judging by the growing concern in Kendi's expression, he saw it, too. A thin sheen of sweat coated the priestess's face, and her skin had paled further with the exertion of traversing the dungeon.

"Does she need more saphyrum?" Ravlok suggested. "She should have a few minutes while we clear these cells."

Kendi nodded once to him and gestured for Sam to attend to her. He called to Anwic. "Stand guard for Orowen and Sam. We'll take care of Rylan and Jessie."

Anwic slipped past Ravlok and took up a spot near the turn in the corridor. Kendi ushered Ravlok toward the other two cells.

The man in the second cell was a broad-shouldered human in his early thirties. Blond stubble dusted his jaw and upper lip, and his skin resembled the color of tanned deer hide. He stood a fingerspan or two taller than Ravlok and regarded him with appreciation as his cell door swung open. When his spellbinders fell to the floor, he offered his hand. "Thank you. Ravlok, is it?"

Ravlok shook his hand. "It is."

"Rylan." He lifted his chin toward the closest cell on the opposite wall. "Jessie is there."

As Ravlok moved to free the dark-haired woman leaning against the bars of her cell, Kendi addressed Rylan. "Have you seen Cheralach or Magnus?"

Ravlok blinked, his key half-turned in the lock.

Cheralach the Deserter was here?

The infamous sorcerer-turned-aethermancer was a legend in Eidosinia. Twenty-five years ago, Cheralach had led the single largest Syljian exodus from Guild-controlled lands since the fall of Astenpor. He'd founded the town of Starlight to accommodate the refugees and joined forces with Koraani, leader of the Alliaansi, to secure the city's supply chains.

It was said Cheralach and his younger brother Jerinoch had both been rewarded seats on the Alliaansi council after doubling the rebel group's numbers.

Starlight became the aethermancers' new base of operations, and its strategic placement still sheltered Syljians and their sympathizers to this day.

"They took them back there." Rylan nodded toward the far end of the corridor.

Ravlok was about to look that way when the woman named Jessie cleared her throat. "If you just want to give me the keys, I can do the rest."

"Right. Sorry." A wave of heat touched his cheeks. He finished turning the key. The lock snapped open, and he soon removed her spellbinders as well.

"Thanks." Jessie gave the cell one last disgusted glare. "I've had some pretty bad accommodations over the years, but this one takes the bacon."

She tried to step out of the cell, but one leg buckled. Ravlok caught her as she fell, gasping, clutching her thigh through blood-soaked skirts. "Chaos curse the bleeding bastards."

"Easy." Ravlok struggled to guide her away from the cell without provoking more pain. What he wouldn't give for one of Yonfé's first aid satchels. That was a lot of blood.

Once there was room, Rylan took Jessie's other side. Together, they lowered her to the floor.

"Let me see." Rylan gripped the hem of her skirts. Without waiting for her approval, he threw up the material.

Ravlok looked away.

Jessie snorted a laugh. "No need to be modest. I was once a courtesan for the entire battalion at Watersgate."

"Jessie," Rylan scolded.

"Well, it's true."

His holy commitment aside, Ravlok was not a prudish man. No one born in Madame's house ever had that luxury. He had seen men and women in countless unfortunate and embarrassing positions during his short service. As for finding any kind of sexual appeal in Jessie's current predicament... he would rather not ponder such things.

"If it doesn't bother you, it doesn't bother me." With her permission granted, Ravlok returned his attention to the source of the blood. He had some mundane healer's knowledge, if only because Yonfé had insisted he volunteer in the Guild infirmary.

Rylan hiked her skirts up to her hips, exposing dozens of long gashes cut into both legs. Blood crusted in gruesome smears over much of her lower half. The worst of the wounds was halfway up her outer thigh. Rylan pried her hand off the wound to get a better look at it. Her palm came away red. He swore at the sight, his expression pained.

A stab wound. Gods knew Ravlok had seen his share of those. A simple bandage wouldn't be enough. He bent down to examine the wound a little closer. It was small, but deep and inflamed. "They've damaged muscle."

Kendi's shadow fell over them. "You're not going anywhere with that. Not until Orowen has seen to it. Rylan—"

Ravlok looked up sharply. "Orowen is in no condition to heal anyone," he argued, drawing all three pairs of eyes. He looked between them, his brows tense. "She can barely walk as it is."

"What choice do we have?" Rylan was already slipping an arm around Jessie's waist.

Ravlok's retort died on his lips as Jessie and Rylan began the slow trek down the corridor.

Kendi followed his gaze. "That sort of wound is easy for her to fix. It shouldn't tax her too much."

Still, Ravlok couldn't shake his unease. Even as a non-adept, he knew casting too much could take a terrible toll on a person. Mage's Folly could be physically debilitating in the short term, but it also affected one's ability to cast for weeks afterward. "This is a bad idea."

"Jessie is an aethermancer. I need her on her feet."

Ravlok scowled. "And you don't need your healer?"

Frowning, Kendi nodded in the direction Rylan had indicated earlier. "If the others are back there, their condition will be even worse. When we encounter resistance, we will benefit from having as many fighters as possible."

Sam roused Orowen from her prayers while Ravlok considered the words Kendi wasn't saying. Their ragtag crew would be much worse off if they had to carry people to the surface. By restoring Jessie's leg, they lowered their liability count from a possible four to three.

Orowen started her work on Jessie's wound, spinning tendrils of white-violet light between her hands. As dire as their situation was, Ravlok still found himself mesmerized by the gods' magic. The dazzling light at her fingertips twirled toward Jessie's wound like smoke. It penetrated deep inside the damaged tissue and healed the wound from the inside out. Within seconds, the flesh had knitted and sealed perfectly. Not even a scar remained.

When the healer's sigil faded, the soft glow from the runes on Orowen's temples was even weaker than before. Ravlok knew little about Syljian runes, but he was certain that did not bode well for things to come. He said a silent prayer of his own to Ordeolas for strength and courage.

He returned his attention to Kendi. "So, what's the—"

The sharp sound of squealing hinges interrupted him. Kendi spun, issuing rapid commands to the others, his harsh whisper lost in the crash of a heavy door closing. He reached for Ravlok's elbow, but Ravlok was already moving.

His palm itched for a weapon—a blade, a staff, something. But a monk's hands, in connection with his own aura, could be just as deadly. He centered his mind around that connection now, feeling his aura ripple with the unbalancing effects of anxiety. In the few seconds it took him to reach the mouth of the corridor, he willed that ripple to calm. Most of his training under Yonfé had focused on immobilizing his opponents, but the same techniques could be adapted. Killing was not encouraged by Ordeolas, but nor was it condemned if done for the right reasons. Ravlok had never taken a life before, but the thought didn't unnerve him. He would do what must be done.

Assuming an open-handed ready stance, he settled beside Anwic, who'd pressed his back against the stone. The youngest Syljian looked prepared to spring forward at the first sign of the enemy, face set with deadly determination. Kendi and Rylan joined them on the opposite wall, sinking into the shadows created by a crevice in the stonework. Behind them, Sam stood guard over Orowen and Jessie as their last line of defense.

The dungeon fell silent. For several heartbeats, no one moved.

Ravlok turned his thoughts inward, steadying his breathing, allowing his belly to expand with each inhale. Sensing the tension in his legs and shoulders, he willed them to relax. With each exhale, his body drew closer and closer to Balance.

At the sound of footsteps, Anwic made a silent gesture and held up three fingers pressed close together. Ravlok spared a glance toward Kendi and Rylan to get a sense of what that meant, but he couldn't see either of them in the shadows. Facing forward again, he resigned himself to following Anwic's lead.

At first, the footsteps seemed to travel away from them. Then they traveled back and stopped roughly where they had started. There were no words exchanged—not even whispers—but Ravlok was certain there was more than one person. He had to center himself again to keep from peering around the corner. They could not chance being spotted and losing their element of surprise.

Behind him, one of the women shifted; there was the softest rasping of cloth against stone. Tension lanced through Ravlok's jaw.

Be still.

Another sound followed. A sort of clicking, nearly imperceptible, but it might as well have been falling stone to Ravlok's ears. His heart pounded at his temples and his fingers curled into fists. Something small and round flashed in his periphery; Rylan's hand shot from the shadows and snatched the tiny reflection out of the air.

Saphyrum.

He was getting distracted. He had to focus. Ravlok steeled his tumultuous aura a second time and exhaled in a rush. Breathing in again, he stilled his mind to all but the task at hand.

The figures approached. Their shadows appeared on the wall, and Anwic tensed beside him, ready to lunge. Ravlok started forward as well—

"Hold!" Kendi's voice was a whipcrack splitting the air. He stepped out of the shadows, white brows furrowed, arm raised. He squinted in the dim light. "Alar."

The shadows stopped. A cautious male voice called out, "Commander?"

"We're here. Who is with you?"

"Val and Jack."

The voice sounded familiar to Ravlok, but he couldn't place it. As he pondered where he might have heard it before, a young man wearing a mage's robe stepped around the corner. His violet eyes swept the scene before him.

Anwic relaxed and Ravlok followed suit, lowering his hands. Another mage and a Guild soldier joined the first man. All three were around Ravlok's age, bruised, bloody, and toting weapons. The youngest-looking one, a black-haired human with a thin, wiry build, bore a grotesque burn that leaked pinkish fluid onto the collar of his uniform. Alar, the center man, sported an enormous bruise over one eye, and he'd split his lip so recently that it still wept blood. The shorter mage looked like he'd been involved in a tavern brawl. Besides the many cuts and bruises on his face and neck, there were massive holes burned in his black robe, exposing singed commoner's clothes beneath.

"We don't have much time." Alar's attention settled on Ravlok. Torchlight danced across the newcomer's face, highlighting familiar features. Tension strained his expression, coupled with the slightest narrowing of discerning eyes. Then Alar looked away. "Is everyone here?"

"We're missing Magnus and Cheralach." Kendi gestured deeper into the dungeon. "Rylan says they were taken back there."

The two dressed as mages shared a look, then Alar shot a glance beyond the small circle of men to the trio of women. His lips parted as if he was about to say something.

His companion spoke instead. "Then we'd better get them out." When Alar grimaced and opened his mouth to speak again, the tavern brawler interrupted him a second time. He turned to Anwic, sweeping his robe to one side. Affixed to the inner lining was a small collection of daggers. "We have weapons for you."

"Finally." Anwic gathered four of them and passed two to Ravlok. "You know how to use these, right, *bashiin*?"

Ravlok took them, familiarizing himself with the weight of the leather-wrapped steel. They were balanced enough for throwing, and the edges were sharp. In answer to Anwic's question, Ravlok spun first one blade and then the other around his fingers. "I might need a demonstration."

Behind them, Sam snorted. She pushed Anwic aside and plucked a dagger for herself. "Careful, Anwic. If you pick a fight with our new companion, my gold is on him." She punctuated her declaration with a wink and a grin at Ravlok.

Anwic side-eyed the woman, lips tightening. Whether a smile or a sneer threatened, Ravlok couldn't say; either way, he was grateful he might have made another friend among these curious allies.

"I don't suppose you have a sword under there as well?" Kendi's eyes slid from Anwic and Sam back to the shorter mage.

While the mage made a show of patting down his black robe, the burned man rolled his eyes and stepped forward. "Take this one." He passed Kendi the rapier he carried. "The soldier I borrowed it from won't be needing it anymore."

"Thank you, Jack," Kendi said.

"There are more weapons out there." The tavern brawler, who must be Val, passed the last dagger to Rylan. "And armor as well. We should stock up before we leave."

"I'll stay with the wounded for now," Rylan offered. "Give Orowen time to help Jessie while you get Cheralach and Magnus."

"Jack can stay, too." Alar stepped toward Orowen and dropped to one knee beside her. "He will also need your healing arts, Devoted. Are you well enough to help us?"

Orowen reached out to touch his cheek with a pale, shaking hand. "I will be fine, *neime*." She managed a smile for him. "Especially now that I can see your face. I have missed you."

Ravlok could not see Alar's reaction, but he did notice the unusual shape of the man's ears from behind. They stuck out from his disheveled brown hair as thick masses of cartilage shaped into curves by the use of assassin's clay. One side had been knocked askew and cracked down the middle where material met skin. Its flesh-colored paint was scraped away in places, perhaps by a fall or a blow to his head.

The man was half-Syljian.

"Let's get moving." Sam started for the end of the corridor. She made to step around Jessie, who was struggling to straighten her leg for Orowen's inspection. "I'm sure Cheralach is already—"

"No." Alar straightened. "You're not going in there."

The change in his tone must have been uncharacteristic for him. Not only did Sam stop short, but the rest of their group stiffened as well. All the air seemed to have been sucked out of the corridor.

It was Sam who spoke first. Her brown eyes narrowed. "Why not?"

"Alar is right," Val said, carefully sliding between them. He shot a disapproving look at Alar before placing a hand on Sam's shoulder. "We don't know what we'll find in there."

Anger rippled across Sam's face. She shrugged him off. "You both still think I can't handle being in the field. I get it. Now piss off."

Val's shoulders sagged as Sam stormed toward the door. He looked to Kendi for support.

Kendi shook his head. "She's as much a soldier as the rest of us, Valaxes."

Kendi's assessment only seemed to make matters worse. Both newcomers cringed and shared another glance. Alar growled and started after Sam with Val at his heels.

Confused, Ravlok looked between the departing trio and Kendi, who sighed. "Come on, then," he said, starting forward.

They caught up as Sam pulled open the last wooden door on the right. A blast of air blew her hair from her face, and she recoiled. The hand not clutching the door's iron handle came up to cover her mouth and nose. Val and Alar faltered right alongside her. Kendi also stopped short, his face pinching.

Death's sickly aroma struck Ravlok like a fist to his gut. He cupped his mouth and doubled over at the waist. It was unlike anything he had ever experienced, even working in the temple dressing bodies for burial. It wasn't just decay and blood, but bile, feces, and urine, too. There was the stench of burned hair and flesh, hot iron and sweat. And beneath it all, something else—something pungent and sinister that Ravlok couldn't name.

His stomach heaved.

The sound was wretched in the otherwise silent space, the splash of sick coating the wall only lending more to the rotten odor spilling into the corridor. Once he'd voided all he could, a palm pressed against his back. Wiping his mouth, he looked up to see Kendi's concern flanked by Val and Alar's steely expressions of detachment. Sam still held her hand over her mouth, but her eyes were sympathetic as she stood with her foot propping the door open.

"Are you alright, Ravlok?" Kendi asked.

Ravlok almost passed the keys to the commander and told him to go on without him. The last place he wanted to be was any closer to the source of that smell, but his new allies were watching him. Yonfé had always said pride was a suit only worn by fools, but Ravlok couldn't help his embarrassment. He spat and sniffed and spat again to clear his nose and mouth of the burning remnants of vomit. Distrusting his seared vocal cords to convey words yet, he nodded.

Kendi looked about to question him again, but Alar spoke instead. "Perhaps you should stay back. It's only going to get worse from here."

Ravlok met Alar's eyes, which had faded from saphyric violet to muddy brown. Again, he was tempted to hand over the keys.

A soft snicker came from behind him.

"Anwic," Orowen warned.

His breath still labored, and his skin felt clammy, but Ravlok straightened despite himself. Anwic's facetiousness sobered him. "I'm fine," he said around a throat full of gravel.

As if to illustrate his claim, he brandished the keys and stepped past all three men to join Sam at the door. He nodded his thanks to her before entering the room beyond.

Torches lit this rectangular chamber, though Ravlok wished the orange glow didn't illuminate as much as it did. Against one wall stood three barred cells. Each one housed a chained prisoner, arms twisted at unnatural angles, white hair matted and limp. All three were Syljian, and all were slumped, unmoving, in heaps of dirty straw. Their figures were bloated and gray, suggesting they had died sometime within the last week. The horrifying likelihood they had been left there to dishearten other prisoners made Ravlok's gut churn again. He looked away.

To his right were two doors. In addition to the same bolt-and-padlock combination found elsewhere in the dungeon, these could also be locked by drawbars that recessed into the wall. Only the closer door's drawbar was in place. A sliver of light came through the gap at the bottom of that door, and a dark puddle seeped across the stone from the room beyond. He approached, careful not to dip his bare feet in it.

The others filed into the chamber after Ravlok. Val moved in his periphery, examining the bodies through the cell bars.

"I don't think they're ours." He cringed. "Though it's hard to tell."

"Baosanni have mercy." Sam's voice was muffled, palm still cupping her face. "We can't leave them like this."

"We'll burn them properly on our way out," Kendi promised her. "It's all we can do."

All four of his companions converged on the door. Ravlok was about to reach for the padlock above the drawbar when the heavy wooden beam moved of its own accord. Alarmed, Ravlok tensed, reaching for his dagger, until a hand on his shoulder stopped him. He turned to see Alar standing beside him.

The half-Syljian's eyes glowed violet once more. They fixated on the door as the drawbar slid into the cutout in the stonework. Once it was seated fully in the wall, Alar blinked his gaze back to brown and patted Ravlok's shoulder.

Telekinesis.

There were only a few kinds of magic-adepts in the world capable of moving objects like that. Powerful mages could do so, but only by speaking certain incantations. Alar hadn't uttered a word. The only other possibility settled like a lead weight in Ravlok's stomach: Syljian masterminds.

His realization must have shown on his face because Alar stared pointedly forward, a little too focused on the door. When Alar glanced at him out of the corners of his eyes, Ravlok did his best to subdue his unease. It was surely unfounded; they were on the same side. His fear was a product of years of exposure to Guild propaganda—nothing based in fact or logic.

Still, it was hard to shake the feeling he'd found himself in the presence of a wolf.

Ravlok sipped at the air, trying to calm himself without breathing too deeply. Now was not the time to lose his nerve. He reached for the lock, and it snapped open with a turn of the key. As his hand settled on the handle, he said a silent prayer for whomever waited on the other side.

Chapter Thirteen

Daeya

Daeya hit the ground with a cry, the air driven from her lungs. The tiffleball fell from her hands. Murtagh cackled, snatching it up. He leaped over her and tried to dash away, but Daeya seized his ankle as he passed. He fell belly-first into the cobbles beside her, feet flailing as she curled her arms around his legs to keep him down.

"Sorcha!" Murtagh called to his teammate.

The wiry young woman caught Murtagh's awkward pass and spun around Annie in a whirlwind of freckles and fire-red curls. She darted toward the tiffle—a metal hoop mounted parallel to the wall—in the eaves of Mr. McCullough's bakery. Sorcha chucked the ball at an angle, bouncing it off a wooden crate, then the bakery wall, and through the tiffle.

"Two points, Red!" Angus called as the ball bounced down the narrow alley. "Green, six. Red, eight!"

Their tie broken, Annie and Sorcha took off after the ball while Daeya and Murtagh found their feet. Daeya shoved him into the side of a water trough. He roared obscenities in Brogrenti as she sprinted away snickering, her white-blonde hair whipping in the wind.

Each round of tiffleball was a race to nine points, with nine rounds in a single game. Teams scored points by bouncing the ball off objects in the surrounding area. The more times the ball bounced before passing through the tiffle, the more points they scored.

Scoring points was simple, but getting the ball and keeping it from the other team was another story. Tiffleball had long been touted as the bloodiest sport played in the Brogrenti Highlands. Even though using weapons and magic went against the rules, serious injuries were common as players punched, kicked, and shoved each other on the court.

They had been at it for six rounds now, with Angus keeping score. Daeya had shed her clothing down to brown leggings and her white, long-sleeved undershirt. Both were heavily soiled from the number of times she'd hit the ground. There was a long gash on her hand from where she'd caught a nail sticking out of a wooden barrel, and both her shins ached with bruises.

The other players were in no better shape. Her cousin's upper lip was crusted with dried blood. Scrapes peppered his knees, and his *aeyak* was ripped in several places. Shreds of green-and-blue-striped fabric trailed in his wake like ragged tails.

Murtagh's teammate, Sorcha, sported a swollen lip and a black eye. Her loose sable shirtsleeves stuck to bleeding cuts from a crash into a crate of glass wine bottles. Her tight leather vest bore scratches from a half-dozen heroic slides across unforgiving ground to retrieve the ball.

Annie's long skirts whirled around her, bearing streaks of mud and blood. Her black hair had unraveled from its tight braid and framed her rosy cheeks in a nest of windswept waves. She had a cut over her left eye and several grisly scrapes on both elbows.

Murtagh was right about her; she was a *braugh* tiffle player, indeed. Though she wasn't Brogrenti, it was clear Annie bore the heart of a clansman. She never once shied from taking a punch or getting her skirts dirty, and her shot-making was exceptional. She had thrown the longest tiffle path of all of them so far, scoring four points with an impossible shot that even Angus couldn't believe at first. Coupled with her lively demeanor and quickness to laugh, Annie was an equal match to Murtagh's bright flame. Daeya could not have been happier for them.

Annie snatched the ball before it rolled into the busy street. She ducked under Sorcha's sweeping right hook and bolted back toward the bakery. Daeya placed herself between Murtagh and the tiffle, acting as guard for Annie's next shot. Murtagh righted himself against the water trough. Daeya's grin was smug even as he glowered at her. Though he was a handspan taller than Daeya, she could still lay him out, thanks to Ravlok's training.

Annie was fast, but Sorcha was faster. The young lutist caught up to Annie and shot out a hand, snagging her friend by her hair.

"Daeya!" Annie called, passing the ball.

Daeya caught it smoothly, dropped to the ground and spun, sweeping her boot in a wide arc that caught Murtagh's legs mid-step. He stumbled, giving Daeya room to escape. She regained her feet and backed up, seeking her best path toward the tiffle.

Sorcha released Annie's hair and darted toward Daeya, but Annie stuck out a foot to trip her. The redhead went down in a heap, swearing a string in Brogrenti. With Sorcha compromised and Murtagh closing in, Annie was wide open and in a better position to shoot. Daeya pivoted, dodging Murtagh's grab for her arm.

"Annie!"

Annie caught the ball and threw it with an expert snap of her wrist. The spinning ball ricocheted off a smooth cobble, bounced off the water trough, and hit the bakery wall. It struck the side of the tiffle before falling through it.

"Three points, Green!" Angus cheered. "Green, nine. Red, eight. And by the gods, great shot, Annie!"

Annie flushed red as a pomitto from the praise and went to retrieve the ball. There was no mad dash for it at the end of the round.

Angus called out the game scores—a tie at three to three—and took the ball from Annie to check the bindings. Murtagh and Daeya took their places at the painted line designating mid-court, facing each other to prepare for round seven.

Murtagh was red-faced and grinning, his dark freckles nearly invisible in the wake of his exertion. "Ye ready to lose this one, Magelet?" he asked, using Po's silly nickname for her. He swiped at a trail of mud on his left cheek. "I've gone easy on ye so far."

Daeya narrowed her eyes. "I thought you were just losing your touch, cousin."

"Only in yer wildest fantasies."

After rewrapping a loose binding on the ball, Angus placed it on the makeshift table—a wine cask turned on its end with a few boards nailed to the top—and waved them all over. "Take five, ye lot, and we'll break the tie after another ale."

Sorcha threw herself onto a barrel beside Angus and reached for the pitcher of ale. Tossing her unruly red curls out of her eyes, she beamed as the dark brew filled her mug. She'd joined them on the way out of Davy's. Her mother, Nessa Allon, was a waitress for Po, and Sorcha played lute for the dinner crowd on most nights.

Daeya liked Sorcha not just for her scrappy temperament and foul mouth, but also for her sense of humor. Some weeks ago, she'd written a catchy tune inspired by Daeya's rival, Normos Beck. Apparently, Sorcha had shared classes with Normos as an acolyte, before the Guild expelled her from the School for poor grades and poorer behavior. Even back then, Sorcha asserted, the stuffy sorcerer had fostered an intimate relationship with the horses in the stables.

Daeya was the last to join them beside the crumbling back wall of Guertie's Bait and Tackle. The fervor of the game drained from her, leaving her stiff and aching from injuries too numerous to count. Her burns especially made themselves known again, and she took the offered mug from Murtagh to stave them off.

She collapsed onto the barrel where she'd left her mage's robe, letting her senses fog with heady elation. "Gods, how I've missed you all."

"Ye'll be able to visit more now that ye don't have classes, won't ye?" Murtagh asked.

She hesitated.

"Unlikely," Sorcha answered for her. "Ye'll be out in the field now, won't ye? Fixin' all the Guild's little problems and such."

Her teasing humor didn't fully disguise the bitter edge in Sorcha's tone. Daeya could tell she still resented the Council for kicking her out, even though she would never admit it.

"That is what I trained for, yes," Daeya said, attempting a sympathetic smile. She looked between Murtagh and her father. "Much as I would like to see you more, Eidosinia comes first."

"Well, you seem much kinder than the rest of them," Annie said between sips of ale. "Don't let them change that."

Daeya frowned. That was a curious thing to say. More curious was the way all three red-headed Brogrenti nodded in agreement—even her father, who always spoke highly of her path to magehood.

The sorcerers were both governors and defenders of the nation. Granted, some mages were tougher on the citizens than others, but they still ruled with compassion. The Guild always kept the people's best interests at heart.

She was about to ask Annie to elaborate, but the sound of a bell chime interrupted her. It rang out across the city—the first of five bells signaling the time of day—and all the warmth drained from Daeya's face. A numbing chill swept through her, and she leaped off the barrel. Swearing a long string in Brogrenti, she shrugged into her robe while the others looked on in bewilderment.

"I'm late," she squeaked. Unceremoniously wrenching the fabric in place, she grabbed her satchel and slung it over her shoulder.

Understanding dawned on her father's face. He would know as well as she did that the passenger vessels were twenty minutes across the city.

As the bell tolled a second time, she kissed her father and hugged her cousin, muttering her farewells in a panicked rush. "I love you both. I'm sorry I have to go."

"Good luck, Daeya," Murtagh said.

"Go, lass. Our hearts are with ye."

Her da reached up to touch her face, but Daeya was already spinning toward the mouth of the alley, chest tight, as if armoring itself against the hammer of fear smashing against her ribcage. She left him there, his hand raised, fingers curling around the empty air, and a pained grimace twisting his expression.

Her feet flew over the cobbles, the ramshackle buildings on either side of the alley threatening to close in around her. The alley spat her out on the street in front of a horse-drawn carriage. Its driver swore, fighting to maintain control of the horses that whinnied and reared with dismay. Daeya twisted out of the way of one horse's raised hooves and escaped being trampled by another team of horses heading in the opposite direction. Angry shouts, screeching metal, and echoing whipcracks were all lost to her as the bell crashed over her again.

How could she have been so *stupid*? No wonder Gregory kept her on such a short leash. If she couldn't even keep track of time—

Racing toward the docks was pointless. She decided this only after running three blocks through riverside traffic and hitching a quick ride on the tailgate of a fast-moving wagon. Her boat would have already disembarked by the time she reached Old River Bridge. She swore again and dropped from the wagon, dodging another carriage team and a group of fishermen who reeked of days-old liver.

Think, damn you.

Spinning toward the wide river, Daeya eyed the fast-moving current. The boat would eventually have to pass this way; she could board it before it left the city. It would be too dangerous to Rift Bend onto such a small moving vessel—not unless she wanted to risk disemboweling herself on part of the boat, anyway. Even if it came close enough for an arcane leap, she couldn't guarantee she would clear the distance without incident. There were fewer ways she could embarrass herself more than missing her boat *and* having to be fished out of the river.

There were always other boats. The port city of Keilliad was the last stop for any vessels traveling downriver. If not a passenger vessel, she could pay any of the fishermen to take her south. Though if she couldn't secure passage within the next hour or two, she risked missing the ship to Orthovia as well. That mistake could set her back a week or more, and the delay would not please Gregory.

The thought of his disappointment in her was enough to steel her resolve. She *had* to get on that boat.

Daeya adjusted her pack and stepped to the edge of the pier as the last bell died on the water. The wind teased hair from her face, bringing with it scents of fish and moss, people and horses, tar and pine. She closed her eyes and let herself breathe. Fear and panic never solved anyone's problem. The best solutions came to a quiet mind. She did her best to find her center, as Ravlok had taught her.

The dockside traffic bustled along behind her. Fifth bell marked the day's end for many, and the crowds grew thicker the longer Daeya stood beside the river. They gave her a wide berth. She knew this even with her eyes closed. Not once was she bumped or jostled, and no one passed close enough to disturb the fabric of her robe.

With the water surging handspans below her boots, its dull roar soothing, her heart rate slowed to a more reasonable pace. She imagined wading into the river at a shallow point, letting the water wash away all traces of those useless emotions clouding her psyche: anxiety, uncertainty, doubt. She imagined them all dissolving under the unstoppable force of nature at her feet.

Daeya opened her eyes. She looked to her right, past the rows of docks and boats populating the eastern shore like barnacles on a ship. Out on the water, only a few small boats cruised along, their narrow bows cutting smooth paths through the current. Each bore a single passenger or two—nothing like the larger boat that would take her and her escorts to Keilliad.

A bolt of annoyance shot through her at the thought of answering to the Vikas for her mistake. She tamped it down. With any luck, they might not have boarded the boat in her absence. She could push on to Orthovia alone, feigning ignorance of their predicament if they caught up to her later.

Daeya looked to her left. All the vessels traveling south passed under the city wall through one of the five river arches. The towering structure filled her field of view. Soldiers in dark green uniforms moved about between the parapets high overhead.

Fifth bell also signaled a rotation of the city guard, and the wall teemed with nearly twice as many people as it normally would on a late summer day. Fresh soldiers took up posts near the winches that controlled the opening and closing of the river gates. The rest of the men and women shuffled off toward the sets of stone steps on either side of the river.

Though she couldn't see where the steps reached ground level over the tops of the surrounding buildings, Daeya estimated they were only a five-minute jog away. She skimmed the wall again, finding a space above the peak of the widest river arch. The boat would have to pass beneath that point to leave the city. Her breath quickened as she considered the immense height of the parapet from the river's surface. It was nearly three times the greatest distance she had ever slow-fallen before. Still, the incantation should keep her bones from turning to splinters when she landed.

Daeya shot another glance upriver. No sign of passenger vessels meant there was still time. How much time, though, she couldn't say.

She turned toward the throng of people and waved down a deeply tanned, middle-aged man wearing a sweat-stained shirt and carrying a box of tackle and a fishing pole. The man froze, eyeing her up and down. When he opened his mouth full of rotten teeth, probably to dismiss her or lament her interruption of his journey home, Daeya gave him her most charming smile.

"Excuse me," she said. "Can you tell me how long it takes a riverboat to reach Southgate from the pier at Old River Bridge?"

The fisherman glanced toward the river behind her. "Depends." His voice was as rough as sandstone. He gestured with the tackle box. "Current like that, maybe ten minutes."

Her shoulders sagged with relief. "Ten minutes. Thank you." That meant plenty of time to walk, rather than Rift Bend, and a chance to further calm her nerves. She stepped toward him and fished for a gold coin from one of her many pockets. It was the least she could do.

The man shied from her. "If that be all, Sorceress, I'll be going now."

Even so, he didn't leave. He looked at Daeya as if he expected her to say something else. She paused in her search for a coin and nodded. Only after he shouldered back into the crowd did Daeya withdraw her hand from her pocket, frowning.

Maybe he'd just had bad luck out on the water today. He was a fisherman on the docks with no fish, after all. Or she supposed he could be heading out for the evening. Being forced to wear clothes that filthy could make even the most cheerful person irritable. She wished he'd let her buy him a shirt.

She took hold of her satchel strap to keep the pack from bouncing against her legs and started toward the city wall. When she reached the stairs and started up them, she glanced back and saw a large passenger vessel flying a red flag round the bend a little way upriver. It matched the description of the boat she was supposed to board, and she hurried up to the top of the wall.

At least, she tried to reach the top.

A uniformed soldier stepped into her path, his hand resting on his sword hilt. "Whoa, there, miss. This area is off-limits to civilians."

Daeya looked up into the man's bearded face. Blue sky and tiny wisps of clouds framed his curly hair. Pockmarked skin stretched taut over puffy cheeks. The three stairs separating them only exacerbated his impressive height, and the insignia on one thick shoulder marked him for a sergeant.

Daeya rolled her eyes and tried to step around him. "I'll let you know if I see any, Sergeant."

He side-stepped, blocking her path again. "Maybe I wasn't clear. Turn around. Take your mischief somewhere else."

"I'm on Guild business." Daeya scowled, setting her jaw. "Now, step aside."

The soldier scoffed. "Nice try, kid, but you're not old enough to be a mage. I mean, what are you? Fourteen?"

Daeya growled. No way was she going to miss her boat for this. She looked over her shoulder, across the rooftops of Southgate, and found the boat had traversed half the distance.

The sergeant's hand closed on her arm.

Daeya whirled, wrenching away from him. "Keep your hands off me."

She tried to slip past him once more, but he caught her by the hair and shoved her back. Daeya stumbled, catching herself on the stonework. Her aching muscles screamed.

"Persistent little shit, aren't you?"

Daeya tried to think logically past the pain as she regained her footing. She did look too young to be a mage. She was also filthy from rolling around in the alley with Murtagh and the others. But assaulting a Guild member was cause for public whipping if she exerted her full power here. There was no time for that. She also had no interest in seeing this man harmed for his misunderstanding, even if he was pissing her off.

Instead, she glared up at the soldier and tucked her right hand into her pocket. "Lucky for you, I have a boat to catch," she told him, slipping her casting bracelet over her wrist.

As puzzlement settled over his face, she fixed her eyes on the point along the parapet above the open river gate. Channeling her power, she began to incant, her glowing fingers tracing a sigil in the air. When she finished the incantation, she slashed the blade of her hand downward, opening a black, violet-rimmed tear in the Aetherial Wall—the veil separating Dessos from the font of all arcane power. A second rift opened at the point along the parapet.

The sergeant paled and stumbled back, tripping over the stair behind him. He fell onto his arse, scabbard raking against stone. "Sorceress! Forgive me—"

Daeya spared an apologetic look at the man, even as the breezy rift tossed her hair into her face. "All is forgiven."

She plunged her arm up to the elbow in the black void, clenched her fist around the slippery, tepid Aether, and *pulled,* as if bending a scrap of metal in a vise. There was a flash of white-violet light, streaks of myriad colors, and suddenly she was standing on the parapet, her back to the river far below.

Wind buffeted her, a thousand greedy, spectral fingers clawing at her hair and clothing. She ignored the surprised cries of the two men stationed beside the gate winch and turned, the combined wind and weight of her pack making her unsteady. Her heart leaped into her throat.

Bleeding Aether. Next time, she would Rift Bend *behind* the parapet.

The boat was fast approaching. There was enough time for another incantation.

Slipping the strap of her pack over her head, she turned back to the nearest soldier. "Hold this for me, will you?" she asked, tossing the bundle toward him.

This soldier was a younger man with dark skin and wide brown eyes. His lips parted to reveal perfect white teeth. He fumbled with the pack and stared at her, fingers tightening around her belongings.

His companion—an older man with a graying black mustache and a hooked nose—reached for her. "Miss, it ain't safe standing up there like that—"

Daeya stopped him with an upraised hand. She was out of patience, and the boat was nearly upon her. "If you make me fall before I can cast, Councilor Gregory will have some choice words for you."

She didn't enjoy using his name to scare people, but it had its intended effect. The man froze. Satisfied, Daeya returned her attention to the boat and the river. With a steadying breath, she began the incantation for a slow-fall. In seconds, two glowing, white-violet orbs of power sprang to life in the center of her palms. The magic hummed and pulsed with promise, and Daeya held them before her with the proper amount of reverence. They were about to save her life, after all.

She took the last few moments to observe the boat, counting the number of heartbeats it took to close half the space between it and the wall. The boat had an open bow, but the middle portion was protected by a slant-roofed canopy. Its stern was also open, and several wooden planks stretched across its width for extra seating.

Daeya had just determined the bow to be her best landing spot when a shout rang out, and six or seven of the passengers surged from under the canopy to gawk at her.

She gritted her teeth. A command to move from this height likely wouldn't be heeded. She couldn't trust them to move if she jumped anyway, and the only other option was landing on the roof. She should be able to slow the fall enough to avoid crashing through the slanted canopy. It was the steep slide to the river on either side of the center ridge she was worried about.

But that was future-Daeya's problem. There were roughly forty-two heartbeats between the boat and the gate. She paced along the parapet, aligning herself with the canopy, aiming for that center ridge. She took twenty-one of those heartbeats to breathe deeply.

Then she jumped.

Screams of passengers below and shouts of dismay from the soldiers above were lost to the wind whistling past Daeya's ears. Too fast, too fast, and still gaining speed. This was a *terrible* idea, but by the gods, she was committed now.

She choked down her panic and released a burst of power from the orbs, angling it downward. An invisible pulse of energy struck the water in front of the gate and rebounded, the river's surface tension working to her advantage. The returning shockwave pushed back against Daeya's body, slowing her descent. She did it again, striking the water right in front of the bow, and again on the bow itself in a space between two passengers. After each burst, her body lurched upward, as if she were a bird caught in an updraft.

With the orbs of light held before her, Daeya curled into a crouch to prepare for landing. The fall was even more terrifying than she had expected, and she spat obscenities as the canopy grew larger below her. She released the rest of the energy in the orbs with five rapid bursts, each one more powerful than the last.

There might or might not have been more curses to accompany each one as she strafed the canopy, shattering shingles in the boat's passage. The last burst stopped her fall completely, and the light in her hands winked out.

Only, she was still three spans above the boat.

Daeya landed hard, smashing feet first into the wood, her hands and knees quickly following. Her limbs shook and smarted. She straddled the canopy's ridge, reeling from the descent as the boat swayed in the water.

Everything hurt. Her ears rang. Her heart thundered in her chest, but it all assured her she was alive. A bubbling, manic laugh escaped her lips.

And I'm on the damned boat.

The shadow of the city wall engulfed her, the sudden change in light stymying what might otherwise be an epic deterioration of her mental state. Rocking back on her heels, she looked up to see the arch masonry and the slot for the gate pass by overhead. If she had been standing, she could have reached out and touched them. Back upriver, the Sorcerers' Towers rose in the distance, their fading amber and brown silhouettes a longed-for sight as the boat left Ryost behind.

"Hey!"

Sharp pounding on the underside of the canopy drew her attention. She crawled to the edge of the roof and leaned over, peering upside down at a Cintoshi man holding an oar aloft. He looked about to beat the canopy with the oar again when their eyes met.

The boatmaster wore a blue cloth cap that flattened an unruly nest of chestnut hair, which bled seamlessly into a magnificent, well-groomed beard and mustache. His leathers were of a fine make, and he carried a shortsword—a longsword, truly, when wielded by a pint-sized Cintoshi—cinched at his waist.

"What's the meaning of this?"

"I have a ticket." Daeya sat up and fished through her pockets. A beat later, she cringed; she'd stowed the ticket in her pack. Leaning back over apex of the canopy, hair hanging around her head like a curtain, she smiled ruefully at the man. "I gave it to the guard on the wall. It will be just a moment."

He sputtered.

In the odd light of the tunnel, a black-cloaked figure rose from a seat behind the Cintoshi. "She's with us," Joss Vika said, his voice dripping disdain.

"She broke off part of my roof!" the boatmaster accused, turning toward him.

"And she'll pay for repairs." Cameron Vika's calmer, smoother lilt caressed Daeya's ears.

"Daeya!" Joss shoved past the Cintoshi. "Get. Down. Here."

Daeya let out an exasperated groan. "A moment, I said!"

The boat cleared the tunnel, and sure enough, both the soldier with her pack and his companion stared down at her from the wall. She rose to her feet, legs still a little shaky on the slanted canopy, and gestured for the guard to toss the pack down to her. He looked at his companion, and the gray-haired man shrugged. The soldier thrust the pack as far away from the wall as he could.

Daeya spoke the three-word incantation that would snag the bag in a telekinetic hold. She had to cast it twice in quick succession because she missed the bag on the first try. Still, she managed to guide it into her waiting hands before it hit the water.

"Thank you!" she called up to the soldier, offering an enthusiastic wave. He returned the wave less confidently. His companion's laughter carried across the water.

Smiling, Daeya unfastened the copper clasps of a smaller compartment in her pouch. She withdrew a crumpled ticket and slipped the bag's strap over her shoulder. Tucking the ticket between her teeth, she swung down over the roof and landed before the elder Vika brother.

Even though Joss was shorter than Normos by a few fingerspans, his hooded brow, dark eyes, and unpredictable temperament made him much more terrifying. The way he glowered at her sent a chill down her spine.

Daeya took an involuntary step back. There were certain unsavory rumors about him among the civilians, but she didn't know whether they were true. As he seized the lapels of her robe and drew her close, lifting her onto her toes, she might have believed some of them.

"That stunt is going to cost you, McVen." His stony face was so close to hers that his breath caressed her face. It smelled vaguely of mint. He sniffed at her, face souring further. "You smell like you've been rutting with the pigs. Why are you so filthy?"

Still with the ticket held between her teeth, Daeya attempted to speak. "Let go of me, Joss."

He smirked. "Make me."

"Fine." She grabbed his wrists and planted her knee squarely between his legs.

He dropped her with a sharp cry and doubled over. Daeya slipped around him and approached the boatmaster. She presented the ticket, but he waved the wrinkled parchment away.

"Just"—he looked between her and Joss—"don't cause any more trouble, alright?"

Following his gaze back to Joss, who leaned, gasping, against the side of the boat, Daeya nodded. "Alright."

Cameron rose from her seat and beckoned to her. Daeya spotted the middle brother, Toby, sitting across from her, observing the entire exchange.

"Come sit next to me, Daeya," Cam instructed, holding her messy blonde curls out of her blue eyes with a forefinger and thumb.

Her smile was enough to ease the tension in Daeya's shoulders. Cameron was not only the youngest and best-looking of the three, but she also had the kindest heart. How she'd ever been born into that family was a strange and unfortunate phenomenon, indeed.

Daeya started forward, but the weight of a hand on her shoulder stopped her.

Joss's fingers tightened. "You can be sure the Councilor will hear about this," he grated out, his voice still raspy with pain.

Daeya forced honey into her tone. "We both know the manner of *how* I got here won't matter to him. He'll only care that I made it at all."

"Joss," Cameron tried, starting toward them, her black robe swirling.

"Shut up, Cam." Joss threw her a dangerous glare, stopping his sister in her tracks. A shudder rippled through Daeya.

Joss spun her around and snagged her jaw in his hand. "You're going to learn some manners on this trip, you little brat—"

A booming rumble sounded from somewhere off to the north, giving Joss pause. His black eyebrows pinched as the reverberation rolled over them. He released her face and turned back toward the city wall, still keeping one hand on her shoulder.

"What was that?" a passenger at the front of the boat asked.

"It came from inside the city," another murmured.

The passengers continued pondering the sound in hushed tones. Daeya wasn't sure why she was holding her breath.

A few moments later, tremendous waves rolled down the river toward them, buffeting the boat from stern to bow, making even the sea-legged Cintoshi sway on his feet. On either side of the shore, trees and bushes trembled, as if frightened by some unseen force of nature.

Daeya tugged herself free of Joss's grip as he staggered. She caught the nearest post and steadied herself against the waves. "An earthquake?"

"Don't be ridiculous," Toby chastised her. She turned to find the hound-faced, ghostly pale brother standing now, staring off in the city's direction. "Only Duerguard and Aivenos are prone to earthquakes."

"An attack," Joss said. "Gregory thought there would be aethermancers coming."

Daeya spun back around, eyes wide. "Real aethermancers? In the capital?"

As if to support his claim, hazy gray clouds plumed over the city wall, twisting into the sky. It was too thin and light to be smoke. Maybe dust? But what would cause that much debris?

Joss turned toward Toby, ignoring her question. "What can you see?"

Toby's arcane skills lay in certain divination arts. He was one of few sorcerers who had mastered Aethersight—a skill that allowed him to cast his awareness into the Aether and see into places as one would with a crystal ball. The casting would take several minutes, however, and it would be even longer before they could glean any answers.

He began the long chant for the spell as Daeya stepped toward the stern. Her hands rested on the railing, its smooth wood grounding her as her thoughts turned dark. The cloud of debris doubled in size in a matter of seconds, and anxiety gripped her chest anew. That sinking feeling she'd had in Master Ulrich's classroom returned.

Whatever had happened, she prayed Faustus wasn't involved.

Chapter Fourteen

Alar

It was one of the grisliest scenes Alar had ever witnessed.

It might even rival the carnage he'd caused in Trivvix. The amount of gore painting the room and its two occupants was almost enough to make him believe in demons and devils. Somehow, it didn't surprise him that such evil would wear black robes.

A table laden with bloody knives, pliers, hammers, and saws sat against the back wall. Smaller tools and a steel tray of mangled body parts filled a wheeled cart. There was a bucket of some unidentifiable liquid in one corner and extra ropes and chains in another. Ruddy stains covered the stone walls and floor. The stench in the tiny torture chamber made his eyes water. The freshness of it was somehow worse than the week-old dead in the other room.

Perhaps it was because these were people he knew. People he considered allies.

"Cheralach?" Sam shook the corpse in the black puddle beside the door. "Cheralach!"

Alar wanted to spare her the sight—her beloved mentor face down in his own fluids, his fingers and toes removed, deep lacerations striping his naked body—but her stubbornness had brought her to this moment. As Sam fell to her knees in the blood, sobbing and shaking the body harder, Alar swallowed his bile and looked away. Powerful emotions would do more harm than good right now. Someone had to remain rational enough to make the tough decisions.

Ravlok moved to the still, naked form suspended by the wrists from a blood-stained wooden frame, and checked Magnus for vital signs.

Alar hovered in the doorway. He didn't need to feel Magnus's pulse to know Cheralach's first officer still lived. His aura lingered about his body like the last glowing tip of a candle wick before it turned to smoke. It pained him to look upon that aura, so he focused on Ravlok instead.

Alar had met the monk in the monastery after one of Daeya's training sessions. He'd also seen him with her several times in the Guild library. A spark of familiarity had kindled in the older man's eyes when they met in the corridor, but Alar didn't think Ravlok realized who he was yet.

Strange a servant of Ordeolas would find himself in a secret Guild prison. Alar couldn't imagine what circumstances must have led to his imprisonment.

"He's alive," Ravlok announced. His hands were already slick with Magnus's blood. "Barely."

While Kendi slipped inside the room to console Sam, Val stepped up beside Alar, surveying the scene with bared teeth. They didn't need a telepathic link for the thought that passed between them. There was truly no end to the Guild's brutality.

"We need to be careful about moving him," Val cautioned.

As if in answer, a weak moan issued from Magnus's lips. His head hung limply, his black, sweat-soaked hair obscuring his face. His arms tensed, as if he were trying to right himself against the chains, but the movement only caused him to sway and vocalize another pained moan. Several droplets of blood fell from behind his short curtain of hair. They joined the gruesome collection of gore on his legs and torso.

"Orowen," Sam hiccupped.

Kendi hiked up his trousers before squatting beside her in the puddle. Sam looked between Cheralach and Magnus as Kendi checked pointlessly for a pulse in the old man's neck.

"We need Orowen." Sniffling, rising to unsteady feet with Kendi's guiding hand, Sam started for the door. "Orowen!"

"Sam!" Kendi spun, his long braid whipping around his shoulder. He drew her back with an arm at her waist, clamping a hand over her mouth. "For the gods' sake, be quiet. You'll bring the whole garrison down on us."

Alar couldn't fault her for her outburst, but Kendi was right. Nothing would alert the enemy better to their position than the sound of mournful screaming. Her outpouring of grief seeped into his aura-sense like the puddle of blood leaching up her pant legs. It made his skin crawl.

He stepped forward to assist Ravlok. "Try your keys."

While Ravlok got to work, Alar examined Magnus's dislocated shoulder. Once they got him down, he would try to reset it. There wasn't much he could do about the deeper lacerations on his chest. Those would require the high priestess's magic if they were ever going to close properly again. Still, he could set bones and patch simple injuries with passable skill.

The keys shook in Ravlok's hands, and his skin went ashen. "None of these are working."

Alar hoped the monk wasn't going to be sick again. "Val." He beckoned his friend forward, gesturing toward the manacles. "See what you can do with them."

Ravlok stepped back to give Val room to pick the locks.

Behind them, Kendi was murmuring into Sam's ear. "You have to keep it together. Cheralach's work is done, but ours is not. I know you won't let his sacrifice be in vain."

"They cut off his *fingers*, Kendi." Tears strangled her voice. "What sort of Chaos-sworn monsters would do that?"

"I hear you. They will pay for this, but we have to get ourselves out first."

Val's lock pick tripped the tumblers on the left manacle. Magnus's head snapped back as that side dropped, wrenching his right wrist and shoulder. His scream was a broken, wretched sound, barely more than a strangled wail.

Alar stared into the remnants of Magnus's left eye. The organ had burst, and the bubbling flesh around the socket was impossibly swollen. Part of his black eyebrow and the flesh spanning the bridge of his nose were burned away, exposing furious red tissue in the shape of a triangle. The skin around the burn bore a curled ridge, as if it was trying to shy from its own injury. Blood and pus wept macabre trails down the left side of his face.

Val covered his mouth with his forearm, his lock pick pinched between his index finger and thumb. Ravlok turned away, dry-heaving into a nearby bucket. Alar continued to stare, marveling at how polite the monk had been to aim for the bucket instead of the floor. A painful void yawned open in his gut. Anger, shock, and disgust abandoned him to an icy numbness that made his entire body shiver.

He fought against the feeling and its ensuing revulsion by giving himself a task. He reached out with his mind to lift Magnus and relieve the pressure on the man's bound limb. Keeping him elevated with telekinesis required pressing him to the cross for stability. If the aethermancer moved at all, he would be much harder to hold.

"Val," Alar said again, his gaze trained on Magnus's blood-slicked clavicle.

Val must have heard the urgency in his voice. Or he might have shared Alar's concern that each minute spent here meant more enemies to pin them down on the way out. Either way, he sprang the latch on the second manacle, and Alar lowered Magnus to the floor.

Nausea settled over him as he released the man, and a viscous haze blanketed his vision. Alar's attention lapsed. Through the red-black curtain, Magnus reached up to touch his missing eye. He was lying on his back now, but Alar couldn't remember seeing him move.

Orowen was there too, pulling a bead of saphyrum from a black bag. She gripped Magnus's wrist and scolded him in Syljian. Alar hadn't heard her enter; he couldn't hear much of anything beyond the linen in his ears. He was doubly surprised to see Rylan, who must have guided the priestess down to her knees beside Magnus. Alar blinked again, dazed, as if waking from a nightmare. Orowen prodded Magnus's shoulder joint.

"Are you alright, Alar?" Rylan's filthy shirt blocked Alar's view. The archer gripped his upper arm. It was like he spoke through several layers of cloth.

No, he almost answered. Cloudy tendrils of his mind's brief, defensive severance from the carnage tugged at his consciousness. Exhaustion crept over him, weighing him down. He fought against it like a diver clawing for the water's surface. They couldn't afford for him to lose focus. Not now.

"I'm fine." A distinct *pop* and a strangled cry punctuated his statement as Orowen reset Magnus's shoulder. "How is Jessie?"

Rylan continued to stare into his face, and for that, Alar was grateful. It gave him something to focus on that wasn't covered in blood. A soft halo of light framed Rylan's tough figure. Orowen's magic.

"She'll limp for a while, but it's mild. She'll be able to fight." Rylan frowned. "Do you need saphyrum? You don't look well."

What he needed was rest. Unlike an arcanist, Alar could pull vast stores of saphyric energy into his body to use over the course of a day. He'd already exhausted his reserves, and it took hours of rest and meditation for a psionist to recover. Pulling directly from saphyrum beads would work in a pinch, but it was even more taxing. Eventually he would succumb to Mage's Folly, just as an arcanist would after casting too many spells.

"I'll be alright."

"We need to burn the bodies." Kendi's voice was close behind them. Alar turned to find the commander standing with one arm wrapped around Sam's shoulders. "Rylan, can you help us with Cheralach?"

Rylan looked from Alar to Kendi and back, keeping his hand on Alar's shoulder as if he feared he might collapse.

"I'm fine," Alar assured him. He gestured toward Cheralach's body. "Take care of our dead."

With a final, scrutinizing glance at him, Rylan stepped away.

"Quickly, now." Kendi guided both soldiers back to Cheralach, and they set to work carrying the aethermancer's body out of the chamber. Alar guessed Kendi would place him among the other Syljians. The commander confirmed his prediction when he returned a moment later. "Ravlok, we need your keys."

The monk had recovered from his latest bout of sickness. He stood aside from the others, watching Orowen trace divine sigils in the air over Magnus. When Kendi called for him, he tore his eyes from the white-violet light. Without a word, he trailed Kendi out of the room, keys jingling.

Val crouched on Magnus's other side. He looked up as Alar's attention settled on him. His face was white-washed by the priestess's power, his curly hair a stark, onyx shadow about his head. Tension simmered in his violet eyes. "They're coming."

Alar nodded. The encroaching danger snapped him out of his stupor. "How many?"

"Dozens."

A copper taste invaded Alar's mouth. "Inform Kendi."

As Val rose and darted away, Alar studied Orowen. Their escape hinged on her magic restoring Magnus enough to get him back on his feet. With Cheralach dead and Orowen suffering saphyrum sickness, Magnus would be the strongest arcanist among them. If he couldn't fight—or worse, if he had to be carried—their chances for a clean escape were slim.

Orowen passed her sigils over Magnus's chest. Red scar tissue followed in their wake, knitting the deepest wounds back together. Shallow impressions remained, but they were no longer in danger of fleshrot. His eye still looked gruesome. It would likely take Orowen several days of healing to seal that wound, but even with the best care, he would never see out of it again.

Magnus coughed, stirring once more. As he came to, Orowen's sigils dissolved into tiny pinpricks of light and evaporated like mist in the sun. The priestess slumped to the stone. Alar knelt and steadied her with hands on her shoulders.

"Cheralach," Magnus croaked. "*Amaa*, where..."

"*Saonis miraar*," Orowen whispered, panting. "I don't think he knows." She reached out to take the aethermancer's hand. "Steady, *neime*. You are among friends."

Alar grimaced.

Magnus struggled to open his remaining eye, his eyelashes stuck shut by crusty, reddish-yellow flakes. The white was steeped in blood, his normally blue iris a muted gray. "Orowen? I-I can't see."

Orowen stiffened beneath Alar's palms. She brushed away the damp hair from Magnus's forehead. "Can you see light, Magnus?"

"A little."

"That's good. Here, let me try this." Orowen spun another sigil and held it a few fingerspans above the aethermancer's face. Magnus squeezed his right eye shut and flinched away from the brilliant white light. She chanted, invoking her goddess to heal his vision. The runes along her temples flashed, and then all the light from her casting winked out at once.

Blinded for a moment, Alar felt Orowen sag forward, her body shaking with the strain. Still blinking away halos, he wrapped an arm around her waist and pulled the tiny priestess back against his chest.

"No more, Devoted," he urged her.

The red-orange haze of the room came into focus once more. Sweat coated Orowen's face. Her eyes were closed, and her head rested on his shoulder. A shadow fell over her face.

"Alar." Magnus sat up slowly, stiffly. "Cheralach was here." His one eye settled on him. "Is he alright? Did you find him?"

Whatever Orowen had done with her magic seemed to have restored his sight, but the image of once-fine features caked in blood and twisted by red and purple scarring made Alar cringe. The left socket was a puckered mass of paper-thin pink tissue. His right eye was still bloodshot, but the murky gray quality was gone.

Alar didn't want to be the bearer of this news. He wanted it even less than he wanted it in the corridor among the others. Cheralach had been like a father to Magnus; the old aethermancer's death would hit him hardest of all. But Magnus must have witnessed his mentor's torture, and he hadn't broken yet. Perhaps he was stronger than Alar thought.

"Magnus," he began.

The door stood open behind him, and an orange glow crept over Alar's shoulders, alighting on Magnus's face. Shadows bathed Orowen between them, and a wave of heat broke against Alar's back.

Scents of burning straw and skin accompanied the heat. When the smell reached Magnus, no more words needed to be said. He gazed past Alar into the flames, rendered speechless. Then, like a mountainside collapsing, the aethermancer's expression caved, his shock giving way to pain.

"No."

Another shadow fell over them. A figure stood in the doorway, blocking the light. When Kendi spoke, his voice was swift and unyielding. "Sorcerers have flooded the tunnels. We need you. Now."

"Wastelands." Alar shifted Orowen in his lap. Her eyes fluttered open. "Orowen, can you—"

A guttural, savage roar cut him off as Magnus shot to his feet. He surged toward the door, stumbling, catching himself on the frame. Kendi's shadow moved, and Alar turned, stunned. Magnus's figure stood against a wall of smoke and fire.

"Saphyrum," he snarled.

Kendi pressed several beads into his palm. Magnus channeled their energy the moment the metal touched his skin. He held out his free hand. Jagged shards of light slashed tiny fissures through the air above and below his fingers. Out of the Aether, a sword made of etched, gleaming steel pressed upon those burgeoning fissures. Wider and wider, the rifts grew as the web of reality tore like tattered cloth. Three heartbeats later, the sword burst through with a shattering wave of light.

The blinding halo faded, and the space where the rifts had been settled like a pool of water returning to glass. Magnus gripped the hilt of his sword and spun toward the fire and the enemy, a shade of vengeance personified.

He screamed, and the walls trembled.

Shivers raced down Alar's spine. In five years with the Alliaansi, he couldn't remember ever seeing Magnus angry. He was both a pacifist and an optimist, like his mentor before him; he rarely showed anything more than annoyance for even the most incompetent people. Now, faced with such thunderous rage, Alar felt a shred of respect for him.

Magnus charged through the gathering smoke and disappeared.

Kendi entered the smaller chamber and knelt beside Orowen. Taking her hand, he pulled her up to a sitting position, where she wavered briefly before shaking herself awake.

"I've got her." The commander's lavender eyes settled on Alar's face. "I need you near the front. Val says there's a staircase in the guard room you can use if you can clear a path."

Alar rose, limbs heavy, as if his bones were made of cast iron. The two elders gazed at him with an air of finality that made his chest constrict.

Before he could voice his protests, the bright curtain of light to his left parted once more. An unfamiliar silhouette stepped into the room. Smoke stung Alar's eyes, and he squinted into the flames. The harmonic pulse of the monk's aura filtered into his awareness.

Ravlok slipped his soot-blackened hands under Orowen's arms and pulled her to her feet. "We're all getting out of this. No one's staying behind."

One look at the determined set of Ravlok's jaw, and Alar understood why Kendi had taken to him so quickly. He was just like all his other incorrigible young soldiers.

The commander opened his mouth, but the priestess stopped him. "Ravlok is right. I think this was part of his vision."

Alar frowned at Ravlok. "You have visions?"

The monk looked equally confused. "Not that I'm aware of."

Orowen shook her head. "No. Cheralach's vision. The reason we came."

Kendi's expression was unreadable, but unease flickered in his aura. "We'll explain later. It's time to go."

Chapter Fifteen

Magnus

Kill them.

The voice in Magnus's head grew more and more insistent. Its rasping whispers urged him forward. He stormed down the corridor, past the cell that had held him, past his companions huddled against the walls. He rounded the corner and met the first group of sorcerers entering the dungeon.

There were five of them, all clad in black and clearly startled by his appearance. Their features were otherwise meaningless to Magnus.

Blinking his one eye clear, he lifted his hand, palm itching, and pure, saphyric energy surged through him. He focused it between his fingers and *pushed.* A burst of raw power leaped from his hand. It rippled through the air, bending light and color with its passage, and smashed into the wide-eyed mages, blowing them backward. Three fell in a heap. The other two kept their feet. They uttered their incantations, only to fall mid-chant with crossbow bolts sprouting from their eyes. Magnus strode forward, sword flashing. The three scrambling to flee his vengeance died on his blade.

His name echoed off the stones, but he paid it no mind. Nothing would distract him from his task. He wrenched open the dungeon door and strode into the guard room.

Kill them all.

Two more mages occupied this room. Soldiers in green and gold flooded through the door behind them, swords glinting and chain mail rattling as they charged. Fire bolts slammed against Magnus's naked flesh. He brushed them off without feeling the burn.

His sword, Malediction, shone like a beacon in his hand. He hacked through the first sorcerer, separating his head from his body. Warm blood sprayed across Magnus's face. The corpse's knees buckled and it fell sideways, exposing his next victim. She fell in the same manner. Magnus stepped over her body, his bare feet sure and steady on the stone.

Normally, using the sword repulsed him. Like Cheralach, Magnus believed the blade was a symbol of a leader's failure—a cold and bloody manifestation of one's inability to seek peace. But with the smell of smoke from Cheralach's funeral pyre coating his skin—with the pulsing ache from his empty eye socket sending fresh stabs into his skull—Magnus did not feel the sting of remorse. Today was not a day to preserve life or tread a path to mercy and understanding.

No, today was a day for justice.

To keep one hand free for casting, Magnus swallowed all five of the beads Kendi had provided him. Unspent saphyrum could be toxic when ingested, but without clothes, he had no pockets. Cutting down the last soldier within reach of his sword, he pulled power from the beads, channeling burst after burst to drive his opponents back. They fell over each other in piles of armor and flailing limbs. Soldiers struck the wall, their helmless heads caved in from the force of the impact. Blood streaked the stone, and bodies sagged to the floor like sacks of grain.

More mages funneled into the room. Several water savants erected vapor shields—glowing, semi-transparent discs formed by transmuting the humid air into white-violet energy. Glimmering particles pulled together from the edges of a wide, circular sigil, as if tugged by a drawstring. The sorcerers pressed close, layering their shields to form a barrier capable of deflecting smaller arcane bursts and physical projectiles.

But those shields would not stop Malediction.

Avenge him, the voice whispered. *Make them bleed as he bled.*

Magnus bellowed a war cry and charged the wall of shields. Blinded by his fury, he didn't heed the distant shouts of his companions. He didn't acknowledge the fact that the mages hopelessly outnumbered him. His only thoughts were of his enemies dying in gouts of blood and screams of pain.

When the first arrow sprouted from his right shoulder, rendering his sword arm useless, Malediction tumbled from his grasp. Before the weapon struck the stone, it returned to the Aether, disappearing into smoky wisps of light.

Snarling, Magnus punched a rift through the Aetherial Wall. Misty black Aether cloaked his skin and erupted into fire around his fist. He thrust the roiling ball of flame toward the mages, scorching the vapor that fueled their shields. Four of the glowing discs evaporated.

The sorcerers hurried to cast again while other shieldbearers moved to close the gap. Magnus drew upon his saphyrum, letting its energy swell inside him like a long, indrawn breath. His fists curled as if to withhold its escape. Heat suffused his muscles, and a dull roar filled his ears. His chest tightened as he built upon that breath, coaxing more and more power from the beads. Within seconds he'd forged it into a violent tempest, a storm to match his rage. When the pressure finally burgeoned in the confines of his body, threatening to burst, Magnus snapped his hand outward, and the storm exploded.

A rippling wave of destruction crashed into the line of mages. Those with shields hunkered down and planted their feet against the buffeting force. Boots scraped and armor crashed, punctuated by screams as those without shields careened backward like swimmers caught in the tide. Some smashed against the wall while others tumbled out the open door into the hallway.

Shouts rang out, and the sorcerers and archers flanking the door flooded the open space, leveling all their attention on Magnus. He reached up to wrench the arrow out of his shoulder, baring his teeth—

His body betrayed him. One moment he was standing on both feet, and the next he was on the ground, his eye blurring hazy red.

Kill them!

Magnus tried to struggle to his feet, but something struck him in the chest, sending him back to one knee. Searing pain and the smell of burning flesh reached him. He was struck again in the leg, and a broken scream ripped through his throat. A body crashed into him from the side.

Magnus felt himself tipping, tipping.

His head struck the ground. Pain. Intense, searing pain. And voices. Voices swimming in his ears. Voices he was certain he should know.

"Get him up!"

"He overcast. I can carry him—"

"Not through all those sorcerers, you can't."

"Magnus!"

Something struck his face. The sting was enough to rouse him with a grunt.

"Chaos-sworn idiot. Wake up!" Sam's voice. "What's wrong with you?"

Magnus tried to speak, but his throat—by the gods, his throat *burned*. Blinking his eye clear, he looked up into Sam's face. To his right was a short wall of wood.

"He's coming around," Sam said to someone.

"Thank Shavaan." Rylan's voice. As he invoked the goddess of healing, the blond-haired archer came into view above him. He was bleeding from a wound on his forehead, and spell burns scorched both clavicles. Floating a few fingerspans above his hand was a glowing red sphere of what looked like molten metal.

From somewhere to Magnus's left, behind a scorched, overturned table, Val called out, "Rift Benders!"

Sam and Rylan both swore, their faces twisting into scowls.

"Stay with him." Rylan rose from his crouch long enough to throw the sphere over the short wall before dropping back down again. "Pray Orowen has strength enough for one more spell."

Seconds after Rylan disappeared, Magnus tried to muster the strength to sit up. He was rewarded with an eruption of pain across his torso. Blistering agony stole the breath from his lungs, and he fell back to the floor with a tortured sob. He looked down to find the source.

He wished he hadn't. Now that his fervor had subsided, the knowledge of his injuries made the pain so much worse. Dozens of spell burns peppered his chest and abdomen. A trio of arrows jutted from his shoulder, a dagger was embedded in his leg, and smaller cuts leaked fresh blood over the dried crust. He reached up to grip the shaft of one arrow.

Sam batted his hand away. "Leave it. I can't have you bleeding out before Orowen sees to you."

Magnus opened his mouth to protest, but a bright flash of white-violet light forestalled any argument. Three black rifts, each large enough for a soldier to step through, slashed the air above him. The instantaneous drop in pressure made his ears pop. A fierce gust whipped his damp hair about his head. Gauntleted hands and helmed faces appeared from out of the rifts.

Sam rose above him, gritting her teeth and clutching a single dagger in her hand.

Then, all around him, there was chaos.

Ravlok stepped into the guard room with Orowen in his arms. A cursory sweep of the scene made his heart sink to his feet. Guild forces blocked the only exit and the stairs. At least a dozen sorcerers stood with hands raised, forming a wall of glowing white-violet shields on the opposite side of the room. More sorcerers and archers filled the space behind the wall, while sword-bearing soldiers waited for the order to enter the battle at closer range.

In the middle of the room, Ravlok's allies had turned three of four massive wooden tables onto their sides to provide cover against the hail of magical and mundane projectiles. The Alliaansi hunkered behind their makeshift barriers, lobbing their own attacks over the sorcerers' shield wall.

Alar steered them toward the closest table on their left. Rylan and Val were already there, providing cover fire for Magnus. The naked aethermancer, who only moments ago might have been knocking at Baosanni's door, seemed to be trying to return to his earlier near-death state with zealous abandon. An arrow struck his shoulder, and his sword fell from his grip. The weapon vanished in a burst of black mist.

Ahead of Ravlok, Alar barked a command. "Stay close to me."

Don't have to tell me twice. Ravlok adjusted his grip on Orowen. It wasn't like he was going to do much fighting like this, anyway.

He ducked a trail of embers from a passing fireball. The orange sphere smashed against the wall behind him, star-bursting with enough force to singe his tattered trousers. Another sphere made of sizzling, white-violet lightning struck the ground in front of him. It exploded outward like shattered glass, and brilliant arcs of static skittered across the floor.

"Watch it!" Kendi's warning came from behind, too late for Ravlok to react.

Tendrils of lightning jolted him, like a thousand tiny needles piercing his bare feet. He recoiled, nearly dropping the priestess. A pungent, metallic smell lingered in his nostrils. He was definitely *not* a fan of that particular use of the gods' magic.

Kendi wrapped an arm around him, simultaneously keeping him upright and steadying Orowen. Ravlok's feet came unstuck from the stone with a horrible tearing sensation.

"Easy," Kendi said. "I have you."

They pressed close to Alar, sheltering Orowen between them. Ravlok tried to focus on the path before him rather than the rawness of his feet.

Arrows flew. The gleaming broadheads turned at the last moment, slipping to either side of them. It took him several seconds to understand what was happening. Alar strode in front of their group, clearing the path with his powers of telekinesis like the bow of a ship parting the sea. The wave of arrows curled out around them and broke against the stone.

Just before they reached the shelter of the overturned table, Alar collapsed.

"You bleeding idiot." Val dropped his crossbow and seized Alar's robe in both fists. He dragged his companion behind the wooden wall as Ravlok and Kendi tumbled in behind them.

Ravlok pressed his back against the wood, murmuring apologies to Orowen for the rough treatment. She waved him off and crawled toward Alar. Blue-green beads of saphyrum glowed between her second and third fingers as she placed hands on his head and chest.

Kendi rose to observe the battle, ducking back down as a gust of heat rolled over them. It whistled through the cracks in the tabletop.

"Fire in the gap!" Kendi shouted.

A rallying cry answered him from the other tables. Val tore himself away from Alar and reclaimed his crossbow with a grimace.

There was little Ravlok could do at this distance, so he set about tending his feet. Blisters had already formed and broken open along his arches, and blood coated his soles and heels. Using one of his daggers, he cut strips of cloth from his ragged trousers to bandage the wounds and cinched the cloth with tight box knots. For now, it would have to be enough.

Fingering the small blade in his hand, he dared a glance over the top of the table. The sorcerers were scrambling to close a gap in their shield wall. Val was using the tiny crossbow affixed to his forearm to fire at the exposed archers. Rylan ducked a sphere of lightning and came up firing a shortbow bearing the Guild's open-handed crest. Ravlok wondered where the bow had come from until he noticed weapons and bits of armor littering the ground beyond the tables. Apparently, the soldiers manning this dungeon were no more orderly than the monks of Baosanni.

Across the aisle, from behind another overturned table, Jack fired a crossbow into the gap while Jessie hurled molten globes of Aether. Sam and Anwic hid behind the third table, darting out now and then to gather the enemies' spent arrows. Sam piled the unbroken ones beside her, and Anwic threw those with snapped shafts like darts back at the soldiers.

Magnus stood alone between them and the Guild forces, motionless and covered in burns. Fire bolts slammed into him, but he might as well have been seated by his own reflection pool for all the attention he paid to them.

"Jessie!" Kendi shouted. "Protect Magnus!"

The globe of Aether in Jessie's hand flickered from molten orange to vibrant purple. She hurled it at a sphere of lightning headed for Magnus's head. Both spells exploded in a shower of brilliant motes of light.

Even as the magical fragments skittered across the stone, Magnus didn't move.

"What is he doing?" Ravlok asked Kendi, who had also started collecting arrows.

The commander spared Magnus a glance as he dropped half a dozen arrows at Rylan's feet, then looked down at Orowen and Alar. The mastermind was still bleary-eyed on the floor.

Kendi retrieved his sword and leveled his eyes on Ravlok, his expression grim. "Buying us time." He turned sharply as a chorus of voices began to chant behind the enemy shield. "Rylan, I need counter-orbs there!"

Ravlok followed Kendi's gesture to a group of sorcerers behind the Guild's left flank. They each drew a spiraling sigil in the air, their hands wreathed by glowing mist.

Too bad I couldn't experiment with Bornen's appropriation theories before all this. Ravlok's desire for true arcane ability was unrepentant. As the others fought for their lives using magic, he just stood there clutching his mundane steel like a common soldier. He *needed* to do something. Even if he didn't have arcane skills, he needed to help somehow.

The other Guild weapons were too far away to reach without cover, but he could throw his daggers with unparalleled accuracy. Though they would only take out a pair of opponents between the two, it was better than nothing. He shifted his grip on the dagger and rose, readying to throw—

Rylan pushed his bow into Ravlok's chest. "Here."

Ravlok's free hand closed on the smooth grip. The bow was not a weapon he knew well, but he used to shoot at rats and ravens with a sling. He glanced over the edge of the table at the thick press of bodies. It couldn't be that hard to hit something.

Grateful not to have to throw his familiar weapon away just yet, he tucked the dagger into his trousers.

"Fire over the shieldbearers if you can," Rylan instructed, passing him a green-fletched arrow. He didn't wait for Ravlok's agreement before turning back to the sorcerers, an orb as black as the Aether itself coalescing in his palm.

Ravlok nocked the arrow and stared down the length of the wooden shaft, taking a moment to familiarize himself with the bow. Breathing deeply, he lifted his eyes above the table.

The draw was heavier than he'd expected. When he yanked back on the string, it rolled off his fingers before he reached full draw and snapped across his forearm. Ravlok yelped. His arrow skidded along the stone ceiling.

Lavender hands appeared from behind him. Kendi adjusted Ravlok's fingers on the bow and pulled his elbow outward. Ravlok looked aside and found the commander holding up another arrow.

"Draw from here," he said, tapping him between his shoulder blades, then squeezed his arm, "not here. And loosen your grip."

Then he darted away, crossing the aisle to reach their companions.

Ravlok took the curt instruction with only a little heat flooding his cheeks. Then he caught Val eyeing him with a perturbed expression, and the feeling became a hundred times worse.

Odes of Ordeolas. You don't have time to feel embarrassed. It was like Yonfé scolding him in the training yard all over again.

Ravlok turned away from Val and nocked the second arrow. There would be time for self-reflection later. He tested the pull on the string, drew back, and rose—just as Magnus's arm swept across the battlefield.

In the wake of some unseen force, the entire Guild army flew backward.

The shieldbearers leaned into the devastating wave as if bracing for a storm wall. Holes opened in their formation, and soldiers and sorcerers were lifted and tossed like limp dolls. Some crashed against the wall, while others slammed against their companions. A few soldiers even flew into the corridor.

A few more blasts like that, and we might actually get somewhere.

But amid the cacophony of voices screaming and metal clanging and bodies scrambling, the aethermancer snarled in pain. He sagged to one knee, clutching his chest. Metal flashed, and a dagger sank into Magnus's leg.

Ravlok took aim and loosed his arrow, snapping his forearm with the string again. This time, the arrow lodged in a mage's belly.

Two more fireballs and a sphere of lightning careened toward Magnus. Rylan darted forward and tackled the aethermancer. They sprawled behind Sam's table, which at some point had been shoved several spans closer to the stairs.

Anwic appeared beside Ravlok. "Quit gawking, *bashiin*. It's time to go."

Ravlok growled. He had *not* been gawking.

Anwic exchanged a few words with Val and hoisted Orowen into his arms. He darted across the aisle while Jack and Kendi pushed their table toward the stairs. Across the room, shouts careened back and forth from the Guild officers trying to untangle their troops.

Val hauled Alar to his feet, regarding Ravlok with unease. He nodded toward the bow in Ravlok's hand. "I'm out of bolts. Can you cover us?"

Alar's eyes settled on him as well. Ravlok cringed. Neither man's gaze was anything like the steady scrutiny Kendi had afforded him. Though the commander knew he'd puzzled out their escape and duped a sorcerer, these two had only watched him repeatedly vomit his guts out and snap his arm with a bowstring. He wouldn't debase himself further by trying to be a hero.

"I should take him instead," Ravlok said, nodding toward Alar. He held out the bow to Val. "You're a much better shot."

To his surprise, the admission seemed to settle them. They shared a decisive look; Val passed Alar into Ravlok's care, took the bow, and snatched a handful of arrows off the floor. Ravlok turned to guide Alar toward the others.

He stopped short as a flash of light erupted in front of them.

Bright as a forge and wreathed in crackling mist, the light forced Ravlok to shield his eyes with his free hand. The sudden breeze tugged at his hair and clothing. Alar muttered viciously in Syljian beside him.

A chasm split the light into two halves, yawning black and infinite at its center. A face, arms, and legs appeared.

"Rift Benders!" Val shouted. He shoved Ravlok and Alar aside to fire at the first soldier. The arrow shot out the side of his neck and disappeared into the void.

"Move!" Alar ordered, stepping forward on unsteady legs.

Ravlok shouldered Alar's weight and took control. "You know, all your thrashing is counterproductive," he said, grunting with the strain. For someone with Syljian parentage, the man was unusually tall—even taller than Ravlok.

They lurched toward the others, only to find more rifts opening behind those tables, too. Rylan and Jessie were palming black, light-devouring orbs that pulled at the edges of a pair of rifts. White-violet tendrils sloughed off from the rifts like wisps of sand from the top of a dune, shrinking them.

Still, soldiers poured through the rifts faster than they could close them. His companions were fully engaged in seconds. The ring of steel on steel filled the air.

A wave of white-blue spheres trailing frigid vapor slammed against Kendi's overturned table. The spheres exploded into branches of glittering frost. Showers of fire bolts cracked the wood apart.

Ravlok drew his dagger and ran for Orowen and Anwic, who landed beside Magnus in a heap. Alar stumbled along beside him.

Three soldiers charged them. One went down with an arrow in his eye. The other two pressed inward, swords slashing. Ravlok threw his dagger, sticking one soldier squarely in the neck. He ducked, dropping Alar beneath the sweep of the remaining swordsman. Palming the hilt of his second dagger, he buried it in the man's knee.

As the soldier fell, his sword leaped out of his hand. Alar snatched it out of the air, his eyes glowing violet. He thrust the hilt into Ravlok's hand. "I know how well you can fight, monk. Don't hold back on my account."

Unlike the bow, the sword felt right in his hand. Ravlok nodded. "Alright. Just try to keep up."

Despite Alar's condition, he didn't hamper Ravlok's movement much. He seemed to anticipate which way they were going to move. He knew when to dodge, when to duck, and even when to fall back while they engaged a more skilled opponent.

Ravlok made a point not to think about how the mastermind was doing that.

He stabbed through a soldier pressing down on Kendi. Ravlok's weapon clashed several times against another enemy's sword and shield before Val took the man out with an arrow. They lent their support to Rylan, who had disengaged from his opponent to help Sam. Ravlok cut down a soldier sitting astride Anwic while Val extended a hand to help the Syljian up.

They fell into a steady rhythm, clearing a path through the melee. When Alar finally tumbled to the floor between Orowen and Magnus, Ravlok was sweating and covered in blood.

But he felt *alive*. No amount of idle reflection or menial work could compare to this feeling—the feeling of *actually* taking a stand against the forces of oppression. *This* was what Mira had made him for. Praise the gods, they actually had a chance!

No sooner had the thought crossed his mind than a white-blue sphere struck the makeshift shelter in front of him. Tendrils of frost skittered across the table-top. The accompanying fire bolts cracked the wood apart, exposing them to the mages beyond.

Wind brushed his neck and Ravlok turned, catching a soldier's sword with his own. The force of metal on metal rattled his bones. His weapon slid along his opponent's, all the way to the hilt. He stepped into the man's space and smashed him in the nose with his fist. The soldier staggered back into Anwic's waiting blade. Ravlok flicked blood off his knuckles and turned—

Sam screamed.

The soldier she'd been fighting pulled his weapon away, covered in blood. Sam stumbled, clutching her thigh as her opponent drew back for the killing blow.

Ravlok charged, battering the man away. He danced him around a rift, dodging and parrying blows, until he found an opening and gutted him. Two more soldiers took his place. He dispatched one, and an arrow took out the other.

But despite their best efforts, they were losing.

The rain of fire and lightning tapered off as the sea of green and gold livery funneled from one side of the room to the other. Shieldbearers advanced, attempting to crush them against the larger force of non-adept soldiers.

A grunt and the rattle of chain mail sounded behind him. Ravlok narrowly dodged a sword that would have cleaved into his side. Another blade scored a hit along his calf. He gasped, striking out blindly from the pain. His weapon found chain mail. Something struck him on the side of the head. Another blow caught his elbow and knocked his sword from his hand. He hit the floor and rolled away from his opponents, pain radiating through his entire arm.

Over the din, Val shouted at their enemies in Syljian, his tone ringing with challenge. It ended abruptly with a choked gasp.

Ravlok's vision swam. He shoved himself to his feet. Nauseated, he stumbled. A pair of soldiers rushed him. In his periphery, Kendi dropped to his knees, spitting blood. A sorcerer kicked Jack in the face.

Ravlok caught one man's arm as his sword came down. He stepped into the soldier's guard and hurled the armored man over his shoulder. The smash of steel accompanied Ravlok's grunt of pain as the second soldier's pauldron slammed into his stomach and drove him to the stone.

Blood coated his tongue. He hooked sticky fingers into the man's helm, but he couldn't get enough purchase to tear it off. His angle was too steep to break the man's neck.

Jessie cried out, and Rylan roared.

Ravlok braced himself for the sword pommel falling like a hammer toward his face. The blow landed; his nose crunched. Pain exploded and blood gushed over his lips.

A soft voice drifted over the noise.
Then everything went white.

Chapter Sixteen

Orowen

Every time Orowen opened her eyes, all she saw was Chaos.

Bodies littered the guard room floor. Blackened starbursts and shattered stones marred every surface. Flames devoured broken wood, belching smoke and heat into the air. The silvery ripple of collapsing rifts distorted the surrounding haze, as if she viewed the place from underwater. The rifts' bright rims left shimmering halos in her vision.

Chaos's oily presence coated her skin, feeding off the Guild's corruption like a boil in need of lancing. The lesser god's influence was thickest here in this suffocating fog of violence and hatred.

It was just as Cheralach had described it. He had seen this. He had seen all of it, and he'd come to his death knowing how it would end.

"I will do what must be done. And when the time comes, you must do the same."

Orowen swayed under the weight of that responsibility.

But what am I supposed to do? And where was the girl? There was no sign of her or those red flames anywhere.

The mages closed the gap between them, leaving the stairs and the corridor loosely guarded. Magnus was mostly healed from his wounds, and he was on his feet again. They just needed to hold on a few moments more while the others fought for an opening to join them.

"Devoted, please." Alar's voice trembled with anxiety. "Sam needs you."

Sam—dear, sweet Sam—was bleeding heavily from a wound on her thigh. Orowen fought down her exhaustion, moving slowly, too slowly, as if she pawed through mud. Her ashen hands wove weak strands of light as she channeled Saolanni's divine blessing. Light fell upon the wound, and the strands coursed into broken flesh. Clutching a saphyrum bead between her fingers, she became a conduit once more for her goddess's power. Torn muscles healed, and severed blood vessels mended. The wound closed, leaving behind a thin red scar.

A scar that should not be.

Her magic was weakening. As her body withered with fatigue, so too did her connection to Saolanni. Orowen sagged under the immensity of her goddess's work, shivering as if from cold. The onset of fever. Mage's Folly would soon be upon her.

Magnus snarled, taking yet another fire bolt to the chest. The level of recklessness he'd displayed after finding poor Cheralach would have been excusable, if she had been in better shape to patch him up. But Mira's mercy, she wished he'd stop getting hit like that.

She was reaching out to him again, her hands weaving the familiar sigil, when Val's strangled gasp and Alar's accompanying cry reached her. Orowen's attention snapped toward the sound.

Sam scrambled to her hands and knees, reaching for Alar, who'd bolted out from behind their half-destroyed shelter. Beside the only upright table, some distance behind them, a soldier had Val pinned by the throat.

Dread gripped Orowen's heart. She saw, but her mind disbelieved.

The soldier had rammed his sword into Val's belly. A savage, teeth-baring grin twisted the man's face. He thrust the gleaming steel up through Val's chest. The spymaster's hands closed around the blade, eyes wide and mouth agape.

Alar's roar of agony reflected reality better than anything Orowen could put into words. Her own scream tore from her throat and echoed across the stone. She reached for the young spymaster with glowing hands.

But her magic could only reach so far.

A psychic blast ripped the Guild soldier's mind apart. He died with blood streaming from his eyes and nose. Alar spat on his corpse and fell to his knees as Sam tried to drag their friend away. Orowen readied her sigils, murmuring prayers to both Shavaan and Baosanni to spare Val's life.

And Saolanni, my goddess, strengthen me as well.

Her prayer to Saolanni was accompanied by another horrifying sight. Kendi struck the ground with a dagger in his side.

No! Please, no!

Throughout her life, Orowen had imparted wisdom to countless families, acolytes, and patients who shied from Baosanni's face. Death was a natural part of life, she would say to them. One not to be feared, but welcomed, when Baosanni called a soul to the Gate. No matter when or how he summoned them, the god of death would care for those whose souls departed, just as Saolanni cared for those in life. The two states of a soul's existence were not to be seen as good or evil. Life and Death were a balance, maintained by Order.

Bile rose in Orowen's throat. There was no Order in this butchery.

It was just as it had been in Trivvix. And Larittrine. And Sessia. Each one a battle in which her people had been made to suffer and die fighting for their families and friends.

"Help him, Devoted," Sam sobbed, hitting the ground in her attempts to drag Val's body by one arm. A bloody trail painted the stone behind her. "Please, you must."

The words stung. She *should* have been able to help him. How often she had prayed she could reverse one sword strike, make one arrow miss its mark, or drive one fire bolt off-target. But even the most powerful magic she possessed could not alter the past. Though she could beseech Baosanni to spare a soul, she could not defy him and restore one to life. Still, Orowen crawled toward Val. Charred Aether collected on her hands and knees, black as soot and reeking of hot metal.

A booted foot slammed into her ribs, driving the air from her lungs. Agony burst through her right side. She saw stars and curled into a ball, shielding her face and chest with her arms. The sorcerer lifted his leg again.

The blow never came. A sharp cry sounded above her. She peered through her hands at the sorcerer and found a sword driven through his chest, his shirt blossoming red. The corpse jerked, spasming and spraying her with blood.

Magnus withdrew his blade and kicked the mage aside. "Go. I'll cover you." He spun to engage a soldier, his sword glittering wet and malevolent in the torchlight.

Orowen pushed herself back to her hands and knees and crawled the rest of the way through the haze to Val's body. His wide, unblinking eyes stared into eternity. His chest didn't rise. He lay there, limp and lifeless. Tears stung Orowen's eyes.

Kneeling at his side, she worked with trembling fingers to find a pulse in his neck. She examined the wound, which, based on the fetid smell, had ruptured his stomach as well as his lungs. Even if she had the time and proper tools to clean the wounds, heal his body, and administer chest compressions, it wouldn't be enough.

Sam watched her through red, puffy eyes. Orowen looked up at the young woman and shook her head. "I'm sorry, *neime*. I'm so sorry."

"He can't be," Sam said, her face twisting with anguish. "He can't—"

"Orowen!" Anwic's voice. He tumbled into view with Kendi's arm wrapped around his shoulders. As they dropped to the floor beside Orowen, Sam turned away, tears spilling down her face. She went back to the battle with a new ferocity, stabbing a blade into the nearest soldier's neck.

Kendi clutched the dagger stuck in his side and grimaced when his eyes found hers. "Apologies, Devoted. I know your hands are full."

For all the sorrow threatening to drown her, Orowen's tears finally overflowed at the sound of his voice. Leave it to Kendi to apologize for getting stabbed. She wiped at her face, forced her pain down, and returned to business. There would be time to mourn their dead later. "Come, let me see it."

Her attention narrowed to the wound while the battle raged around them. Distantly, she was aware of Anwic, Magnus, and Sam guarding them as she worked. She placed one hand beside the wound, letting Saolanni's magic course into the punctured tissues. With her other hand, she carefully removed the dagger. The puncture closed behind the bloody steel until it was a deep red scar on the surface of his skin.

The scar sent sweltering anger through her. A wound like that should not have sealed so badly. Her control was getting sloppy.

Saolanni's magic took its toll. A mortal body could only endure so much before it broke down. Orowen was close. The trembling in her hands worsened with each spell; it spread up her arms and into her core with a persistent shiver that no amount of warmth would quell. Fever sapped her strength, even as sweat ran in rivulets across her runes and down her neck. Muscle aches would come next, with dizziness and vomiting soon afterward. Her spells would grow less and less effective, until she could no longer cast at all.

One of the heavy wooden tables went flying, hurled into a group of approaching sorcerers. Orowen's irritation bubbled to the surface. Alar was in no condition to be doing that. He couldn't keep casting from beads like an arcanist. He knew better.

Her eyes fluttered closed. A low, dull roar filled her ears, and her fatigue threatened to pull her under. She was spinning, falling, like a maple seed with its one brittle wing twirling on the wind.

A sudden, firm grip on her shoulders jolted her. "Stay awake, *neime*." Kendi's voice sliced through the roar buffeting her senses.

Orowen blinked her vision clear. Jessie and Jack stood before them. A spell burn in the shape of a hand scorched Jessie's shoulder. Jack's left eye was swollen shut, and blood spotted his stolen uniform. Both young humans wasted no time returning their attention to the enemies around them. Orowen reached toward Jack—the closer of the two—and called on her goddess's power. The glow of healing magic warmed her fingertips.

"They're boxing us in," Magnus said.

"If we're summoned to the Gate, we're taking as many of them with us as we can." Kendi's declaration was loud and fierce in Orowen's ears. She vaguely acknowledged his palm on her shoulder as the only thing keeping her upright. He was gripping her wrist. "Save your strength, Devoted."

Jack stepped away from her, grunting his agreement through the crossbow bolt in his teeth. Jessie was too far away for Orowen to reach. The dark-haired arcanist stood shoulder to shoulder with Anwic, fighting a trio of soldiers. Orowen's hand fell to her lap.

Her crawl toward Val had placed her roughly in the center of the guard room. Most of her friends stood with their backs to her now—a loose circle of defense against the sorcerers and soldiers. There were still so many of them. Without cover, they didn't stand a chance.

Where was Alar? Rylan? Ravlok?

Another table flew through the air, answering her first question easily enough. She looked through Anwic's legs to find Alar surrounded by a pile of green-liveried bodies, each with eyes and noses running red. The psionist was shaking, gasping for air, and down on one knee. Through his tangled brown hair, he stared down a group of five sorcerers who circled him like wary crows. One mage summoned a sphere of lightning and hurled it like a stone. The sphere struck Alar in the back, and he collapsed.

No!

Jessie screamed beside her. Orowen ripped her attention away from Alar as a soldier's sword came away from Jessie's leg. She went down, and Rylan charged into view with an axe. The archer roared, swinging his weapon into the soldier's shoulder, shattering chain mail. Anwic finished the man off by snapping his neck.

Orowen started to shove herself forward to help Jessie, only to feel Kendi holding her back. She rounded on him, bewildered. "What are you—"

She stopped.

Varkendios Emaaris had fought by Orowen's side for over a century. They had both been young adults when the Crystal Towers of Astenpor fell and their families were butchered in the flight through the Syljian floodplains. They'd witnessed the horrors of the Blood Crusades led by Father Durn and his inaugural troop of Light Paladins. They'd built villages and towns together, only to see them gutted by fire, their crops burned, their people slaughtered. Over and over, they had faced suffering, starvation, saphyrum sickness—and never once had Kendi borne the look of defeat, of utter hopelessness, that was on his face now.

"You're giving up." She stared at him, at the solemn guilt that overcame him.

He reached a hand up to touch her cheek. "It's been an honor, Devoted."

Orowen shook her head. Anger hot as a smith's forge settled in her chest. "No. No, I don't accept this."

"I should have told you this years ago," Kendi pressed on, his eyes conveying a sorrow that words never could. "I love you, Orowen Evallier."

There was a suspended moment in which her warring fury and pain kept her from processing his words. They fumbled around in her mind like coins in a jar, a disjointed medley of sound. As she drew a series of shallow breaths, they started to make sense.

Orowen knew. She had always known. And of course his admission would come here, on a battlefield, as he prepared to die.

"Ravlok!"

Sam's cry wrenched them both back to the present. Orowen followed Kendi's eyes to the girl as Sam tried to dart through the press of soldiers. Two men caught her by the arms and threw her back into Rylan, sending them sprawling. Through the press of bodies, Orowen caught only a glimpse of the monk lying under an armored soldier, getting his face smashed with the pommel of a sword.

"When the time comes, you must do the same."

It was time.

"We're not going to the Gate." Orowen started to rise to her feet. Her legs and arms protested. Her body screamed with pain. Exhaling sharply, she sank back to her knees. She gripped Kendi's arm. "Help me up."

His expression was pained. "Devoted—"

"I said help me up!" There was no time to argue. Not in the precious few minutes they had left. Not while she could still give them a chance. "I'm going to end this."

Orowen had been many things in her life. Sister, daughter, healer, teacher, priestess. There was only one role she had given up in service to the Temple of Life. Only one name she'd sworn—as part of her oath to do no harm—that she would never use again.

Aetherian.

It was to that title—that set of skills—that she turned now. For Cheralach, for Val, and for all the warriors who'd died during their capture, so they had not died in vain. For Kendi, whose love she returned. For Rylan, Jessie, Anwic, and Sam, who deserved to see their families in Starlight again. For Alar and Jack, who'd risked their lives and defied all the odds to reach them. And for Ravlok, whose presence was a blessing from the gods.

Kendi hauled her to her feet and held her steady. Orowen reached into the bag of saphyrum and pulled out a fistful of beads. It was a dangerous move, especially in her condition. One she likely would not survive. But, for this last desperate attempt, she would do what must be done.

She chanted to a new cadence. A terrible cadence. One not spoken since before she had taken the Oath of Saonis.

Soldiers circled them, the lethal tips of their blades held forward like the teeth of some savage beast, pressing her companions close. Sorcerers filled the gaps, their expressions hungry, menacing. They spun their sigils, readying for the kill.

Orowen summoned the gods' magic from the beads, but this time, there were no glowing sigils or ribbons of light. This time it was a single, concussive explosion of power. Her beads shattered, filling her hands with white-violet light. The sound was a deafening crash of static, like a thunderclap in the palms of her hands. A churning flame of white plasma formed between her fingers. Her hair stood on end. Gooseflesh swept across her arms. The electric hum of magic was a penetrating force from the base of her neck to the seat of her spine.

Muffled screaming and the call for counter-orbs barely reached her.

If she had been more practiced, or perhaps if she hadn't been on the verge of collapse, she could have directed the magic into something more stable, more controllable. She didn't have that luxury right now. Instead, she shaped the light into dozens of spear-like shafts. Arcs of plasma snapped and buzzed as they whipped the air around her. They were so bright that she averted her eyes even as she readied to wield them.

The power of an Aether rift for short- and long-distance travel was well known to most arcanists. But to an Aetherian, who possessed the power to shape Aether in ways both sorcerers and aethermancers could not, a rift could also be a devastating force of destruction. It could sink ships, cause avalanches, swallow fields, and even collapse fortress walls.

Orowen spun the shafts of light into a loose ring around her quaking hands. Each shaft was less than half a span long and no thicker than an arrow, but each one could tear a rift in reality large enough to pull a man through it. She pushed the shafts high overhead, feeling resistance as the magic crackled against her fingers. Her body trembled under the immensity of that power.

Counter-orbs black as ink carved thin trails into the white halo surrounding her. Most dissolved like chips of ice thrown into a hot bath when they breached her stronger magic. Others met with her companions' counter-orbs and broke into glimmers of light.

She wavered on her feet, but steadied under Kendi's hands again. Forcing herself to focus against her rapidly waning strength, she squinted up at the shards. Unbidden tears filled Orowen's eyes.

Goddess, forgive me.

She released her hold on the magic, and the shafts burst apart.

They slammed into the ground like streaking comets. Red, molten rock splashed upward as the beams burrowed into the stone at her enemies' feet. Sorcerers scattered. Soldiers screamed. Orowen slumped to her hands and knees, vomiting hot, acrid bile. The room spun as the magic left her and the light from the shards vanished. Darkness crept into her vision. The dull roar from the magic subsided to panicked shouts and confused cries.

"What was that?" Rylan asked.

"I don't know." Kendi hesitated. "Orowen?"

Beneath Orowen's hands, the ground shook. She looked up into Kendi's face and forced out a single word.

"Run."

An echoing crack resounded off the guard room walls. It was followed by several more as the floor around them broke apart. Beneath it, a yawning black void stretched wide, glowing white-violet where its edges touched the stone. Huge sections of rock fell into the chasm and disappeared into black, Aetherial mist. A tremendous wind howled into the rift. Braziers, weapons, and stools tumbled into the cracks. Soldiers and sorcerers were sucked in after them.

The roar of magic returned tenfold as more of the rift was exposed. Kendi's orders came in clipped, curt sentences barely discernible above the noise. Rylan, Anwic, and Magnus exploded into motion.

Guild forces broke into panicked flight; some of the more practiced sorcerers cast rifts to flee the buckling floor. Other sorcerers and soldiers caught themselves on the broken ledges. Their bodies dangled over the Aether before their fingers slipped off the blood-slicked stone. They fell screaming, their voices quickly swallowed by the void.

A strangled sob slipped through Orowen's teeth. Yes, they were enemies. Yes, their people had killed Cheralach, Val, and so many others. They would have killed the rest of them without a shred of remorse. She could hate them for all the suffering they caused. But they were still Mira's creations. Misguided creations, tainted by Chaos, but still born of Saolanni's will. Orowen had sworn an oath to protect all life, to do no harm.

And she had killed them anyway.

Magnus took hold of her. Though he hauled her up with ease, her legs turned to water when she tried to stand with his help. She couldn't even wrap her arms around him. Orowen sagged back to the floor like a marionette with cut strings. Movement was impossible now. Nausea left her blinking back unconsciousness, sound took on a muffled quality, and the figures darting across the guard room blurred. She emptied her stomach a second time, right onto Magnus's feet.

"I'm so sorry."

"It's alright. I've got you."

His voice was like gravel in her ear, as if his throat still pained him. She would have to examine his vocal cords for any damage she might have missed—

Another snap of stone sounded. A huge fissure appeared in the far wall near the dungeon door. Torchlight and smoke poured in from behind it. The floor caved beneath that wall and the fissure widened, stretching for the ceiling. Massive stones fell into the void, further exposing the dungeon corridor beyond.

Horror ripped through Orowen. *That wasn't supposed to happen.* The rift should not have extended that far. If it damaged too much of the structure, the remaining sorcerers would be the least of their problems.

Magnus hefted her in his arms and started for the stairs. A line of enemies took shape in front of them. Even the collapsing room wouldn't deter the more zealous ones from trying to stop them.

"Samara!" Magnus barked. "Clear the way."

"With pleasure, *Amaa*." Sam appeared beside them, bloodied and brandishing a sword.

She darted ahead, making quick work of the first guard. Jack was close at her heels, having traded his crossbow for a sword and shield. The pair of youngsters clashed with another soldier while a trio of sorcerers took up positions in front of the stairs. Orowen could only look on, her head heavy on Magnus's shoulder.

The rift was still growing. Stone cracked open in front of them. Sam and Jack dispatched their opponent and leaped the gap in the floor. Magnus drew up short as the crack widened. The slab he stood on tilted back the way they'd come.

Something flew past them—the arrow-laden remnants of their tabletop shelter—and lay perfectly flat across the crack, bridging the gap for Magnus to cross. He wasted no time stepping over the chasm as the wind cemented the table into place. Air tore at their hair and Orowen's clothing, but Magnus's footing on the wide planks remained sure. She spared a glance into the rift as it loomed below them, infinite and vast. The scent of Aether, like the redolence of air after a lightning strike, turned Orowen's stomach again.

So much death.

But it was the only way.

Chaos has touched me.

No. No, she mustn't think that.

Charlatan. Oathbreaker.

Molten orbs of Aether flew over Magnus's shoulders, meant for the sorcerers. The mages fired off their own spells. Jack blocked some with his shield. Others were intercepted by counter-orbs, courtesy of Rylan or Jessie. The first sorcerer fell with a dagger in his eye. A second took a dagger in his chest. The third fled up the stairs. Sam gave chase, gutted him, and kicked him over the side of the stairway.

Orowen's people would live.

The ceiling cracked. Dust and debris rained down. Another wall collapsed, tumbling into the Aether. The wind was a living presence now, pawing at them as they mounted the stairs. They ran round and round until they reached the opening at the top. Beside them, the ceiling gave way in earnest, breaking off in small chunks, growing larger.

The rest was a blur. They fled through storage rooms and catacombs and laboratories until they found another set of stairs, rows full of books, and windows that shattered. Late afternoon sky, still bright and blue, and the caress of cool, late summer air. Behind them, stone crashed down. Booming echoes rattled the ground.

Orowen trembled.

Such destruction. Such devastation. It might have been worthy of Chaos himself. She turned her face into Magnus's chest.

She had done her part. Her people would live.

But at what cost?

Chapter Seventeen

Daeya

Night settled over the ship as it cut a path across the sea. Waves rasped along its hull, pounding out a steady beat. White sails snapped and ropes creaked, adding to the rhythm and creating a percussive symphony of soothing sound. The air was cold and condensed, magnifying the brightness of the stars in the endless black sky.

Daeya breathed in the smell of salt and sea. A fine mist coated the bowsprit where she sat with her back against the forestay. One of her legs was folded under her, while the other hung over the water.

A boisterous cacophony of sailors' voices carried across the deck. Despite Daeya's best attempts to engage the crew of the *Breigh Maiden* in conversation, they'd given her and her babysitters a wide berth. Not that she blamed them. Joss had already threatened the captain in order to obtain an officer's cabin for himself and his siblings, far away from the other passengers on the ship. He claimed they needed the privacy to gather further information on the aethermancers' attack through Toby's Aethersight.

The last time Daeya passed by their room, however, they had been more invested in their game of piccara than discussing the collapse of the School of High Sorcery.

According to Toby's report, the middle portion of the west wing—which housed dozens of classrooms and laboratories—had been completely leveled. It was unclear how exactly the bastards had done it, and Daeya didn't care. What she *did* care about were the hundreds of students who had been in those classrooms at the time of the attack. Such a senseless and unprovoked massacre of children would not go unanswered.

Before they'd set sail, Daeya had considered returning to the capital. She was a mage now, and it was her duty to hunt down the aethermancers responsible. But if Gregory had wanted her to return, he would have delivered word to Toby through a Conduit or sent Normos to Rift Walk her back from Keilliad. Until he took such drastic measures, it was her duty to follow orders and go to Orthovia.

She rested her head against the forestay and looked up at the stars. It was still a marvel to her how bright they were out here, away from the city. Osa and Ortana, the mother bear and her cub, were a cluster of stars to the south, while the five stars of Eioden's Blade pointed the way north over the Nohri Peninsula. There was also the Riftweaver and the Archer in the east, and the Corridian Twins behind her to the west.

She was contemplating Tiior's Aspect—the dragon goddess who stretched her great wings across the sky to the southeast—when the creak of wooden boards sounded behind her.

"Does the captain know you're out there?" The voice was soft, amused, and accented with the perfect elegance of Ryostian nobility.

A smile tugged at the corners of Daeya's mouth. She glanced over the bowsprit at the churning ocean far below her. It was too dark to see the white-capped waves battering the hull, but she could hear them. She could taste the salty spray on her lips. "I'm certain if he did, he would have hauled me back on board by now."

Cameron Vika chuckled. "And by your bootstraps, no less."

Daeya turned toward her, holding the forestay for balance. Cam stood behind the bowsprit, arms folded across the railing. Wind teased her messy blonde curls off her forehead. Shadows obscured most of her features, but her silhouette was framed against a sailor's lantern moving across the bridge.

"You couldn't sleep either?" Cam asked.

Daeya snorted. "No. Something about hundreds of children being murdered by aethermancers has been keeping me awake."

Unwilling to sleep in the same space as Joss and Toby, Daeya had chosen to remain in the passengers' quarters. Every time she closed her eyes, she kept imagining all those little bodies buried under hundreds of tons of stone, wood, and glass. Toby's description hadn't been much more than a sketch of the disaster, but it was enough to fill Daeya's thoughts with vivid scenes of gore and blood, the likes of which she had seen only in her nightmares.

"A malady you and I both share." The humor was gone from Cam's voice, replaced by weariness. She studied her in the starlight. "Will you come off of there? You're making me nervous."

Daeya might have refused if the request had come from anyone else, but she liked Cam. Despite the ten years separating them, she was at least friendly, if not a true friend.

And, truthfully, her arse was starting to hurt. "Well, since you asked so nicely—"

She channeled a trickle of power from her casting bracelet, settled her attention on a wide open point behind Cam, and wove a glowing sigil in the air. Perfectly timing her spell for maximum effect, she flung herself off the bowsprit and fell into a rift over the ocean.

Streaky, starlit mist swallowed Cam's cry of alarm. When Daeya dropped from the Aether and hit the deck, she found Cam throttling the railing and leaning over the side of the ship.

The sorceress rounded on her, clutching her chest. "Gods, Daeya!"

Laughter bubbled out of her, and the exit rift overhead vanished in a burst of light. Daeya rose from her crouch and socked Cam on the arm. "Oh, come on. You surely recognized that sigil."

"Aether take you." She heaved a breath, shaking her head. "You'll be the death of me one of these days."

Still chuckling, Daeya brushed grime from the bowsprit off her trousers. "If I do, I promise it won't be intentional."

"Is that supposed to be a consolation?"

"Well, yes, in a manner of speaking." In the brief seconds the rift had illuminated them both, Daeya had spotted a small, wax-sealed letter tucked under Cam's arm. She gestured toward it. "What's that?"

Cam turned the letter over, ran her thumb over the seal, and passed it to her. "Master Ulrich asked me to give this to you. She said it would be important."

Daeya took the letter, lifting an eyebrow. "Did you read it?"

"No. I wouldn't." Her tone was indignant. "I'm not Joss."

"Thank the gods for that."

Cam settled against the railing. "Need a light?"

"Please."

As Daeya broke the wax seal and unfolded the letter, Cam slipped the catch on her casting bracelet and removed a bead of saphyrum. "*Luminos,*" she murmured, and the bead began to emit a dim white-violet glow.

She held the bead over the parchment, illuminating Master Ulrich's stylized script. A few errant drops of ink stained the note, as if the master instructor had written it in a hurry. There were only two words written on it: '*Trust him.*'

Daeya frowned and turned the parchment over. The other side was blank. "Bleeding Aether, that's vague." Some obscurity was expected from divination magic, but this was ridiculous.

Cam shifted on her feet. "May I?"

Daeya held it up for her.

She cringed. "Yeah, that's vague, alright."

Daeya's sigh was more of a growl. "It would have been nice if she'd warned us about the attack instead."

Cam looked sharply at her and Daeya winced, regretting the words as soon as she spoke them. It was too much like an accusation, and that wasn't fair to Master Ulrich.

"I'm sorry. That came out wrong."

"It's alright," Cam assured her, softening once more. "I can't say I disagree with you, but you know she can't choose what she sees in the Aether."

"I know."

Daeya looked over the letter again, silently praying its author hadn't been teaching at the time of the School's collapse. Ulrich was always quick to offer advice for problems Daeya would never have brought before Gregory. As tough as her curriculum was, Ulrich cared about her students and devoted herself to teaching in a way few other instructors could. To think the Guild might have lost her in some baseless act of terrorism...

She swallowed the stone in her throat and tucked the letter away. "Did she say anything else?"

Cam pursed her lips with an expression both pained and apologetic. "I'm afraid not. She just caught me in the hallway, stuffed the letter in my hand, and said to give it to you." She shrugged. "Normal Master Ulrich behavior."

It was true. No one would ever applaud the Cintoshi professor for her tactful delivery of future knowledge. She often opted for abrupt, unnerving episodes of insight, which sometimes made her appear unstable. It was to be expected, though; immersing one's consciousness in the eddies of Aetherial time flow would make anyone a little eccentric.

Daeya leaned against the railing. "We can always count on her to keep life exciting, I suppose."

Cam made a noncommittal noise and turned to follow her gaze out to sea.

Daeya glanced aside to her. Cam's profile was thrown into stark relief against the blackness of night. The shadow of a dimple adorned the left side of her face. Her jaw was tensed, and waves of unease rolled off her, sending echoes of the same emotion prickling down Daeya's spine.

There was a secret the older sorceress kept, rather than endure her brothers' incessant ridicule and lewd commentary. She'd shared it with Daeya as a sort of peace offering after discovering her runes at Belden Abbey.

"Have you heard from her?" Daeya asked.

Cam's blue eyes leveled on her, gleaming in the bead's light. At last, she allowed her fear and anguish to show. "No."

Cam's partner, Killian, was a junior instructor of Political Science and Diplomacy at the School. Her classroom was one of many in the middle portion of the west wing.

Daeya looked down, then out to sea again. A stiff wind snapped at the lapels of her robe. "I'm sure she's alright."

"Silonas willing," Cam said, invoking the god of fortune.

As word of the aethermancers' treachery spread, thousands more would vie for Silonas's attention while the Guild took stock of its dead and prepared notices for the victims' families. If Faustus was found among the wreckage, Daeya would insist she handle the notice to be sent north to Sarton. He would have been in class, too.

Only something told her he wasn't. It was too much of a coincidence to hope he hadn't been involved.

She shoved aside that unsettling ache between her shoulder blades and flexed her hands. Cam sidled closer, letting their shoulders touch. Daeya's chest constricted at the rare display of comfort and leaned into the older mage. For long minutes, it took everything she had just to breathe normally. Silence borne of uncertainty, anticipation, and grief settled between them. Rage loomed like shoals beneath the dark waves.

Clouds built in the distance, formless and black as Aether. They blotted out the tip of the Archer's arrow like a premonition of darker times to come.

Though there were still many sleepless hours until dawn, Daeya longed for the sunrise. "Do you think the Council will finally declare war?"

"I hope so." Cam's response came fiercely, her voice saturated with emotion. "Surely not even Sarikkian can talk his way out of it this time."

Councilor Isa Sarikkian, Killian's mentor, was the Guild's most adept ambassador and an old class rival of Gregory's. The two could never agree on anything, especially when it came to the Alliaansi and their host of blanker sympathizers. Gregory had been pushing to invade the Northlands and wipe them out for years. Sarikkian, on the other hand, cautioned that such aggression could spell disaster for the Guild's resources and for their relationships with other nations.

The Council at large had split the vote for war several times over the last decade. Its declaration was stymied mostly by arguments from Sarikkian and his newly appointed protégé, Councilor Shei-Gwen Mar-Pol.

There was little argument to be made now. That the Alliaansi would target the Guild's youngest and most vulnerable—the future of Eidosinian leadership—was cause enough for Daeya to throw her lot in behind Gregory and his loudest supporters, Councilors Tressa Blake and Nash Ferren.

"They'll pay for this, one way or another." Cam's fingers tightened around the bead, its glow red through her skin. "Even if I have to do something about it myself."

The same anger and hurt—the same need for retribution—gave Daeya focus as she reflected on every child she had ever cared for in the Guild nursery. Every student she had ever tutored. Every friend, however fleeting, she had ever made. "You won't be alone."

Cam gave her a curious look, her brows furrowing.

Daeya gazed back at her, hardening her expression, hoping it properly displayed the seriousness and strength of her resolve. "I will stand beside you."

The sorceress appraised her a moment more before letting her face soften. She nodded, giving her an appreciative half-smile. "You've grown up, McVen."

Daeya mirrored the look and leaned in conspiratorially. "Promise not to tell?"

Cam's smile twitched wider. "I promise." She nudged Daeya in the ribs. "And just between you and me, I think black looks good on you."

That simple compliment made her heart soar. Daeya couldn't help but grin back, warmth blooming in her cheeks. "Thanks, Cam. That means a lot."

Cam looked down at the bead between her fingers. She must have been casting from it for some time; its glow faded to that of an ember. Her smile faded with it. "Just watch out for Joss, alright? I'm afraid he's out for blood."

Daeya scoffed. That wasn't surprising. Joss was likely as jealous of her as Normos was. She rested her boot on a lower rung of the ship's railing and leaned against it. "He'll have to get in line. I'm sure Normos will want first rights."

Cam put her hand on her shoulder. "I'm serious. He's going to do everything he can to make sure you fail in Orthovia."

The thought of failure, of what Gregory would do to her if she disgraced him in the eyes of the Council, sent a spike of fear through Daeya's chest. Phantom pressure against her wrists and the iron scent of Aether made her heart beat faster.

"He'll only succeed in making himself the fool." Her attention strayed toward those ominous clouds again. "I'm not going to fail."

"I've seen you do some pretty amazing things." Cam returned her hand to the railing. "I'll do what I can to help."

Though she spoke with good intentions, her promise was hollow at its core. If she wouldn't tell her brothers about Killian, Daeya couldn't count on Cam to stand up for her. But she also wouldn't call her out and risk ruining whatever tenuous friendship they had.

The light from Cam's saphyrum died. With the bead's magic spent, it crumbled to dust. She bared her palm to the sky, and the glittering remnants blew away on the wind. "You should try to sleep. See the captain's healer for some poppy wine if you have to."

Black clouds swallowed the Archer. They continued their slow march on the hands of the Riftweaver. "Is that what you're going to do?"

It was a shame poppy wine, like many medicinal herbs, didn't affect her as well as it should. Convincing any healer worth his salt to provide her with a near-lethal dose would be a fool's errand. But Cam didn't know that; only Gregory did. It was more knowledge she was supposed to keep to herself—part of a long and exhaustive list of secrets.

"I think I'll have to." Cam turned from the railing.

Daeya looked away from the sky. "Good night, Cam."

"Good night, Daeya."

Her black silhouette retreated across the deck until it blended with other shadows. Soon, the only sign Cam had been there at all was the rectangular shape of Master Ulrich's letter pressed against Daeya's abdomen.

Trust him.

She couldn't imagine a scenario in which she would be made to trust Toby, much less Joss. Could Ulrich have meant Gregory? Maybe she knew more about the Councilor's activities than she let on. Perhaps she wanted to reassure Daeya all was well. Then again, it could mean someone else. Someone she had yet to meet.

Trust him. Daeya groaned aloud.

Trust *whom*?

Chapter Eighteen

Alar

Alar drifted.

The tiny room beneath Clover 386 had fallen away hours ago, leaving him floating in the center of a still, clear lake. It was a place of quiet serenity, of infinite possibility, far removed from the clutter of conscious thought. Especially in times of stress, his mind craved this openness and clarity, just as the body sought comfort in wide open spaces. He could create rolling meadows, shoreless oceans, and vast stretches of cloudless sky with only a thought. He could create any place he desired. In this meditative state, he was unfettered by the fragile constructs of reality.

If the gods existed, he imagined they lived in places like this, where omnipotence and omniscience seemed not only possible, but probable, if built by a skilled enough hand. Someday, he would master this skill.

Someday he would understand why good men died.

The thought was intrusive. Subversive. It caused a ripple in the surface of the lake he'd constructed, dampening his sense of control. He forced it aside.

Weightlessness. He let his body rise above the surface of the lake until he could see a distant shore. Rather than moving toward it, as he might in a dream, he asserted his will on the space so the world spun beneath him. Then he stepped down on the sand.

He didn't like the gritty feeling of real sand between his toes or how it lingered in every crack and crevice, so he made this sand better. It was soft without sticking, fine but not dusty, and it didn't have that dirty, piscine smell. It was superior to real sand in every way.

Alar stood on the beach, populating it with perfect palms and tropical flowers. He allowed a light breeze to blow through the leafy vegetation, just enough to set them swaying. White citrus flowers, orange and pink yarrow, fragrant lavender, all free of browning or decay. With no more than a thought, he planted delicate Aivenosian lilies with stunning blue petals, tropical hibiscus trees laden with golden blooms, Skriian orchids the color of blood—

Blood.

The sky overhead changed, no longer a cloudless blue, but a deep shade of purple, streaked with red.

Purple like bruising. Red like blood. *There was so much blood.*

He hadn't deserved to die like that.

Alar stiffened. Grief rose inside him like the tide. His meditative vision took on a life of its own, the ocean surging, threatening to drown him. The clouds churned, darkening, blotting out the sunless light.

Enough.

He breathed deeply. The beach, the sand, the clouds all fell away. He was left at the center of a void of gray. Seated once more, legs crossed, hands on his knees, and beads of restorative saphyrum between his fingers.

Free of emotion.

Drifting.

Ravlok started when a shadow emerged from the tiny room beneath the stairs. The crooked wooden panel posing as a door banged shut behind it.

"Now that we've all had a chance to rest," Alar said, stepping into the candlelight, "would someone care to explain why one of our most powerful aethermancers came on a routine supply run and got himself killed?"

The dusty cellar under Morren Berridell's jewelry shop fell silent. Some of Ravlok's new companions avoided glancing in the mastermind's direction at all. After several hours of meditating under the stairs, Alar barely looked injured, aside from a fleeting stiffness in the way he moved.

Ravlok was sitting as still as he could on top of a barrel while Laerin Riverdale sewed up a gash below his collarbone. The red-haired woman was no surgeon, but she sold her working knowledge of non-adept healing techniques with all the confidence of a Duerwisti stage performer.

That was probably why her freckled nose wrinkled when he flinched. "Will ye stop moving?" she hissed at him, her heavily accented Eidosinian breaking the silence.

"Sorry," he said, his voice distorted around the linen stuffed in his nostrils. Pain pulsed across his face from the broken tissue. At least ice had brought the swelling down.

He'd been surprised to see Laerin here, considering the number of times she'd looted Berridell's when he was younger. She had taught Ravlok much of what he knew about life on the street after he'd left Madame's. Based on the vicious way Laerin stabbed the needle into him, she still hadn't forgiven him for choosing the monastery over her thieves' guild.

"Laangor's breath, ye smell worse than Southgate on tannin' day," the ill-tempered woman grumbled.

It wasn't Ravlok's fault they had run out of soap before his turn to bathe, but he stayed his tongue. If he upset her too much, her needlework might grow even more vengeful.

Laerin held up her needle and frowned at the too-short length of thread remaining. "Rammie, I need more catgut."

Her younger sister—who was tending to a slash on Anwic's face—shoved the sack of medical supplies across the floor with her foot.

Alar folded his arms and cleared his throat, wordlessly demanding an answer to his question.

It was Magnus who finally spoke. "Cheralach insisted," he rasped.

The aethermancer had been bathed, bandaged, and clothed, but until Orowen was well again, there was nothing to be done for his ravaged throat. Speaking obviously pained him, but his one-eyed gaze was steady as he regarded the mastermind.

"Why?" Alar's face was made of stone, as if he faced a group full of unruly children. As if he felt no compassion at all for the ragged state of his companions.

Ravlok *had* seen him before, and now that he was no longer at immediate risk of being beheaded or burned alive, he finally knew where. He went by another name in the Guild: Faustus Crex. An older initiate who'd recently enrolled in the School of High Sorcery. He had been assigned to Daeya for private lessons. Though it was obvious now that Crex was an Alliaansi spy, Ravlok still struggled to reconcile the charming and good-natured Faustus with frosty, sarcastic Alar.

Magnus sat with his elbows on his knees, hands hanging limp between them. "He was having visions again."

"What kind of visions?" Alar asked.

Magnus tried to respond, but an intense bout of coughing overcame him. Ravlok cringed at the grating sound. When the man's arm came away from his mouth, blood misted the sleeve of his shirt.

Kendi spoke up from beside Orowen's makeshift bed—two crates shoved together and covered with straw and blankets. "The kind he could never ignore. He believed they were messages from Tiior."

The mention of the goddess of knowledge piqued Ravlok's interest. There were many stories of Ordeolas's only daughter appearing in visions to luminaries throughout history. Stories claimed King Ellian Orthalas of Aivenos had been given visions by Tiior when his regent, Leoro Adzeras, sought to steal his throne. There was also Reordis Oakenforge, a Cintoshi whose visions had predicted the fall of Eiode to the Aetherian, Sedrion Riftbreaker, during the time of the Great Schism. And there was the story of Nyxavhara Stormheart, one of the last dragons to stand against the Denorian priests of Chaos before the extinction of her people some five hundred years ago.

The implication of Tiior's involvement in Cheralach's visions had Ravlok straining against a hundred thousand questions. There was much he could learn from studying those visions.

But to his dismay, Alar only scoffed and rubbed his temples. "Fantastic."

"He was certain the future of the Alliaansi depended on their interpretation," Kendi said more cautiously, leaving Ravlok to wonder how Alar fit into the Alliaansi's command structure. Did masterminds somehow outrank even seasoned commanders, or was Kendi just too weary to correct him?

Alar lowered his hand from his face. "And what was their interpretation?" he asked, as if he was only humoring him with the question.

"He only spoke with Orowen about them." Kendi hesitated. "She wasn't able to glean much before we came south."

The mastermind's face twitched. For a fraction of a second, he looked on the verge of imploding. Then his eyes closed, and he breathed a slow, exasperated sigh. "So, we have one dead spy, a dead aethermancer, half a troop of our own dead soldiers, and nothing to show for it but a bunch of cryptic messages we can't interpret."

"Alar, don't be a prick," Sam said, looking up from changing Jessie's bandages. The Guild soldier's sword had cut deeply, and Jessie had been in and out of consciousness, sweating and shivering with fever all night.

"He's right, though." Rylan held a damp cloth to a burn on the side of his neck. "We shouldn't have let him come."

"It wasn't a matter of letting," Magnus asserted. "You try talking him out of things—"

"We can't, now, can we?" Alar spat.

Magnus winced and fell silent, squeezing his one eye shut as the scar tissue puckered around the empty socket.

Laerin paused in threading her needle. She turned away from Ravlok and addressed the room. "What's passed is past. Ye should start thinking about how ye're getting out of the city. The Guild has it locked down tighter than a hangman's noose." She glanced toward her sister, adding, "It's too dangerous for my people to help ye any more than this."

Rammie's hands stilled over Anwic's wound. "I promised Val I'd help them. I intend to see them safe, if for nothing more than to honor his memory."

Laerin's jaw tensed, as if Rammie's words struck a nerve. Her hand tightened on the needle. "An unfortunate thing, that. Don't think I don't feel his loss. But I see what the Guild did to that one." She nodded toward Magnus. "I don't want to imagine what they'd do to ye."

Rammie spared a glance in the aethermancer's direction, no doubt studying the gruesome state of his face. Then she returned her attention to Anwic. "I'm helping them just the same."

Laerin sucked in a sharp breath. "Rammie—"

"Ye'll not change my mind," Rammie said, tossing a scowl over her shoulder. "Best save yer moaning."

"We appreciate everything you've done for us," Kendi said diplomatically, looking between the sisters. "We'll not ask you to put yourselves in any more danger on our behalf."

"Ye don't have to." Rammie lifted her needle again. "It's my pleasure. I'm happy to do it for friends of Val's."

Ravlok was relieved when Kendi didn't argue further. With Rammie on their side, Laerin would feel obligated to help them, if only to ensure her sister didn't get caught. If they were to have any chance of leaving this city alive, it would be with the master smugglers of the thieves' guild.

The cellar door creaked open, and morning light spilled in from the shop above. Ravlok gripped the edge of the barrel on which he sat, stifling a grunt as Laerin drove the needle into his flesh. He focused on the set of boots that appeared at the top of the stairs.

Alar also looked up as the leather-clad figure descended. "How bad is it?"

"Bad," Jack said as he reached the short wooden landing. He turned left down the last three stairs before reaching the cellar floor. "They've tripled the guard on every wall. They're conducting searches on every crate and barrel leaving the city, and no boats are leaving the docks."

"And the Towers?" Alar asked.

Jack shrugged. "Looked like the entire west wing was destroyed."

A sickly numbness settled over Ravlok. "The west wing?"

In their desperate escape from the dungeon, his internal compass had been thrown entirely off-kilter. He remembered the huge rift in the floor and stone crumbling. He remembered winding catacombs and dozens of stairs and tumbling out of a secret door in the Guild library. A heart-pounding dash through back alleys and old tunnels had brought them to this safe house. But in all of that confusion, he hadn't stopped to ponder where exactly they had been beneath the Towers.

Jack and Alar both spared him looks, neither of them friendly. Jack's was wary and disdainful. Alar's was simply cold.

Ravlok pulled the bloody linen out of his nose, sparing himself the indignity of facing off against these two while sounding like a duck. "You're saying the School was destroyed?"

"Nothing left but a pile of rubble." There was a smugness in Jack's tone that made Ravlok bristle. "Good riddance to it, I say."

Before he could stop himself, Ravlok launched off the barrel, fury blooming in his chest. "There were *children* in there—"

Rylan rushed to intercept him, one hand against Ravlok's bare torso. "Now is not the time, *amii*."

"Ravlok, please." Kendi lent his support toward keeping the peace, rising from his own barrel. His movement, more than Rylan's touch, snapped Ravlok out of his advance. The commander had refused to leave Orowen's side, much less release her hand, since their arrival last night. Now, Kendi stepped up beside him. "You must keep your voice down."

He was right. Of course he was right, but Ravlok still simmered, glaring at Jack, hands closing into fists. Delvin curse him if he was going to let that comment go. "Guild or not," he said, his jaw tight, "those children were innocent."

Jack's upper lip curled. "There is no such thing as an innocent sorcerer."

Twenty-four hours ago, Ravlok wouldn't have hesitated to deny such a damning generalization. Most Guild members were decent people, but after what he'd witnessed in the dungeon—the torture, cruelty, and malice—he struggled to find the right way to respond. He needed to think about it logically, to reason with Jack.

He didn't get the opportunity.

"That's enough." Kendi's head snapped toward Jack so suddenly that even Alar recoiled. The commander's eyes swept the room, settling on each of them one by one.

"Let me make this perfectly clear for all of you," he said, his voice made of iron. "What happened last night was a tragedy. We may have escaped, but the destruction we left behind us will have lasting consequences."

That he didn't mention Orowen's part in the destruction was not lost on Ravlok. He tore his attention away from Jack and looked toward the sleeping form of the tiny priestess. The way she'd wielded the gods' magic yesterday had only been heard about in songs and stories, and those from the mouths of musicians and storytellers with an inclination toward hyperbole. They spoke of a time before the Schism when aethermancers and sorcerers were all simply called magi, and Aetherians were the ones to fear.

Evil is no cure for evil, Orowen had said, quoting the Book of Life. But her actions could be considered evil, couldn't they? Bringing down the entire building to escape, heedless of the unsuspecting victims on the floors above?

Unless, perhaps, that hadn't been her intention. Though he had only known Orowen for the length of his dungeon stay, Ravlok couldn't believe any devoted follower of Saolanni would have purposely destroyed a school full of children.

"Surely you all realize what is to follow," Kendi went on.

"War," Alar said.

Kendi's expression was grim. "If what Jack says is true, I would expect the declaration to come before we reach Starlight."

"Then it's inevitable," Rylan said. "Even if the Guild doesn't declare war, without Cheralach, Koraani and Nemaala will push for it."

"Jerinoch wouldn't let that happen," Sam said. "Nor would Tipori."

"Jerinoch is only one man, and Tipori has abstained from choosing sides for his own reasons." Kendi sighed. "The vote will likely come down to whoever fills Cheralach's seat on the council."

The person he expected to fill that seat became obvious as Ravlok followed his gaze to where Magnus sat hanging his head, fingers clenched in his hair, palms over his ears, as if to block out the sounds of their voices. The titan of a man who could toss guards about like dolls with his magic now seemed to be on the verge of a breakdown. All the horrors he must have witnessed, the pain he'd endured—it was impressive he'd lasted this long without crumbling.

Alar also glanced toward Magnus, his face a mask of neutrality. "We can worry about that later. Right now, we need to gather what supplies we can and get you out of the city."

Rammie finished closing Anwic's wound and wiped her hands on a towel. "Our supply caches should have what ye need. If ye've the beads, I have a contact who can rift ye through the wall near West Riddle."

"Beads won't be a problem." Alar reached down and opened the pack at his feet, withdrawing a sack of saphyrum bearing the Guild's senior acolyte blue and black coloring. Ravlok's eyes narrowed, and the corner of Alar's mouth lifted.

He poured out a handful of beads and passed them to Rammie. "Tell your contact we'll want to move during the shift change at fifth bell. The sun should still be high enough to disguise the light from the rifts."

Orowen's frail voice cut in. "We can't leave. Not yet." The priestess coughed, the sound little more than sandpaper on wood. She shifted on her pallet of straw and struggled to sit up.

Kendi was at her side in an instant. "Devoted, you need to rest."

Orowen reached for him, but only to pull herself further upright. "We have to find the girl."

Anwic groaned. "Not this again."

"What girl?" Ravlok and Alar asked at the same time. The mastermind glanced toward him, but Ravlok's focus remained on Orowen as Kendi helped her take several slow sips of water from a skin.

"The one in Cheralach's visions." Orowen ignored Anwic's continued, inarticulate grumbling. "He believed she was in danger."

Alar might not take the visions seriously, but Ravlok did. "What did she look like?"

"He said she must be around sixteen. White hair. Green eyes. Exceptional with magic."

Ravlok's pulse quickened. That sounded like...

Alar had gone still; Ravlok met his gaze. The way the mastermind studied him, he could tell they were both thinking of Daeya.

Ravlok shifted his focus back to Orowen. "What kind of danger?"

Orowen's brows furrowed. "The visions weren't clear. Cheralach wouldn't tell me everything. He kept saying he had to find her. He was certain the fate of the Alliaansi was inextricably tied to her."

"I don't suppose he got a name," Alar said, as if even now he loathed to make such a leap of faith.

She shook her head, her strength already flagging. "No, I'm sorry."

Alar's gaze settled on Ravlok again. He looked contemplative, as if he were considering what to say. It was possible they were both wrong, and the visions meant someone else. But Ravlok didn't know any other white-haired, green-eyed sixteen-year-olds, and everyone in the Guild knew Daeya possessed exceptional skill. It was too perfect a match to be coincidental. She was also prone to getting herself in trouble, both intentionally and not.

What sort of misfortune was destined to find his friend if Cheralach the Deserter had seen her in his visions?

Kendi seated himself on the crate beside Orowen, holding the waterskin in his lap. He frowned, seeming to note the silent knowledge passing between them. "What is it?"

Ravlok gave the mastermind the slightest nod. These were Alar's people. He would leave it up to him to decide how much they should know.

Alar lifted his chin. "A mutual acquaintance of ours matches that description."

Orowen's eyes widened. Kendi's followed suit. Sam and Rylan shared wary glances. Even Magnus looked up from his feet. Jack, however, leaned against the wall with his arms folded, looking bored.

"Good," Anwic grunted. "The sooner you fetch her, the sooner we can get back home."

Alar scoffed. "I'm afraid it's not that simple." He lifted the drawstring bag of saphyrum and gave it a shake. "She's a senior acolyte at the School."

Whatever warmth the meager candle provided might as well have been sucked out through a rift. The silence that followed could have been the same as that following a death knell. It was a tangible thing—a tension that built steadily, irrevocably, until a single word sliced through it with the lethal accuracy of an assassin's blade.

"*What?*"

Ravlok took an involuntary step back as Anwic found his feet. The rage rolling off the Syljian was akin to the fiery heat emanating from an oven. He advanced on Alar, teeth bared. "You mean to tell me Cheralach *died* trying to rescue a *sorceress*?"

"Anwic." Orowen struggled to keep her eyes open. "I know this is hard to accept." Her words came slowly, like she was having trouble remembering how to speak the trade tongue. Even so, no one dared interrupt her. "We have all lost loved ones to the Guild. But if Cheralach believed this girl was important, then I trust him."

Jack came away from the wall, his scowl lethal. "You must be mistaken."

Ravlok placed himself between Orowen and the two men. Not that he thought they would harm her, but arguing with them would not help her condition. The move incidentally brought him closer to Alar's side. He gestured toward the mastermind as a show of solidarity. "It's not a coincidence Alar and I both thought of the same person. If she's in danger—"

"Visions can be misinterpreted," Jack broke in. "What if *she's* the danger, and it's up to us to eliminate her?"

Ravlok's blood ran cold. Without Cheralach to refute it, they would have to consider the possibility. Daeya *was* training to become a sorceress, and a powerful one at that. Still, she had her own mind, and with proof of the Guild's cruelty and corruption, he knew they could convince her to listen.

"No response to that, *bashiin*?" Anwic waved toward Jack. "This one has the right of it. These visions are clearly misunderstood. If the girl is a sorceress, she can't be trusted."

"Cheralach was once a sorcerer," Sam pointed out. She set her jaw stubbornly, one hand resting on Jessie's bandaged leg. "So was Jerinoch." Her attention fixed on Anwic, her expression one of cold rage. "You of all men should know better than to condemn an entire people, Anwic."

Anwic's fists balled at his sides. "That is different—"

"It's not." Sam jerked her chin toward Ravlok and Alar. "If they can convince their friend to come with us, then I say we bring her to Starlight."

"Not Starlight."

Ravlok turned toward Kendi, incredulous, tensing to argue.

The commander held up a placating hand. "Not without the council's approval." He looked at Alar. "You know this girl. Do you think she can be trusted?"

"Maybe." Alar's response was casual. "Just this morning, she was questioning Guild doctrine."

For once, it seemed Daeya's problems with authority were working *for* her. Sam's sudden, pleased grin bolstered Ravlok, despite the dubious look that passed between Jack and Anwic.

Kendi's reaction was no more than a subtle lift of his white eyebrows. "Can you extract her without drawing attention to yourself?"

Alar gave a noncommittal shrug. "Assuming she lived through the collapse."

The thought left a sour taste in Ravlok's mouth. Of course Daeya was alive. He would not consider any other alternative.

"Collapse?" Orowen blinked open her eyes, lifting her head from Kendi's shoulder. There was another silent pause as the priestess surveyed the room. "What collapse?"

The words had barely left her mouth before she sagged back against Kendi. He wrapped an arm around her shoulders. "I'll explain later," he promised, fixing the rest of them with a warning stare over Orowen's mess of tangled white hair.

Realization hit Ravlok like a blow from his mentor's staff. Orowen didn't know she'd destroyed the School.

"We'll take her with us as far as Fawn's Breath." For Ravlok's benefit, Kendi added, "It's a neutral town, just over the border. We can hold her there and send word to the council. If she is a threat to us, she'll be out of Guild hands."

Alar nodded, gathering his pack from the floor. "I'll be right back."

It was the best solution, and one that left Ravlok selfishly excited by the prospect of Daeya going north with him. Still, it was possible she might choose not to come. If they accepted her wishes and left her behind, she might fall prey to whatever danger Cheralach had seen. If they decided she was a threat to them, they might not accept no for an answer.

While it was never explicitly stated in the Book of Order, Ravlok was certain Ordeolas would not approve of kidnapping.

Chapter Nineteen

Alar

The west wing of the Sorcerers' Guild hadn't quite been reduced to a pile of rubble, but it was close. The five-story building bowed in the center like a bone cleaved almost entirely in half. Its two ends still stood untouched by the rift, which by its very nature would have long since closed beneath the tons and tons of shattered stone littering the square.

Civilians and sorcerers picked through the mountain of rubble, searching for survivors. Their faces were grim and covered with dirt, their clothes similarly stained. They spoke only in low murmurs to one another, interrupted occasionally by the barked commands of sorcerers or quiet sobbing from nearby onlookers.

Wagons and carts lined the west wing, half full of debris waiting to be carted off to rifts standing open near the square's center. The small, stable rifts—ones meant to transport, rather than devour—were vertical slashes of violet-rimmed black against the backdrop of the east wing and market district. Those rifts would carry the destruction away into the Aether, where arcane maelstroms and unrelenting currents would eventually break it into its smallest parts.

The central tower's shadow cooled the heat of the sun on Alar's gray robe. He had taken great care to reapply his Faustus disguise, especially taping down his ear points and covering them with new assassin's clay. Since none of the sorcerers in the dungeon seemed to have recognized him as Faustus Crex, nor had he recognized any of them, it was safe to assume his alias was still intact. He'd simply chosen a proper alibi for his absence yesterday—a misplaced bag of commissary coins that led to an hours-long search through the city—and practiced his look of devastation in one of the jeweler's mirrors before departing. It was that look he wore as he crossed the mosaic leading up to the Guild's grand entryway, surveying the wreckage with not entirely feigned astonishment.

He would be certain to stay on Orowen's good side after this.

He paused for a pair of mages who were guiding a chunk of stone too big for a wagon through the air with telekinesis. They grunted and strained beneath the mental weight before heaving it into a rift. The stone vanished and they both nearly doubled over from the exertion, hands anchored on their knees and sweat glistening on their brows.

Amateurs, Alar thought with a sniff, his jaw twitching. Just when he was certain he had mastered his anger, seeing the mages' frailty inflamed him all over again. They weren't guarding their minds against him while they worked. It would be easy to slip inside them and rip them apart.

The thought was tempting. Almost too tempting.

For Val's sake.

For Finn's.

Picturing Finn's horrified face when he brought news of her husband's death nearly undid him. He didn't even have a body to return to her. Val's remains were lost to the Aether, swallowed up as the stone buckled beneath them. Alar could still hear the scrape of Val's boots against the floor as he made a grab for the body and missed, nearly tumbling in after it.

He steeled himself against the memory—against the bite of the stone beneath his palms, the hair-raising pull of the Aether as he stared into the rift, watching his best friend's dead eyes slip into the black mist. With several slow breaths, he shoved his grief and pain far, far down inside him, ensuring the anger simmering in his blood didn't show on his powdered face. There would be time for vengeance later. Right now, he had to find Daeya.

He smiled politely and dipped his head to the sorcerers as one of them—the one with an unfortunate mole on the side of his nose—straightened.

Mole returned the nod and gestured for him to pass. "As you were, Initiate."

The voice that responded was all Faustus—deferential, amiable, submissive. "Thank you, Sorcerer."

Alar slipped around the pair and ascended the wide stone staircase between the square and the hedge-wrapped veranda. The Guild's main entrance loomed in front of him. Four pairs of wood-and-iron doors tapered to pointed arches some eight spans above the ground. Their iron bracing was freshly oiled, and the hinges, too, had been tended recently. The door Alar chose opened easily despite its size, without a single chirp of protest.

He braced himself for the resplendence, the glittering tapestries, and the gilded banisters. He'd tried to avoid all this grandiosity by coming through a side entrance closer to Daeya's room, but the entire complex was under lockdown. The sentry who'd turned him away had explained the main doors would be the only source of entry or exit until the Council said otherwise.

For once, a fine layer of dust muted the splendor. It was thickest on the floor to his left, where dozens of trails already carved the grime into various shapes. More dust clogged the air and blotted out the sparkle of gold and gems even as shafts of sunlight pierced the haze.

Not only were there sentries at each set of doors, but they were also posted in evenly spaced intervals inside the rotunda. An extra pair lingered on the threshold leading to the west wing, likely to keep people from venturing into the wreckage. A long-eared Feridian—even shorter than the average Cintoshi, but with the sleek, short fur, and reed-thin, wiry build common among his people—stopped everyone beside the greeter's desk, ensuring they checked in and out with the senior acolyte stationed there.

Alar didn't recognize the Feridian sorcerer, but he knew the acolyte. Lucinna, he recalled, studying the human's dark eyes, round nose, and full, pursed lips as she recorded the trio of mages at the front of the line. Lucinna was a skilled student of elemental magic. While most sorcerers could produce only one of the four elements, Lucinna could produce three: fire, water, and wind. Her temperament was just as mercurial, especially when her desire to please everyone brought her into direct conflict with one of her many social circles.

Determining there was no way around waiting in line, Alar decided he would press her for information while he was here. Talk on the way over suggested the Guild was framing this as an unprovoked attack from Alliaansi rebels. As connected as Lucinna was, she might be able to tell him more.

The line moved swiftly, and more students and mages filed in behind him. Unless he wanted to draw attention to himself, he would have to ask his questions quickly and be on his way. Alar stepped up to the desk when the senior acolyte in front of him departed. With a forlorn look down the hall of the west wing, he asked, "Do they know who did this?"

Lucinna's attention snapped up from her parchment, the delicate chains of her saphyrum earrings slapping against her onyx cheeks. Her feathered quill hovered a finger or two above the inkwell. She lowered it as she studied him, her lips parting. "Faustus Crex."

The tightness in her voice sent a cold jolt down Alar's spine. Faustus was well-known among the students, and he had a great rapport with most of them, including Lucinna. For her to look at him that way—

Something was wrong.

There was no retreat, though. Things were already in motion as the Feridian mage turned. Reedy, Alar decided to call the child-sized man. His features were almost wolf-like, exacerbated by the dusting of black fur framing wide-set amber eyes, slightly hollowed cheeks, and a sharply tapered chin. Reedy stalked closer to the greeter's desk, his long, fur-covered ears twitching. Even when he drew himself to his full height, he barely came level with Alar's hips. "You're Faustus Crex?"

Alar looked from the mage to Lucinna and back, letting his brows furrow and leaning into Faustus's innocence. "I am. Is..." He hesitated for effect. "Is something wrong?"

Lucinna's eyes darted toward Reedy before she reached for a note half-buried under a stack of books. Alar studied her face closely. Unease lingered there, and beneath it, a stronger sense of duty. She passed the note to him.

As Alar took it, Reedy's brows lifted, sending an impressive set of wrinkles marching toward his furline. "Your Councilor left us a message. You're supposed to see him immediately."

Wonderful. Gregory was the last person he wanted to see right now.

The note was a shorthand version of that very message, written in Gregory's own script. Such a note was a rarity. He would save it to study for later. His ability to forge documents in a Councilor's hand could be invaluable.

"Did he say why?" Alar allowed himself to sound nervous. Any student unaccustomed to visiting Gregory would be. He'd only had the displeasure of being inside Gregory's office twice: once when he'd arrived, and once when he was assigned to Daeya. She'd run interference between him and the Councilor ever since.

Lucinna only motioned the next student in line forward, ignoring him.

"No." Reedy took Alar by the elbow and tugged, attempting to lead him away.

Alar might have growled in frustration. This was a delay he couldn't afford. He only had a few hours to find Daeya and explain things before they were supposed to meet Rammie's contact. Delaying the others' escape risked not only their safety, but Jessie's and Orowen's health as well. Mage's Folly had claimed the priestess's strength. Orowen would have no magic for several weeks. Both women needed the care of other healers, and while finding one for Jessie wouldn't be difficult, there were only a few healers in Eidosinia willing to help Syljians.

The entrance was right behind him. A breeze ruffled his robe as one door opened and closed. Every instinct urged him to run. Perhaps if he claimed to have forgotten something outside. Maybe he'd left a book—or worse, his saphyrum—at a nearby tavern. But Reedy's pull was too insistent. Tearing his arm away and bolting would end badly with this many mages around him. So, he allowed himself to be led toward the viper's pit.

When the sorcerer realized Faustus was following him without resistance, he released his sleeve and quickened his pace. They journeyed in silence toward the commissary and the stairs while Alar turned over the last twenty-four hours in his mind, searching for mistakes he might have made that would have attracted the Councilor's interest. Gregory was usually too busy to meet with Faustus personally. He normally sent Daeya to speak with him over trivial matters, like failing a test or forgetting to file an excusal—

Icy dread ripped through him. His own words clanged through his mind. *Assuming she lived through the collapse.*

Alar stopped and turned back, staring down the row of arch-paned windows and doors, past the sunlit rotunda, and into the haze that cloaked the west wing. He recalled Lucinna's disquiet and the grimness set like stone in Reedy's face.

What if Daeya *hadn't* lived through the collapse?

He'd voiced the possibility earlier only as an attempt at nonchalance, but Daeya would have been in Aetherial Elements III around that time. It was her last class before departing for the Guild nursery every Mirasday afternoon.

That class was hosted on the ground floor, near the center of the west wing. He spun back to the sorcerer.

"Is Daeya alright?" he blurted out. He didn't bother to elaborate further. Everyone knew Daeya McVen.

Not that he should care if she was okay. She wasn't really his friend. As Faustus, he only kept her close to get the protection a troublesome girl could offer. Most people made concessions for Faustus because they believed Daeya made his life difficult. They saw her endless pranks and sharp wit as a source of constant stress, and so his failures were often overlooked. They blamed the rest on Daeya herself.

Reedy paused halfway up the first flight of stairs. His ears flattened. "She's fine."

Even as clipped, as *disappointed*, as the sorcerer sounded, the tension in Alar's gut uncoiled, and he released the breath he'd been holding. *Just keeping up appearances.* Of course Faustus would be relieved. It was nothing more than that.

"I take it you haven't heard," Reedy went on, tilting his head. "She got promoted yesterday."

Alar blinked. "She did?" That was what her meeting with Gregory must have been about. It also explained why Normos Beck had been so agitated. His days as Gregory's right hand were numbered now. "That's great news."

He hoped the joy he mustered sounded genuine, because in truth it was anything *but* great news. Daeya's time as a student was split between classes, studying, and attending tasks of her choice. He'd been counting on knowing her schedule if he couldn't find her in her room. Even if classes were interrupted, her other activities allowed for plenty of chances to catch her alone. As a mage, her time would be subject to the Councilor's whims, leaving little slack in her lead for anything else. Unless he caught her between errands, it was going to be easier to extract an infected tooth than Gregory's newest pet sorceress.

Reedy made a face. Clearly, he wasn't happy with her promotion either. Few mages would be, considering most didn't obtain the rank until their mid-twenties, and Daeya's promotion at only sixteen made them all look bad. The sorcerer said nothing, however. He made an impatient gesture with his chin before continuing up the stairs. Alar followed a few steps behind.

If Daeya had been promoted, Faustus would have to be assigned a new mentor. It was possible this meeting was only that. But a simple reassignment didn't align at all with Lucinna and Reedy's reactions to his appearance. Unless Lucinna was supposed to be his new mentor, and the prospect upset her that much. The thought nearly provoked a smirk.

No, it was more likely Gregory had been notified that he hadn't filed an excusal for missing his classes, and the Councilor wanted a full accounting of his activities to absolve him of any part in the collapse. It looked bad for him, disappearing the very day his classrooms were reduced to dust, as if he'd had some prior knowledge of the aethermancers' plans—

Wastelands.

What if Gregory was setting him up? He could easily spin the lowly Faustus Crex into the Guild's web of lies surrounding their escape. He could use him to prove the collapse was premeditated, completely covering up the Guild's part in it. Or—

Bleeding, cursed Wastelands.

What if Gregory was onto him? What if he'd guessed at his involvement with the Alliaansi?

But how? None of the mages in the dungeon had recognized him. Surely skipping class on a single unfortunate day couldn't have tipped him off. To make that sort of connection, Gregory must have been watching him for some time, scrutinizing his every move—

The realization knocked the breath from him.

Daeya.

Daeya had rarely left his side these past eight months. The nightly tutoring sessions, the dogged determination to meet him for every meal, her sob story over Gregory's attention... it had all made him feel at ease with her. Even the block on her mind had played a part. Not only had it shielded her motives from him, it had lured him into her web like a weaver spider's sweet thread attracted fruit gnats.

She'd known about Cheralach. She'd baited him with that knowledge. That meant she knew what the Guild was doing to his people in that dungeon. When she'd suggested they go meet Cheralach, she might have even led him down there to watch him be mutilated.

Alar had hoped that spark of rebellion in her might work to the Alliaansi's advantage. He had hoped it might be enough to kindle a flame and convince her to join their cause. Instead, he'd let his feelings for her interfere with his mission.

She was supposed to be different—

He didn't allow himself to finish that thought. This was not Trivvix. He refused to liken the sting of Leah's betrayal to what he was feeling now. Daeya had played her part admirably, making him believe for a moment that any goodness could exist in an order as foul as the Sorcerers' Guild. She deserved her promotion. Without a doubt, she had earned it for her masterful deception of him.

Reedy turned east when he reached the second floor and continued on toward Gregory's office. Alar took care not to step on the little mage's trailing robe.

He pushed his bitter thoughts aside and forced himself to calm. Cheralach's visions be damned. They were no more than the delusions of an aging mind. Alar certainly didn't believe Daeya's fate was tied to the Alliaansi. Even if he saw merit in removing a powerful sorceress from Guild hands, he couldn't do it if they arrested him in Gregory's office.

He was walking into a trap. He needed to stop this confrontation and get out of the Towers immediately.

He took a quick inventory of his surroundings, searching for something that could cause a distraction. The bank of windows on his right faced south and overlooked the mage-littered square. Several shorter hallways on his left led to more rooms and a second, longer corridor. A steady stream of students and instructors filled the space. Acolytes and older initiates toted boxes, chairs, and desks down the wide hallway, helping their gold- and red-robed instructors convert the east wing's office spaces and conference rooms into classrooms.

There were plenty of options. One strategically placed tumble and the entire wing would stir like fly-infested carrion. The ensuing chaos would allow Alar to slip down a smaller corridor and flee out a north-facing window.

A curt Cintoshi voice rose above the din. "Mr. Bennick, do not jostle my mirrors!"

The students all around Tom Bennick shied from that voice, forming a bubble around the blue-clad acolyte. Reedy slowed, hesitating, and even Alar straightened at the sound.

Mardis Ulrich's every word rang with distaste. She stepped into view perhaps thirty spans down the hallway, heading toward them. Her dark braids tumbled down the back of her red robe, swinging with every step as she hounded Tom down the corridor.

"Sorry, Master," Tom mumbled. He hefted the wooden box in his arms, earning another growl from the Divinations Master.

Alar fought the urge to grin. Nothing good ever came from the master instructor's anger, and she protected her trove of magical items like the dragons of legends past. He could use that to his advantage.

"Miss Stans," Ulrich said to a human in initiate gray. "Get the door for Mr. Bennick."

The girl—Mouse, Alar named her, for her mousy brown hair and nervous demeanor—scurried to obey as Tom and Master Ulrich approached a room on Alar's left. Twenty spans between them now, and perhaps ten spans from Mouse.

Reedy seemed to have recovered from the instructor's unnerving appearance. He picked up his pace again and shot Alar a scathing look. "Hurry up. I haven't got all day."

Alar complied while addressing the finer details of what he was about to do. A smaller corridor split off beside the room where Mouse waited. Students bustled around her, carrying other items. The open door she held would block their view of Tom. It was the perfect place for a mishap.

He slowed his steps to better time his escape with Tom's approach. Reedy didn't seem to notice. When the mouth of the corridor came up on Alar's left, Tom was five spans from the door with Ulrich nipping at his heels. Alar focused on the box in Tom's arms, the way it shifted and swayed as he walked. With his eyes trained on the object, he subtly *pushed* it downward.

The power of his mind became gravity itself. Tom labored with the box, suddenly grown too heavy for him to handle.

Alar *tugged* it to the side just as a gold-robed instructor rounded the door. Mouse squeaked a warning too late, and the instructor collided with the corner of the box. Tom's face twisted with horror as both he and his burden crashed to the floor.

One side of the box exploded, spilling its contents into the hallway. Students leaped backward, some too slow to avoid stepping on and shattering the delicate scrying mirrors. Reflective shards caught the sunlight and skittered across polished white tile.

Ulrich swore a stream in Cintoshi. "Tiior's torment, Mr. Bennick, have you no grace at all? No, no, don't try to pick them up. Fetch a broom, now. I'll see to the globes myself. By all the gods, I've never..."

Alar didn't stick around to hear the rest. While his Feridian escort and the students gaped at the wealth of broken mirrors, he slipped down the narrow corridor.

Having memorized the layout of this entire building months ago, he knew exactly where his best chances for escape would be on every floor. He made for the closest maintenance closet on the north side first. If it was occupied, there was another storage room closer to Gregory's office he could try.

There was a rare break in the crowd as he passed a windowless closet on his right. The door was slightly ajar, but the room beyond it was dark inside. He made to steer around it.

A hand shot out, clamped around his arm, and hauled him into the closet. He caught a flash of red robes and brown braids before the door snapped shut and locked behind him.

"What—"

"Shh!"

Alar was so stunned that he obeyed and fell silent. He righted himself on a nearby shelf and then simply stood in the darkness, heart pounding. For several moments, there was only the sound of his breathing.

The hand on his arm loosened, but didn't let go.

"Who—"

The hand tightened again. "If you value your life, Mr. Crex," Master Ulrich whispered, "be silent."

Surprise didn't cover the extent of it. There were so many questions burgeoning at the tip of Alar's tongue that it was a miracle he heeded the instructor's warning.

One question, at least, was easy enough to answer while he pondered this new and unexpected ally—if that was indeed what she was. The little room stank of Aether, which meant Ulrich had used magic to get inside. She must know the Towers well enough to Rift Bend blindly, despite its risk. It was the only way she could have gotten here from the hallway so fast.

He took a calming breath, and another, and another, until he had mastered himself once more. He was in a closet with the Divinations Master for a reason. All would be made clear soon enough. He just had to be patient.

Voices came from down the corridor.

"I don't know how he got past me," Reedy said.

"Idiot," Normos Beck snapped.

Alar gritted his teeth, though a shadow of fatigue echoed in his bones. He still wasn't fully recovered from the fight yesterday, and he could do without crossing paths with Normos right now. Glancing aside to Master Ulrich, whom he could make out now in the sliver of light from under the door, he supposed he owed her thanks for sparing him from that unpleasant experience.

"Your wards are weak," Gregory's right hand continued. "He probably touched your mind."

So, they knew what he was. The confirmation might have been more harrowing if he didn't find Normos's words so offensive. He hadn't even used psionics on Reedy. Leave it to the sorcerers to believe they couldn't be tricked by good, old-fashioned guile.

Alar shifted on his feet. Master Ulrich's grip tightened a third time—a silent command to be still.

"He can't have gotten far." Reedy's voice grew louder as they approached the door.

"Send for the Enlightened. I want Paladins on every floor." As the sound of their footsteps retreated, heading north, Normos growled, "We're going to find that blanker if it takes the entire Church."

Indeed, Alar vowed it would. His lip curled at the thought of the Light Paladins. It was they who had hunted his family down outside Trivvix after Leah sold him out to the town constable. They could track Syljians through aura tracing, using the imprint his people left on the Aetherial Wall like footprints in the sand. Fortunately, the skill relied on multiple factors that could be obscured by heavy magic use, the presence of other powerful arcanists, and his own ability to dampen his aura. Knowing how to escape the Church's zealous Paladins was one of the first skills his mentor Ashaara had taught him.

When they were gone, Ulrich let out a sigh beside him.

"*Luminos*," she incanted, and the room filled with soft light. Shelves full of cleaning supplies, waxes, polishes, and oils sprang from the darkness. Ulrich muted the bead's glow with her fist, tinting it red as it passed through her fingers. Her expression was stern, and her beard cast soft shadows on her neck. "You shouldn't have come back."

He fought the urge to roll his eyes. "It's a little late for that, don't you think?" Faustus would have never spoken to her that way, but they were beyond such games at this point, and he was in no mood to be lectured.

If she was taken aback by his boldness, she didn't show it. Short as she was, she had to crane her neck to look up at him. "Just as well. I have need of you, Mr. Crex."

Alar chuckled. "I'm flattered, Master, but I'm afraid you aren't my type."

Ulrich didn't smile. The wrinkles around her mouth only deepened. "I would not be laughing if I were you. Every other escape attempt I've Foreseen ends with you hanging from your neck in the gallows."

Alar immediately sobered. While he put little stock in divine prophecies and visions, Foresight was another matter. It was the rarest gift among arcanists, and a talented seer who could sort through multiple futures was rarer still. Tipori, the Alliaansi's strongest Aetherian, and his daughter Riisii were the only other people Alar knew who possessed the ability. They could predict events with unnerving accuracy, even weeks or months into the future. If Ulrich's skills were anything like theirs, Alar would take it seriously.

"You know what I am." He regarded her coolly. "Why would you help me?"

"As I said, I have need of you." She reached into a pocket and withdrew a small scroll tied with a red ribbon. "I need you to deliver this to a man in Orthovia. A man named Vortanis."

"You want me to play messenger boy for you?"

Her eyebrows lifted in challenge, her spine as straight and unyielding as steel. "In exchange for your life, yes."

Just when he'd thought his situation couldn't get any more ludicrous. There was no way he was going to Orthovia for a sorceress. Still, he was tempted. Ulrich was offering a way out that didn't involve more risk to himself. Once he was beyond the city walls, there was nothing to ensure he kept to such an arrangement. He could simply agree to her task and leave for Starlight with the rest of his companions.

"Alright." He reached for the scroll.

She placed it in his hand, but didn't let go. Her dark eyes searched his. "Do not open it."

"I won't." He was absolutely going to open it.

Ulrich relinquished the scroll, satisfied by the earnest look he forged to hide his amusement. She bent down to retrieve a small satchel from the floor. "And don't wait until fifth bell. The thief you're going to meet will betray you." She pressed the satchel into his abdomen.

A chill shot down Alar's spine. His free hand closed numbly on the satchel. "How did you—"

Ulrich didn't let him finish. "The reward for your heads proves too tempting." Her words were brisk as the autumn breeze. "Two hours from now, take the Southgate tunnel under the wall."

Alar opened his mouth, but no sound came out. The Guild was *not* supposed to know about that tunnel. It was the same tunnel Jack and the Riverdale sisters used to smuggle goods in and out of the capital.

"The guards will be distracted long enough for you to flee into the forest. There is a woman there who can help your friends. Just don't harm the bird."

"What bird—?"

Ulrich shushed him again. Her bead winked out as she began to cast from it, shaping the sigil for a Rift Bend. The sigil seared the darkness, a trail of white-violet light at her fingertips. She slashed through it with the blade of her hand, cleaving a man-sized hole in the Wall. It blotted out the back of the little closet like ink pooling on parchment.

Alar sidestepped her attempt to grab his arm and pull him into that Aetherial darkness. He bumped into several cans of paint on a shelf close by. The rusty, metallic taste of Aether coated his tongue, and a wave of nausea from memories too fresh had him grappling for purchase on the door and shelves. He fought for breath as his clothes and hair whipped toward the rift.

Somewhere in that whistling void, he would have sworn he could hear Val screaming.

He seized control of his breathing, in through his nose and out through his mouth, ignoring the hammering of his heart. He refused to see Val's face sinking into the Aether beside him. Instead, he focused on getting help for Orowen and Jessie.

"How do I find the woman?" he asked.

The whites of Ulrich's eyes reflected the shimmering violet light emanating from the rift. She extended a hand. "You don't."

Alar forced himself to nod, the static hum of the rift vibrating the jugs and jars around them. In close quarters, it was nearly unbearable. He tucked the scroll away and shouldered the satchel, taking care not to knock the cans of polish and tubs of wax off the shelves. He would consider Ulrich's motives and whether to trust her directions later. Right now, he had little choice but to go with her. He just hoped there wasn't a prison cell on the other side.

His hand closed around hers, and she pulled him into the void.

Chapter Twenty

Daeya

"And then we adjust the aft sails with this rigging here when we want to correct our course back to starboard," Belio said.

Daeya held her hair back while she listened, squinting up at the ship's sails through a web of ropes and knots. Bright sunlight reflected off the white cloth, which was stretched tightly in the blustery headwind. "So you zigzag back and forth across the ocean. That's how you sail into the wind?"

Belio's face lit up. "That's right! It's called tacking."

"But the ship is still going sideways." She frowned. "How does it not tip over?"

"Ah!" Belio held up a dirty, callused finger. "Because of the keel."

He demonstrated the shape of the keel mounted against the bottom of the ship with the blades of his hands. His kohl-black hair whipped around him in a tangle, sticking to his teeth as he grinned. "It extends below the sea. The water pushes against the keel as it tacks, acting in counterpoint to the sails."

"That's really clever." The rugged sailor was so eager to share his knowledge that Daeya couldn't help but grin in return. "You must really love to sail."

He flashed her another smile that was all teeth and looked out upon the white-capped waves. They piled atop one another all the way to the horizon. "It's as close to flying as a man could ever dream."

Daeya followed his gaze across the starboard side of the ship, toward the small, puffy clouds that floated like cottonwood plumes in the distance. It was like she could see all the way to the lands of Duerguard beyond.

She'd dreamed of flying last night. Sometime between Cam's departure and dawn, she'd closed her eyes and imagined herself in a time, centuries ago, before the last of the dragons had surrendered the skies and perished from the world. As the wind slashed at her clothes and snapped at her hair, the ship had faded away, replaced by a great, fire-breathing beast that flew above the clouds.

It was a vision she had often—a vivid one, even while waking—in which she could feel the bite of hardened spines against her thighs, the heat and strength of golden scales beneath her hands.

"What about you?" Belio asked, drawing her back to the present. "What do you dream of?"

Daeya looked up into his face, noting the way his eyes mirrored the teal-blue of the sea. Her cheeks flushed at the intensity in his gaze. "Nothing, really."

The lie tasted sour on her tongue, but Belio was the first sailor who'd bothered to say more than a few words to her since she'd set foot on the ship. His company helped distract her from her thoughts of the atrocity back home. The last thing she wanted to do was chase him off by telling him about her crazy dreams.

Belio lifted an eyebrow, disbelieving. "Something draws away your thoughts. I would like to hear about it."

Daeya studied him as he reached up to inspect a fray in the rope tied to the aftmost mast—the mizzenmast, he'd called it. Belio was handsome in the sort of roughshod way no mage or acolyte could ever be. His skin was weathered and tanned from his days in the sun. Like many of the sailors, he went without a shirt, and his muscled chest and abdomen were slick with salty mist. His sable trousers hung loosely around his hips and grew progressively darker below the knee, as if the grit and grime on the ship had a mind to creep up his clothes. A tattoo of swirling lines and complex shapes cascaded over one shoulder and down his left pectoral.

She wanted to ask him what the tattoo meant, but he kept glancing her way, expecting an answer to his question, even as he climbed partway up the mast and tagged the frayed rope with a bright red sash. Marking it for replacement, no doubt.

He dropped back down to the deck and wiped his hands on his trousers. More dirt. More grime. Daeya could smell it on him, the mixture of soil and sweat—the scent of good, honest work.

"Well?" The corners of his mouth turned upward. "Don't tell me you're speechless now. You've been asking questions all morning."

Color heated her cheeks further. It was true; she had gone below deck only to shed her mage's robe as the early morning warmed beyond her tolerance for the double layer of sleeves. She'd kept her usual high-collared white shirt to hide her runes and traded the robe for a simple brown vest fashioned with pockets stitched along its front. After breaking her fast alone on the main deck, she had spotted Belio climbing the ratlines with the sun and found a seat on a barrel to watch him work. Much to her surprise, *he* had engaged *her* in conversation when he noticed her there. He hadn't shied from her first few questions about the ship, and before she knew it, they were eating lunch over his explanation of various sails and their purposes.

"Alright, I'll tell you, but you can't laugh," she said.

Belio nodded seriously, but merriment still flitted about his face like light on the waves. "Sailor's honor." He pounded his fist twice against his chest.

The display made the other sailors around them snicker and gesture suggestively among themselves. Daeya narrowed her eyes at them with mock severity. They hurriedly went back to their business.

"It seems your fellow sailors don't think much about your honor."

"They're just jealous because I hold the attention of the prettiest maiden on board, and they don't."

Daeya laughed, and Belio grinned again. She wasn't naïve enough to miss the hunger present in that look. *Da would flay him alive.* "Certainly, a noble sailor such as yourself has nothing more nefarious in mind."

He bowed at the waist with a flourish. Despite the grime on his pants and the hand still wrapped in the rigging of a nearby sail, his gesture was so unabashedly flamboyant that Daeya laughed again.

"Milady, I assure you," the scoundrel purred, offering his arm to her, "I only seek the chaste pleasure of your company."

"Like a child seeks only a sniff at the cookies in a jar." She placed her hand in the crook of his elbow and allowed him to lead her to his next station. "Mira forbid you be left unattended."

"Fine, fine, point taken. But you still haven't answered my question." When she shot a pointed look at him, he added, "I won't laugh, I promise."

He seated her on another barrel and returned to his rigging. Daeya considered her response while he knotted the trailing end of a rope on the yardarm overhead. She wouldn't tell him about the dragon, but telling him what she thought the dream represented couldn't hurt. The flight, the stars, the wind all held meaning.

"I dream of freedom."

He'd climbed partway up the shrouds to reach another set of ropes and now looked down at her from above. "Freedom?"

She nodded.

Belio frowned. "But you aren't a slave."

Daeya fidgeted with the hem of her sleeve. How could she explain her thoughts to him in a way that made sense? Of course her experiences didn't rival those of actual slaves, like those who dwelled in Rillion across the sea. But she lived in a prison nonetheless, its bars gilded and warded by the very magic that should have set her free. At times, there was no price she wouldn't pay to be rid of it—to be normal like her father, like Murtagh and Belio, who lived fulfilling lives doing the mundane work they loved.

"No." She scratched absently at the back of her neck. "But freedom to choose where I go and what I do, without having to answer to others."

Belio paused in his inspection of the rigging. The ropes creaked under his weight. "Now that, I can understand."

Her brows furrowed. "What do you mean? You have one of the best jobs. You get to see ports all over the world."

"Ah, but not ports of my choosing." Belio climbed higher, the shrouds swaying with the wind. "Captain Arnes makes those decisions for me."

Daeya squinted up at him through the glare of sails, bracing herself against the barrel with one hand. "Perhaps one day you'll have your own ship. Your own crew."

"Aye, if only a man had coin for such a thing."

"Arnes pays you well, doesn't he?"

"Better than most. At least, that's what I hear."

Belio finished his work and climbed back down, dropping the last few spans to the deck. There was a new smudge of dirt on his stubbled cheek. Daeya withdrew a kerchief from one of her many pockets and passed it to him, pointing to her own face where he should wipe himself.

Belio took the kerchief with another extravagant bow. "Many thanks, milady." He scrubbed at his face, smearing the greasy dirt more than removing it.

Daeya slid off the barrel, boots thudding on the deck. "If it's something you want, I think you should pursue it. Start setting the coin aside now, rather than wasting it on cards or dice."

"But I *like* gambling." He drew out the words in a whine of protest. Grime streaked the kerchief, but he folded it neatly and handed it back to her. The light in his sea-blue eyes guttered. "Besides, I'd have to save for lifetimes."

Tucking the kerchief away, Daeya took his arm once more. He steered her toward the bow, and she let the matter drop.

"Freedom to choose, eh?" Belio asked. "Say you had such a thing. What would you do with it?"

A good question. If she hadn't been born with magic, Daeya would have been a blacksmith like her father. But as her powers grew and her tethers to the Guild tightened, the only dream she'd nurtured since childhood was her desire to see the world.

"Perhaps I'd become a sailor, too."

A low, rumbling laugh answered her. Belio swept a hand across the ship to the sailors attending to their various tasks. "It's awfully hard work."

Daeya took in the sight of the men and women, how their busy, callused hands set about repairing sails, scrubbing boards, hauling lines, and checking pulleys. It was demanding work, yes, but the sailors seemed in good spirits. They likely slept well after the long, grueling days at sea. There was something invaluable about nights when both body and mind fell into such exhausted sleep that they left little room for nightmares.

"Not many chances for a bath, either." He elbowed her gently and wrinkled his nose as if his own scent offended him. "You sure you'd want to throw in with a smelly lot like this?"

She scoffed. "I don't mind the smell."

Belio's sure steps faltered. Somewhere ahead of them, a bell rang out. It struck five times, signaling both the time of day and the shift change. He turned to face her. "Really?"

"Really."

He tilted his head, brows knitting together. All around them, sailors roused themselves from their work and chatter filled the air. "You know, I didn't think to ask what it is you do for a living."

A shadow moved in Daeya's periphery. Even as he spoke, her focus slid from Belio to the glint of golden curls. Cam stepped into the sunlight, her lips a thin, grave line. The edges of her black robe snapped in the wind.

Belio fell silent. In fact, the entire ship seemed to fall under a spell of silence at the sorceress's approach.

"Daeya," Cam said in greeting. Her blue eyes flicked toward Belio before resettling on her. "Toby's received word from Ryost. You are needed."

Belio released her arm like Daeya had burned him. His salt-chapped lips parted, looking between her and Cam as if they had transformed into Nohri blood wraiths. "You're one of them."

Daeya frowned as Belio sidled away from her. He stammered an apology—for what, she didn't know—and was gone seconds later, disappearing among the ropes, wood, and canvas.

What in the world...

Tearing her gaze from his retreating back, she looked around at the other sailors, who tiptoed around them as if they feared so much as stepping on their shadows. Her chest grew painfully tight.

Cam tossed a glance in Belio's direction, clasping her hands before her. "He's handsome."

Daeya's throat constricted. Despite Cam's attempt to lighten the mood, the tension squeezing her lungs didn't abate. Belio hadn't known she was with them. That was why he deigned to speak with her at all. He hadn't associated her with Joss, who'd been making a total arse of himself by belittling the sailors and bullying Captain Arnes. Now that Belio was aware of her affiliation, it was likely he wouldn't speak to her again.

Cam's expression softened. She moved to Daeya's side and placed a hand on her lower back. "Come on. Best not keep them waiting."

Toby Vika's too-long face pinched into a scowl.

Daeya crossed her arms, glowering at the middle brother, who sat before her at a table bedecked with an array of salted meats, soft cheeses, and colorful fruit. Even if their own journey was a mere three to five days, it was an absurd display of decadence while the rest of the passengers lived on jerky and bread.

Joss sat next to him, leaning back on two legs of his chair. He crossed his ankles over one corner of the tabletop and rested an elbow beside an open bottle of wine. The sound of his chewing on a bright red apple made a muscle in Daeya's jaw twitch. She did her best not to look at his slovenly form, even as his eyes raked over her body.

"They can forget it," Daeya said.

Toby's lip curled upward, revealing square teeth too large for his mouth. His pin-straight hair framed parchment-thin cheeks. "You will do as the Council decrees, whether you agree with it or not."

She shook her head, setting her feet apart and balancing her weight, preparing to ride out this storm. "No. It's wrong. *They* are wrong. Who voted for this madness? Surely Gregory didn't."

Behind her, Cameron sighed. Daeya's eyes flicked toward the older sorceress as she sat heavily on one of two cots flanking a bed box set into the wall. The cot was topped with blankets so soft that Cam's hands sank entirely from view.

Joss bit into the apple with a resounding crunch.

"Gregory proposed the decree," Toby drawled, "and the vote was unanimous."

The decree in question had been issued an hour ago, delivered to Toby through one of the Guild's Conduits—mages who could relay messages to those with the same skill through the Aether. It stated that any person known or suspected to be working for the Alliaansi could be apprehended by any means necessary, up to and including the use of arcane force on those without magic.

Searing acid filled Daeya's stomach. Such a decree went against the most basic of Guild principles—the very reason the magi had brought their power to bear against the followers of Noven Ivaeys during the Great Schism. Magus Ivaeys had used his magic to maim and murder his wife—a non-adept and the youngest daughter of King Eioden, for whom Eidosinia was later named. Her murder had precipitated the deadliest war to take place on Dessian soil in over a millennium. Millions had died. No place on Dessos was safe. The resulting fear the non-adepts had of even the magi who fought for them had turned allies into enemies. The only way the magi could staunch the blood flow was to make a promise.

A promise that no mage would ever use magic on those who could not use it themselves. With that promise came the assurance of only self-destruction, should a war between magic adepts ever be fought again.

Daeya clenched her fists. She could not abide this, not even for Alliaansi dogs. "This is ridiculous. I will *not* harm non-adepts with my magic. It's barbaric—"

Toby huffed a laugh. "Barbaric? What's barbaric is the way the aethermancers attacked us in our own classrooms, bringing the very stone we hold sacred down upon our heads." He rose to his feet, bracing his hands on the table. "You would defy this decree and see them revel in our cowardice, rather than tremble at our power?"

"They are not the only ones who would tremble. Our own people will fear us." Why couldn't he understand how disastrous this would be?

Joss waved his half-eaten apple in a languid gesture of dismissal. "To fear us is to respect us."

Daeya's horror and disgust only seemed to amuse him. He brought the apple to his mouth with a self-satisfied smirk, his dark eyes gleaming in the light from the saphyrum lantern on the table.

She struggled to keep her voice even. To let it break would be to widen the cracks in her composure—to let the stinging hurt behind her eyes become full-fledged tears. How could Gregory do this? How could any of them not see? "To fear us is to turn from us. If we follow this path, we will become no better than the aethermancers."

"The point is to find the scum responsible and prevent others from suffering at their hands." Toby straightened, stepping around the table. Daeya kept her feet rooted to the spot. "Do you not think they would use our own reticence against us? Take hostages? Fortify their position with non-adepts so we couldn't attack it except with common soldiers?"

"It's the first step in declaring war, Daeya," Cam said. "In seeking vengeance."

Daeya whirled on her. The resignation with which Cam spoke cracked something vital in her chest. "You mean you agree with this?"

There was guilt in Cam's expression when their eyes met, but it morphed into something darker. Something colder and more deadly, like the icy spheres she wielded in elemental combat. *For Killian,* the look seemed to say.

"Of course she does." Toby stepped into her space. He was so close Daeya could smell the sweetness of Feridian oranges on his breath. "She is not a child blinded by pretty idealism."

The insult struck home, rendering her mute for a beat too long.

Joss cackled at her floundering and tossed the apple core onto a pile of scraps beside the lantern. He uncrossed his ankles and rose, straightening the front of his black tunic with a deft swipe of his hands. His swagger was nothing short of predatory as he closed the distance between them. Daeya could feel the menacing intent crackling off him. He smiled as she ceded a single, involuntary step backward.

"Speaking of blindness," Joss said, his voice slithering around her ears, "shall I tell her the rest, Toby? About how Gregory is very unhappy with her?"

Toby sneered. "By all means."

Daeya shifted her stance so she could keep them both in her sights, acutely aware of the only door to the room at her back. She tried to swallow, but her mouth went desert dry. "Let me guess," she said, lifting her chin and injecting as much venom into her voice as she could. "Someone finally found what was causing the rotten fish smell in Councilor Tallion's office."

But no, this wasn't about any of the harmless pranks Gregory let her get away with. Whatever it was, it was making Toby positively gleeful.

Joss slipped his hands into his pockets. "Turns out your little friend Faustus was an Alliaansi spy," he said. "And you, dear Daeya, missed all the signs."

Her stomach hit the floor.

No.

She'd left Gregory the note about her suspicions, but she had still held on to the hope there was another explanation for Faustus's disappearance. "I—"

She had been wrong. So incredibly wrong.

The note would have come too late to make any difference. Faustus had spent eight months by her side. He'd endured eight months of the Councilor's subtle tests—tests Gregory had trusted her to carry out—and she had failed to recognize him for what he was. She'd ignored all the little things Faustus did that should have sent up saphyric flares. If she had discovered him sooner, she could have stopped him.

She could have foiled the attack.

The weight of the realization nearly drove her to her knees. She dared not look at Cam, lest she see the accusation in her eyes.

Joss leaned in, and Daeya recoiled. Snakes writhed in her stomach as he reached up to brush her white-blonde hair behind her ear. "It seems to me, *my sweet*"—he hissed the term of endearment, mimicking Gregory's accented 'v' sound in place of the 'w'—"that you are to blame for what happened."

Tears stung her eyes. She bit down on her lip so hard she tasted blood. Crying was *not* an option. She tried to spin for the door to hide her shame, but Joss caught her by the shoulder, holding her in place. The promise of violence in his touch ripped the sob from her chest.

"I'd start praying to the gods if I were you."

Just watch out for Joss, alright? Cam's warning rang loud in Daeya's ears as she stared into that hate-filled gaze. *I'm afraid he's out for blood.*

Joss stroked his thumb through the tear sliding down her left cheek. The smile on his lips was a mockery of tenderness. "When word of this gets out, only they can save you."

Chapter Twenty-One

Magnus

They don't trust you, the voice whispered. *How could they?*

Magnus pressed his hands over his ears, trying to block out the sound. His fingers threaded into his hair. Sweat beaded on his brows, his neck, his chest.

Even Cheralach didn't trust you. He was right not to.

"Stop. *Please.*" His ravaged throat burned as he hissed the words into the silence. He had hoped removing himself from the others, retreating from the main cellar to the tiny, dust-filled room under the stairs, would bring him some respite.

You would have spilled all his precious secrets to the sorcerers just to make them stop.

The voice spoke louder than ever. It was not his own voice, nor was it Nicolas's. It was someone else, some*thing* else, that tormented him.

Each time he tried to rise from the dusty floor, each time he tried to return to his friends, he found he couldn't. His body shook with the strain of remaining upright, and he couldn't keep his feet. He was clenching his jaw so tightly he might have cracked his teeth. Every ragged breath was made of shards of glass. His eye—gods, his eye *hurt*. If he could just stop the pain—

You don't have what it takes to lead them.

"Stop, stop, *stop*!"

He couldn't let his people see him like this. They all expected him to take Cheralach's place—to be as strong and implacable as the legend himself. They would never follow him if they saw the trembling wretch he'd become.

I can help you.

This time the voice was a gentle caress, like a cool hand placed on the back of his sweltering neck. Magnus stilled. He looked up, scanning the room, as if he expected to see someone standing there.

There was no one. His only company was the single lantern at his feet and the dusty crates and boxes piled to the joists around him. For long moments, there was only the sound of his own raspy breathing. Yet a subtle change in the air prickled the hair on his arms and legs.

"Who—" Magnus coughed, tensing at the stab of pain. The presence waited. Wheezing, Magnus scanned the room again. "Who are you? Show yourself."

There was no response.

Seated on a crate beneath the jewelry shop, Alar groaned to himself and rubbed his temples. The scroll Mardis Ulrich had given him rested in his lap, its neatly flowing script illuminated by tallow candles. He had to hand it to the old witch: she truly was a master of her craft. He'd already read the scroll a few times, marveling at just how much of his future she had Seen.

'Mr. Crex,' it began. *'Thank you for remaining consistent in your inability to follow directions. It is a wonder you ever passed a single test in my class.'*

Her jab had caught him off-guard the first time through, and he'd laughed aloud.

'Fortunately, this message is not for Vortanis. It is for you.'

Of course it was. How silly of him to think otherwise.

Sandwiched between that line and the next, she'd written in smaller script, *'It is shameful you didn't bother to ask for a description of the man before running off. What kind of spies are the Alliaansi sending these days?'*

It made him wonder how long she had known. Why hadn't she reported him to the Guild Council? Neither Ashaara nor Koraani had informed him of other Alliaansi agents secreted away in Ryost. Koraani wouldn't want to risk his other spies being compromised if one of them was discovered and interrogated.

'I would apologize for my deception,' the scroll continued, *'if I didn't suspect you planned to renege on our arrangement.'*

She had him there.

'I must caution you against such action. You must go to Orthovia and find Daeya McVen. She is no longer safe in Eidosinia. Take her north with you and see that she never returns.'

She signed it with her initials. *'MU.'*

"Well," Kendi said, having read the scroll a few moments earlier, "it seems there is something to Cheralach's visions."

He sat on a barrel beside Orowen and Ravlok, running a whetstone over his stolen sword. The gentle rasp of the stone along the blade's edge appeared to have soothed the rest of the warriors to sleep. Anwic and Rylan dozed on the floor next to Sam, who slept with her head propped against Jessie's pallet of worn blankets. Magnus had retreated into the tiny room under the stairs. Only Jack, Ravlok, and Kendi had been present and alert when Alar returned.

Kendi turned the blade over to work the other side. Metal caught the candlelight and reflected a stripe of gold across his face. "The seer didn't tell you more about the danger the girl might face?"

Alar shook his head. "She didn't say anything about her." Likely because she knew he would have refused her task otherwise. He didn't explain to the others how Daeya had blindsided him. Since no one was likely to trust her anyway, he planned to keep that little detail to himself.

"I don't see how she's our problem," Jack groused from the base of the stairs. The Ryostian thief had picked the spot strategically, as Val had taught him. From there he could likely see all the way up the stairs at Alar's back, with a clear view of the cellar door at the top. The small crossbow strapped to his arm was loaded and trained on the floor. It would take only the smallest movement to greet anyone who came through that door with a bolt to the heart.

Kendi lifted the whetstone from his weapon and rested an elbow against his thigh. "Cheralach saw something in her. Something he was willing to risk everything for."

Alar returned to the scroll while the two continued arguing. He lingered on the last few lines of Ulrich's message, turning them over in his mind: *She is no longer safe in Eidosinia... see that she never returns.* Much as he could sense the teasing reproach in the first part of the scroll, those last words bore a fundamental shift in tone. Ulrich truly believed Daeya was in danger, and the proof of her powers of Foresight was right here in his lap.

What if Ulrich had Seen something that did, in fact, validate Cheralach's visions? What if Daeya somehow changed the outcome of the approaching war?

But Daeya knew about Cheralach.

The thought pained him more than he cared to admit. She'd informed on him while he posed as Faustus, and there was no doubt she had raised the alarm the moment he disappeared. Despite her very convincing performance to the contrary, she'd proved herself to be Gregory's creature.

There was something else, though. Ulrich and Gregory were often at odds with one another. So why would Ulrich care about one of Gregory's most prized students? Did she seek to weaken him by removing his most powerful sorceress? Not that Alar wouldn't mind seeing the old bastard knocked down a few pegs, but the urgency and concern permeating the last few lines of Ulrich's message didn't feel political. They felt personal, and Gregory certainly wouldn't approve of a personal connection between Daeya and Master Ulrich.

Alar was missing something.

"...and I cannot, in good conscience, dismiss the girl outright," Kendi was telling Jack. Though his voice remained neutral, it rang with steel. "It's our duty to help those in need."

Jack stood with feet spread, red-faced and scowling. "She is a *sorceress*—"

I can't believe I'm doing this.

"I'll go to Orthovia," Alar said.

The room fell silent.

He took great care to roll up the scroll as he considered his next words. The parchment chafed beneath his fingers. "Regardless of whether she finds herself in danger, she may be of use to us." Jack opened his mouth to disagree, but Alar held up a hand. "Should she prove untrustworthy, she will still make a valuable hostage."

Ravlok looked up from his vigil over Orowen. He, too, was about to voice his protest when Alar turned to him. "I know she's your friend, but you must make a choice. You're either with us, or you're not." When Ravlok hesitated, Alar let his voice soften. "You know Daeya will make a powerful sorceress. If she stands against us in the coming war, many people will die."

The monk swallowed, jaw twitching, and the creases lining his brow threw stark shadows across his forehead. Then those shadows vanished. "I'm going with you." Ravlok glanced toward Kendi as if seeking the commander's approval. "I know she'll disagree with what the Guild has done. I can help you convince her to join us."

Us.

Alar studied him, tapping into his aura-sense to search for signs of deception. What he found was a halo of stillness surrounding the monk, like the placid waters near the banks of a stream. It could have been exactly as it appeared—quiet resolve—or it could have been a calming technique to disguise Ravlok's true intentions. Alar should have expected as much from a follower of Ordeolas. Without dipping into Ravlok's mind, his control of his emotional state would make him harder to read.

He would concern himself with more invasive psionics later. Ravlok had been invaluable to them in the dungeon yesterday, and he might continue to be so in the weeks and months to come. Alar would not risk offense by entering his mind without permission—at least, not until he was given cause to do so. For now, he greeted Ravlok's fierce declaration with a nod of acceptance.

"If he's going," Jack said, flashing his teeth, "so am I."

The two men glared at each other across the cellar, Jack's hand flexing on his crossbow, Ravlok's fingers curling into fists. They were more likely to kill each other than be of any use in the Old City, but Alar wouldn't turn down extra protection.

"It's settled, then." Kendi's air of authority could have corralled even the most hostile soldiers. "The three of you will go to Orthovia and find the girl. The rest of us will await you in Fawn's Breath."

As Ravlok and Jack murmured their agreement, Alar tucked the scroll away and sighed to himself. It seemed he was going to Orthovia for a sorceress, after all.

Chapter Twenty-Two

Ravlok

"Po's tunnel not rescue service!"

The squat, bald-pated owner of Davy's Tavern shook his finger at Rammie. His thick Rillanese accent obscured much of his broken Eidosinian, and his eyes were largely hidden by a thick slab of flesh that folded three times along his forehead. "Freckles take trouble somewhere else."

Ravlok set Orowen down on a narrow stool and held her steady while she regained her balance. Kendi murmured his thanks and took Orowen's face in his hands, speaking softly in Syljian. She gave him a tired smile, and Ravlok retreated to Rammie's side to give them a sliver of privacy.

The rest of their companions dropped their provisions on the floor, heaving sighs of relief and exhaustion in equal measure. After traveling through a series of cellars and underground tunnels, and then a swift dash aboveground dodging Guild patrols, they'd tumbled through the back door of the tavern and into Po's kitchen.

Alar claimed Rammie's man couldn't be trusted, so their next best option was the old mine shaft that ran under the city wall. It could only be accessed inside the capital by a secret entrance in the cellar of Davy's Tavern. Ravlok remembered it from his time in the thieves' guild. Though he'd never used it himself, the tunnel had been an extraordinary boon to the smugglers when Laerin had finally negotiated with the surly barkeeper for its use.

Rammie—or Freckles, as Po called her—gave the Rillanese man a saccharine smile. It was her signature look, and one to which not even Ravlok was immune. "Come on, Po. I've never known ye to turn down someone in need."

Po's ears reddened. His lips parted as if he were about to relent. Then he huffed and placed his hands on his hips. "Pointy ears bad for business."

"All the better to move them along." Rammie waved toward the back door. "Ye don't want them seen leaving yer fine establishment, do ye?"

Po gaped at Rammie through his mass of sun-weathered wrinkles, lifting his finger again.

The door to the bar room swung open. Nessa Allon, Po's waitress, stopped short in the entryway, balancing a tray of dirty dishes. She stared at them for several seconds, letting the door hit her as it swung closed. Frazzled hair sprawled in a fiery red halo about her head, having come loose from the short braid at her nape. A thick dusting of freckles peppered her nose, and her cheeks were flushed from exertion.

Movement in his periphery sent a jolt of alarm through Ravlok. He glanced aside to find Magnus, Rylan, and Sam forming a defensive wall around Orowen and Jessie. Jack and Anwic loomed in the shadows, reaching into their cloaks, while Alar stepped up on Ravlok's other side.

A molten ball of anxiety settled between Ravlok's shoulder blades. He held up a hand to stay Alar's advance, hoping to prevent any overreaction from plunging the room into chaos.

"Hello, Nessa," he said, attempting a smile.

"Gods be good." Nessa hurried to place her burden down on the sink and swept toward Ravlok, taking him by the shoulders to examine him from head to toe. "What sort of trouble have ye gotten into?"

Ravlok opened his mouth, but she didn't wait for a response. She looked at Rammie, then Alar, and finally at the rest of their ragtag group.

"Laangor have mercy, ye all look a fright." She pulled a towel out of her apron and snapped Po's arm. "Posenka Malik Evalsemahr Naftalli, why didn't ye say we had guests comin'? I'd have prepared more ham 'n' hash."

Po turned a deeper shade of maroon, clutching his arm. "Po not give free food! Needle knows is—"

"Bad for business. Aye, I *kinnich*." Nessa rolled her eyes. "Mira, Shavaan, and Caelyn, ye're worse than me ma."

Alar relaxed beside him. Ravlok spared him a glance and offered a grin. He had spent a lot of silvers in Davy's Tavern over the years, and Nessa and Po were good people. Though Po had the mind of a Rillanese businessman, always looking for ways to profit, he allowed Nessa to temper his tight fists with her tender heart.

Po tapped a finger against his temple. "Needle not think. What if Guild catch pointy ears in kitchen? Po be ruined, and Needle back on street."

Rammie let out a dramatic, shoulder-sagging sigh. "Let them use the tunnel and be gone, then. They won't trouble ye any longer."

Nessa glared at Po. "That's all they're after? And ye kept 'em waitin'?"

If Po's eyes widened any further, Ravlok worried they might fall out of his head. "They just get—"

Her face darkened. "Ye know better than that, ye crotchety old man. Take 'em down to the cellar, and I'll rustle up some food for the road. Why, I've never in all me years seen such a blatant disregard for hospitality." Nessa swept out of the room again, still muttering to herself. The door swished closed behind her.

Relief and amusement settled Ravlok's nerves. He had never asked Nessa about her thoughts on Syljians, but Rammie had assured him the former courtesan wouldn't sell them out to the Guild. It warmed his heart to find she wished them no ill will.

Rammie clapped a hand on his back. "Ye see? Nothing to worry about."

Po crossed his arms. "Pointy ears still pay for tunnel." His narrowed eyes settled on Ravlok. "And Lockpick still owes Po three coppers."

Ravlok's cheeks warmed. Lockpick was the name Po had given him when he'd run with Laerin's crew. The name had stuck even after the botched heist that had landed Ravlok in jail eight years ago, when Yonfé had let him join the monastery as penance. Those three coppers were for the window he'd broken on a night of shameless drinking, shortly before Yonfé added temperance to his monastic studies.

He withdrew the coin purse Rammie had provided. Silonas damn him if he wasn't going to settle the last of that debt before he left.

When he placed a fourth copper in Po's hand, the man blinked and beamed up at him. His fingers closed around the coins, and he cuffed Ravlok on the arm. "Agh, Lockpick not so bad. Have drink on Po next time."

Ravlok snorted. "Water, you mean."

As quickly as it had appeared, the friendliness on Po's face evaporated. "Of course, water. Po not moron."

Rammie held up another small coin purse. "This should cover their passage and the food. Ye can count it if you like."

Po snatched the purse and weighed it in his palm. When his expression turned sour, Ravlok sighed again, pulled out a few more coppers, and looked aside to Rammie. "You really thought you could short him?"

Rammie shrugged. "It was worth a try."

Po slipped the purse and the extra coins under his apron and waved them away with both arms. "Agh! Freckles lucky Po in good mood."

"Wouldn't want to see him in a bad mood," Rylan mumbled under his breath. Sam shushed him with a glare.

Rammie giggled and stepped aside for Po. "Ye should see him over the Solstice. He guards his coffers like a dragon."

Po ignored them and made for a storage area behind Orowen and Kendi. With a grumbled string of obscenities in Rillanese, he shoved aside a crate of red-skinned potatoes and an unmarked barrel, then rolled back a burlap canvas and lifted the trapdoor underneath. Po swore again, dropping the wooden panel hard against the floor. Wiping a sheen of sweat from his brow, he gestured to Ravlok. "Come now. Bring pointy ears."

While his companions roused themselves and collected their packs, Ravlok returned to Orowen. "Are you ready, Devoted?"

She lifted her exhausted gaze and nodded, reaching for him. "*Ciir, neime.*"

She was too tired to even speak in Eidosinian. Ravlok hesitated, grappling with that knowledge as he took in the shadows under her eyes and the sunken pallor of her cheeks. He exchanged a look with Kendi, whose gloomy expression only amplified his concern.

Ravlok shook the thoughts aside and hoisted her up. The best way he could help now was to get her as far away from Ryost as possible.

Po led them down a narrow staircase and into the stone-walled cellar. He snapped his fingers twice; flaming sconces blazed to life, illuminating shelves housing more torches and a few nondescript crates. Ravlok paused at the bottom of the stairs, marveling at the expense such enchantments must have cost. Compared to the rest of the dilapidated tavern, he would have never guessed anything magical existed down here.

"Go, *bashiin*," Anwic said, hovering on the last stair behind him.

Annoyance sparked hot in Ravlok's belly, but Kendi's sharp words in Syljian—whatever they were—silenced the retort on his lips.

"Take care, ye lot," Nessa called down to them. Ravlok glanced over his shoulder to where she stood stuffing a bundle into Sam's satchel. "And don't get this bread wet!"

Her warning left Ravlok confused until Po slid aside a false section of the wall and tapped a pair of wardstones behind it. The illusion of a dusty crate at his feet shimmered, then winked out, revealing another trapdoor. Hoisting the panel up, Po exposed a ladder leading down into a foul-smelling, half-flooded hole.

Rammie pecked him on the cheek and squeezed his bicep. "Don't ye be a stranger, Lockpick. I'll expect a bird when ye get where ye're going."

"Thank you, Rammie," Ravlok said. "We couldn't have done this without you."

"Nay, I reckon ye couldn't." She winked at him, then turned to Alar with a meaningful look. "Ye're doin' right by him, ye *kinnich*. He'd be proud of ye."

Torchlight flickered across Alar's face. There might have been pain in his expression, but it was gone when Ravlok blinked. Alar nodded wordlessly to Rammie, shouldered past her, and peered into the hole.

The mine shaft was a remnant of Syljia's original trove of saphyrum mines. Syljian rebels had collapsed most of them during the destruction of Astenpor. Others were lost when they burned the maps of the remaining tunnels. This one had likely been forgotten for decades before Po bought the place.

Alar cleared his throat and reached for a nearby torch to light their way. "Magnus and I should go first in case we run into anyone hostile."

"Lead the way." Kendi nodded to Rammie and Po. "Thank you both for everything."

"Fare ye well." Rammie gave them one last once-over, leaning against Po with an elbow on his shoulder.

Po made an impatient gesture, and Magnus started down the ladder. The rest of them followed, hissing and muttering about the chill as they lowered themselves into the hole.

Cracks along the tunnel walls leaked river water into the old mine. Stagnant pools rose to Ravlok's hips in places, and the stench of rot and mold was an unyielding companion. Stone walls pressed in on all sides, leading to frequent complaints from the taller members of their entourage. The tunnel had obviously been constructed with much smaller Syljian miners in mind. More than once, the ceiling became so low that Ravlok was forced to stoop into the water for several spans—no easy task while carrying Orowen on his back.

She stayed conscious enough to grumble about the surrounding filth and Jessie's mounting risk of fleshrot in the waterlogged tomb. To placate the half-lucid priestess, Rylan and Anwic carried Jessie above the waterline for as long as the tunnel permitted. Still, it didn't stop the bandages from getting wet when Anwic slipped once on slick stone, smashing himself and Jessie against a jutting turn in the wall. Jessie let out a bark of pain, quickly muffled by Rylan's hand.

Silonas must have heard Ravlok's prayers because they eventually made it out on the other side, well into the forest surrounding southern Ryost. The shaft emptied into a creek bed flanked by stands of reedy, blue-barked cavae trees, interspersed with thicker ashes and maples. From this side, the opening was little more than a cave, half-collapsed and strewn with moss-laden rock and leafy vegetation. They paused for several minutes, watching for signs of Guild patrols. While they waited, Ravlok said another silent prayer to Caelyn to see them safely through her forest.

Once it was deemed safe enough, they climbed up the creek bank and limped due east. The Alliaansi set a dogged pace, even weighed down with wounded and provisions. Fire mounted in Ravlok's calves and thighs until each step was a struggle. Sweat coated his skin, drenching his back where Orowen's body contacted his. Wet clothing chafed in the most miserable places, and at least three of Laerin's stitches had torn away from the wound on his chest. Breathing became his central focus to distract himself from the pain.

His fatigue was reflected in the faces of his companions, but none of them complained. In fact, none of them had spoken at all for over an hour since reaching the surface. It was clear they all sought to put a greater distance between them and the city walls before turning north.

As they trudged through the understory, dozens of rodents and small reptilian creatures skittered aside to let them pass. Birds flitted from branch to branch. Deerlike ullopie with smooth, striped antlers grazed in a nearby meadow. A few horned selka—the ullopie's sleek, black-and-tan cousins—darted through the gaps in the trees. There was even a flash of ringed spots from some kind of feline creature—likely a native chaagra or a more invasive leopard—before it slipped away into the brush.

A piercing shriek cut through the haze of Ravlok's thoughts.

He started, spinning toward the sound, heart leaping into his throat. Kendi's sword was half drawn, Sam's daggers flashed into her hands, and Jack brandished his crossbow.

The scream hadn't come from either side of them, but from above. They all looked up.

Tiny projectiles pelted their heads and shoulders. Jack loosed a bolt into the canopy, and another earsplitting shriek sounded—this one far angrier and accompanied by another hail of projectiles and leaves. The Alliaansi swept into battle stances, baring teeth and clenching weapons. Ravlok hoisted Orowen higher on his back and stepped off the game trail, single-minded in his promise to protect her.

When he dared a look back at the narrow trail, he choked on his laughter.

"Acorns," he breathed.

"What?" Orowen lifted her head from his shoulder.

"Acorns," he repeated. "Look." He nodded toward the projectiles littering the ground.

The priestess was quiet for several seconds. She snorted a laugh. "*Saonis miraar.*"

Sam was next to laugh—the sound one of pure joy and relief—as she lowered her daggers and peered up into the tree. Rylan and Kendi followed suit. Even Alar cracked a smile.

Perched high above them on a wide oak branch was an enormous falcon with needle-sharp talons and white-and-brown mottled feathers. The falcon shrieked a third time, and Ravlok could have sworn the bird was glaring at them. It stretched its wings and flapped several times, shaking loose more acorns.

"You could say that bird has gone a bit nuts," Orowen murmured, prompting more laughter from their companions.

As terrible as it was, hearing her crack a joke at all brightened Ravlok's mood. He stepped back on the trail, still grinning. Even his steps felt lighter as they resumed course. From the lingering smiles on his companions' faces, they must have felt it, too.

Finally, when twilight approached, Alar called a halt in a sheltered grove of trees. Ravlok took care not to crush Orowen's legs beneath him before dropping to the ground.

"We're still too close to the city," Kendi said, eyeing the fading light through the canopy. "We'll press on in half an hour."

While Anwic and Rylan passed out bread, hard cheese, and waterskins, Sam set about changing Jessie's bandages.

"Laangor's blight," she swore as she unwrapped the bloody sword wound. "Ravlok, give me a hand here."

Ravlok forced his body to move, kneeling down beside Sam and offering what skill he had with mundane healing. Jessie was at least conscious, but her skin was pale, and her green eyes were glassy and unfocused. Sam had cauterized the wound with help from Magnus's Aetherial flame last night, but the soaked bandages had softened the tissue enough to open the scab again. They needed to find a healer, and soon, or she would be at risk of losing her leg.

"We should let it dry before rewrapping it," Ravlok suggested.

Sam nodded her agreement, then commanded Jessie to eat.

Ravlok's attention strayed to Orowen, who was sipping at a waterskin with Kendi's help. The priestess had attempted a single sigil of healing to seal Jessie's wound, only to summon a tiny spark of light before collapsing again. Her overtaxed body simply couldn't handle the strain of pulling any more from the

Aether. It ate at Ravlok that he could do nothing to help her. If he only possessed magic himself, he could at least mend Jessie's leg and restore some of Orowen's vigor.

One heard stories all the time of feats of otherworldly strength borne of desperation, or fonts of godlike endurance manifesting in times of deepest need. Grendel of Sessia was one such story—the tiny Feridian soldier who'd lifted a horse off her commander while they battled with the Alliaansi forty years ago. There was Mascha of Rillion, the infamous, slave-born pit fighter, who had defeated six men in a single death match to win his freedom. And everyone knew Magus Illustria Stormflight, whose elemental powers of wind had manifested the day she filled the sails of her family's fleet to outrun a deadly storm on the West Aivenosian Sea.

Grandulli Bornen, the professor Ravlok had been researching in the Guild Archives, was particularly fascinated with Magus Illustria. Bornen often used her as an example of the undiscovered magical potential hidden within ordinary men and women. He believed the gods bestowed magic on all mortals, regardless of birth, and it simply required more incentive for some to access it. Ravlok had devoured all of Bornen's essays on the subject and taken extensive notes on the mind-immersing techniques from the primitive Skriian peoples that Bornen recommended. All tribal Skriians, the professor claimed, had magical aptitude.

Ravlok returned his attention to Jessie and the wound weeping from the broken scab. If there was any better time to unlock his magical potential, he couldn't think of it. He breathed deeply and reached out to touch Jessie's leg below the wound.

Okay, remember the steps.

Sam gave him a curious look, and Jessie frowned at him while she chewed her bread. Ravlok gave them both what he hoped was a reassuring smile.

His eyes closed. *Master your breathing.*

That was the easy part. He'd spent years mastering his breathing with Yonfé, even during the most rigorous physical training. If he'd made any progress on attaining Balance, it was right here as he fell into the familiar rhythm. In through the nose, out through the mouth, creating even circles of life-giving breath.

Still your aura.

Harder, but still a well-practiced skill. It had taken Ravlok nearly two years just to visualize the slippery, tumultuous aura—the essence of life itself, gifted to him by Mira and blessed by Saolanni. Once he could finally see the mirage-like rippling of his aura tucked in close to his skin, the real work had begun. Taking control of one's aura was much like trying to grasp a fish in a raging mountain stream. It required endless patience, strict discipline, well-attuned reflexes, and a heaping dose of luck. Nearly half a decade had passed before he'd reaped the benefits of aura mastery, and it was a skill he would continue to hone throughout his life.

Touch the Aether.

The hardest part, and the key to unlocking his magic, if he so possessed it. There were still hundreds of arguments over what the Aether was, exactly. This strange force, which could be shaped into elements by sorcerers, wielded directly by aethermancers, and utterly controlled by the most powerful Aetherians, remained a mystery to all but the gods themselves.

His studies of the Skriians' mind-immersion were vaguest here, and no part of his training at the monastery could prepare him for it. The only notes of worth regarded the way his aura should flow from his body to the Aether and back. Whatever that meant.

Touch the Aether.

He had seen the Aether through rifts and understood that a Wall of some kind separated their world and the infinite, inky plane of magic. Ravlok tried to visualize that Wall. He imagined himself running his hand along the barrier, coaxing it aside like a veil.

But there was nothing. No wave of magical energy. No static force of divine power. Not even a whisper of existential might.

A twig snapped.

Anwic gave a shout, and Alar swore. Ravlok's eyes flew open as three Guild soldiers crashed into the grove.

This is your chance.

Magnus curled his fingers into fists as Rylan, Kendi, and Anwic dropped into fighting stances, ready to defend their camp. The monk rose to his feet, and Alar, Sam, and Jack fell back to protect the wounded. Steel slid from scabbards, and shouts tore from throats. The cacophony of sound barely reached him over the thundering of his own heart and the voice inside his head.

He could not be weak.

Show them you are strong.

They had already lost so much faith in him.

Forge it anew.

Magnus stepped forward, blood roaring in his ears. Fury kindled in his chest.

Summon your blade.

Aether flashed, wind snapped, and Malediction was a force of death in his hand. The blade's icy grip made his lips curl with contempt. He hated this sword. He hated its purpose. Its promise of violence.

He hated the Guild more.

Kill them.

For what they had taken from him. For what he still had left to lose.

Magnus stormed past Ravlok, past Rylan, past Anwic. Kendi engaged the first soldier while the other two ran past. Magnus lifted his sword, and Malediction swung true. Flesh parted from muscle and bone. One man fell. The second closed in.

Their weapons clashed. Magnus grunted, rocked by a blow to the face with the soldier's shield. He summoned the Aether into his next swing—an arc of rippling smoke and light that cleaved the air—and the impact shattered chain mail. Malediction scraped bone. Coppery blood and reeking viscera stung his nostrils. The second man died with a howl of pain. Magnus moved on to the third.

The last soldier crossed blades with Kendi twice more before Magnus drove Malediction into his back, skewering the man until the tip of the sword jutted out of his chest. The full weight of the soldier slumped forward, and blood gushed across Magnus's hands. He let the corpse drop to the ground before wrenching the weapon out.

A hush fell upon the grove. Magnus looked from the corpse to Kendi. Cheralach's most trusted commander gazed back at him, white eyebrows nearly touching his hairline, face splattered with blood. Behind Kendi, Rylan and Anwic were staring, too. They had barely even lifted their swords.

Magnus dropped Malediction back into the Aether, disgusted, doing his best to ignore the sticky blood between his fingers.

A necessary evil.

"A necessary evil," Magnus echoed aloud.

Anwic's grin was feral. Approving.

Kendi clapped Magnus on the shoulder, face solemn. "Indeed. Good work, Magnus."

Take command.

"We can't stay here any longer." Magnus looked at each of his people in turn, letting the weight of his words linger in the space between them. He straightened, hardening his expression as Cheralach once had. "It's time to move."

Chapter Twenty-Three

Daeya

The heat was stifling. Daeya's palms grazed rough stone. Cave walls loomed on both sides, neither narrowing nor widening as she walked. Flickers of golden light trailed from her fingertips and reflected off obsidian veins in the rock. Her skin glowed like the embers of a campfire. Sulfur and smoke clung to her nostrils—scents of a mighty forge, or the heart of a volcano. An orange glow suffused the end of the tunnel, around a bend past which she couldn't see.

"Nashanett."

A word she had never heard before. A word she understood. Its meaning stopped Daeya in her tracks. He couldn't possibly be addressing her.

"Who are you?"

The deep, rumbling voice answered in a language so guttural and ancient that it was less like actual speech and more like a series of grunts and growls. But she understood: "That remains to be seen."

Daeya knew that voice, like a memory called to the surface. She tried to recall a name, but it slipped from her like smoke. Someone waited for her there, around the bend. She started toward it, stepping cautiously.

Cool air caressed her skin. It might have been a comfort, except it stood in stark counterpoint to the heat and made her shiver. Ice trickled down the back of her neck.

"You must be fearless," Gregory purred behind her.

"Councilor—" She choked on the word as she spun back the way she'd come, the phantom bite of a blade against her chest.

There was no one there. The cave behind her was as black as Aether. Her panting breath raked heat into her throat. She tried to swallow, but not enough moisture remained in her mouth. Daeya turned again, quickening her pace toward that light until her feet flew over the stone. The darkness followed, but she dared not look back. Something terrible lingered in that darkness.

She rounded the bend and slid to a stop at the mouth of a cavern bathed in fire.

"You must forge the bond, Nashanett*."*

"What bond?" she demanded, squinting into the inferno. That fire would surely incinerate anyone standing within. "And why do you call me that?"

"I've been waiting for you."

Well, that was entirely unhelpful. She scowled. "You'll be waiting a lot longer if I don't get some answers."

The voice turned reverent. "Withstand the Test of Flame, and I will serve you."

Daeya jolted awake to a mighty surge of magic raging through her like wildfire. Golden light arced over her fingertips, straining at the confines of her body as if seeking a way out. Breath hitching, heart stuttering, she closed her hands around that power to hold it back. The light winked out, and blackness swallowed her whole.

For a moment, it seemed the darkness in her dream had overtaken her. She shot upright in a panic, struck her head on something wooden, and slumped to the floor with a groan.

"Bleeding—gods," she murmured, rubbing at the rapidly swelling knot. Just a dream. It was just a dream. But it seemed so real.

Where...

Memory slowly returned to her as the lingering thrum of magic faded. After retreating from the Vikas' room, she'd folded herself up inside a storage closet, Sealed the door, and cried uncontrollably until exhaustion had dragged her down into sleep. Her cheeks were dry now, but they still bore the tightness of tears.

Daeya wiped her face and drew in lungfuls of musty air, resting her head against the wall. Shameful as it was, she felt better after crying like that, as if all the emotional turmoil had blown open the doors to her mind, letting her guilt and misery spill out in one cresting wave. Stillness followed in its wake. For once, Daeya felt empty, and she would savor this nothingness as long as she could. It was only a matter of time before the self-condemnation and loathing took root once more.

It was her fault, after all. She had ignored the signs of Faustus's treachery, and hundreds of children had died for it. She wouldn't be surprised if Gregory recalled her early to bestow punishment. Whatever the Councilor did to her after this would be well deserved.

The ache from several hours of being crowded into a corner crept into her awareness, but she couldn't find the courage to move yet, to rise and face the world, knowing what she had done—what she'd failed to do. Nothing would change if she lingered here another hour, or two, or the rest of their journey. It was best, perhaps, if she stayed out of sight and refrained from kindling any more animosity from her companions.

When she closed her eyes, the fiery cavern alighted in her memory. That voice rumbled in her ears.

Withstand the Test of Flame, and I will serve you.

Daeya didn't know what the Test of Flame was, nor did she care to be served by some incorporeal voice that refused to answer simple questions. Never mind that it spoke a language she shouldn't understand and called her by a title she didn't possess.

Nashanett. It was difficult to translate into the trade tongue, much less Eidosinian, but she knew its meaning. The closest she could come in either language was 'blessed leader,' or more terrifyingly, 'blessed mistress.'

Daeya scoffed. She was no more a mistress than Joss was a charitable gentleman, and she would make a worse leader. The only thing she had ever blessed was the training staff she'd accidentally hurled into a font of holy water. Yonfé still wouldn't let her practice in that wing of the monastery.

Things were complicated enough. Such dreams were better left ignored. Daeya opened her eyes to the pitch-black closet and reached for her pendant to light the tiny space.

That voice from her dream sounded again. Daeya paused, frowning, but she couldn't make out the words.

The floor dropped out from under her.

"Ach!"

Her temple bounced off the wall, and wood scraped her cheek. She floated for a split second before slamming into the deck. Boards groaned and creaked. The entire world shuddered before the ship righted itself. Fortunately, the objects on the shelves above her had been secured to keep them from crashing to the floor.

The sound from her dream came again.

Only it wasn't the same. Daeya held her smarting head and listened. There were no words or cadence of speech at all.

It was thunder.

Of course it's thunder, idiot.

Footsteps pounded above Daeya, followed by shouts and another peal of thunder. The tension left her shoulders, and she sagged back against the wall. The sailors were just preparing for a storm.

Storms at sea weren't uncommon, especially as summer gave way to fall. Temperatures could fluctuate wildly from day to day and even hour to hour, with powerful winds driving monstrous swells. The crew would be well-equipped to handle rough waters. No doubt Belio and the others were already taking care of the sails and doing whatever else sailors did in conditions like these.

She braced her feet against the wall to keep from being tossed about like a copper in a jar. Folding her arms across her stomach, ignoring its inconvenient growl, she hunkered down and resolved to go back to sleep.

Moments later, the closet twisted until 'forward' became 'down,' and most of her weight rested on her propped legs. She flung her arms out to catch herself, and the ship rolled back in the other direction. Daeya narrowly avoided smashing her head a third time. More shouts rang out above deck, and something *cracked.*

The sound was tremendous. She looked upward, though there was nothing to see in the blackness. The ship's bell clanged, an arrhythmic sound that reverberated through the walls and floor. She reached for her pendant.

"*Luminos.*"

The closet filled with light. Daeya blinked until her dirty white shirt, the grime coating the floor, and the cobwebs in her hair came back into focus. A shelf was directly above her, so she leaned forward to see around it.

Water splattered onto her nose. She jerked back, startled, the sting of salt on her lips. Seawater—not rain—had soaked the ship enough to drip through two decks to reach her down here.

A bolt of alarm shot through her. She wiped at the droplet, letting it glisten in the light. Her eyes strayed back to the ceiling.

Oh, that can't be good.

Thunder boomed. Shouts grew more urgent. More desperate. Daeya considered going up to help somehow, but she hesitated. There was little help her inexperience at sea could offer them. She didn't know which ropes to pull or what sails to trim or when to do any of those things. Her presence would likely be more of a distraction than anything.

The ship bucked and thrashed. More water dripped from the ceiling and dribbled in thin streams from a larger knothole to Daeya's left. Water soon soaked the seat of her trousers. Despite the heat earlier in the day, she shivered with the chill and longed for her robe's extra layer of warmth.

Something struck the side of the ship hard enough to throw her sideways. She yelped, splashing palms-first into a full fingerspan of water. Shadows swung around her, mimicking the motion of her glowing pendant. She reached up to steady it, and a scream punched through the walls of her tiny shelter.

The sound was pure terror, chilling her blood and prickling the hair on the back of her neck. It cut off abruptly, and a clamor of voices rose all at once, calling out in panic.

Someone had gone overboard.

An image arose in Daeya's mind. The ocean rising to sweep the sailors from their vessel, blasting them over the sides and pulling them into its churning, black depths. The ship rolling with the waves, masts shattered, boards broken, sails bubbling against the surface.

Her imagination, perhaps... or a foretelling of things to come.

Daeya was no seer, but she believed in the power of instinct and premonition. There must be something she could do. As a mage, it was her responsibility to serve and protect. She couldn't sit idle and let the ship and its crew break apart. Even if she knew nothing about sailing, her magic could at least push back some of those waves. Perhaps she could keep them from sweeping anyone else overboard.

With aching limbs, she pushed herself upright, fighting the force of the waves. Her shirt sleeves trailed dark jets of water. Another *crack* sounded, and something crashed above her. A discordant, metallic clanging rang through the air loud enough to rattle her teeth.

The ship's brass bell must have broken loose. Daeya shoved herself to her feet, pendant clenched in her fist. A whisper passed her lips, and the invisible Seal on the closet door broke apart. Water sloshed against her boots as she heaved it open. Her pendant illuminated dozens of crates and barrels on this level. Nearly all of them were lashed together, but some had broken loose. Several barrels rolled toward her as the ship listed again.

She sprinted for the nearest ladder and threw herself up the rungs. She was nearly at the top when the barrels slammed one after another into the bottom of the ladder. Wood splintered beneath Daeya's hands. She leaped the short distance to the next deck, heaving herself onto it as the broken wood bowed beneath her weight.

She crouched at the opening, trying to catch her breath. Below her, two of the barrels rolled out of sight while the third spilled its contents over the floor. Some kind of wine. Its sweet scent cut through the ship's usual amalgamation of mildew, sweat, and pine tar.

Lightning flashed, highlighting the outline of the closed hatch that would take her to the main deck. Daeya dismissed her Light spell and checked the beads on her casting bracelet. Then, rising, she reached for the next ladder, scaled the slick wooden rungs, and pushed on the hatch.

It met her with so much resistance that at first she feared the sailors had locked the bleeding thing from the outside. With both hands flat on the hatch and all the strength she could muster, she shoved upward. The door lifted a few fingerspans, hung suspended for a moment, and snapped clean off its hinges.

Ocean spray tried to blast Daeya back down the ladder. She caught the top rung even as her feet slipped on wet wood. Heart in her throat, she ducked her head against the lash of rain.

A passing sailor saw her struggle. "Are ye crazy? Get yer arse back below!"

She didn't give herself time to contemplate the wisdom of his words. Her boots found purchase on the rungs, and she hauled herself out, one arm over her face to shield against the wind.

If she'd thought the storm was rough below deck, being up on the main with the rest of the sailors was like stepping into a cyclone. Perhaps that was exactly what she was doing. She questioned the soundness of her decision again, then stomped down the inklings of self-doubt and turned her thoughts outward. She was a mage, and she wouldn't cower in the dark while all these brave non-adepts fought for their lives.

Squinting against sheets of rain and driving wind, she took in the devastation that had already befallen the *Breigh Maiden*. Broken and splintered wood lay everywhere. The huge brass bell was partially embedded in the deck beside the forecastle. Shredded sails whipped overhead. The shortest yardarm on the main mast swung freely, tangling in ropes and threatening to slice into the largest sails still intact.

A few sailors clung to the rigging, working to get the broken yardarm under control while others struggled to roll up the sails on the mizzenmast. Daeya summoned power from the beads around her wrist and reached up toward the yardarm. She could hold it steady for them while they worked—

The ship bucked, tossing Daeya to the deck. A wave crested the hull, dousing her entire body and forcing her backward. Water swept into her lungs and drowned out her scream.

She tumbled across the deck and slammed against something hard and round. The wave left her coughing, clawing at her throat and chest. When she finally purged the last of the sea and drew a ragged breath, she was lying against the mizzenmast, staring up at the roiling sky. Arcs of lightning zipped through black clouds, painting her vision with branching halos.

An object struck her chest. Daeya started, eyes wide as her hands closed over coarse, coiled fibers.

Rope.

"If you plan to stay aboard," a voice shouted over the howling wind, "tie yourself to the mast or get the fuck below!"

Dizzy, throat raw, Daeya groaned and rolled over. She sat up with the rope, turning toward the sailor to thank him, but he was already gone.

"Heave to!" The captain's voice, furious and authoritarian, barreled over the deck. "Heave to, I said! Bleeding, Chaos-sworn whelps! Keep the ship in line! And someone secure that bleeding spar!"

If he saw her here, the protective bastard would try to send her below. She threw herself into motion, tying one end of the rope to the mast and the other around her waist. Simple box knots only; nothing as fancy as the knots the sailors tied. She tried to summon the power of her saphyrum, only to snarl with frustration. Her casting bracelet was gone. It must have broken off when she fell.

"Sorceress!"

Daeya flinched. Captain Arnes stormed into view, bringing the fury of the wind with him. The man's usually tidy brown hair had come loose from its single braid and blew about his head and beard in a mad tangle of wet locks. His tricorn hat was gone, and his olive-green waistcoat and black trousers were completely soaked through. The soft brown eyes and amiable smile he'd greeted her with upon boarding were a far cry from friendly now.

"What in Caelyn's name are you doing up here? Get back to your quarters!"

Daeya's anger rose to match the captain's. She'd be damned if she was going to be sent below like a scolded child. She reached for her pendant. "No."

The captain's eyes widened, then narrowed. "You'll get below, or I'll—"

Daeya summoned power from the pendant, lifted her free hand, and spoke the three-word incantation to *seize* the swinging yardarm. She clenched it against the wind, the strain pulling at her mind and hand in unison.

The sailors working in the shrouds gave confused shouts over the wind. One made a grab for the beam and whooped victoriously as he secured it with a quick tether.

Captain Arnes jerked his head up toward his men and back down at Daeya, anger giving way to more surprise.

Daeya leveled her gaze on him and released the yardarm from her spell. The ship swayed beneath her feet, but she rode it out. "Are you going to complain about my help, Captain, or are you going to let me do my job?"

Lightning flashed between them. Another swell struck the hull and Arnes rocked with the ship, lifting his arms to keep his balance. He motioned to the rope around her waist. "You'll just cut yourself in half on your way overboard like that. Here."

He stepped into her space and wrenched her knot loose, looping the rope over her shoulders and around her chest like a harness. Taking up the slack, he looped that around the mast and secured it as well, leaving enough room for her to move about.

"Thank you," Daeya told him with no small amount of amazement.

"You've already done more than the louts you travel with. It's the least I can do." Cinching the rope around the mast, Arnes looked back at her. "Have you a dagger?"

Daeya shook her head. Her knife was back in the passengers' quarters, bundled in her robe.

The captain reached down and pulled a long, serrated knife from his boot. He presented it to her, holding the blade between forefinger and thumb. "Anything happens to my ship, you cut yourself free."

She tucked the blade into a loop on her vest and swallowed the stone of fear the possibility provoked. She wasn't a strong swimmer; if she went overboard, she would drown.

"Nothing's going to happen to it." She pulled out a pair of saphyrum beads, tucked one inside her cheek, and cast a Light spell on the other. She pressed the glowing bead into the captain's hand. "Take this. It may be of use."

His bushy eyebrows lifted. White-violet light washed over his dark beard and glinted off crooked teeth. "I can't take your—"

The ship canted sharply as it crested a swell and tipped down the other side. Daeya pitched forward, but Arnes caught her and the mast to keep them both upright.

Daeya huffed a sigh as the ship leveled out. She fought to keep her nerves steady, pretending the quaking in her limbs was from the cold. "You can, and you will, Captain. I insist. I'll take it back once this is over."

It wasn't like she was selling it to him, after all. Only receiving money for saphyrum would have made the exchange illegal.

Arnes squeezed her wrist. Somewhere near the bow, boards snapped, and the fallen bell rattled. "Caelyn's blessing upon you, Sorceress."

The sailors often invoked the temperamental goddess of nature during their journey. Daeya repeated the phrase she'd heard often. "I pray she sends fair weather."

Arnes cut loose a throaty, somewhat deranged laugh. "Aye, lass, pray she does."

His silhouette retreated with the bead's light. Daeya returned her attention to the ropes creaking and swaying above her. Sailors on the main mast hurried down the ratlines. The next flash of lightning illuminated Belio among them. He dropped to the deck and strode toward her, mouth gaping.

Whatever he was going to say was interrupted by a massive swell that struck the bow and broke against the deck in a mighty surge.

"Look out!"

It wasn't clear who called the warning, but all the sailors dove for handholds as the surge swept toward them.

Daeya stood firm. She channeled her bead and spoke an incantation, her voice clear and strong. Sigils of white-violet sliced the air, swirling around her as she gestured with wide, sweeping movements of her hands. Smoke-like Aether poured from the sigils, and she shaped its power to her will. A shimmering, opalescent wall formed before the main mast, curving around her and the sailors. The wave smashed against the Aetherial barrier and careened back over the sides of the ship.

"Aetherian," the sailors muttered in awe.

Daeya winced, but she didn't have time to correct them. As the glowing, translucent barrier fractured into spears of light and returned to wisps of smoky Aether, the hairs on her arms and neck rose.

Bleeding Aether. It was the same feeling she got against Normos's elemental lightning when they sparred, only no counter-orb could negate nature's power. With no lightning affinity of her own, she couldn't ward against it. She could only guess at where it would strike.

Looking up through the few intact sails on the main mast toward the highest point on the ship, Daeya wove a sigil of protection. She backed toward the mizzenmast, placing herself in front of the largest group of sailors.

"We need to—" Belio began.

Daeya cut him off. "Stay behind me."

She didn't pause in her movements to see if he obeyed. She worked faster, layering her first sigil of protection with a second, and then a third. Each spell amplified the one before it until an enormous web of white-violet light stretched away from her in all directions, shielding the sailors. It was no easy feat; the sigils sought to intertwine and become a useless, deadly tangle, but she had practiced layering spells with Gregory since she was nine. It took discipline and focus, and most mages couldn't layer more than two spells. Daeya could layer up to six.

The fourth sigil took all her focus to draw. Her arms shook with the strain of magic, and her hands dragged through the air like it was made of sap. This last sigil, woven all throughout the rest, was made to channel raw energy.

Static tingled along her limbs. She tasted metal on her tongue.

"Get down!"

The cry scarcely left her throat before the world around her exploded. Daeya turned her face away and thrust out her hands, pouring all the saphyric energy she had left into that fourth sigil. Her bead turned to dust in her mouth. Gods willing, it would be enough to prevent any more loss of life.

She braced hard against the concussive burst of light and noise, instantly deafened by the crack of thunder. Even behind her eyelids, her vision flashed white-violet, and a searing sensation against her palms ended almost as abruptly as it began.

Dead silence replaced the sound of the storm. There wasn't even the slightest ringing in her ears. Daeya *felt* the crew surge forward around her, boots pounding on the deck, and slight interruptions in the current of air rushing across her skin. She opened her eyes to find her sigils completely burned through and her skin glowing.

Just like in her dream.

She jerked back and stared. The golden shimmer took on the look of spidery webbing, or a latticelike network of fine lines, as if her skin were shattered glass, painstakingly pieced back together and lit from within. It traveled across her palms, over her wrists, and beneath her wet shirtsleeves, where the glow could still be seen halfway up her forearms.

Someone grabbed her shoulder.

Daeya looked up. Her breath came in shallow gasps, and grit from the bead still clung to her tongue. Belio's face was creased with awe and concern. He looked unharmed, thank Caelyn, but she couldn't hear a word he was saying. An orange glow lit the side of his cheek; for a moment, it mimicked the glow from around the bend in the tunnel. But no, that dream hadn't come with the smell of charred wood and smoke. Daeya shook her head to clear it and looked in the direction the other sailors were running.

They rushed about, collecting whatever buckets and soaked cloth remained on deck. Though none of them looked seriously injured, their efforts to smother the fires would amount to little. The main mast had split down the middle, its topmost section nothing more than charred wood. All the way to the deck, the mast glowed from the inside out. Scraps of sails blazed, and fiery embers rained down. More flames crept along the rigging, threatening the other two masts and the remaining sails.

Belio's mounting panic showed in the firelight as he gestured to the mast. Even if Daeya couldn't hear him, she understood what he was trying to tell her: if the storm didn't sink them, the fire would.

It was dangerous magic—something she'd never done on a scale as large as this—but she could save the ship.

I can put it out. Her lips and tongue formed the words, but the vibrations in her vocal cords and Belio's shoulder-sagging relief were the only indications that she had spoken at all.

Belio nodded, his expression hardening with purpose. He turned away, conferring with the nearby sailors and pointing once at Daeya. Whether *they* could hear him was difficult to say. His companions balked at her, but whether in astonishment or disbelief she couldn't say. Daeya didn't spare them another look. She dug out another bead, tossed it into her mouth, and started weaving more spells.

Fire was as familiar to her as the Aether itself. It was the only elemental affinity Daeya possessed, but her skill rivaled that of even the most powerful water savants. She could summon, shape, and even snuff out fires by manipulating its energy.

Containing it, however, was the first step in battling these flames. It would take too long to ward the entire ship, so she began by casting simple wards on the rigging and remaining sails to keep them from burning. The sigils shot from her fingers as ribbons of white-violet light. They coiled around their targets until they butted up against the flames, tossing out glittering clouds of Aetherial mist when they began to burn. Her wards would last just a few minutes. It had to be enough.

Rain was pummeling the smaller fires along the sails and ropes into extinction, but the mast still smoldered from within. It was too great a surface to smother. Daeya would have to draw the flame out of the wood.

She took a deep, steadying breath. There was no sigil to guide the flow of her magic through this. Every year, many fire savants succumbed to Mage's Folly, and some even died while quelling wildfires on the western highlands. It required perfect control of the element, and Daeya tried to ignore the fact she had suboptimal conditions in which to work.

As if to remind her just how bleeding awful the conditions were, the ship pitched sideways and nearly threw her off her feet. Someone snagged her by the rope harness and wrenched her upright. She looked up into the face of a scruffy, waterlogged sailor, whose grin was as wide and lopsided as the gap in his front teeth.

He mouthed something, but all she heard was a faint ringing in her left ear. He kept a firm hold of the harness and thrust his chin toward the mast, indicating she should continue. His grin somehow put her mind at ease. She gave him a smile and a nod of thanks.

The smile faded as she returned her attention to the mast. She lifted her palms toward it. White-gold lines still laced her skin, but she would ponder that oddity later. Her mouth formed ancient words, and power coursed through her.

Vuurmas seluu.

Daeya *seized* the fire and willed it into her body. Both the glowing mast and the light beneath her skin flared brightly. Flames erupted from the wood as if stoked by a strong wind, licking sideways toward her. Waves of heat turned rain to steam, surrounding her with a burgeoning cloud of mist. Like sand through an hourglass, the fire formed a channel, slipping from the burning mast into her outstretched palms. It pooled within her as molten energy, its intensity building in her hands, arms, and chest, but it didn't burn.

She craved more.

The feeling startled her. Scarlet embers sparked to life in her palms as waves of heat poured off the mast.

Careful. The power was intoxicating. It was so easy—too easy—and if she pulled too fast, she could wind up at Baosanni's Gate. She slowed the flow of her magic to a maddening trickle and forced herself to be patient.

Daeya wavered on the deck. Not one, but two sailors held her now. Belio stood on her other side, face aglow with the strange scarlet fire.

She had never seen its like before, but it sang to some deeper part of her, like a melody that resonated with her soul. It felt good. It felt *right*, as if she had exhumed some innate power long buried within her.

Could this be the Test of Flame?

Something rumbled underfoot and the ship bucked again. A sudden tremor, as if from an impact, traveled through the wooden planks. Through the veil of smoke and rain, Daeya couldn't see what had caused it. She kept her eyes fixed on the mast and that brilliant shaft of orange-white fire sprouting from its side, light-blinded to anything beyond the shadows and the trail of rippling heat. The fire on the mast was shrinking, its inner glow nearly extinguished.

Her limbs buzzed with the immensity of all that energy, as if she was drunk with it. A single wrong step could send her tumbling. She steeled herself against the feeling. There was only a little more. She could do this. She *had* to do this.

The ship's bow struck another wave and pitched upward. Daeya staggered. One set of hands on her rope harness tugged sideways as the sailor was thrown. Belio heaved her back up and held firm.

She bared her teeth in a silent snarl. Her fingers curled as if she could cling to the channel of fire, rather than allow the connection to break. Fatigue crept in, and a frigid knife of exhaustion twisted between her shoulder blades. If she had to recast, she might not have proper control of her affinity the second time.

The tremor beneath her feet shook the deck like thunder. Sailors dove to either side of her, taking shelter in her periphery. She dared a glance away from the mast and caught sight of the cockboat tumbling toward them. Behind it loomed the larger shadow of the wave that carried it. The boat was almost on top of them, riding the surge that crested the bow. Belio pulled on Daeya's harness as if to drag her to safety.

But there was nowhere safe from that massive wave, and the boat was many times longer than Daeya was tall. With the power of the water behind it, it would crush them. There was no time to summon a barrier or use telekinesis. All she had was the torrent of fire energy stored inside her.

No, not fire. Aether. It was *Aether* she held.

And it had nowhere else to go but out.

There were no spells. There were no sigils. No training she had ever received could have prepared her for this. She acted on reflex, turning toward the wave. What erupted from her body was raw, unquenchable power, devoid of discernible shape or color. The boat and the wave blasted backward, curling, rolling, tumbling off the sides of the ship.

When the power left her, Daeya hit her knees, gasping and shaking, mouth full of dust. The golden light that had suffused her hands and arms went out.

Belio knelt beside her, one hand on her back. She lifted her eyes to the blackened mast and sobbed with relief.

The fire was gone.

CHAPTER TWENTY-FOUR

RAVLOK

The bird was still following them.

Ravlok peered through the trees when Magnus signaled a halt to their northeasterly march. Sure enough, the beat of wings and a whisper of leaves soon followed. The falcon settled down on a branch over their campsite. It was too dark to see anything more than its massive silhouette nestled between two limbs, but it had to be the same bird.

He lowered Orowen to the ground next to Kendi and sat beside them. "It's back again."

He couldn't see if Kendi followed the subtle movement of his chin toward the tree, but the old Syljian nodded. He had asked Ravlok to keep an eye on the creature after it followed them from the clearing where Magnus had slain the soldiers. They hadn't come across any more Guild agents, but the bird's unnatural interest in them set Ravlok on edge.

It had once been believed that some magi could see and hear through the senses of animals. There were also records of masterminds possessing certain animals in the Saphyrum War. Ravlok had never heard of a sorcerer using such a spell, but in a way, that made it even more plausible. It was the sort of ability a tyrannical government wouldn't *want* anyone to know it possessed.

"Alar." Kendi tapped a finger to his temple and tipped his head toward the tree.

The mastermind had been quietly simmering since Magnus had assumed command of their entourage. It was obvious Alar was used to getting his way, and Ravlok had caught him staring too intently at the back of Magnus's head more than once.

Seated across from them, next to Jack, Alar followed Kendi's gesture. He stilled, staring at the bird. Ravlok studied his dark shape. Could he possess animal minds, too?

When Alar spoke, his voice was hushed. "Someone's communing with it."

That seemed to be all the confirmation Jack needed. In one smooth motion, the thief rose to his feet and leveled his crossbow at the bird.

Ravlok started, swearing under his breath.

"Wait," Alar began, but the bowstring *snicked.* The bolt whizzed over Ravlok's head—

And froze in midair. The metal bolt levitated, glowing a soft purple for two full heartbeats, before dropping to the ground.

The bird screamed. Its horrible, piercing cry made Ravlok recoil. He reached for his own sword as the sound cut through the buzz of insects. Sam palmed a dagger and rose, her white teeth flashing in the near darkness.

Behind her, the foliage parted. A feminine voice, haughty and laced with anger, wafted into their small circle. "I wouldn't do that if I were you."

Sam and Jack both spun. Ravlok leaned to one side to get a look at the newcomer through their legs.

"Who speaks?" Magnus rasped, his hand held away from his hip, likely to summon his sword.

Dim light filtered through the canopy as if in answer to his question. Ravlok's eyes widened. There was no moon tonight. The stars themselves seemed to have brightened to flood the clearing.

The woman was of a height with Magnus and as lithe as a whip. Roughhewn fabric wrapped low around her waist, gathering on her left hip with a series of white, bone-like fastenings. The hem of her skirt hung in stringy tatters down to one knee. Her feet were bare, but not dirty, as if the ground itself dared not soil her. Her bodice was made of woven vines that left her midriff and its series of striped tattoos exposed. When she stepped forward, the foliage parted further, clearing a path for her. Shafts of starlight painted the flower petals in her hair.

Odes of Ordeolas.

She was mesmerizing. A servant of Caelyn, no doubt; Ravlok took in the elegantly carved wolf's head—the symbol of the Guardians—at the top of her wooden staff. He rose, feeling his heart quicken in his chest.

Though her skin looked gray in the meager light, he guessed it held the olive-green hue of Aivenosian ancestry. Her short, sharp ear points and severely angled cheekbones indicated the same. She didn't smile at them. Her fingers only flexed on her staff, and her close-set eyes lifted to the falcon.

"Paelic," she said. "Why are you harassing these people?"

The falcon shrieked.

The corners of the woman's mouth turned down. "I'm certain they didn't mean to scare away your dinner."

Ravlok tossed an uneasy look over his shoulder at the bird. It was known some Guardians had the power to speak with animals. He had never expected it to be so unsettling to witness.

The bird, Paelic, squawked and puffed up its wings.

"Well, I suppose I don't blame you. Now, come down here." The woman extended her free hand toward Paelic, and the falcon leaped from the branch with an indignant chirp.

It flew over Ravlok's head, extending its feet toward the woman. Before its sharp talons tore into her bare forearm, a bark-like substance emerged from beneath her skin. She held the enormous bird as if it weighed little, though it stood nearly half as tall as she did.

Kendi rose to his feet, looking as perplexed as Ravlok felt. "Forgive us, my lady. We meant no harm."

"Two of you did." She glared at Sam and Jack.

Sam at least had the sense to look cowed. She tucked the dagger away. Jack only grumbled to himself and went to retrieve his crossbow bolt. A flash of annoyance seared Ravlok's nerves as he side-stepped the ill-tempered thief, who narrowly missed clipping him in the shoulder.

"Not to mention," the woman went on, "your graceless traipsing through my forest damaged many saplings, and you now stand in my newest grove of sickleberry bushes, stomping all over the young fruit."

Ravlok looked down at the ground and grimaced, lifting his feet. The boots Rammie had given him were indeed stained with the remnants of green, crescent-shaped berries. With his attention drawn to them, their sour aroma was almost overwhelming.

He sighed to himself. This was why the monks of his Order went without shoes. While the boots offered protection for his blistered feet, they also left him feeling disconnected from the world around him, unable to experience the simplest and most important sensations.

Like stepping on sacred berries.

"You have our sincerest apologies." Kendi held up an arm to prevent Jack from stalking back through the same patch of berries. "We will be more careful."

The woman looked unconvinced. She raked her eyes over their group, lingering on Orowen and Jessie, both unconscious at their feet. Her gaze settled on Ravlok with the same intensity of an approaching thunderstorm. "I would have you on your way sooner, rather than later. Come."

"You expect us to just follow you?" Magnus croaked. "We don't even know who you are."

She paused. The falcon on her arm squawked again, its feathers bristling as if it didn't like Magnus's tone.

The Guardian gestured toward Jessie with her staff. "I can smell the rot setting into your friend's wound." She shrugged. "But it makes no difference to me whether she keeps her leg."

When she turned away, the grass and shrubs parted once more. She disappeared into the trees; her path remained open in silent invitation. The starlight that had suffused the clearing dimmed with her departure.

Indecision gripped Ravlok. He didn't like that she hadn't given them so much as a name. Even a fake name would have been better than nothing. But he supposed they hadn't provided their names, either.

"Magnus," Kendi said, "I think we have to trust her."

"She has healing skills." Alar looked distracted as he gazed down the path. "We need her help."

Magnus nodded his agreement. "Remain vigilant, Commander."

"*Ciir, Amaa.*"

They gathered their packs and rose with a chorus of grunts and groans. Ravlok wiped damp strands of hair from his forehead. He bent to pick Orowen up and willed his legs to move.

For several minutes, they followed the Guardian through even denser, darker forest. The path she shaped through the foliage closed behind them, leaving little sign of their passage. At one point, when the forest grew so dark Ravlok could barely see Orowen in his arms, something strange passed along his skin, like the zap of static off a wool blanket. The coppery tang of Aether lay thick on his tongue.

Dizzying nausea overtook him. The air cooled several degrees in an instant. He stopped, reeling from the foreboding sense that he'd just stepped over a bottomless chasm—the kind where a fingerspan in the wrong direction would have sent him plummeting to his death. His head pounded, and a shrill whistle blew in his ears.

When he regained his wits and looked around, the forest was different. The trees were taller and thicker. Grass and brush had given way to springy moss. He couldn't see the stars through the canopy.

Up ahead, Alar doubled over and retched into the grass. Sam and Magnus steadied themselves against nearby trees, and behind him, Anwic cursed. Apparently, his companions felt that nauseating disquiet, too.

Moss gave way to hard-packed ground, and they descended into a small valley by way of a series of wide, stone slabs. Water rushed over rock somewhere below them—a curious sound. Tired as he was, Ravlok couldn't recall a creek running southeast, away from the capital.

Soft light glowed near the bottom of the gully. Through thick trunks, he spotted a small stone cottage nestled against a wide creek bed. The stream beyond was a sheet of black obsidian flanking a well-manicured garden of shrubs and ferns. Smoke spiraled up from the chimney, its plumes distorting the reflection of firelight on the water.

It was a welcome sight. With the promise of rest so close, Ravlok set aside his thoughts on the magical manner in which they'd arrived and ignored the lingering scent of Aether on his skin.

As they approached the cottage, a shadow slipped along one ivy-covered wall. The black shape shot toward them, and Ravlok froze, clutching Orowen. Two rows of gleaming white teeth flashed in the darkness.

The wolf growled.

The Guardian's rebuke came swiftly. "They are guests, Corra. Be at ease."

She sent the wolf inside the cottage first and gestured for Paelic to do the same. The falcon leaped from her arm, and the bark covering her skin dissolved.

Ravlok's heart was still hammering as he approached the door and stepped inside. A small fireplace bathed the room with orange light. He blinked, allowing his eyes to adjust. A long wooden table and one lone chair stood at the room's center. A silver vase sat atop the table with blue and purple flowers bursting from its mouth. Leatherbound books and sprigs of dried holly adorned the mantle. A spiral staircase in one corner led up to a narrow loft. Rows of cabinetry and two short countertops flanked the round window in the back wall. Beneath the frosted pane was a wash-basin too small to be called a sink.

Paelic perched atop the mantle, next to the stack of books whose titles were too faded to be read from where Ravlok stood. As his companions filed in around him, the falcon began preening its feathers. Corra, the wolf, lay down on a woven rug before the fireplace, her pink tongue lolling out of her mouth.

Ravlok gave the sleek black creature plenty of space. She turned her head to track the woman's movements like a dog watching its master, but there was no mistaking the predator behind that easy posture and the keen intelligence in her ochre-brown eyes.

Their hostess spoke to Rylan, who held Jessie in his arms. "Take her to the table."

As Rylan obeyed, she withdrew several jars of herbs and pastes from a cabinet, as well as a bowl and a mixing spoon. When she turned back, her gaze slid toward the fireplace.

Her expression soured. "Corra, make room for the priestess."

The wolf made a noise that sounded like indignation. With his mind in such a fog, Ravlok almost expected the creature to argue aloud. Instead, Corra rose and padded over to lie beside the door.

His attention fell to the rug. The allure of an end to the ache in his arms and legs became too great. He took three trembling steps and might have collapsed with Orowen had Kendi not caught him by the arm on their way down.

"Easy, *amii.*" The commander eased them both to the floor, his white brows drawn together with concern.

"The poultice will take some time to prepare." The woman gave them a sideways look and nodded toward the stairs. "I suggest you all rest while you can. You'll find spare blankets in the chest upstairs. I'll wake you when it's time to leave."

Ravlok knelt beside Orowen, his body too heavy to heave up the stairs. It was tempting to pass out right here on the floor. Sam seemed to be of like mind and settled beside him, her back against the gray stone surrounding the fireplace.

Alar leaned toward Jack. "Scout the perimeter—"

"That won't be necessary," the Guardian cut in. She set about mixing pastes for the poultice, and a soil-like scent undercut the smell of woodsmoke. "No one can find this place unless I wish it. You are safe here."

"You're a Walker," Magnus said, eyeing her. "Where have you brought us?"

They'd Walked through the Aether to get here.

Ravlok had started to drift off, but that made him jolt fully awake once more. That odd spark, the static sensation tingling against his skin—that had been the Aether. He'd felt it as they pierced the Wall. He knew what to look for now.

"Aivenos," she answered.

Aivenos? The name bounced around in Ravlok's mind. A continent a thousand leagues across the ocean from Guild-controlled Eidosinia, and a monumental display of the Guardian's power. No wonder he'd been so dizzy.

Stunned silence permeated the room. What that meant for them all—

Beside him, Sam barked a laugh. The sound was contagious, infecting Ravlok and taking root in his own smile. It was a heady realization, like the first show of spring after a brutal winter. Relief and euphoria bloomed in his chest.

They were safe.

They were free.

Behind him, Anwic let out a whoop of joy and clapped Kendi on the back. "Let those Guild rats chase us now, eh, Commander?"

Kendi's reaction was more subdued, but when Ravlok looked up, the commander was smiling too. "Indeed." He addressed the Guardian. "Thank you, my lady. If there is any way we can repay you, you need only name it."

Her lips twitched upward at that. "I doubt you have anything I want, Syljian. Just plant a few trees in the Northlands when you return." She set the bowl down and picked up another jar.

"We'll see it done," Kendi promised.

Magnus gave the room an assessing sweep. "We're months away from home out here. I pray you'll Walk us back to the Northlands as well."

The Guardian added more herbs to her greenish paste and stirred. "If it keeps you out of my berry gardens, I'll drop you off wherever you wish to be."

"Fawn's Breath," Kendi said. "Though three of us are bound for Orthovia."

The woman snorted. "What business have you in Delvin's city?" Before anyone could answer, she relented. "Never mind. I'm sure I don't want to know."

Ravlok shifted from his knees to his backside and crossed his legs, resting his hands on his thighs. The derision in her tone was puzzling. Was it the city itself or the god of law that drew her ire? He remained silent, watchful, thinking it best not to risk upsetting their only way back to the Eidosinian continent.

He sighed and closed his eyes, trying to ignore the pulsing along his temples. He would take this opportunity to meditate and rest while the ones in charge deliberated on their next step. It wasn't like he could offer much insight on where they were going anyway.

Their voices fell away as he focused on his breathing. He willed his mind to calm, and soon the weight of his exhaustion pulled him down.

A dog barked.

Ravlok shook himself awake. With a soft groan, he became aware of stone digging into his back. The heat of the fire warmed him. It took a moment to remember where he was.

Corra barked again, and he struggled to open his eyes. The wolf was standing at the door, hackles raised.

Apprehension wriggled down his neck. He blinked and scanned the room. It was still dark outside the round window. Rylan, Anwic, and Jack must have gone to bed upstairs. Kendi, Magnus, and Alar had rearranged themselves about the room. Sam's head rested on his shoulder, and a blanket was draped across them both. She was mumbling in her sleep.

The Guardian stood at the table, applying her poultice to Jessie's wound. She lowered the bowl of green paste, watching the wolf.

Ravlok cleared his throat. "What's wrong?" His voice sounded much louder in the stillness.

She glanced at him, frowning, hazel eyes glinting like flecks of granite in the firelight. Saying nothing, she strode to the door.

Kendi roused himself and sat up on Orowen's other side, reaching for a weapon. Magnus turned from where he stood at the back window, dropping his arms from across his chest. Alar opened his eyes but remained unmoved, cross-legged in his own meditative pose in the corner.

A wave of the woman's hand placated the wolf. In the same gesture, she summoned the strange layer of bark upon her skin. Paelic launched himself off the mantle, stirring embers in the hearth. He landed on her upraised arm in a flurry of wings as she pulled the door open.

The cottage glow illuminated her olive-green skin for several paces into the garden. Ravlok leaned as far forward as he could to watch her through the open door, stiff muscles straining to obey his every move. There were no obvious threats he could see.

The Guardian spoke to the falcon. Her voice was little more than a caress of wind, too soft to discern any real words. She stroked Paelic's cheek feathers with the knuckles of her free hand. The bird began to glow a soft white-violet and burst into flight. He disappeared high above the treetops.

Corra paced to her side, and the woman reached down to place a hand between the wolf's ears. They stood that way for a full minute, staring after the falcon. When they finally returned to the door, the Guardian looked troubled.

Ravlok settled against the stone, Sam fast asleep on his shoulder. Kendi lowered his sword, still in its scabbard.

"Is everything alright?" Magnus rasped.

"An anomaly in the Aether." She shut the door behind her. Corra circled once and lay down at the threshold. The Guardian returned to Jessie's side and began wrapping the paste-covered wound with cloth.

"What does that mean?" Alar asked.

She shrugged. "Most likely nothing."

Ravlok noted the tension in the woman's shoulders. "And if it's not nothing?"

The Guardian eyed him with a new intensity in her face—a sharpness of focus reminiscent of a hawk. If Ravlok hadn't already been pressed to the stone by Sam's weight, her expression would have pinned him there.

"Then the world as we know it is about to change," she said. "And not for the better."

Chapter Twenty-Five

Daeya

"I bet ye don't know this one, lass."

Cordy cleared his throat with a loud hacking sound and thumped his chest with a fist. The scraggly, gap-toothed sailor wobbled on his feet and launched into another tune.

Daeya grinned over the rim of her bottle. She absolutely knew the song; her cousin Murtagh sang it every Midsummer. It was called "Winds of Fair Fortune," and it was a classic in the Brogrenti Highlands. After harmonizing the chorus with him—much to Cordy's delight—she took a drink.

Brandy sprayed out of her nose the moment Gavin added his rich tenor to the next verse, dirtying the lyrics. The sailors howled with laughter.

Gavin excelled at parodying popular tunes and lacing them with innuendo. Even Murtagh would have been impressed by the black-eyed sailor's impeccable use of rhyme and rhythm.

One-Hand Dan pounded Daeya's back with his weighty palm, twisted black locks falling into his face. He shouted over the raucous cheers. "There, now, you've gone and made the lady blush!"

Gavin lifted his bottle. "A fine color befitting such fair cheeks."

Daeya choked on her laughter, one palm over her mouth. Her eyes and nose burned with the strong spirits. Aivenosian brandy was a viper of a drink. It struck hard, and it struck fast, but it certainly tasted better than Po's watered-down ale. If not for pacing herself with meticulous care, she'd have been lying on the deck next to Quinn by now.

Belio leaned into her, his eyes sparkling in the lamplight. He offered his shirt sleeve. "Here, let me help you with that."

"Oh, you're too kind." Daeya cringed at his grimy sleeve, swaying with the effects of the alcohol. She rubbed her face on his shoulder.

He chortled and took the bottle from her. "The kindest."

"And the humblest, too." Her cheeks ached from smiling so much.

"That's it. Get him, Daeya." Cordy sauntered over and shoved between her and Dan, nearly sitting in the bigger man's lap to make space for himself. He reached across Daeya to grab the bottle from Belio.

She couldn't have imagined such close contact with him days ago. Her camaraderie with the sailors had begun the morning after the storm. Once they'd paid their respects to the three sailors who perished, Daeya had insisted on staying above deck to help repair the ship. Belio and his mates had invited her to dine with them that night, and every night since had been full of rowdy singing and drunken storytelling.

Now, after a full day of repairs and four days of sailing without the main mast, they were just twelve hours from limping into port. Captain Arnes believed they should reach the Orthovian harbor by third bell tomorrow.

"Alright, I've got one," One-Hand Dan said in his rumbling baritone. His rough accent, midnight skin, and single orange stripe across the bridge of his nose bespoke his Skriian ancestry. "It's a story you've never heard."

"We've heard all your stories," Belio argued, holding the bottle away from Cordy, who draped himself across Daeya's lap and strained to reach the brandy, "at least a dozen times each."

"Not this one." Dan held up the stump where his left hand used to be. At the end of the stump was a three-pronged metal fork. He thrust the curving tines toward Belio, one eye widening to show a ring of white all the way around his chestnut-brown iris. "This one is about a dragon."

The word burst through Daeya's fog of liquor, her curiosity piqued. "A dragon?"

"Aye, a copper one. The ones that breathed lightning, they say."

"Ow!" Daeya winced as Cordy's elbow drove into the nerve cluster on her thigh. She shoved at him, swearing in Brogrenti. "Get off me, you *napher gought.*"

Cordy overbalanced, one arm pinwheeling, and hit the deck beside Quinn. The curly-haired woman groaned in her sleep and rolled over, empty bottle cradled in her arms.

Belio howled again. "Gods, I never thought I'd hear such words from a sorceress." He passed the bottle back to Daeya while Cordy spluttered and flopped about the deck like a fish.

The vapor-slicked glass cooled her palm. "You've not been around the right ones, I guess."

"Cheers to that." Gavin leaned over Cordy to clink his bottle against hers. "I rather like this one."

Cordy made a show of brushing himself off before rising. New streaks of grime appeared where his hands passed over his shirt.

Daeya sipped from the bottle, feeling the liquor burn all the way down to her belly. She looked past Cordy into the oil lantern hanging from the hook over their heads. The fire danced in the night wind. "I would hear your story, Dannicus."

Dan's white teeth flashed. He liked it when she used his full name. "It has a fancy Aether mage in it, too." He winked at her.

Daeya groaned and rolled her eyes. It had taken three days to convince them she wasn't an Aetherian. Rumors of what she'd done during the storm departed from reality in such outlandish and fantastical ways that slowing their momentum was as impossible as trying to slow a rockslide. One told of how she'd levitated the ship above the waves. Another suggested she'd calmed the winds themselves, like Illustria Stormflight. The most farfetched of them claimed she had sent the entire ship through an Aether rift to clear the storm.

Belio jabbed her with his elbow and took the bottle. "You know he does that to get a rise out of you."

"I'm aware." She side-eyed him. "Who put him up to it, I wonder?"

Mischief danced in her friend's gaze. "Truthfully, I couldn't say."

Dan tapped his metal cuff on the deck railing to get their attention. "It all took place in the tree city of Pananmai."

As he spoke, the sailors quieted, their expressions eager. Dan was the best storyteller among them—and likely the source of the wildest rumors about her magic. Cordy reclaimed his seat next to Daeya, pushing Quinn back over with his callused foot. Shadows teased their faces. The lantern between them swayed on the breeze.

"It was a little city in Aivenos, known for its rolling rice fields and hearty fish. Its people worshipped Caelyn and cared deeply for her land. They were friendly, and they never turned away strangers, except"—he held up a finger—"for one week of every year."

Belio's arm curled around Daeya's shoulders. She leaned into him, welcoming his touch. Even if she would likely never see him again after this journey, she indulged his friendship and affection. Gods knew the more she had of it, the more she wanted.

"It was called the Week of Reaping, and it was Pananmai's most closely guarded secret. Every Reaping, the Blight would awaken." Dan's face darkened as he leaned away from the lantern's glow. He held up his hand and weaved it back and forth, mimicking the motion of a snake. "His shadow would slither down from the mountains. His great wings would blot out the sun, plunging the forest into darkness. He came to collect Pananmai's yearly offering of riches beyond our wildest dreams."

Belio and Gavin traded grins, murmuring about where the townsfolk would have gotten such treasure.

Daeya attempted an admonishing look. "Bleeding pirates."

The men both laughed.

"Years passed. Pananmai grew poorer and the Blight grew hungrier, until one Reaping, the people had no riches at all."

Water lapped at the hull. Ropes creaked. Sails fluttered in the wind. Dan leaned back into the light. It reflected off the sheen of sweat on his brow and made the whites of his eyes glow. "It just so happened that on the night before that fateful Reaping, a man came to the city.

"'We have no rooms for you,' the innkeepers said, but the man would not be deterred. Somehow, he knew about the Blight of Pananmai. He promised to stop the dragon from taking everything they had. The keeper of the smallest inn allowed him to stay just for one night, but he made the man promise to leave by sunrise."

Dan met Daeya's gaze. His eyes pinned her to her seat as they transformed, shifting from brown to rich, ruddy copper. They smoldered like coals, pupils formed into slits, like those of a snake.

Her heart beat harder in her chest. An illusion. A bleeding good one.

"True to his word, the man left the inn before sunrise, but he did not go far. When the Blight came to his favored grove, expecting his riches, there the lone man stood, instead.

"'These people have nothing left for you,' the man said."

Dan's voice took on an otherworldly sound, like air being squeezed through a gap. His face twisted into a horrible, teeth-bearing snarl, sending chills down Daeya's spine. "And the Blight replied, 'If they will not pay what I am owed in gold and gems, then they shall pay with their lives.'"

"Tiior's tits," Cordy swore, the tip of his bottle poised halfway to his mouth.

Despite his crudeness, Daeya shared the sentiment, gripped as she was by all the haunting ways One-Hand Dan was bringing the story to life. "Did he destroy the city?"

"He tried." Dan's expression smoothed over. His eyes—dark once more—swept his audience before returning to Daeya. He held up a thick finger. "But the Blight made a grave mistake in underestimating his adversary. For he was something much more than any ordinary man. Stronger than your mages. Stronger than any Aetherian yet living. This man was known as a dragon rider. A draegion. And he was not to be defied."

Daeya had heard of the dragon riders. Ancient beings that once commanded the greatest predators to have ever lived. There was a well-loved children's book about them in the Guild nursery. They were a myth, of course, but tales of their bravery and heroism had inspired initiates for as long as she could remember.

"The Blight leaped into the morning sky, his ruddy scales glinting like pools of blood. As he opened his maw to lay waste to the city, the draegion spoke a single word, and the dragon crashed to the forest floor. Trees and hilltops shattered in his wake. But when the draegion came for him again, the Blight was ready. He summoned a storm of lightning that split the sky apart."

A fork of lightning flashed in the clear sky above them. Daeya's attention snapped upward, eyes widening. The others recoiled in awe and fear. Echoing halos lingered in her vision, and she shook her head to clear it. Dan's skill was masterful. How was he doing that without spells? Had he studied at the School? And where was he getting his saphyrum?

When Dan spoke again, his tone was grave. The tattooed stripe across his nose pinched at its center. "As the forest went up in flames, the Blight brought his lightning to bear on the man, certain his power would prevail. But in his hubris, he sealed his fate."

The flame in the lantern guttered. At first Daeya thought it was another illusion, until the ocean wind caressed her skin. While the fire struggled to stay alight, Dan's face was lost to shadow and darkness. Belio shifted beside her, squeezing her shoulder. She glanced aside to him and giggled at his harrowed expression.

Light returned to them. The fire's orange glow chased the shadows away. Dan held his hand and metal cuff before him, gradually spreading them apart. "A churning ball of crackling death swelled between the Blight's teeth. He reared back—"

Thunder crashed.

The sailors started. Even Daeya flinched. How was he *doing* that?

"—and the draegion threw up his hands before the dragon's lethal breath." Dan lowered the cuff, resting his elbow on one knee. His hand lifted, palm out, as if to mimic the dragon rider's gesture. "Into his palms the lightning flowed, like a river pooling in a basin. When the Blight's mighty attack expired, the man's eyes were globes of copper. His flesh glowed with the same ruddy light."

More shadows flitted across One-Hand's face. Daeya's lips parted. Dan gazed back at her with a steadiness built of mortared stone. She relished the staggering intensity of it.

Her voice came out little more than a whisper. "Then what happened?"

"Well, you see, the draegion knew the dragon's scales could not be pierced by any manner of mundane steel. Because the man took the dragon's very essence into himself"—a feral smile stole over his black lips—"it became his weapon. In his hands, the dragon's breath reformed. Hotter. Stronger. Able to punch through the dragon's own defenses.

"The dragon now understood the man's power. He even tried to negotiate, but for the Blight of Pananmai, the draegion's justice was swift. The first sphere of scarlet lightning punched through the dragon's metallic hide. The second stopped the dragon's heart."

Gavin whistled, long and low. "Chaos be damned."

Belio shook himself. "That's quite the story, Dan."

"And it's all true." Dannicus straightened, looking very pleased with himself.

It absolutely couldn't be true, and it pawed at Daeya's sensibilities to allow Dan to claim otherwise. The dragon riders were a myth. Dragons had gone extinct long ago. And the magic he spoke of—stopping a dragon's devastating breath with only one's hands—was impossible. If any part of the story was ever true, it had been embellished beyond all recognition.

Narrowing her eyes, she took a gentle approach at calling him out. "So, what happened to the city? I've not seen Pananmai on any maps."

Dan chuckled. "That's because the city was destroyed. Trees don't like lightning, you know."

His teasing warmed her cheeks. She wrinkled her nose. "You mean to tell me after all that, the city was still destroyed? That's not a very satisfying ending."

Cordy choked on his liquor. When Daeya glanced his way, he looked like he'd swallowed an apple whole. "You're saying old One-Hand's left you unsatisfied, lass?"

It took Daeya a full three seconds of Gavin's uproarious laughter before she caught the innuendo. Her ears burned even as a sheepish smile threatened. She'd walked right into that one. *Bleeding sailors.*

Belio took a playful swing at him. "Mind your manners around the lady, you toad-faced cad."

"You wanna fight for the lady's honor, eh?" Cordy's gap-toothed grin was enormous as he lunged for Belio.

Daeya let out a mirthful yelp and leaped away from them. She hunkered down on Dan's other side while the two men tussled, rolling about on the deck like boys. Gavin rose from his seat to cheer them on, sloshing liquor on himself as he gestured wildly with his bottle. Daeya's abdomen ached from laughing. It was almost like being at home in Southgate again.

Dan reached across their small circle of crates and barrels for another bottle of brandy. "You can be sure Caelyn was not happy with the draegion." He pulled on the cork, and it gave way with a *pop.* "She banished him from Aivenos for it. Might have banned the rest of the draegion, too, if Tiior hadn't talked her out of it."

Something about the way he spoke pulled Daeya's attention from the rowdy brawl. Dan was so cavalier speaking about the goddesses, it was like he knew them personally.

He's been eating too many talotibas. Gods knew those mushrooms could make a person see the divine. Ravlok and the monks used them in their rituals.

Daeya decided to humor him, anyway. "And how do you know the goddesses so well?"

When Dan leaned toward her, his breath smelled of Aether and Aivenosian brandy. He lowered his voice. "Can you keep a secret?"

She stifled a snort at how his words slurred. The liquor was doing its work even on the brawny storyteller. She lowered her own voice to match his. "Yes, of course."

He leaned closer still, his stubble scratching her cheek. He whispered in her ear. "I serve Tiior. I'm a dragon."

Daeya stilled.

Her humor evaporated. A heavy feeling settled in her gut, as if the brandy had turned to stone. She leaned away from Dan, studying his features in the firelight. That wide, flaring nose. The flat planes of his cheeks. His prominent jaw and pouting lips.

Snake-slitted, copper eyes. Lightning in the clear sky, the absence of spells. Thunder.

Fear sank its talons into her.

No. You are fearless.

Daeya made to rise from her seat and retreat from him. Whether or not he was a threat to her—

She was halfway to her feet when Dan bared his teeth, squeezed his eyes shut, and doubled over. He roared with laughter. "You should see your face," he forced out, gasping for air.

The breath she'd been holding blew out of her in a rush. Relief, sweet and cool as any orange, coursed from her chest to the very tips of her fingers and toes. She lowered herself back down, lips twitching. "You bastard."

Belio and Cordy, both bleeding from mouths and noses, paused in their spirited game of male dominance, watching her.

Her reaction only made Dan laugh harder. He clutched his stomach, pounding his cuff on his knee. Daeya covered her face, shoulders shaking with silent mirth.

"I really had you going, didn't I?"

Gods, did he. When she regained control of herself, she lowered her hands. Her cheeks were aflame. "You really did," she breathed. "That was well done."

He beamed and tipped his bottle toward her. "Thank you, Sorceress."

"You're going to have to tell me how you did all that." Daeya reached for the last unopened bottle and tapped it against his. "Those are some of the best illusions I've ever seen."

Lifting his chin with pride, Dan opened his mouth to say more, but stopped. A shadow fell across his face. The other sailors went silent, staring at the source of that shadow.

Daeya turned. Cold, calculated malice stared back at her.

"Nice to see you having such fun with the dregs of society, Daeya. It suits you." Joss curled his lip as he took them all in. His icy gaze sliced her open like a razor. "But it's time for you to go to bed now. Big day tomorrow."

She lowered the unopened bottle, glaring at him. "I'll go to bed when I'm ready. You're not my keeper."

"Oh, but I am." His grin was sharp. Feral. "And I need you fresh for your debut in front of the Magistrate."

A whisper of foreboding slipped down Daeya's spine. It was followed by confusion. "The Magistrate?"

"Yes. It seems the auxiliary Council in Orthovia agrees with our assessment. You are to stand trial for your part in the collapse of the School."

It might have been because of her lowered inhibitions. Or perhaps it was because she'd grown tired of being pushed around and made to feel guilty. But the next thing she knew, Daeya had risen, stepped into Joss's space, and drawn herself up to face him.

"You know I had nothing to do with that." She cursed the slight tremor in her voice. "I followed Faustus for months. I accept that I failed in that mission, but it wasn't on purpose."

Joss tilted his head with a mocking look of surprise. "Is that so? You weren't aiding the blanker spy because you, too, are working for the Alliaansi?"

Daeya blinked. "What?"

The word was as much a conveyance of her shock and outrage as she could muster. How could he think that? Her loyalty had never been called into question. Why, all of a sudden, would anyone—even Joss—think she would betray her people?

His poise didn't so much as flicker. She longed to slap that haughty look right off his face.

"We know what they've been calling you." Joss waved a hand toward the men gathered around the lantern with her. Another cold smile twisted his face. "Aetherian."

Shocked protests and assurances they had only been joking rose among the sailors, but they were a background din against the roaring in Daeya's ears.

"We also have reports of your ostentatious use of Aetherian magic last week. Eleven people so far have come forward, willing to take the stand against you."

Her chest grew tight. She had used only the simplest wards and spells alongside her elemental affinity that night. None of those were in any way like the devastating force of magic Aetherians could harness. Whatever those witnesses thought they saw must have been misconstrued.

The blackness of night closed in around her, narrowing to a single point—that cruel, triumphant gleam in Joss's eyes. He'd likely bullied the statements out of them. Certainty of her suspicion sparked hot against her fingertips. Now she understood why he and Toby had left her alone for the past few days.

They were setting her up.

He's going to do everything he can to make sure you fail, Cam had said.

Her nails pricked her palms. He wouldn't get away with this. There was no way the Council would fall for it. "Gregory will—"

"Ah, yes." Joss placed his finger against her lips. His expression was almost apologetic. "I'm sorry to say Gregory has been called away on a most pressing matter in the north. He won't be coming to save you this time. But, rest assured, you will still have our Councilor's representation. Normos has elected to stand in for him."

There it was. The true master behind this plot. She should have known Joss wasn't cunning enough to have acted alone. Their jealousy had united them, even though Normos's contempt for Joss ran deep. If Normos was her only defense against the accusations of murder and treason she now faced, she might as well walk herself to the gallows when they reached port.

Daeya fought back the tide of helplessness threatening to swallow her. She struggled to keep her voice even. "Joss. Please. Don't do this."

Joss closed the last of the distance between them. One hand cupped her cheek. His other disappeared between the folds of their black robes. Daeya stiffened, biting back a whimper. The sound of his soft laughter in her ears made bile rise in her throat.

"There is one way you can persuade me to undo this."

Only tangentially did Daeya register Belio's snarl of outrage and Gavin and Cordy's warnings not to interfere. All her focus was on that hand between her thighs. No one had ever touched her there, and the wrongness of it threatened to turn her stomach out on the deck.

Joss's grip tightened on that intimate spot. He ran his tongue along the curve of her ear. "What do you say, McVen? Make it worth my while?"

She was tempted to let the bastard have his way. She could see the matter dropped, go on with her mission, and never think about it again. But that wasn't how this worked. There was no guarantee he would keep his word, and no chance with Normos involved.

There was also the matter of what he would find beneath her robes. If a rigged trial didn't send her to the Gate early, then hundreds of runes found only on blankers and half-bloods surely would.

No. She couldn't. She wouldn't agree to this. She had to trust that the Councilors stationed in Orthovia would see this plot for what it was. Daeya reached up, placed her palms on Joss's chest, and shoved.

He stumbled back, wide-eyed, barely keeping his feet.

She spat on the deck between them, bristling with rage. "Go fuck yourself, Joss."

As he righted himself, his laughing eyes caught the light. "Suit yourself."

Joss dipped his chin sharply, and Toby stepped into the light. He seized her left wrist. Cold metal slapped against her skin, and the spellbinder clicked shut.

Daeya wrenched her wrist away with a snarl, pulling the sturdy chain and the second manacle with her.

"There's nowhere to go, Daeya," Joss purred. "Where are you going to run from us on a ship?"

In her periphery, Gavin and Cordy were holding Belio back by his arms and shoulders. Good. At least they wouldn't be charged with assaulting a mage on her behalf. She stepped over Quinn's prone form and tugged at the binder on her wrist.

"You're only making this worse for yourself, resisting arrest," Toby pointed out.

The brothers took up flanking positions on either side of her, their figures fully illuminated by the lantern. The open manacle bounced off her knee, provoking a wince.

They were right. There was nowhere on this ship she could hide. If she tried to fight, she would only incriminate herself further. But gods, the last thing she wanted to do was submit to this.

Cam. Where was Cam? She wouldn't stand for this. She knew Daeya was loyal—

But no. Her obvious absence spoke tomes. She either didn't realize her brothers had planned this, or she had chosen not to get involved. Daeya was alone.

Her gaze settled on Dan, who hovered at the edge of the fire's glow, half in shadow behind Toby. He was watching the display with an expression cut from stone. His eyes shone like copper coals. The sight was comforting, somehow bolstering her courage, like a promise that everything would be alright.

In Daeya's distraction, Joss lurched forward and seized her free wrist. Toby was right behind him, clamping the second cuff in place.

Metal chilled her skin. Chain links clinked as she shifted to make the manacles more comfortable. Though the spellbinders cut her off from her magic, there was no shroud-like sensation or dampening of her perception like she'd expected.

She kept her eyes on Dannicus as Joss hauled her forward by her wrists. There was the barest flash of pointed teeth against Dan's black lips before she lost sight of him behind Joss's taller frame. She stiffened again as the mage pressed his body against hers.

His lips brushed her neck. "Now, be a good girl, *my sweet.*" He ran his fingers through her white-blonde hair, and worms crawled up her spine. "You'll get some rest and shine like gold in the morning."

"You're going to burn for this," Daeya told him, her voice surprisingly steady.

She didn't know why she said it. But the knowledge settled deep in her bones, and the taste of smoke coated her tongue, as if the fire she'd drawn from the ship's mast still raged inside her.

This I promise you.

Chapter Twenty-Six

Orowen

Orowen walked out of the cabin under her own power, though she held the Guardian's arm as they traveled down a stony trail to the brook's edge. Corra loped along beside the path, slipping silently through the brush like a shadow.

Orowen's legs trembled and her lungs labored, but the herbal tea the Guardian had provided at breakfast helped soothe her weary nerves. It had also granted her a reprieve from the symptoms of Mage's Folly and filled the aching hollow in her chest that her magic left behind. The brew wasn't the most palatable concoction, but the recipe the Guardian had shared was worth passing on to her students at the Temple.

Water chattered against the rocks. Brightly colored fish darted in and out of fallen leaves. Orowen breathed in the scent of autumn and relished the gentle breeze that teased her white hair across her cheeks. Warm sunlight filtered through the towering trees. She tipped her chin up to bask in it. The Guardian was right; a walk was just what she'd needed.

The trail ended in a small circle of logs blanketed by red-dappled mushrooms and emerald-green moss. Their vibrant colors and rich woody scents stood in such stark contrast to the stale Guild prison that Orowen's eyes brimmed with tears.

She breathed out, taking it all in as she blinked away the sting. "Caelyn be praised for such a beautiful morning."

"Mm." The Guardian's smile rivaled the sun for its brilliance. She planted her staff and assisted Orowen in sitting down. Springy moss cushioned Orowen's gracelessness as her legs gave way beneath her. "It could be a little cooler. My chrysanthemums and equinox daisies are taking their time blooming this year."

Orowen's attention strayed to the vines spiraling up from the ground to hold the staff in place. White flowers blossomed along their lengths, and a lovely aroma wafted on the air. "I'm certain they will bloom when they are ready."

The Guardian gave her hand an appreciative squeeze before releasing it. "Such is the nature of all growing things."

There was something enamoring about the Aivenosian woman's wild and savage beauty. It was as if she embodied the spirit of nature itself. Life seemed to bloom wherever she walked. Even the autumn grasses seemed to stand a little straighter, and a trick of the light might have darkened them to their prior summer green. There was no doubt Saolanni's light shone brightly within her.

The thought tightened something in Orowen's chest. A sense of longing, perhaps, or of loss. She had forsaken that light such a brief time ago, but it felt like ages since she'd felt its warmth and purity for herself. The others assured her Saolanni's magic would return in time, but they didn't understand the grievousness of her betrayal. It wasn't simply Mage's Folly that had taken her light, but a broken oath for which the only penance could be the withdrawal of the goddess's blessing entirely. If Saolanni could not forgive her, Orowen would never wield magic again.

Corra glided into the clearing and settled at the woman's side. The black wolf looked up, and the Guardian placed a hand between her ears.

"Rest here for a time." The Guardian's voice was soft, despite the curtness of her instructions. "Send Corra to fetch me when you are ready to depart."

Orowen bowed her head, still unable to banish the shade of discomfiture her own envy produced. "We are in your debt, my lady."

"Think nothing of it, priestess. It is our mother's will."

The Guardian reached for her staff, and the vines uncoiled from the wood as if by some sentient force. They lay in a tangle as the flowers wilted and petals littered the ground.

As the woman departed, Orowen carefully extended a hand to the wolf in invitation. Corra stepped into her palm and turned her enormous head in a silent demand. Another smile came unbidden to Orowen's lips, and she obliged the creature with firm scratches behind her ear.

"You knew just what I needed, didn't you?" she asked.

Corra panted quietly, closing her eyes as she sat, leaning into Orowen's leg.

Time passed, and the sun crept higher. Corra remained at her side, eventually settling her bulk against Orowen's feet. She perked up only at the sound of footsteps on the trail. As the wolf's ears turned toward the newcomer, Orowen followed her intelligent gaze to Kendi, who was making his way down the hill.

He'd washed and braided his hair, and changed into fine but simple clothes so unlike his usual austere attire that he could have been mistaken for a young man again. Bell sleeves rippled in the wind, and brown leggings fit snugly against his muscular thighs.

It was the haunted look in his eyes that aged him—eyes that had seen far too much suffering and death to belong to anyone but a military commander. Still, he managed a smile for her, though with an uneasy glance toward Corra when she fixed him with a keen stare.

"She's taken a liking to you." Kendi reached the bottom of the trail and hesitated at the edge of the circle, as if deciding whether to approach.

Orowen scratched the wolf once more, and Corra gave a contented sigh. She chuckled. "I think you might be right."

The slightest tensing of his jaw betrayed his anxiety. Kendi was rarely so unsure of himself. Orowen sobered, her smile fading. Those words he'd spoken in the dungeon, just before she had summoned the rift, still lingered between them. He'd been preparing to die when he said them; the only question now was where they should go from here.

Her life as a priestess and his as a soldier had always come first. A romantic partnership was so far removed from Orowen's thoughts that her students always joked she was more likely to marry the goddess herself than any mortal.

Kendi approached, his boots scraping stone. He gestured to the space beside her. "Do you mind if I sit?"

Orowen slid over to make room. "No, of course not. Please."

As Kendi sat, Corra returned to her feet and sauntered away down to the water's edge for a drink. The awkwardness of the moment stretched on, and Orowen twined her fingers in her lap.

Anxious to end the silence, they spoke at the same time.

"About what I said—"

"I love you, too."

Warmth flooded Orowen's cheeks, and she lowered her gaze.

"You—" Kendi stared at the side of her face, mouth hanging open. "You do?"

Mira's mercy, it was like she was sixty-five again. She tried to squash the butterflies in her stomach, only to find they'd fluttered up her throat. Summoning her courage, she reached for him.

"Of course I do. I always have."

It was true. She had remained aloof not out of fear, but out of love. Kendi had always wanted children, and that was something Orowen wasn't able to give him. Not after a Light Paladin's blade had pierced her abdomen and damaged her womb beyond repair. She'd prayed that in time, he would move on and find love with another, and Mira would bless him with the family he always wanted. But he hadn't moved on; he'd been waiting for her this whole time.

Kendi let out a shaky exhalation as he twined his fingers with hers. His smile was relief and joy in equal parts. "As have I. I'm just sorry it took me so long to say it. My timing was terrible."

Tears flooded her eyes. "It suits you, *nei ama're*."

My love. What a strange and wonderful name for him.

His eyes gleamed in return. He cupped her cheek. "It suits us."

"*Ciir*." Gods, did it. His forehead came to rest against hers, and Orowen let her tears fall.

"No matter what happens now," Kendi said, his breath a caress against her lips, "there is no one else I would rather share my years with."

Something in his voice roused Orowen from the heady elation of their confession. She pulled away just far enough to search his troubled face. There had been talk of war this morning among their companions, but there had been talk of war for decades.

"Surely Tipori can stay the vote." Her sister's husband had spent nearly twenty years ensuring the council remained deadlocked in Koraani's push for war. "And Magnus will uphold Cheralach's visions for peace. We must have faith."

Kendi straightened, retreating further, but he kept a firm hold on her hand. The haunted look in his eyes returned, and he opened and closed his mouth a few times. Orowen's unease redoubled.

"What is it?" she asked. "What's wrong?"

"Orowen." He drew in a breath and spoke with the same caution he used to deliver ill-fated news to his troops. "It's not our council I'm worried about."

She frowned. "The sorcerers have been dragging their feet for years. They know they can't touch us on the Plateau. Especially not with such dense forest between us and the mountains. Even with their greater numbers, they would lose too many."

He shook his head, his expression grim. "I'm afraid they can't ignore us any longer."

Trepidation prickled the back of Orowen's neck. The memory of distant, crashing stone echoed in her ears. "Speak plainly, *neime*. You know I can't stand suspense."

Kendi took a long time answering. He busied himself by examining the back of her hand, still clutched in his. His throat bobbed. "Do you remember much of what happened in the dungeon? How fast your rift grew?"

"*Ciir.*" Her anxiety gave way to remorse. "It wasn't supposed to leave that room."

His shoulders sagged with another breath. When he looked up again, the entire world ground to a halt. The burbling brook became white noise as she stared into his harrowed eyes. "It went much farther beyond the guard room. Devoted, it—"

She waited, her body rigid as a spear held under tension and ready to break.

"It destroyed the entire west wing."

Her heart seized. The noise that left her barely shaped a word. "What?"

"I know it was an accident. I know you didn't mean—"

"The west wing," Orowen cut in. An excruciating knot formed in her throat, making it hard to project her voice beyond a whisper. "You mean the School?"

He cringed. "*Ciir.*"

Icy horror sluiced all warmth from her veins. "You're saying I murdered a school full of children?"

Kendi took her by the shoulders, but the answer was plain in his expression. "No. No, Orowen, listen to me..."

His words faded away. The entire world grew muffled, and Orowen reeled as her mind attempted to process the inconceivable truth.

The ground came up to meet her as she sagged in Kendi's hold. A slow blink later, she found herself staring up into the trees. Kendi's face appeared, backlit by bright shafts of sunlight. He spoke to her and touched her cheek, but Orowen felt only numbness and pressure on her skin. A wolf's howl punched through the fog of her awareness as she spiraled down, down into some dark recess of her mind.

She had forsaken her oath.

She had forsaken Saolanni's light and chosen death over life.

And hundreds of children had paid the price.

Chapter Twenty-Seven

Alar

Crabby dropped Alar, Jack, and Ravlok off at the edge of the Old City in a swirl of shadow and mist. As soon as the rift closed behind them, Alar's organs violently rearranged themselves. He retched, vomit searing every part of his mouth and throat.

The Wastelands take him if he ever Walked again.

Val would have had a quip for the occasion. He would have cracked a joke perfectly timed to shoot vomit straight into Alar's nose. But Val was gone, his body likely eroded into dozens of pieces by now. Nothing ever stayed whole in the Aether for long.

When he straightened and wiped his mouth, he found Crabby watching him. The Guardian's olive skin blended with the low-hanging palms of the Orthovian oasis. A hint of a smirk lingered on her moss-green lips.

"Next time, close your eyes. The nausea won't be as bad."

"I'll have to remember that," Alar rasped. She could have told him that three Walks ago. She'd surely kept the knowledge from him on purpose.

Her haughtiness grated. If her aura hadn't been like staring into the sun, Alar might have suppressed her emotions to a numbing indifference just for some respite. He would never have agreed to accept her aid without Master Ulrich's instructions.

Now, looking around, he was glad he had. Not only had his people reached their respective destinations, but they'd all managed at least one night of restful sleep, and in relative safety and comfort compared to the woods outside Ryost.

Jessie's wound had succumbed to fleshrot, but Crabby's mysterious poultice had worked wonders to banish the disease. All evidence of rot was gone this morning, and the healers in Fawn's Breath would further seal the wound. Crabby had also given Magnus a tonic for his throat, and Orowen some herbs to regain her strength. She claimed the worst of the danger was already past, and the priestess's arcane abilities should return in a few weeks. They would all be in capable hands until they could meet again.

Alar offered a hand to the woman. "Thank you."

Crabby looked disdainfully at his palm before extending her own. As her fingers closed on his, she thrust her chin over her shoulder. "Orthovia is just over the ridge. I trust you can find your way from here."

Again with that arrogant tone. At least she wasn't spouting world-altering, cryptic nonsense anymore. "Yes, I think we can manage."

She released him. Her gaze lifted to the monk at his left shoulder. "The gods have heard you, servant of Ordeolas. I've seen you safely through the forest."

Ravlok recoiled. Wide-eyed and blinking, he fumbled a bow and muttered an Aivenosian platitude in return.

She summoned a rift and vanished.

Alar glanced at him; surprise was a static uproar in the monk's aura. "Looks like you made a friend."

Ravlok opened his mouth, but no sound came out.

Jack checked the weapons at his belt. "Now what?"

"Now we find Daeya."

Alar started for the ridge. With the sun cresting the rise ahead, the air breezy and cool, they made their way along the Eidosinian coastline. Dry, leafy debris mixed with sandy soil and crunched under their boots, making a stealthy approach to the northern gate impossible. Fortunately, Alar had reapplied his assassin's clay and make-up to hide his ears, and he wore a simple blouse and tunic suggestive of a wealthy craftsman. The others wore the garb of mercenaries—leather vests over plain white shirts and sword belts well-fitted and buckled low around their hips. Alar would have to send Rammie something special for the attention she'd paid to their attire.

The city of Orthovia was a sprawling expanse of tan stone buildings with gray slate roofs and awnings in shades of red, yellow, and green. Squat structures clung to the curvature of the city walls, with two-, three-, and even four-story buildings marching toward an enormous central keep—the famous Tower of Law, home of the Jurists' Order and some of the stuffiest individuals Alar had ever met.

The Jurists were worshippers of Delvin, god of justice, and the mediators of all trials overseen by the Magistrate in Eidosinia. Known for their strict adherence to the law, they were the perfect, passionless force to carry out sentences on Syljians and criminals alike.

In the shadow of the Jurists' Tower was the Guild embassy and an array of service buildings, barracks, and training yards for mundane soldiers. That sector was to be avoided at all costs.

West of the city stretched the glimmering blue waters of Narisett Bay. To the north spanned a second sea made of sand. They would have to decide later whether to brave the sweltering heat and unforgiving terrain of the Denorian Desert, or if they would take the longer road home through the forests of Nohr.

Alar turned his attention to the western portion of the city, which boasted the largest port in the country. Ships of every size crowded the harbor, sail-bedecked masts jutting proudly into the sky. A hundred docks stretched like spindly wooden fingers into the bay, riddled with smaller boats tied in an endless web of ropes. Scents of briny water and sweaty sailors carried on the wind. Insistent cries of seabirds and the ring of ships' bells only added to the bustling ambiance of the city.

Daeya's ship from Keilliad should arrive at the docks that evening, pending fair winds. With any luck, they would be on their way to the border by nightfall. Alar turned to his companions, who flanked him atop the ridge. "We'll try the docks first."

Ravlok looked across the city, brows furrowed. "How are we going to find her in that mess? We don't even know what ship she's on."

"The harbormaster should be able to help us. Just let me do the talking."

The road to the northern gate was lined with carts and carriages waiting for admittance. They approached a smaller gate admitting foot traffic, posing as Jaime Ellington and his pair of bodyguards, Raff and Turk. The soldier manning the gate barely looked twice at them before ushering them through the wall.

Markets teemed with vibrant colors. Merchants sported wares of every kind, from bolts of richly dyed cotton to exotic fruits and vegetables. Horses and carts crowded the main thoroughfares, directed at intersections by soldiers in bright green. Side streets and alleyways were impassable to all but those on foot. Even then, it was slow going to reach the port.

The city's coastal scent was even stronger at ground level—a combination of fish, sweat, and sulfur. Smaller than Ryost by only a fraction in physical size, Orthovia boasted busier, more crowded streets due to the number of visitors and temporary residents. It was easy to blend in among them, and easier still to avoid the few mages they encountered.

Alar sensed Jack's irritation growing with each passing moment. The younger man didn't like being stuck in crowds or jostled about. He finally dismissed the dour-faced thief with a gesture he'd seen Val use, silently instructing him to take to the rooftops but stay close.

"Where is he going?" Ravlok asked when Jack slipped into the crowd.

Alar caught the subtle gleam of a knife as Jack slit the strap off a passing nobleman's purse. He smirked to himself. "He's going to secure supplies for the journey north."

Ravlok sighed. "You mean he's going to steal supplies."

Alar looked back at him, his grin widening. "Not the supplies, no. Those he'll purchase. Come on."

The monk rolled his eyes, but voiced no protests. They skirted the city and stepped onto the boardwalk as the four noonday bells echoed across the port.

Shops lined the boardwalk. Many were taverns and inns full of half-clad courtesans and rowdy sailors. Others were bait-and-tackle shops and ship supply stores. A few signs advertised smithies and armories. Alar even spotted a cobbler's shop.

Like everywhere else in Orthovia, the place was crowded. Tourists of a dozen races and nationalities surrounded them. Some meandered about, gazing in wonder at the street performers and musicians. Others strode with purpose, trailed by servants hauling their luggage to nearby coaches.

Sand clung to Alar's skin and made every cobble rasp beneath his boots. He repeatedly wiped his hands on his clothes, longing to return north, where the crisp, clean air was heavy with the scents of evergreen, and the only irritation was fast-melting snow.

They swerved around a group of children running barefoot across the mist-dappled planks, their trousers stained and tattered. Most were several fingerspans too short, and the boys were all shirtless. One had a gruesome, crescent-shaped scar on his cheek, as if he'd been kicked in the face by a horse.

Alar caught Ravlok staring after them and paused. "Turk, we have little time."

Pained blue eyes shifted to him. Then Ravlok turned on his heel and stalked after the children.

Bleeding heart monk. Alar sighed, but there was no venom behind his annoyance. At least someone cared.

He stood waiting as Ravlok coaxed the scarred boy out of the shadows and passed him a few copper coins. Soon more children darted out, claiming their own coins until the purse Rammie had provided him with hung empty, and Ravlok lifted his hands in defeat.

The children disappeared as he turned and made his way back. There was a challenge in his face, as if he was daring Alar to complain.

Alar kept his tone conversational. "Why did you do that?"

"'Give freely to those in need, and find the scale is balanced at the Gate.'" The tension in Ravlok's shoulders eased. He shrugged. "I was like them, once."

It was all the explanation offered, and Alar didn't press him. Though he wasn't surprised the monk had come from the streets—many of the most devout did—his story was his to tell. He nodded and turned away. "It was kind of you."

They continued toward the harbormaster's office. The single-story building was made of wood, rather than stone, and located at the end of a wide pier laden with craggy fishermen and garish merchants. Tables full of trinkets and jewelry crafted from shells and beads flanked them on both sides. Alar ignored a brightly clad hawker trying to sell him a strand of shiny clam shells and approached the ill-fitting wooden door.

The hinges creaked, and a spring at the top of the door groaned as he pulled it open. A human woman greeted them, looking up from some sort of manifest. Her frizzy brown hair was pulled tight and wrapped into a bun at the back of her head. Several thin strands had come loose and framed her face, giving her a haphazard look. Despite the sheen of sweat on her brow from the warming day, her collared shirt was clean and only slightly wrinkled.

"Can I help you, gentlemen?" Frizzy's hazel eyes surveyed them, lingering on Ravlok's sword.

"I certainly hope so," Alar said with a smile. He tapped into his aura-sense while her gaze was on Ravlok. "My name is Jaime Ellington. I am expecting someone to arrive in port from Keilliad this evening. I just wanted to ensure her ship was on schedule."

Frizzy sat back in her seat and sighed. "You and every mage this side of the Nohri." Her aura buzzed with annoyance. She made a flippant gesture with her quill. "All ships from Keilliad have been delayed."

Of course they have. Alar forced a look of concern to override his exasperation. "Oh? What happened?"

"Cyclone on the Kjaltemore last night." She spoke wearily, like she'd reported this same information several times. "Damaged a few cargo vessels. Sank at least one shoallie. A pair of galleons limped in early this morning, and the men were reporting twenty-span waves."

His look of surprise didn't have to be manufactured. "Gods be good. Well, is there any way you can tell me if her ship survived? I know it sailed out of Keilliad on Mirasday—"

She flipped open a well-worn book full of loose parchment. "I suppose I can see if it's reported in. What was its name?"

Alar hesitated, feigning embarrassment. "Well, I'm not exactly sure what the ship was called."

"What time was departure?"

"After fourth bell, I think."

Frizzy looked up from her register. "You think, but you don't know?"

Alar cringed, dropping his gaze, attempting his best sheepishness. "That's right."

Through his lashes, he saw her face scrunch. "Do you know how many ships leave from Keilliad every day?"

"Apologies, milady. I know I'm asking a lot." He gave her his most earnest look. "But if the storm was as bad as you say, I'll be worried sick until I know she's alright."

Frizzy sighed again and looked back down at the register. Her aura returned to a steady pulse of annoyance. "You don't know the time of departure or the ship's name. Do you at least know the passenger's name?"

He let out a laugh. "Yes, of course. Her name is Daeya McVen."

The woman froze.

Alar's chest tightened. The harbormaster's aura expanded outward like a cloud, denoting awareness. Suspicion. He fought the urge to ball his fists.

Frizzy looked from Alar to Ravlok and back, her expression guarded. "Are you with the mage that was just here?"

Alar examined her aura carefully before responding. It made sense there had been a mage asking after Daeya. She would stay at the embassy while she was here; the mage was probably sent to escort her from the docks. Another complication Alar couldn't afford.

Frizzy must know Daeya was a sorceress. How the harbormaster felt about the Guild would determine how Alar played his next few cards.

"That depends," he said, letting his own unease and suspicion match the woman's. "What can you tell me about this mage?"

Frizzy tapped the quill against the parchment. After a moment, Alar pressed ever so slightly on her aura to ease her suspicion and slipped a single thought into the woman's mind. *He's worried about her. Just tell him.*

It was enough to loosen her tongue. Frizzy's face softened. "He told me to hold the *Breigh Maiden* at anchor and disallow unloading until the prisoner was brought to shore."

All the color drained from Ravlok's face. "Prisoner?"

Alar cringed. If the monk messed this up—

"Aye. The sorcerer said Daeya McVen was a threat to national security. He ordered me to suspend all nonessential activities once the ship makes port. This whole place'll be shut down until the mages clear out."

"Did the sorcerer say what she did? She's never been one to cause trouble before." Alar almost choked on the words as he said them.

She shrugged. "Can't say I asked. Ain't privy to questioning mages."

Smart woman.

The suspicion left Frizzy. Her aura settled into a slow, undulating wave of sympathy. "You gentlemen must be her family."

"Yes," Alar agreed. It was always easier to let them make their own assumptions.

"I'm sorry." The weight of her apology could have anchored a galleon.

"Thank you, milady." He gave her a courtly bow at the waist, using the guise of stemming his emotions to make a quick exit. They had everything the harbor-master could provide them. There was no point hanging around.

"What are we going to do?" Ravlok asked as soon as the door shut behind them.

"I'm thinking." Alar strode down the pier, once more dodging the woman with the string of clam shells.

"We can't just give up. We have to—"

Alar stopped so suddenly that Ravlok collided with him. He spun, taking the shorter man by the shoulders. "Stop."

He had never missed Val's unshakeable faith in him more.

"But you heard the—"

"We're not giving up." Alar released him, letting out an exasperated sigh. "We'll likely have a few days to plan before she reaches port. But you have to trust me, *Turk*." He emphasized the name to remind him they were still under cover. "Can you do that?"

Ravlok drew a deep breath of his own. He closed his eyes, exhaled through his teeth, and nodded. His gaze leveled on Alar, steadier and more focused. "Yes."

He had the makings of a soldier; Alar couldn't help but notice it. Kendi would do wonders with him. "Good. Let's find Raff and buy a room. I saw several inns on the boardwalk. Then we'll decide what to do next."

He turned away from the harbor. Ravlok fell in at his side.

If whatever trouble Daeya had gotten herself into was bad enough to get her arrested, perhaps it wouldn't be a matter of convincing her to leave after all, but helping her escape. She would be a fugitive like the rest of them. For some reason, that put Alar's mind at ease. He wouldn't have to harm her or force her into anything.

He smirked to himself. The *Breigh Maiden* would shut down the entire port when it arrived.

Leave it to Daeya to make such a grand entry.

CHAPTER TWENTY-EIGHT

DAEYA

"*Come,* Nashanett."

Fire illuminated the cavern. Sheets of flame licked the walls, and waves of heat roiled across the ceiling. What was not bathed in fire was burned black or made molten. Lava flows spilled into glowing chasms that cleaved the chamber into pieces. Daeya stood at the mouth of the tunnel, gazing inward. The lethal maelstrom threatened to consume all who entered.

"Do not be afraid."

The voice rumbled through the rock and into the soles of her boots. It spoke in the language she understood, but had never learned.

"Who are you?" she asked the flames. Then, as if sensing the impending reply, she added, "And don't say it remains to be seen. I know you have a name."

Another rumble. This time, it sounded like a laugh. "You know my name."

Irritation prickled her skin. Yes, she was supposed to know it. She could feel *their connection like a tether, tugging at her. Drawing her toward it. Daeya resisted. "Remind me."*

Her hands tingled. That strange, smoldering light danced across her palms. Sparks of scarlet flame teased her fingertips. As if in response, the maelstrom inside the cavern shifted and writhed, curling toward her.

"My name is Telerion. I've been waiting for you."

Finally, an answer. With it came the remnants of a memory long-forgotten. Glass shattering. A flash of gold, bright in the sunshine. A gust of wind heavy with smoke. That same voice calling to her.

She peered into the flames, trying to spot a figure among them. "Where are you, Telerion? Will you show yourself?"

"You will find me where the three sisters touch the mountain."

A riddle. Daeya growled aloud. Now was not the time for riddles.

The flames flared in answer to her annoyance. Another tug pulled on her senses.

"Come, Nashanett. *The Test awaits."*

Daeya became aware of three things upon waking. The first was the numbness in her hands from the spellbinders against her wrists. The second was the shooting pain in her neck—her reward for the awkward way she'd slept chained to the bunk. And the third was that she was alone.

Telerion's voice echoed in her ears, his summons like a peal of thunder heard in the distance. It stirred something inside her. A feeling, an instinct, which bore the same resonance as the power she had felt on the night she saved the ship. She wanted to heed that summons—*yearned* for it. But there was the small matter of her captivity, impending trial, and possible execution.

She grimaced and exhaled in a rush. The chain connecting her binders scraped against wood as she rolled over and sat up. Everything ached. She flexed her fingers to work some feeling back into them. As the telltale needling sensation began, her eyes slid across the room to the desk.

Cam had been there since first bell, but her chair sat empty now. A bead still glowed in a crystal sconce above it, throwing rainbow-colored slivers on the walls.

If Cam was still cross with her for refusing to abide by the new decree, she hadn't shown it. She'd even voiced her disapproval of Daeya's treatment and assured her the Magistrate would see her freed from all charges if she simply stood trial and told the truth.

Frustrated as Daeya was by Cam's naiveté, she couldn't fault her for being optimistic. Nor was Cam altogether lacking in her awareness. When the older sorceress had first suggested she keep watch last night, Daeya thought it was because she no longer trusted her. Now she understood Cam was standing between her and Joss.

Daeya shuddered. The pressure from that bastard's hand still lingered between her legs. A phantom jolt of pain shot through her at the memory. Those long, harrowing seconds where her fear and anger had both given way to shock, leaving her vulnerable to his touch, were a disgusting smear of unwanted sensations and jumbled thoughts.

She desperately needed a bath.

Voices sounded outside the room. She tensed, certain she'd be hauled out of the ship in a humiliating procession of shouted jeers and rotten fruit, like a criminal being led through the streets of Ryost. But the voices passed by, laughing, and faded down the corridor. Her muscles unspooled.

They must have reached port by now; her babysitters wouldn't leave her alone for long. She tugged on the spellbinders, but the cross brace supporting the bunk didn't so much as flex beneath the pull. The manacles were tight enough that she couldn't slip them over her thumb joints. Even if she could get them off, running would be an admission of guilt—one even Gregory would be hard-pressed to explain away, when he returned from wherever in the Wastelands he'd gone.

The Councilor's threat to her father was another concern. Would it warrant Angus McVen's ruin if she fled only temporarily for her survival? Surely Gregory would see through the coup that this was.

Another clamor of voices carried down the corridor. These were louder than the last ones, and their streams of curses marked them for sailors. One of them shushed the others almost as loudly as another swore. They stopped outside her door.

Daeya peered around the wall locker, frowning. That sounded like—

Something crashed against the wood, rattling its hinges. She flinched.

"Heave, you slimy snatch!"

Cordy.

They struck the door again. It splintered inward, pulling the top hinge from its framework. With a third blow, the door swung open, and Belio, Cordy, and Quinn tumbled into the tiny cabin. As they fell over each other, a heavy piece of charred timber clattered to the floor and landed on Cordy's hand.

"Scabbing ball sacks!" The gap-toothed man swore another colorful streak and sucked on his fingers.

Dan stepped into the room behind them. The one-handed Skriian held a satchel slung over his shoulder, and he wore fighting leathers rather than his usual shirt and trousers. He shook his head, reached for the door knob, and turned it easily. "It was unlocked, you Aethershites."

Daeya found herself gaping and snapped her mouth shut.

As they rose and brushed themselves off, Belio stepped toward her, pulling an axe from a loop on his pants. "Good morning, Daeya."

She stared at him, uncertain whether she should laugh or scold him for carrying around an axe in his trousers. "Good morning, Belio."

He flashed her a smile and hefted the axe. "We're here to rescue you."

Her eyes widened. "I can see that."

Curly-haired Quinn approached the bunk on which Daeya sat. The youngest of the sailors had a sheepish demeanor about her. She was a year or two younger than Daeya, but over a handspan taller and with an unusual broadness through her shoulders. "Morning, milady. If you'll kindly move to the far side of the bunk, please."

"Just pick the locks," Dan suggested. "There's no need to—"

Belio raised the axe. Daeya hastened to press herself against the wall, as far from the fall of that gleaming blade as possible. Splinters flew and wood snapped, severing the cross brace.

Quinn grabbed the chain between her spellbinders and beckoned to her. "This way."

Too stunned to refuse, Daeya allowed Quinn to drag the chain along until it reached the break in the cross brace. She stood on stiff legs and stretched her muscles with a wince.

Dan rubbed his temples. The sigh that escaped his lips sounded more like a growl. "Someone will have heard all of this."

"Then we'd best be off." Belio took Daeya by the arm. "Freedom awaits you, Sorceress."

He made to pull her along, but Daeya roused herself from her shock and stood firm, chain links rattling. "I can't."

All four sailors shared incredulous looks.

"Of course you can." Cordy waved a hand at her spellbinders. "We'll get those off later."

He was so sure of himself, Daeya almost believed him. Spellbinders were supposed to be tamper-proof. "You don't understand. If I go with you, I'll not only condemn myself. My father—"

"You are condemned if you stay." The cold certainty in Dan's gaze was harrowing. Daeya's resolve crumbled as he spoke. "The mages mean to harm you, *Nashanett*. This, I cannot allow."

He might as well have struck her in the gut. All the wind rushed out of her in an exhale so intense that her abdomen cramped. The weight and reverence of that title settled over her like the vestments of a priest. "W-what did you just call me?"

Belio, Cordy, and Quinn shared confused glances among themselves and looked toward Dan. Their Skriian friend paid them no mind; his attention was for her alone.

"There is no time to explain. We must go. Now."

The tug of power from her dream wrenched at her senses, compelling her to go with them. She took an involuntary step toward Dan, and the man's eyes flashed copper.

Belio gave another pull on her arm, almost as insistent as the tugging sensation wrapped around her heart. She started to move with him. "Dan has a friend in the city who can help you. He's going to take you to him."

They made it to the door before Daeya's sense of duty cemented her feet again. The way his voice lowered made her uneasy. This friend was likely someone a Guild sorceress shouldn't trust. "If he's a friend of the Alliaansi—"

"Baosanni's breath, woman," Cordy snapped. "Would the Alliaansi really be worse than getting strung up by your neck?"

Daeya swallowed. She didn't know how to respond to that.

"He is not of the Alliaansi," Dan reassured her. "His name is Vortanis, and he serves Tiior, as I do."

Vortanis.

The name rang through her like a gong. Tension eased from her face. The man she had been sent to find was a friend of Dan's. He was willing to take her to him.

Gregory would understand. He wouldn't lay waste to her father's career if she brought him exactly what he'd requested. By the time he returned to deal with her trial, the Guild would have all the answers from Vortanis that Gregory desired. He likely wouldn't even be angry with her.

Dan offered his hand. "Come, *Nashanett.*"

She could take a risk and trust in the Magistrate. She could hope he saw through Joss and Normos's plot in time for her to circle back and allow Dan to lead her to Vortanis. Or she could complete her mission right now and deal with these false charges later.

The choice was an easy one.

Daeya spun back to the wall sconce and collected the bead Cam had left. Unable to dismiss the Light spell without her magic, she dropped the glowing bead into a pocket of her vest. Joss had taken her saphyrum when he'd chained her up last night. He'd forgotten to take the bead in her pendant, but it would need to be replaced soon. All of her other supplies—and her last two oranges—were back in the passengers' quarters.

They left the broken bunk and shattered door behind and made their way along the corridor. Sunlight refracted through glass prisms embedded in the deck above them, lighting their way. The walls were set close on this level, leaving barely enough room for them to walk two abreast. They passed several more cabin doors while Daeya tried to orient herself. They were heading for the back of the ship.

"The mages are waiting on deck for a boat from shore to come get you," Belio told her. "You'll be long gone by the time the boat gets here."

While they walked, Cordy pulled Daeya back to investigate her spellbinders. "Can you swim, lass?"

Panic knifed through her. "*That's* your way off the ship?"

"Well, you sort of threw the cockboat overboard in the storm."

Right. The truth was, Daeya couldn't swim. Gregory had started his rune work when she was very young, and the Guild had never made swimming part of its curriculum.

She nodded to her spellbound wrist in his hand. "If you can get these off, I have magic that can get me to shore."

Cordy grinned and elbowed Belio hard in the ribs. "Told you she would. You owe me ten silvers."

Belio's grunt of pain was followed by a grumbled curse and the clink of coins as he fished in his pockets.

Daeya gaped at the two of them, incredulous. "You're rifting through the Aether on this entire rescue, aren't you?"

Belio gasped, recoiling from her. Cordy's brows furrowed and his lips parted in outrage, but it was the bright touch of color in Quinn's cheeks that gave them away.

"Sorry, milady."

"Maybe we ought to put you back where we found you, lass."

"Forgive us if we aren't planners, Sorceress."

It was all too much for Daeya. Laughter and joy as pure as spring water bubbled up out of her. She steadied herself on Cordy's arm to keep from losing her footing.

Quinn was the first to join in her laughter. Belio's barking laugh soon followed. Cordy cuffed her on the shoulder, and Daeya only laughed harder. Dannicus shushed them all and stopped at a ladder leading upward. They quieted but for a few stray chuckles.

Daeya wiped at her eyes. She tried to hold still as Cordy took her wrist again. He slipped a metal pick in the lock of her right manacle, and it came free with a *snick*. He moved to the left manacle and made quick work of it as well. She marveled at the ease of it; the newest batch of spellbinders was certainly not as tamper-proof as they'd been led to believe.

The binders fell into Cordy's hands. He stuffed them into his trousers. When Daeya gave him a curious frown, he shrugged. "They're popular with some of the ladies in port."

She cringed. "Gods, Cordy."

"What?"

"Quiet," Dan barked. "Or we won't hear when Gavin gives the signal—"

A single concussive explosion followed. Daeya rocked backward, steadying herself on Cordy's arm.

"Don't know how we'd miss that." Cordy pushed her toward the ladder as Dan started climbing. "After you, lass."

Wood creaked under her weight, the once-square rungs of the ladder worn smooth and round by years of use. Above her, Dan raised the hatch and climbed out. Midmorning sunlight poured in, leaving her blinking and shielding her eyes. Dan reached down to offer his hand again.

When he pulled her out, two more explosions sounded off the portside bow. The noise was tremendous. Daeya flinched away from the bright flash of red and clapped her hands over her ears. Dan pulled her toward starboard, muttering to himself about the cost of all those saphyric flares. Though the flares were notoriously expensive, most Guild-commissioned ships kept a small supply on hand to signal for aid from nearby vessels. Several of them wound together made a spectacular grenade.

All was chaos behind them. Sailors rushed about, trying to find the culprit behind the blasts. Dan dragged Daeya further aft, ducking behind the starboard wall of the captain's quarters. He slipped the satchel strap over his head. "You should take off your robe so you don't draw attention to yourself."

Daeya hesitated, but obeyed as Belio, Cordy, and Quinn formed up behind her. Dan withdrew a simple brown cloak from the satchel. He held it up for her, and she turned to let its light weight settle over her shoulders.

"Since I assume you can Bend to shore, I won't bother carrying you." Dan took her mage's robe, stuffed it in the satchel, and pushed the bag into her chest.

She frowned. "What do you mean, 'carry' me?"

He ignored her confusion and gripped her shoulder. "We'll have to deal with the fallout from all this before we can unload the ship. Meet me at the Lighthouse Tavern at sixth bell. I'll take you to Vortanis from there. Stay out of sight until then."

Sobering at the unusual severity in his tone, Daeya nodded. Gods knew she wasn't going to argue with that solemn face. She slipped the bag's strap over her head. "Sixth bell. Lighthouse. Got it."

Dannicus released her, and Belio pulled her into his arms. "Good luck, Daeya."

"Thank you." She returned the embrace with a fierceness worthy of her father. Then she gazed at the rest of them, gratitude constricting her throat. "All of you."

Belio stepped away, and Cordy thumped her on the back. "Would that all those purple-eyed bastards were like you."

She scoffed. "I know plenty who would disagree with you."

"Well, they're bleeding morons, aren't they?"

Quinn gave her a shy smile and kissed her hand. "It was a pleasure, milady."

The gesture was so innocent and sweet that a telltale sting pricked Daeya's eyes. She touched Quinn's cheek. "I'll never forget this."

"Course you won't. No one could forget us." Cordy snorted. "Now get going. We'll have company soon."

Daeya squared her shoulders and looked out across the port. It was a long way to the nearest dock, but she could make it. Grasping her pendant, she stepped toward the railing and began to cast.

The first rift opened, and the second one was a slash of light in the distance. She sank her arm into the Aether and *pulled*. Colors streaked by, shot through with black. When she came out on the other side, she breathed in the coastal air. Wood creaked and swayed underfoot as she started down the dock.

There was a shout and a flash of white-violet off to one side. Daeya froze, head snapping toward the sound. Light filled her vision.

A sphere of lightning slammed into her chest.

Chapter Twenty-Nine

Ravlok

Ravlok scowled. "Don't kill them."

Jack looked up from the sights of his crossbow, snorted with derision, and lowered his chin back to his task.

Annoyed, Ravlok reached across the slate rooftop and put his hand in front of the sights. "Seriously. If she sees you killing her people, she'll sooner jump into the Aether than come with us."

The thief jerked his weapon out of Ravlok's reach. "We don't have to convince her. We just have to subdue her."

"No, Ravlok is right." Alar spoke up from Jack's other side. "She's going to be mad enough with me as it is. If you have to shoot, then shoot to wound."

Ravlok's anxiety lessened a fraction with Alar's support. He returned his hand to the warm slate ridge and breathed to steady his aura. Lying on the inn rooftop, they had a clear view of the three mages loading into the boat. Bright red explosions off the sides of the not-so-*Breigh Maiden* had spurred them to action, but three others hung back on the dock. One of them was Daeya's rival, Normos Beck.

He didn't need to recall all the rumors. Just by watching the man, Ravlok could tell he was dangerous. The mage paced the boardwalk like a caged innix, and the languid motions of his black robe accentuated the feline movements. His focus on the ship and surroundings was absolute—worthy of the most skilled warrior.

"That's twelve mages between here and the ship," Jack pointed out. "You saw all the guards outside. They're not taking any chances. We're going to have to kill some of them."

"No. Not unless it's our only option. Ravlok, are you ready?"

Ravlok nodded. "Ready."

"At your leisure."

Quietly and carefully, Ravlok shimmied back down the steep slope and lowered himself to the window ledge outside their room. From there, he dropped the last few spans to the ground.

The alley behind the inn was deserted. Harbor patrol had cleared the port of all foot traffic that morning when Daeya's ship dropped anchor. Ravlok's new friends had kept to the shadows during the clear-out. There was no sign of them among the refuse.

Ravlok whistled, trilling and soft, mimicking the sound of a skylark. An answering chirp came from his right, and a black shape detached from a trio of rain barrels. The dark figure moved from building to building, never once casting a shadow against the gravel in the midmorning sun. It rounded a wooden loading platform beside the inn and materialized into Olly, the leader of the Docksiders Gang.

Olly's dirty face split into a wide grin, made ghastly by the unfortunate scar on his cheek. A small sack hung over his shoulder; he set it down at Ravlok's feet. "This is gonna be the heist of the century. My boys ain't never stolen from mages before."

The boy's eagerness sent a pang of sorrow into Ravlok's heart. If he had been in Ryost, he would have taken him to the monastery for new clothes and a pair of shoes that fit his feet. He could have offered a free bed and meals in exchange for sweeping the training halls and scrubbing pots and pans. But here in Orthovia, all Ravlok could offer were coins pilfered from unsuspecting nobility.

Coins that had been the source of another argument between him and Jack, but Alar had been surprisingly on his side then, too. If Ravlok was going to be complicit in more thefts, he would at least make sure the things they were stealing went to people who needed them. It was all about finding a balance, after all.

Alar had seen the merit in enlisting the locals to help them. He hadn't even protested when Ravlok insisted he be the one to organize the children. The frosty mastermind was growing on him, little by little. Beneath all those layers of indifference and cynicism, there was a softness in the man. Even if Alar justified his acts of kindness as acts of necessity and logic, he had mostly good intentions at heart.

Ravlok withdrew a bag full of coins from his pocket. "Let's not make a habit of this. There's a reason no one steals from the Guild."

Olly scoffed and took the bag, weighing it in his palm. "Aye, that's what old Cob Bigby said, too. Ain't nothing to be scared about, boss. Me and my boys'll help you get your girl."

Your girl. Ravlok and Daeya both would have laughed at the thought. She knew about his reservations with romantic involvement—how difficult it was for him after his time at Madame's—and a huge draw of her friendship was her lack of such expectations. He admired her in many ways, but there was nothing more between them.

He cleared his throat. "Did Bigby give you the leather strips I requested?"

Olly shoved the sack across the space between them. "It's all there. Why'd you want nails in 'em?"

Ravlok bent to open the sack. Inside were several wide strips of leather with nails driven through one side. He pulled one out to inspect it and nodded his approval, testing the sharpness with a finger. He took out two more strips for himself and pushed the sack back toward Olly.

"It's an old trick I learned. When the guards come for you, throw a few of those into their path." To demonstrate, Ravlok tossed one of the strips on the ground. It landed with a soft thud, nail points up. "If they step on them, the nails go right through their boots and give you more time to escape."

The boy's dark eyes bugged as if Ravlok had just revealed one of the greatest mysteries of life. "That's bleeding scabby, boss."

Ravlok picked up the strip, tucking all three under his arm. "My old crew called it the cobbler's trick."

Olly hefted the sack over his shoulder, the smaller bag of coins nowhere in sight. "You bet your arse we'll be using that one."

A shout drew Ravlok's attention. It was followed by a loud *crack* and a cry of pain. He glanced around the corner of the inn, but there was nothing to see but the harbor. Ravlok hurried around the side of the building. Olly followed close behind, sand and gravel whispering under their feet. They stopped before leaving the shadow of the inn's gray awning.

Normos was striding toward a prone, blonde-haired figure on the dock.

Odes of Ordeolas. Lungs constricting, Ravlok spun back to Olly. "The others are in position?"

The boy's owl-eyed fear was poorly masked. "Aye."

"Tell them to fire the pitch and release the livestock." When Olly didn't move, Ravlok gave him a shove. "Go. Now!"

Olly stumbled back through the narrow gap between the inn and the tackle shop, kicking up gravel as he ran.

"And keep your slings handy," Ravlok called after him. When the boy was out of sight, he dropped the cobbler's leathers and took out his own sling.

He took aim and fired.

Her cloak was burning.

Daeya gazed up at the sky, vision swimming and clouds warping. Flames licked her clothes. She had to put the fire out. She had to get the fabric off. Her vest was on fire, too. Gods, but everything hurt. Her back. Her chest. She couldn't breathe. Had she hit her head? Why was she on fire?

Normos.

His sphere of lightning had set her cloak on fire. She had to get up. Had to get away—

A strangled cry escaped her as she struggled to sit up and failed. The water. Water would put the fire out. She struggled to roll over and drag herself toward the edge of the dock. The ringing in her ears muffled sounds of creaking wood and lapping waves.

Boots appeared in front of her, followed by the edge of a black cloak. "I thought you might try something like this." Normos's voice burgeoned with reproach. "You're becoming predictable, Daeya."

"Forgive me." She fought for every croaked word. Her lungs still refused to obey, or she might have deigned to laugh. "If I'd known you'd be here, I would have just waited for you to fuck up. Saved myself the trouble."

Normos reached down and gripped her by the arm. He flashed his perfect white teeth, blue eyes icy as they met hers. "You have agents working for you on the ship. I'll expect their names, along with your confession of illegal magic use and consorting with the Alliaansi."

She coughed. The acrid taste of smoke coated her tongue and singed her throat. "If you think you'll get away with this, you're a bigger fool than I thought."

Normos hauled her to her feet, even as her cloak continued to smolder. "You helped murder hundreds of childr—"

Something whistled passed Daeya's ear and struck Normos in the face. He recoiled with a yelp, and Daeya stumbled. Her head was still spinning, but she dared not waste his momentary distraction. She flung the flaming cloak off her shoulders, gripped her pendant, and incanted.

"*Vuurmas seluu.*"

The embers still smoldering along her vest pooled like water in her hands. She flicked them into Normos's face.

"Agh!" He threw up his arm to shield his eyes.

Daeya whirled away, fingers glowing white-violet as she channeled magic. She began the sigil for a rift, focusing her exit point on a nearby rooftop.

A counter-orb smashed into the sigil. Both broke into dazzling motes of light.

"Bleeding Aether." Daeya clenched her teeth.

As the fragments winked out around her, two more mages stalked toward her from the boardwalk. One male. One female. Both human; she recognized neither. The woman's sneer chilled Daeya's blood.

As the man reached for her, Daeya stepped backward, only to find herself pressed against Normos's chest.

"The Magistrate will see to—" the new sorcerer began.

A crossbow bolt sprouted from his shoulder. Agony contorted his tan features. He dropped to the dock with a cry when a second bolt struck him in the leg. Daeya's confusion was reflected in the woman's eyes. The bolts had come from behind them. She searched for the source as Normos clamped his hands around her arms.

"Whoever is helping you will suffer for it." A trickle of blood seeped from a gash on his cheek. He pushed her before him like a shield. "Get moving."

Daeya dug her heels in against the forward movement and scanned the port again. Who *was* helping her? Dan hadn't left the ship, and none of the others had magic.

"No." The older sorceress whimpered. "No, no, no."

Normos jerked Daeya to a stop and stared back at the female mage. "Aneece, what's wrong with you?"

Aneece clutched her close-cropped auburn hair in her fingers, eyes bulging with terror. "He's in my head."

Warmth drained from Daeya's face.

"He's in my head. He's in my head!" Blood gushed out of Aneece's nose, over her lips, down her chin.

No. Gods, no, this wasn't happening. This couldn't be real. Why would a blanker—none of this made any sense—

Paling himself, Normos spun Daeya around, nails biting into her shoulders. "This is low even for you. Where's the blanker? Tell him to let her go!"

Fear seized her by the throat. Daeya shook her head furiously. "This isn't me. I didn't—I'm not—"

Aneece crumpled beside the other sorcerer, still clutching her head and sobbing. Normos spared her a look of pity before all his attention leveled on Daeya. Hatred as cold and black as a northern night in winter promised her destruction—a slow and excruciating march toward death.

"I can't risk taking you through town." Normos kept one hand on her as he began to weave a sigil. "We'll Walk instead."

Tears stung her eyes. Hot trails slid down her cheeks. She strained against his bruising grip. How could she even begin to explain this? "You know I would never do this."

The slightest softening of his fingers sparked hope, but he didn't spare her a glance as he completed the sigil. "Save your lies for the Magistrate."

It couldn't end this way. She had to clear her name and make things right. At least, she had to stall long enough to see Gregory's return. He would fix this.

But with evidence of a blanker's involvement, whether feigned or not, her trial would be expedited. Punishments for them and those working with them were always swift, and the Magistrate's decision was final. She could hang in the gallows by sundown. Hopelessness crashed down on her—a landslide of despair so implacable she feared it would bury her.

There was only one thing left she could do.

Daeya sniffled, twisting in Normos's grip. Her fingers curled around her pendant. "I'm sorry."

Normos had a limited ability to Walk through the Aether. Though it could take him much farther than a Rift Bend, it was a taxing ability to summon, and even more challenging to control. If she interrupted this attempt, he couldn't summon it safely again until she was far away from here.

She wrenched her arm free and summoned her counter-orb in the same breath. The crackling, black-violet sphere crashed into his sigil, and Daeya bolted down the dock as the fragments burst apart. The bead in her pendant crumbled to dust.

Boots pounded across wet wood. If she could gain enough ground to Rift Bend out of sight, she could lose him. When she hit the boardwalk, she veered sharply left and leaped over—

A chicken?

Daeya crashed back to the ground, narrowly missing a chicken that shot from underfoot. A pair of goats sprang across the walkway; hooves clattered. Pigs poured out of an alleyway, and down the street, a chicken coop lay on its side. The animals squealed and screamed as they flooded the boardwalk, filling the spaces between abandoned carts and idle wagons. Further along, children dressed in rags heaved barrels of pitch into the street and set them alight.

What in the gods' names was going on?

"Daeya!"

She whipped around. There was no mistaking that clear tenor. "*Ravlok*?"

He was dressed in mercenary fighting leathers and roughshod linen. Black stubble smattered his cheeks, and his nose bulged as if it had been recently broken, but his broad shoulders, close-set eyes, and muscular stature were unmistakable.

He beckoned to her from the shelter of a nearby inn. "Come on. This way."

Lightning flashed in the darkening sky, and a peal of thunder sounded. Daeya spared a glance over her shoulder; Normos's eyes were glowing violet as he summoned his element. Sigils whirled around him, snapping outward—wards to protect the nearby buildings.

"Come on!"

She needed no further urging. Daeya darted for the inn.

A sphere of lightning slammed against the stone wall beside her. She stopped short, hair standing on end as another blast careened toward her. Daeya spun aside, shielding her face from flying shrapnel. The scent of Aether grew heavy and the sound of chanting filled her ears.

Normos strode down the dock, arms outstretched, robe billowing behind him. Against the backdrop of sea and gathering storm clouds, two balls of white-violet lightning shone brightly in his palms.

She wouldn't make it to the inn. Not without dealing with Normos first.

"Daeya!"

A new voice. A familiar voice that came from above and behind her. She ignored it and reached into her pocket.

"You're making a mistake," Daeya said. "Just give me time to prove it."

Normos bristled. "Your blanker friend can try all he wants, but he won't penetrate my mind."

Gods, he was the most obtuse, infuriating bastard in all of Dessos. Her fingers closed around Cam's bead as she tried one last time to reason with him—to appeal to the friendship they'd once had. "I don't know who he is, or why he's helping me. I know how this looks, but you have to believe me. I'm not an Aetherian, and I'm *not* working for the Alliaansi."

Normos scoffed. "You think I'd believe a child murderer."

His accusation stung. Daeya stepped backward and lifted her arms in a placating gesture. Cam's bead glinted reassuringly between her middle and ring fingers. "I don't want to hurt you."

It was true. Despite how badly he'd treated her, a sliver of her still clung to her earliest memories of their relationship, back when sharing strawberry tarts and counting stars mattered more than impressing Gregory. "Please, Normos. You know me." Her throat tightened. "I wouldn't harm children."

Pools of fiery pitch crept closer. The boardwalk blazed on both ends, trapping them in. Shouts rang out, followed by the sound of swords drawn; the city guard seemed to have found their way blocked by flames.

Normos stopped on the dock, just shy of the livestock fleeing the fire. He glowered at her, shifting one foot forward, one foot back, into a battle mage's stance. "Stand down, Daeya."

Sorrow and fury warred in Daeya's heart. It was all she could do to project strength and confidence into her voice. "I can't do that."

"Then you'll die where you stand."

His magic brightened to a blinding intensity, fingers spread wide to guide the bolts forward. Wind snapped his blond hair about his head. Lightning coursed from his palms.

Daeya incanted, calling the power of the Aether to her command. She pulled from the bead so fiercely that it cracked. Energy poured out of it, guided into sigils drawn so frantically that her limbs themselves seemed to be made of light. The five-layered, opalescent barrier she constructed took the force of his lightning—

And shattered.

Hundreds of prismatic shards sliced trails of heat through the air. The force blew Daeya backward. Feet skidding across wet wood, she barely remained upright trying to hold the onslaught back. A scream ripped from her at the searing intensity of his magic, and Aether buffeted her in clouds of black-violet mist.

When the blast finally subsided, she searched for Normos through the dissipating fog. Reality itself rippled in the space between them, as if she were viewing him from underwater. The dock writhed like a snake in the harbor. Boats, carts, and wagons wavered as if they were made of ephemeral shadows.

An Aetherial warp.

A dangerous anomaly caused by weakening in the Aetherial Wall where two powerful magical forces collided. Daeya's gaze met Normos's through the warp. The harrowing knowledge reflected in his eyes. If they struck the Wall like that again, they could open a rift the size of the port itself.

Normos set his jaw and reached toward the sky instead.

Existing elements wouldn't break the warp. As he prepared to harness lightning from the storm clouds, Daeya reached out and *seized* the fire at either end of the boardwalk. It bent toward her in rivulets, heeding her call as it had on the night of the storm. Golden light flickered over her skin; fire coursed across the space and pooled between her fingertips. She thrust the two pools inward and *twisted* the fire before her. The flames reformed hotter, brighter, and took the form of two twining spirals of scarlet death. She shoved them toward Normos with all her strength. Both halves of the broken saphyrum bead turned to dust.

Her hair stood on end. An intense static charge built up from the ground where she stood. As soon as her attack was sent on its course, Daeya dove behind a vacant wagon and covered her ears.

Lightning spiked down with a thunderous crash. The wagon exploded. Wooden shrapnel blasted outward, and Daeya pressed herself to the boardwalk with a prayer to all the gods who would listen.

For long, harrowing seconds, she couldn't discern the roar of flames from the ringing in her ears. She lifted her head and squinted through the scarlet-tinged haze. An enormous gust of superheated wind stirred ash and smoke into the sky. Her entire body radiated mind-numbing pain.

Warm arms wrapped around her, lifting her. An odd feeling of weightlessness.

She looked up into a man's face. Black hair. Blue eyes. Her brows furrowed as she struggled to concentrate.

"Ravlok," her voice sounded far away, "what are you doing here?"

Chapter Thirty

Alar

Daeya's hand cracked across Alar's face so hard he tasted blood.

He'd always known she was smart; it hadn't taken her long to deduce exactly what he had done and why. Alar licked blood from the inside of his cheek and straightened, careful to keep the satisfaction off his face. She could be angry. She could rage at him all she wanted for immobilizing that sorceress with psionics, but it didn't change anything. Daeya was like him now. A fugitive. A rebel.

Condemned.

Clasping his hands in front of him, he squared his shoulders and fixed her with a reproving look. "Are you quite finished?"

He didn't need his aura-sense to read her. She was positively seething. Her fists clenched and her breath came in short, furious bursts. The way her nose scrunched into a scowl was almost endearing, like a kitten's attempt to be threatening.

If she'd been at her best, that anger might have made him uneasy, but right now she could barely stand, and she'd run out of saphyrum—a fact confirmed by the absence of her casting bracelet and the empty stone setting in the necklace she always wore. At least temporarily, Daeya McVen was harmless.

She thrust a finger at him. "You have no idea what you've done."

Amusement tightened his cheeks. "On the contrary, I'm pretty certain we just saved your life."

The single candle in their basement hideout flickered. It teased shadows across Daeya's delicate features. Her eyes were still violet from her incredible display of magic, and the light painted her white-blonde hair a deeper shade of gold. A smudge of soot colored her left eyebrow. She'd stripped down to her close-fitting undershirt, which was no longer white but dingy gray, and the sleeves were blackened in several places by remnants of Aether.

Even spell-burned and furious, she still managed to be pretty.

"I had it under control," she said.

"Not from where we were standing." He gestured to Ravlok, who sat cross-legged on an old wine cask, watching them. "If we hadn't stepped in, you would have been overwhelmed."

"If you hadn't stepped in, I would have been able to explain myself to the Magistrate and fix all of this." Some of her vehemence faltered. Her anger turned to pain. "Now my father stands to lose everything."

Further argument died on Alar's tongue. The tension left his face, and he blinked twice to absorb that implication. He hadn't expected her concern to linger on her father.

Ravlok's brows furrowed. "What do you mean?"

"The others will report to Councilor Gregory that I've run away. He'll make certain Da pays for this."

Alar frowned. "Why would Gregory have cause to hurt your father?"

"Why else?" She spat the words with disgust.

Realization dawned, and he became acutely aware of Mardis Ulrich's scroll pressed against an inner pocket of his tunic. "To punish you."

Candlelight reflected off a sudden wetness in her eyes. Her lower lip trembled, and her teeth clamped down on it. She nodded.

For once, Alar didn't know what to say. He'd convinced himself her aversion to Gregory was an act, but that looked like real fear in her expression. He had to proceed carefully. "The Alliaansi can help your father, but I have some questions for you first."

"What makes you think I would accept your help? You'd probably enslave his mind, too."

Alar sighed. So, she was going to be difficult. Great.

Ravlok held up a placating hand. "Daeya, please, just listen to him."

She rolled her eyes skyward. "And while we're at it, you can release Ravlok. You didn't have to bring him into this."

"He didn't." The monk unfolded his legs and slipped off the barrel. He came to stand between them, closing their small circle. "I'm here for the same reason you are. The Guild is corrupt. They had me slated for execution."

In her bewilderment, Daeya's jaw nearly fell to the floor. "You've got to be kidding me. *That's* the story he sold you?"

It was too soon for this. Alar cringed. "Thanks, Ravlok."

"It's true," he insisted. "Gregory caught me in the restricted archives. He used magic on me, and I threatened to report him."

A laugh burst out of Daeya. She shook her head, her face a mask of disbelief.

Alar groaned and rubbed his temples. Even though it was true, he'd prefer to avoid this conversation until she was more firmly rooted on their side. "Please stop talking."

Ravlok finally seemed to realize his claims weren't helping. He winced. "Sorry."

Daeya wasn't about to let it go. She pursued it with the same dogged determination of a Light Paladin. "He's a blanker, Rav. He's twisted your memory to believe what he wills."

"He hasn't manipulated any of my memories." Ravlok glanced at him, brows pinching. "Have you?"

"No, of course not. I can't even do that."

Not yet, anyway.

Daeya folded her arms and lifted one white-blonde eyebrow. "I'm sure that's what you want us to think. Meanwhile, this could all be some construct of your mind, and Ravlok and I are lying on the floor drooling all over ourselves."

Irritation welled. He shouldn't have been surprised she held such prejudice, but it still rankled. Her willingness to speak to him at all was a good sign, however; even if she held to Guild ideals, she likely didn't hold to those of the Church, which vilified Syljians and claimed they were all infernal agents of Chaos. The question was whether time and exposure to his people might change her opinion, or if she was too brainwashed to ever see them as anything more than blankers.

He was glad Jack wasn't here to witness this.

"I'm a psionist, not a mastermind. There's a difference." Alar caught the puzzlement on Ravlok's face, but he ignored him. "And even if I could manipulate memories, I can't touch *your* mind at all."

Confusion wrinkled her forehead, lending even more to Alar's frustration. Of course she would be untouchable by psionics and have no idea why.

Rather than elaborating further, he closed his eyes and took a calming breath. "Look, let's just start over. You want the truth, and so do I. You answer my questions. I'll answer yours."

"Sounds fair." Daeya leaned back against another wine cask. "Let's start with your real name and what you're doing here, because I'm sure Faustus Crex wasn't just out for a stroll to the Orthovian port."

It had taken time to settle on how to explain things to her when they finally met up again. He wasn't about to prattle on about Cheralach's visions. While they waited for her ship to reach port, he had decided on the most succinct answer possible.

He reached into the folds of his tunic and pulled out Ulrich's scroll. "My name is Alar Fellman, and I really am here to rescue you."

"Fellman?" Daeya scoffed. "That's not a very Syljian name."

Alar ignored her overly perceptive remark and presented the scroll to her. His true family name was much more than either she or the monk needed to know.

Daeya took the creased parchment and unrolled it. Silence settled over the dusty basement as she read. The exact moment when the shock set in was visible seconds later. Her brow smoothed over, her lips parted, and her eyes traveled slower over the message, likely rereading as Alar had. She lowered the scroll and looked up, studying him intently.

He'd expected she might accuse him of forging the note. If he had been in her position, it was what he would have done. Instead, she spun aside and knelt beside her pack on the ground.

Alar shared a curious look with Ravlok as Daeya tore out a black garment and rummaged through its pockets. She pulled out a folded piece of parchment and rose, offering it to him.

"What's this?"

"Just open it."

He did. There were only two words written on it: '*Trust him.*'

"Ulrich gave this to you." Alar looked up from the instructor's initials. "When?"

Daeya seemed to consider something for a long moment, staring down at the note in his hands. "My first night on the ship, by way of Cameron Vika."

She returned to the scroll she still held. Alar was silent as she examined it again. Finally, she let out a breath and met his gaze. "Alright. You have my attention, Mr. Fellman."

"Alar, please." He passed the note back to her and offered an easier smile. One obstacle cleared. Even Ravlok's shoulders sagged with relief. But there was another matter that needed to be addressed before Alar could allow himself to feel the same. "My turn."

"By all means."

Alar braced himself, determined to keep his emotions under control. "How much did you know about Cheralach?"

"The Deserter?" Her brows drew inward. "Not much. Why?"

A spark of anger flared in his chest. He snuffed it out by balling his fist and slowly releasing it. It was a feat of immense mental fortitude to keep his voice steady. "You knew he was being held by the Guild. You told me he was to be executed."

The tension left her face. She shook her head. "That was just a rumor. We didn't really have him. Gregory just wanted to see how you would react."

How he wished at that moment he could communicate telepathically with her. Examine the flow of her thoughts. See her aura. Anything that might assure him she was telling the truth. Even if she appeared sincere, he had to rely on too little evidence to know for certain. His jaw tensed. "But you were going to see him."

"If you'd gone with me, I was to take you to the city jail, where we would have found a man bearing his description. It would have raised further suspicion if you knew he wasn't the right man." Her face darkened, her gaze sharp as a razor's edge. "Is that why the aethermancers destroyed the School? Because you thought we had Cheralach?"

The accusation drew him up short. "The Guild did have Cheralach."

"The—" More confusion. Daeya recoiled. "We did?"

"In a secret dungeon beneath the School." Alar did nothing to alleviate the bitterness in his tone.

Daeya swallowed. It was hard to tell if the dungeon was news to her, but he almost believed her little act of fumbling for words. "When you say they *did*—"

"They killed him. But before that, they tortured him. They removed all his fingers and toes, one knuckle at a time, and sliced him open in more places than I could count. They also burned out another man's eye and stabbed my best friend in the heart. Now I have the delightful task of telling his wife why her husband isn't coming home."

Alar let the words hang suspended, cold and forbidding between them, like a chasm yawning wide. He expected she would mutter some empty platitude for his loss, but she didn't. She simply stared at her feet, her grip creasing Ulrich's letter.

"Daeya." Ravlok touched her arm. "What happened to the School was an accident. I know that's not what you want to hear. I know it's not what they want you to believe, but I was there. I saw what the Guild did to his people. It was gruesome and inhumane." Ravlok took her other arm in hand and looked down into her face. "I know if you had seen it, you would have been disgusted and ashamed."

Red blooms of emotion colored her pale cheeks and rimmed her eyes. Her words were strangled, as if she had to wring each one out through her tears. "I thought evil was no cure for evil, Rav."

Orowen said the same thing. It was a sentiment meant to mollify the devout and the weak, deterring them from seeking vengeance on those who'd wronged them. While Alar thought it foolish, it seemed to strike a chord in the monk.

Ravlok's jaw worked for a moment before he sighed and released her. "You're right. It's not. But it wasn't evil that drove us. It was an act of survival made in desperation. We didn't know the stakes, and we didn't care. We simply acted, and people died for it. If there had been any other way, I can't say we would have found it. We just wanted to survive."

It wasn't the most eloquent speech Alar had ever heard, but it served its purpose. Daeya searched Ravlok's face, and then his own. She must have found what she was looking for, because she drew herself up and gestured to the monk. "Tell me what happened. Don't leave anything out."

Alar remained silent while Ravlok recounted their escape from the prison cells, the battle in the guard room, and the rift that had led to the School's collapse. Daeya seemed particularly disturbed that mundane soldiers had been present for the fight, and she turned a light shade of green when Ravlok confirmed the torture Magnus and Cheralach had endured. She alternated between listening to his account and watching Alar, likely for signs of his psionic influence. When the monk finished, she stared at them for a long time, then looked down at Ulrich's note again.

Finally, she scrubbed her palm across her face and nodded. "I believe you."

Relief uncoiled the knot in Alar's chest. He let out a breath, surprised by how deeply those three words affected him.

It only meant his mission should succeed. Nothing more.

The basement door creaked open and shut. Jack descended the stairs a moment later, his hand crossbow still loaded and leveled within a fingerspan of Daeya. Alar stepped between Val's man and the sorceress—a silent command to stand down. "What did you see?"

Jack glowered at him, but he lowered his weapon. "Some soldiers still picking nails out of their feet. A few burns. No fatalities. Looked like the bastards jumped into the harbor to avoid the fire. The whole port's gone up, and they're locking down the city."

"Bleeding Aether," Daeya swore.

Alar nodded to Jack. It wasn't good news, but it came as no surprise. "Did you get the rose madder?"

Jack untied a small sack from his belt and tossed it to him. The finely ground root powder shifted between his fingers. Alar turned to Daeya.

"We're going to have to dye your hair. I know you speak Brogrenti, and red should take well over the blonde. Do you have fresh clothing in your pack?"

Daeya's attention was on Jack. "Yes." She slid her focus back to Alar. "But we can't leave yet. I have somewhere to be at sixth bell."

"They'll send for Light Paladins within the hour if they haven't already," Alar said. "We don't have time to run errands."

She scoffed again. "Then we'll make time. Before you showed up, I had plans with a friend I made on the ship. He just happens to know the very man I was sent here to find."

He shouldn't even entertain the thought. They couldn't afford any more distractions or setbacks, and here she was baiting him with information—a weakness he had been unable to hide even as Faustus. But it would be worthwhile knowing what the Guild was up to; the Alliaansi would need every advantage in the coming war.

"Who?"

A spark of victory lit her face. She held out the scroll to him. "Vortanis."

The person in Ulrich's message. He took the scroll, tapping it thoughtfully with one finger. It was a clue, not a coincidence. Either Ulrich knew Vortanis personally, or she had Foreseen their meeting with him and wanted to steer them that way.

Ravlok's eyes widened at the name. Alar held up a hand to acknowledge the monk's awareness. He took in Daeya's straight-backed posture, her lifted brows, and uplifted chin. The message was clear.

She had him, and she knew it.

Alar schooled his expression into one of indifference. "What does the Guild want with this man?"

Her response was equally cool and composed. "He claims to be an Aetherian. The Guild wants him for questioning."

Exactly the wrong thing to say in front of Jack. Rage clouded the thief's aura and blanketed Alar's senses. Whatever tenuous truce they'd established cracked like glass. Alar moved to intercept Jack. Ravlok pushed Daeya behind him.

With a dark look and an insistent hand on Jack's chest, Alar halted the younger man's advance. "Easy."

Hatred simmered in Jack's brown eyes. He glared around Alar's shoulder. "We all know what that means, Chaos-sworn witch."

"She isn't insinuating anything, Jack." Alar's tone was heavy with rebuke. He tapped into his aura-sense and *squeezed* the dense fog of anger surrounding Jack. "She was only answering my question."

"She still does the Guild's bidding even now. How do you not see this?" Jack shoved his hand away, his fury burgeoning at the confines of Alar's psionic hold. "You think she wouldn't seize the opportunity to arrest a man to get back in their good graces?"

Alar tightened his grip on Jack's aura until the tension in the man's posture eased a fraction. He spoke calmly and extracted his mental touch. "I think she's smart enough to realize that's no longer possible. Sorcerer Beck would sooner see her hang."

"So would I." Jack spat on the ground between them and stormed toward the stairs.

Alar made no move to stop him. A bone-deep weariness settled over him as he turned back to Daeya and Ravlok. She peered out from behind the safety of Ravlok's larger frame, watching Jack leave.

After the basement door had opened and closed again, Alar cleared his throat. "Apologies. He's been under a lot of stress." As if that would salvage the tattered remnants of her trust.

Ravlok bristled. "He's a tinderbox."

Though his assessment wasn't unfounded, Alar couldn't help his twinge of annoyance. Ravlok would be, too, if he'd suffered half as much at the Guild's hands.

Daeya stepped out from behind the monk, her hand brushing his arm in thanks. Her attention lingered on the top of the stairs before she faced Alar once more. "What happened to him?"

It wasn't his story to tell, but a strategic unveiling of just how badly her people treated their subjects could make the difference between naming her an enemy or an ally. If nothing else, he could use it as another measure of her character. "He lost his father to the Guild's questioning many years ago."

As he had hoped, Daeya looked pained. "That's awful."

He took a risk and stepped toward her. She didn't shy from him. "If we go to meet Vortanis, can you assure me he won't end up the same way?"

"He won't." Her voice was surprisingly steady. She looked up at him. "If you can assure me you'll help my father."

His entire world narrowed to the spark of rebellion that caught fire in her eyes. The sight of it made his chest constrict, and for a moment, he found it difficult to speak.

Alar shook himself. It was unlikely the Alliaansi would agree to spend valuable resources on rescuing an old blacksmith, but her father's skills could be useful. He could make an argument on Angus McVen's behalf, if nothing else. And right now, Alar needed her compliance more than anything.

He nodded. "You have my word."

Chapter Thirty-One

Daeya

A sickly crescent moon sliced through the haze clinging to the Old City. Coastal wind whispered along the cobbles and stirred clouds of smoke. Ash mingled with dust and sand, coating the beachside buildings with a gritty film.

Daeya slipped down the alleyway with her companions, grateful for the Brogrenti *taenach* wrapped around her mouth and nose. Not only did the scarf-like garment obscure her face below her freshly tinted eyebrows, but it also filtered out the acrid smell of burned wood and pitch.

City curfew would go into effect in a few moments. Through the gap ahead, people bustled home along one of the major thoroughfares. Those on foot were further harried by the curt demands of city guards. Lanterns blazed in their posts, and a steady orange glow bathed the Orthovian street.

While the others paused to observe the flow of traffic, Daeya glanced up toward the darkening sky. Tall, stone-faced buildings rose on either side of her, their upper floors obscured by grimy fog.

Jack was supposed to be up there somewhere, skimming the rooftops and keeping watch. She suppressed a shudder, trying her best not to imagine herself between the sights of his crossbow. He'd been furious when Faustus—Alar, rather—armed her with a trio of beads to aid them in their escape. After declaring that the only trustworthy sorceress was a dead sorceress, Jack had stormed out of the cellar again, slamming the door behind him.

Alar assured her Jack would come around with time. Daeya found it difficult to believe him.

Trust him.

She let out a sigh. Trust a blanker. That was like asking her to trust a starving chaagra with a wounded rabbit. What had Master Ulrich Foreseen that demanded Daeya flee Eidosinia with an Alliaansi spy? Could Alar have taken control of Ulrich's mind? Forced her to write a pair of messages so ironclad and irrefutable that Daeya's only choice was to accept them? If so, what in Baosanni's name did Alar want with her?

Maybe he meant to take her hostage. She was close enough to Gregory that he could ransom her in exchange for supplies or money. Perhaps he planned to interrogate her for Guild secrets.

No. He knew how skilled she was. He wouldn't have given her saphyrum if his goal was to kidnap her. There had to be another reason. She'd been over and over a dozen other possibilities in the hours they'd waited for the rose madder to take hold. Eventually, she was left with only one—the simplest and most logical one.

Maybe he was telling the truth.

As Alar crept along the side of the building in front of her, Ravlok's warmth pressed in from behind. His steady presence eased her tumultuous thoughts. Even if he wasn't mind-controlled, even if he didn't exhibit any of the signs of a mastermind's psychic imperium, she owed it to him to find out for sure.

Once they'd met with Vortanis and secured a path out of the city, she considered trying to convince Ravlok to part ways with these Alliaansi and go north with her to find Gregory. The Councilor could confirm whether Ravlok's memory had been compromised. He could also sort out the mess Joss and Normos had made of her mission. She could explain her encounter with the blanker to him, prove she hadn't run away or committed any crimes, and guarantee her father's safety without the blanker's help.

Still, something nagged at her. Something Ravlok had said. If Gregory had used magic on him, if he'd betrayed the most fundamental principle of the Sorcerers' Guild...

Daeya wasn't certain how to feel about that.

It could be argued that he'd acted within the law, but the timing wasn't right. The decree stating magic could be used to apprehend Alliaansi non-adepts hadn't come until after she'd set sail. Ravlok would have been imprisoned before then. In a secret dungeon, no less.

She wanted to believe Ravlok was lying, but he'd never lied to her before. Worse, Gregory's history of bending rules and keeping secrets left too much room for doubt. If Ravlok was telling the truth, the Councilor could easily deny the accusation and hang him for treason—a fate Daeya would never allow to befall her closest friend.

Alar slipped into the flow of traffic. She linked arms with Ravlok and followed a respectable distance behind the blanker. To any onlookers, Alar was a lone merchant, and she and Ravlok were a couple of young lovers hurrying back to their lodging for the night.

As they left the wide lanes of the city proper, closely packed buildings gave way to rocky coastline. Cobbled streets became a single lane of mist-soaked gravel worn in by wagon wheels. The constant press of people relented, and Daeya welcomed the encroaching blanket of night.

The Lighthouse Tavern was a busy establishment standing alone at the end of a short bayside peninsula. True to its name, the main entrance beckoned from a tall cylinder of white-washed stone. Fire blazed near its summit, though only its bright glow could be seen through the haze. A rectangular structure nestled beside the lighthouse, two stories tall and covered with gleaming windows.

The first of six bells reverberated through the city as they approached. Alar entered first, paying his respects to the guards at the door without incident. He had shaved his stubble and applied chassick oil to darken his skin to a rich bronze. With the oil and new make-up, he looked nothing like the young man Daeya had known in Ryost. Ravlok was similarly disguised, his hair cut short and the beginnings of his beard darkened with soot to give the illusion of fullness.

More bells chimed. A flurry of movement caught Daeya's eye. An enormous shape landed atop a gnarled tree beside the road. She squinted into the darkness as they approached it. Sitting on a low, swaying branch was the largest falcon she had ever seen. The creature's black, beady eyes reflected the meager light, unsettling in its focus.

Ravlok nudged her with his forearm. "You alright?"

Did he not see it? Daeya nodded toward the falcon. "Look at the size of that bird."

His steps faltered. "Paelic."

"What does that mean?"

"That's his name."

They stood in awkward silence while Ravlok studied the bird. It continued to stare at them, even tilting its head as if deep in thought.

"A friend of yours?" Daeya asked when the pounding of the surf and the pulsing in her ears became too loud.

"You could say that." He finally tore his eyes away, his expression troubled. "He sort of helped us escape the sorcerers in Ryost."

Her lips twitched; she suppressed an inappropriate snort. Ravlok had always been a little eccentric. Maybe she'd been worried about psionics for nothing. "Maybe he'll help us out of Orthovia, too."

Ravlok's frown deepened and he started forward again, seeming to have missed her jest. "Maybe."

Unease wormed its way along her spine, and her smile faded. Daeya would have never described Ravlok as an easygoing man; he was prone to long moments of silence, even when nothing seemed to be amiss, but the extended length of his brooding sessions concerned her. She allowed herself to be led, overjoyed to leave creepy Paelic and his unnaturally intelligent gaze behind.

The guards ushered them through with disinterested waves, and they stepped into a wide, circular room that spanned the ground floor of the lighthouse. Clinking glassware, clattering dice, raucous laughter, and even the badly played lute were a welcome change after hours cramped in the quiet brewer's basement. Coupled with the strong scent of sweat, spirits, and courtesans' perfume, the place reminded her of Davy's. At least, if Davy's had been in a more affluent part of town.

Oil lamps spilled flickering light over old maritime paintings and threw long shadows off benches and tables. Floorboards creaked underfoot. Most patrons appeared to be sailors who'd run aground while the port was closed for repairs. A smaller number were mercenaries with worn leathers and sheathed weapons. Others bore no sign of their chosen professions at all. There were no robed mages present. Only a few off-duty soldiers had taken up stools near a set of doors to Daeya's right.

Jack had somehow beaten them there. He held a mug of ale and leaned against the bar, his crossbow for once nowhere in sight. Alar made his way toward him. They would wait there until Daeya found Dan and signaled for them to move.

Fortunately, Dan was easy to spot. He was the only sailor with a Skriian tribal stripe across his nose. Daeya pointed him out to Ravlok, slipped off his arm, and made for the dicing table. Belio and Gavin were bickering over whose turn was next when Daeya stepped up beside them.

Across the table, Cordy adjusted the front of his trousers and let out a low whistle, eyeing Daeya's disguise. "Damn me if it didn't just get hotter in here."

Daeya pulled her *taenach* below her chin, shooting him a playfully affronted look. "Charming, Cordy."

Belio started. "Dae—ugh!"

Gavin's elbow connected with Belio's ribs, driving the air from his lungs. "Shut up, idiot."

Pained, holding his side, Belio looked Daeya over. "Apologies, my lady."

He shot Cordy a pointed look, but the gap-toothed sailor only puffed from a pipe and raised his hands. "I said what I said."

Dan eyed them all with a mixture of weariness and disdain. He tapped his three-pronged hook on the arm of his chair before rising. "They're waiting for you."

They?

Daeya glanced behind her at Ravlok. "There are others with me."

Dan paused, already two long strides from the table. He didn't bother to follow Daeya's gaze. "Do you trust them?"

That was the question of the day, wasn't it? Daeya closed her eyes, breathing in and out to calm herself. Jack would sooner slit her throat than watch her back. Ravlok could be under the influence of a blanker. Alar had been lying to her since they met. And yet, without them, her own people might have hung her for treason an hour ago.

With every beat of her heart, Ulrich's message echoed through her mind. *Trust him.*

Her fingers curled. Daeya growled to herself and glared at the floor.

Dan returned to her. He smelled of salty sea and heated metal. His fingers slipped under her jaw, beneath the *taenach*, forcing her chin up. Copper, snake-slitted eyes gazed down at her. They were comforting, even mesmerizing, in their measure of safety and warmth. His voice was a quiet rumble among the din. "*Nashanett*?"

Nashanett. Blessed leader.

Those eyes were no illusion, but the absence of one—a peek under the mask.

A force, deep and implacable in its strength, rose within her and chased away all doubt. She steeled herself. "Yes. For now."

Dan didn't question her. "Then come."

She followed him through the maze of drunken patrons, past the off-duty soldiers, and through the set of doors. Ravlok and the others fell in behind them.

A long corridor stretched away from her, separating two rows of doors. Each door had a brass number hanging from its center. Dan stopped at one marked with the number twelve and knocked three times. A curt male voice called out.

"Enter."

Inside, the room was modest and clean, flanked by a narrow closet and a spacious washroom. Sensible, tan bedding lay undisturbed on the bed. Two chairs sat unoccupied at a small table adorned with a vase of wildflowers.

The room's only occupants were a man and a woman, both dressed in tailored robes of white and silver. The woman stood beside the stove, resting her hands on the back of the man's chair. She studied them as they entered, but it was the man who caught Daeya's attention.

Frazzled gray hair ringed his liver-spotted head. His beard ended in a sharp point that brushed the plate of food in his lap. He only looked up after Dan closed the door behind them. His weathered face seemed permanently set into a frown.

The entire space smelled of Aether. Power rolled off him in staggering waves that rocked Daeya's senses. His physical presence was even more substantial and imposing than Gregory himself. Daeya fought the urge to bow to that power, but she failed to stop herself from lowering her eyes to the floor.

The reports of an Aetherian in Orthovia might not be rumors after all. Even if she hadn't given her word to Alar, she wouldn't have been able to subdue this man. Not on her own.

The man snorted and looked at Dan. "You're certain? She trembles like a fawn."

His derisive tone sent a hot wave of embarrassment through her. Daeya tensed and forced her gaze back upward. She clenched her jaw so hard her teeth ached. *Be fearless.*

Dan dipped his chin toward the man. "*Vheth*, Magisei. I saw it with my own eyes."

The humility and deference with which he spoke the ancient Aetherian honorific was so unlike the sailor Daeya had come to know that she found herself staring at him.

What was he talking about? What had he seen?

The woman regarded Dan with a smile that pulled the two trios of white stripes on her cheeks upward. As the Aetherian grumbled obscenities under his breath, her smile deepened, wrinkling the blue stripe that ran the length of her nose.

"Peace, Vortanis."

Her voice was little more than a caress of air, but it carried like a bell made of finest crystal and stilled the old man's tongue. He glared at her over his shoulder, and she matched him with a look of amusement. Despite the man's arcane strength, it was clear which of them held power over the other. Daeya shifted her focus from Vortanis to the woman.

Like Dan, she was of Skriian ancestry. Her rich umber skin bore over a dozen tattoos, including half a sunburst in yellow across her forehead—an homage to the rising sun. Sleek oiled hair the color of midnight was pinned into elaborate curls and waves beneath a white kerchief adorned with silver embroidery. She had a presence about her, something Daeya struggled to identify, like familiarity without knowing. As if she should recognize this woman.

As if they had once been good friends.

"We've been searching for years." Vortanis turned fully to look at the woman, his elbow draped across the back of the chair. "And you think it's proof enough when some whelp shows up on a ship and burns the entire port to the ground?"

Daeya grimaced at the reminder. "It wasn't the entire port. Most of that wasn't even me."

Vortanis's attention snapped back toward her, eyes wide and incredulous.

The woman's laugh mimicked the soft, melodious strum of a harp. Her dark eyes danced as she looked at Daeya. "No, it was not." She nodded to Dan. "You've a keen eye, young one. Well done."

Her praise seemed to electrify the air around Dan. The sailor bowed low at the waist. "*Zhev annivhosh, Saonivhatt.*"

Thank you, Goddess.

Daeya's mouth fell open. She understood the mixture of sibilant and guttural sounds just as well in her waking hours as she did in her dreams. Dan was embellishing, surely. Perhaps she'd misunderstood. She was bound to make mistakes with a language she had never studied.

It was probably just her name. Saonivhatt. People named their children strange things all the time. Yes. That had to be it.

She caught the woman watching her again. A warm but knowing smile lingered on her lips.

Alar stepped into Daeya's periphery, breaking her out of her thoughts. It was a good thing, too, because her knees might have buckled without his distraction. He gestured to the pair opposite them, his annoyance thinly veiled. "I have to admit I'm a little confused. Would either of you care to explain what's going on? Preferably in a language we all can understand. And an introduction would be nice. You are Vortanis, I assume?"

"Watch your tone, boy," the Aetherian snapped.

Alar lifted placating hands. "I'm only asking your name."

Vortanis sucked his teeth before answering. "You'll call me Magisei. You'll call her Saonivhatt."

Saonivhatt ignored them both. "Daeya, what can you tell me of your parents?"

Daeya spared a look at Alar before answering. Gods help the blanker if he said something stupid enough to provoke the old man. "My father is a blacksmith. He fills the Guild's commission for weapons and armor." At least, until Gregory decided to leave him destitute. "My mother died when I was ten. She was a seamstress."

The woman's expression softened. "I mean your birth parents. Did you know them at all?"

Daeya resisted the need to reach for her pendant. How did this woman know they *weren't* her birth parents? "No. Da says my mother died not long after I was born. He buried her on the farm they owned before he and Ma took jobs in Ryost." She still visited her gravesite once a year. Da encouraged her to take flowers there to honor her.

Saonivhatt nodded. "What was her name? Did he tell you?"

Daeya shifted from foot to foot. Her response came slowly. "He said her name was Neri."

The Aetherian's attention settled on her again. Daeya glanced toward him before training her eyes on Saonivhatt.

"And your father?" she asked.

"Da never said much about him." She didn't mean to mince the words through her teeth. "Only that he must be a sorry sod to leave a woman alone in the woods so close to giving birth." Angus never spoke ill of her father in front of her, but she'd overheard plenty of conversations.

Two small wrinkles appeared between the woman's dark eyebrows. She looked as if she was about to say something, but Vortanis coughed, interrupting her thoughts. Those wrinkles smoothed over. She clasped her hands before her. "Dannicus tells us you saved his ship from a lightning storm a few days ago. Would you please explain how you did that?"

Daeya shrugged. "I just used elemental magic."

Saonivhatt tilted her head. "Lightning, then?"

"No. I can only wield fire."

"And Aether," Dan added.

Daeya groaned aloud. "I told you, I'm not an Aetherian. I can't wield Aether. Not like that."

Vortanis scoffed. "Of course, the Guild would fill your pretty head with rubbish."

"What do you mean?"

He waved the hand still casually draped over his chair. "Everything is Aether, child. The only difference between magi and Aetherians is my understanding of how to shape it. To blend one element into the next and back again, if I wish."

It was the simplest explanation of the Aetherians she'd ever heard. It also explained why they were so dangerous. Having the ability to ward and wield every element would make them immensely powerful, but the more elements one could wield, the more time it took to master each one. Deadly mistakes happened often during elemental training.

"While you were using your element, did anything unusual happen? A change in color, for instance?" Saonivhatt asked.

"It did change color." Daeya remembered thinking that was odd. She'd thought it was from the sheer quantity of the element she'd had to take in. "And these odd lines showed up on my hands. It happened again on the docks."

Vortanis straightened, sobering, his gaze as sharp and unsettling as Paelic's. "What color?"

She wasn't sure if he meant the fire or the weird lines. "The fire was sort of a deep red. The lines were gold."

"Gold." Saonivhatt let out a soft sigh. Gods, everything she did was soft and graceful. "Is that proof enough for you, Vortanis?"

Daeya looked between them, puzzled. "Proof enough for what?"

"Can you summon it?" Her question went unanswered. Vortanis leaned forward in his chair, his dinner forgotten in his lap. "Can you show us?"

A chill passed down Daeya's spine at the intensity of that stare. She shook her head. "I don't think so. I didn't summon it. It just happened."

"Try—"

"She may need guidance," Saonivhatt broke in. "If her power only manifested during a moment of crisis, it is possible her memories have been buried too deeply. We'll need to unlock those sooner, rather than later. If Caelyn felt her magic awaken, Chaos will not be far behind."

Ravlok's voice came from behind Daeya's right shoulder. "Chaos? You mean Anordis?"

A sound eerily close to a growl issued from Dan's throat. "Some would say you invite him in to spy on us by speaking his name."

Alar sniffed. "Someone's paranoid."

Saonivhatt gave him a reproachful look. "Unfortunately, some of his servants do have the power to call upon him."

Ravlok paled. "That wasn't my intention—"

"Peace, servant of Ordeolas. I know you mean well." Saonivhatt stepped toward him and placed her hand on his temple. She, too, bore the strong scent of Aether, along with something Daeya could only identify as sunlight on a bright summer day. "She is going to need your protection in the coming months. Chaos would do anything to get his hands on her."

Alar groaned aloud and rubbed his temples. "You can't honestly believe—"

"They'll all need wardstones." Vortanis rose from his chair and crossed the room to retrieve a small pack.

Daeya reeled as the information flooded in. Tension constricted her lungs. She clenched her fists to stop their shaking.

While she had always borne faith in the abstract idea of divinity, all this talk of gods and goddesses made her want to side with Alar in his disbelief. Things were happening too fast. Decisions were being made, and all she could do was turn circles around the idea that the gods were real people *and* held an interest in her. Yet the truth of it was standing right in front of her. A name lay poised on her tongue, the true name for this Saonivhatt—Tiior, lesser goddess of knowledge, the patron deity of dragons—but she dared not speak it aloud. She feared the reality that confirmation might bring.

At last, she couldn't hold back the questions any longer. "What power are you talking about? What have you been searching for? Why would Chaos want *me*?"

All eyes turned to her. Even Vortanis paused in rummaging through his pack.

Saonivhatt slipped away from Ravlok and took Daeya's hands. "All valid questions, *Nashanett*." She drew in a breath, giving Daeya's fingers a squeeze. "You are becoming what you are meant to be. The soul that resides in you is the last of an ancient people whose magic is older than written history. Older than the lesser gods themselves."

She reached up to cup Daeya's cheek. Her dark eyes were kind, even apologetic, as if she sensed the monumental weight that was coming to rest on Daeya's shoulders. "Do you remember the story Dannicus told you? The one of the draegion?"

"I wish I didn't." It was hard to force the words out around the sand in her throat. The draegion's lightning had turned scarlet when he faced the dragon. Just as her fire had on the ship and at the docks. Had Gregory known about this? Had the Council? "You're saying I am one?"

Saonivhatt nodded. "You are the only one left."

Chapter Thirty-Two

Ravlok

Ravlok took in Daeya's tear-streaked expression and scoured his memory of every ancient text he'd ever read. He forced aside his thoughts of Chaos, of Caelyn, and of how this woman knew his faith even when he was in disguise. He steadied his tumultuous aura by controlling his breathing and focusing only on that one word.

"What's a draegion?"

Vortanis snorted and resumed the search through his pack. "Ancient beings, boy. Weren't you listening?"

The old man reminded him so much of Yonfé that Ravlok took his deprecating tone in stride. "I've studied hundreds of ancient tomes and scrolls, and I've never encountered that word."

"Well, of course you wouldn't. The only stories left on Dessos are outlandish fae tales that belittle their influence. I'm sure you've heard of the dragon riders."

Acid leached into Vortanis's tone. Ravlok nodded, albeit uncertain he *should* admit how compelling he'd found those heroic stories from his youth.

Vortanis scoffed. "See? Shameful, especially for a member of Ordeolas's order. If anyone should remember the truth of them, it would be his monks." He pulled out a smooth, palm-sized stone and placed it on the table beside his pack. "The most important texts were lost in the Shadow Era succeeding the fall of Xavkavhosh."

"Who?" Ravlok knew only sparing details of the Shadow Era—an indeterminate number of centuries from which only a few stone and metal accounts survived. Scholars believed it had been a time of worldwide desolation—wars, wildfires, cyclones, and earthquakes—that brought Dessos to its knees.

"Xavkav—oh, forget it. You're too young to appreciate it, anyway."

Ravlok dared a step toward him. "Please." He took another step, hoping he looked as earnest as he felt. If he was supposed to help Daeya, he needed to know more. "If it helps me understand what's happening, it may be important."

He reached the old man's side as Vortanis placed three more wardstones beside the first one. Veins of saphyrum ran alongside smaller stripes of gold and silver. Even one of those stones would be worth a fortune; Ravlok had stolen a few in his day from Madame's patrons. With the right enchantment, they allowed a bearer to disappear from every manner of arcane scrying until its magic wore off.

Vortanis dropped one into Ravlok's hand. "Knowing the draegion emperor won't help you much," the old man admitted. "But I suppose if you want to know more, you'll need to learn Ancient Draconic first."

Jack spoke up from behind them. "Are these draegion dangerous?"

Vortanis barked a laugh. "Oh, yes. They were once the most powerful beings on Dessos." He gathered up the remaining three wardstones and approached Jack, placing one in his hand. Ravlok slipped his own stone into a pocket. Vortanis nodded toward Daeya. "This one's only an infant. Soon, she'll have the power to command dragons."

A dark look stole over Jack's face. Ravlok returned to Daeya's side, placing himself between the younger man and his friend. The one-handed sailor, Dannicus, eyed Jack as well, with a fierceness Ravlok found unsettling.

Alar crossed his arms, one flaxen eyebrow lifting. "Isn't that power sort of pointless if dragons are extinct?"

The thought had wormed its way into Ravlok's mind as well. Aside from that, if Ancient Draconic differed from the more modern forms of the dead language, the texts he would need to learn it would likely have deteriorated by now.

Dannicus looked over Daeya's head. Ravlok started when his dark eyes flashed a vibrant copper. The grin he spared Alar was a thing of feral bemusement. "I assure you, we are far from extinct."

Alar's bronze skin paled in every place his chassick oil was thinnest. His gaping mouth and wide-eyed astonishment might have been comical if Ravlok's own heart hadn't tried to seize in his chest. Ravlok looked toward Saonivhatt, who offered him a wink and the slightest smile—confirmation of his suspicions of who this woman was. Her appearance, her knowledge, the presence of dragons—

His knees grew weak, as if to lower themselves of their own accord to the ground, but Saonivhatt gave the barest shake of her head, still watching Ravlok with that tiny smile. It took everything he had not to prostrate himself at her feet.

Daeya, however, took the news of dragons without so much as a batted eye. She regarded Dannicus without fear or disbelief for a full three seconds before returning her attention to Saonivhatt. "With all due respect, I don't want to control dragons. I just want to live my life in peace."

"Too late for that." Vortanis dropped a wardstone into Daeya's hand. He stepped around her and offered Alar the last stone. "If it's any consolation, Baokryn didn't want her responsibilities, either. She eventually ruled as queen."

"Vortanis," Saonivhatt warned.

"What?"

Dark amusement tugged at one corner of her mouth. Though she didn't speak, she nodded toward the chair by the stove, and Vortanis grumbled under his breath. He reclaimed his seat and folded his arms like a scolded child. With her companion subdued, Saonivhatt's expression softened once more. She looked between Ravlok and Daeya.

"I know this is a lot to take in, but I must be frank with you. A war is coming, and not just in Eidosinia." She side-eyed Alar as he recovered from the momentary lapse in his haughty persona. His mouth snapped closed before whatever insolent retort he'd thought of passed his lips. "Chaos's power grows. It is rumored among his servants that he will make a play for the Greater Throne against Saolanni. With the last draegion's power—*your* power—tied to his, he could destroy the entire pantheon."

Daeya chuckled, the sound thin and reedy in Ravlok's ears. "The last thing I want to do is get involved with a war between gods."

Before Saonivhatt could say more, Ravlok clasped Daeya's shoulder. He could feel the weight levied there as tension coiled in the muscles beneath his palm. It was so much to take in, and he could only imagine the pressure she was feeling. He felt it to a lesser degree, having been charged with her protection. There was no better time than now to start acting the part.

"I know it seems impossible, but you won't be alone. Whatever the gods need of you, I will stand by your side."

Daeya's eyes finally returned to their usual shade of new-leaf green. She fixed him with a baffled stare and shook her head. "You're not listening. I don't want this." She glared at Saonivhatt. "Choose someone else."

Saonivhatt winced. "It isn't a matter of choosing, I'm afraid. Mira and Shavaan created you with the remnants of Baokryn's magic. I can explain more later, but—"

"I would rather you didn't." Golden-white ribbons of light threaded about Daeya's fingertips. Her hands curled into fists as lattice-like tendrils crept up past her wrists.

Vortanis stood from his chair so quickly it scraped against the floor. "Tiior."

"I see it." Saonivhatt's melodic voice bore the slightest edge. As if in response to Daeya's light, her eyes flickered from warm brown to shining quicksilver. A spike of dread shot through Ravlok as her pupils narrowed to slits. She motioned to Daeya's hands, her expression hardening. "Come to Draeconis. There are dragons there who can teach you to control this."

Again, Ravlok scoured his memory for references of the term 'Draeconis,' but there was nothing.

"No." Daeya's ire radiated from her like heat from a wildfire. The sensation thrummed down Ravlok's spine, making him shiver as if from the threat of a deadly animal. If what they said was true, then she was more dangerous than even the supposed dragon on his other side. He stood in Tiior's presence—the goddess of knowledge herself—and yet he was more daunted by the girl who'd shared her oranges and read forbidden texts with him. The girl who'd wiggled into his heart and become nothing short of his best friend.

"Daeya, breathe. Please." He steadied his nerves with his own deep breathing. "Just like we've practiced."

Daeya stared at the goddess without flinching, though tear streaks gleamed on her fair cheeks. For a long time, it seemed she didn't hear him, until she drew a single shuddering breath and let it out. Ravlok counted that breath to six seconds and might have wept with relief. She did it again, and the light faded. Her fingers uncurled.

Tiior's lips parted at the sight. It was the only sign of anything akin to surprise she had shown all evening. She nodded once at Ravlok to acknowledge his part in quelling Daeya's temper before returning to her, brows furrowed. "Chaos will come for you whether or not you accept your calling."

Alar swept between Daeya and Tiior, heedless of all decorum or respect in his blasphemy. "You have her answer. If there is nothing else, we'll take our leave of you."

Vortanis bristled. He moved like mist to Tiior's side and hovered at her right shoulder. "It is the wrong answer. A draegion without a dragonbond is unpredictable, and few gold dragons reside outside of Draeconis."

Daeya fixed him with a heated stare. "What of Telerion? Is he a gold dragon?"

Genuine shock seized Vortanis as he recoiled. "Aethersworn? Aliri's boy? How do you know him?"

Tiior's expression changed. Quiet contemplation replaced her unease. She turned away to pace the room in a slow circuit, silver-embroidered robe whispering against worn carpet.

Daeya spared her a glance before answering. "He haunts my dreams like a flaming specter. So far, he's yet to show himself, but I know his voice. He says he can be found where the three sisters touch the mountain. Whatever in the bleeding Wastelands that means."

"Of course." Tiior touched a delicate hand to her chin, deep in thought.

Vortanis scowled. "Telerion's been exiled. In any case, he's only a wyrmling. You will return with us and meet a proper dragon—"

Tiior spun on her slippered heel. "*Vhash*. We cannot make her return with us. We must respect her choice."

She lifted her hands, and soft white light pooled between her palms. It brightened to a blinding intensity, forcing Ravlok to look away. When the light faded, Tiior stood before him, holding an enormous tome. The book was bound in brown leather and bore a clasp of metal, perhaps silver or platinum.

"I cannot give you the knowledge of magic for which you have long prayed, little brother. However, I can give you the magic of knowledge. The Tome of Eolaan will open only for you, and you may summon it or dismiss it with a word. Study it each day, and it will teach you all you need to know."

Eolaan. That was a name he *did* recognize. The first dragon created by Mira in Tiior's image—the Mother of Stories, whose wisdom and knowledge were said to rival Tiior's.

As the goddess pressed the tome into his hands, the word he needed became known to him as surely as he knew his own name. His heart thundered in his ears as the weight of his responsibility settled upon him. Though there was a twinge of disappointment at knowing the goddess herself could not bestow magic upon him, she had still answered his prayers.

She had given him purpose.

Ravlok stumbled over his gratitude while his tongue tied itself into knots. He bowed. "Th-thank you, Goddess."

She dipped her chin in return. As he straightened, she said to Daeya, "The Three Sisters is a constellation you will find in the north during winter. Alar can show you where it is."

The psionist started at the sound of his name. He shifted on his feet before hardening his expression and lifting his chin as if he might refuse. When Daeya looked at him, he hesitated. "I suppose I can."

Daeya's smile lit her face. "We'd best get going, then. I wouldn't want to be any more unpredictable."

Alar smirked. "Indeed."

She looked back at Vortanis. "Are you going to activate these wardstones, or shall I?"

"Caelyn's not going to like this," Vortanis grumbled aside to Tiior. When the goddess didn't offer a response, he sighed and made a flippant gesture with his hand. The wardstone instantly warmed in Ravlok's pocket.

Jack tossed his stone into the air and caught it with nimble fingers. The turquoise stripe of saphyrum flashed in the candlelight before the stone vanished up his sleeve. "I don't suppose either of you have a faster way of getting us out of town."

Vortanis scoffed. "You want to go gallivanting around the country rather than listen to reason, that's up to you."

"Then it seems we're done here." Alar touched Daeya's shoulder and started for the door. She followed with little coaxing, murmuring her thanks to Dannicus on the way out. Jack trailed in their wake, departing without a word.

Ravlok lingered, watching Dannicus and Tiior share troubled frowns. Hefting the book in his hands, he spoke the word to unsummon it and jumped when it vanished in a puff of shimmering black-violet mist. With his burden lightened, he caught Tiior's gaze and bowed to her. "I'll keep her safe, Goddess."

A small, sad smile touched her lips. "I know you will do your best."

The knowing, haunted look in her eyes made Ravlok's chest ache. They should go to Draeconis. If Chaos was really involved—and Ravlok believed every word Tiior and Vortanis had said—then there was nowhere safer for Daeya than among people who had some idea of what was coming.

But his charge was already out the door, and her footsteps receded down the hallway. With a last reluctant nod, Ravlok turned to follow her.

Chapter Thirty-Three

Orowen

Fawn's Breath, or Ru'Kaari'uu, as it was known to Orowen's people, nestled in the foothills of the northern Palisadic Mountains. The tiny village had grown tenfold since her last visit many years ago. Stone streets and structures had taken over old dirt roads and wood-and-thatch dwellings from decades past. A school had been built near the town hall, and new rooms were added to the abbey and the temple.

Despite its remarkable growth, the town still bore the same sense of peace and camaraderie that had inspired its foundation. Here, the circumstances of one's birth didn't matter. It was what people brought to the community that made them welcome in Ru'Kaari'uu.

Though the town had never officially joined the Alliaansi, it was the first stop on the road to Starlight for refugees fleeing western Eidosinia and the Brogrenti Highlands. Because it was free of Guild oppression, and because work and land were both plentiful, many families decided to settle here rather than journey farther into the frigid Northlands.

Orowen's breath clouded the glass before her. The window radiated an icy cold that bled through her woolen shawl and made her skin prickle. Outside, snowy moonlit mountains loomed like ghostly silhouettes. Evergreen cedars and pines stood like dark blades buried hilt-first into the rocky hillsides. A thin layer of fog crept over the abbey as twilight faded into night.

Three weeks had passed since Alar and the others had departed for Orthovia. There was no word from any of them, and Orowen had begun to fear the worst. Rumors swirled around an attack on the Orthovian port. Reports of scarlet flames consuming the boardwalk—flames that matched the ones in Cheralach's visions—were the only common thread among them. Some described an Aetherian and a mastermind teaming up against a group of sorcerers. Others suggested the mastermind had used a psychic imperium on the local children and commanded them to kill the city guard.

It was hard to sort the morsels of truth from the lies. Nearly every report agreed the Alliaansi were responsible. So soon after the destruction Orowen had caused in Ryost, it was no wonder unrest brewed in Eidosinia. Scouts reported movement of Guild troops near the mountain pass. A few even spoke of Guild Councilors in Trivvix.

The creak of a door preceded the soft footfalls of her dearest friend. She turned from the window. Light from the fireplace threw stark shadows across Kendi's straight nose and angular cheekbones. He was balancing a plate on his forearm and carried two steaming mugs. Scents of hot cider, spiced selka, and roasted vegetables wafted toward her.

He attempted a smile and placed his offering on the table. "I thought you might be hungry."

His voice was the first she'd heard in hours. It warmed her thoughts, but it did little to thaw the icy grip of her despair. "Thank you, *neime*."

Orowen feigned a smile in return, but she couldn't make it feel honest. Things between them had been tense since he'd told her about the collapse of the School of High Sorcery. Chivalrous as he was, Kendi sought to mitigate her responsibility for the act, but his attempts only frustrated her more. She was an oathbreaker, after all. She deserved to feel that pain.

Kendi sighed, likely sensing her mood. Their friendship spanned over a century, and there was little he was bound to miss. "You're brooding again, Devoted. You must eat."

She ignored his veiled command. "Has there been any news?"

"From Alar? No." He stepped around the table. When he lifted his hand to touch her face, she stiffened. Kendi hesitated and returned his arm to his side. "What can I do? How can I help you, *nei ama're*?"

The hopelessness in his voice gutted her. How could she explain to him that she was undeserving of his love? His affection? Her grief for the children and her disdain for herself left her hollow inside. There were no more tears she could cry. No more prayers she could pray. Her knees were chafed from all the time she'd spent at Mira's altar begging forgiveness. She would never feel whole again.

Kendi searched her face. He reached for her hand slowly this time, giving her a chance to pull away. Warm fingers interlaced with hers. "There's still no sign of it?"

Her throat constricted. That hollow space inside her yawned further. "No."

Her magic had not returned from the worst case of Mage's Folly she'd ever suffered. Not even the strongest healer in the town abbey could offer much beyond kind words and assurances, but Orowen knew the truth. Because she had forsaken her vow to do no harm, Saolanni had turned from her.

Kendi kissed her knuckles. "It was an accident. There's no way you could have known."

"Tell that to their mothers." Anger prickled along her spine, but it wasn't directed at him. Never at him. "I accepted the risks when I opened that rift. All those little lives paid for my mistake."

"We all make choices we regret."

Orowen's chest felt like it had been caved in by a hammer. Every breath was one of agony. "I broke my vows. I used magic I swore I would never touch again, and I hate myself for it."

His lavender eyes brimmed with tears. He listened without interrupting, and when she finished, he tugged her into his arms. Her half-hearted resistance broke against his greater strength, and she went limp against him. The blended smells of blade oil, leather, and woodsmoke enveloped her.

"I refuse to leave you alone in your grief." Kendi leaned back and gripped her chin with gentle fingers. A slight but insistent pressure encouraged her to look up at him. "I know you would have never intentionally harmed those children. You may hate yourself right now, but know that I love you, and I'm right here when you're ready to hear why you should love you, too."

Orowen had thought there were no more tears to cry. She'd thought wrong. His words tore through the nettles surrounding her heart, ripping open the fresh scars there. Her hands clenched around his tunic, anchoring herself to him.

Kendi bowed his head until his forehead touched hers. "Saolanni will forgive you, but you must forgive yourself as well."

She closed her eyes, her nose brushing his. Tears fell freely down her cheeks. "I'm not sure I can."

"You will." The words were a whisper against her lips.

Orowen closed the last of the space between them, capturing his mouth with hers. He returned the kiss with patient care, stoking her longing for him with each passing moment. They had danced around their love for decades, both too stubborn and proud to admit it to the other. It surged forward now, as relentless and implacable as the tide.

She broke the kiss to draw a ragged breath. "I love you."

Kendi's strong hands cupped her face. His thumbs stroked the long tapers of her ears. "And I love you."

He kissed her again. Orowen gave herself over to his passion, matching his fervor with her own need to feel something other than misery. She pressed herself tighter against him, letting every span of her scarred body take comfort in his firmness and warmth. Heat pooled in her belly. His hands slid down her white dress, coming to rest on her hips in a grip that was equal parts protective and possessive.

A primal sound escaped him—the first sign of his restraint breaking down. His voice grew husky. Pleading. "Orowen."

"*Ciir, nei ama're.*"

Her acquiescence shattered the last of his resolve. He hoisted her up and parted her thighs to hold her to him as he carried her to bed. Her breath rushed out of her when her back hit the bedspread, and her eyes closed against the press of his mouth to her neck. More kisses scorched a trail across her clavicle, and she lifted her hips as searching hands slipped beneath her modest skirts.

Desperation built with every touch of his lips, every caress of his fingertips, until her core burned like the hottest forge and the ache inside her at last elicited a need that he could fill. Orowen slipped the stays of her dress, and Kendi parted the simple bodice and skirts from her, tossing them carelessly into a heap on the floor. Her shift and his clothes soon joined them.

Cool air washed over her skin, soon replaced by the press of his body over hers. She clutched at his shoulders, legs wrapping his thighs in a possessive vice. A sudden, violent sob escaped her when, at last, at *last*, she felt whole again.

Misunderstanding the sound, Kendi stiffened and made to withdraw, his expression one of shame and guilt intermixed. "I'm—"

She pulled him back down with a ferocity that took him by surprise. "Don't. I'm okay. Don't stop."

He stared owlishly, then settled over her again with painstaking gentleness. "I'm here. I'm here, *nei ama're*." He claimed her lips with the softest kiss. "You need never weather your burdens alone again."

Orowen sniffled and nodded, even though she knew the truth. Her palms smoothed the expanse of his chest, and she tipped her chin in silent offering. He obliged her with more kisses down her neck. They moved as one, even as silent tears spilled down her face.

Later, as the fire burned low and the room descended into darkness, she lay in Kendi's arms and listened to the sound of his steady breathing beneath her cheek. For the first time in long weeks, she didn't agonize over her magic or her path forward as a priestess. But neither did she feel at peace, like when she meditated in the garden or led the acolytes in prayer. Instead, she felt numb, as if she were lost to the Aether in a tangle of fur throws and midnight shadows.

A sound reached her through her half-conscious haze. It was far off, like a whistle in the distance. Orowen blinked open her eyes. Orange light spilled across dark trusses, steadily brightening as she stared upward.

Another whistle sounded, closer this time. Then another, louder, like a scream.

Gooseflesh swept across her skin, despite Kendi's heat. She rolled over, following the glow to the window, where at first, it appeared to reflect light from the hearth. Only, the fire there had nearly gone out.

Kendi stirred beside her. "What is it?"

Curious. Foreboding knotted in her chest, and Orowen sat up to get a better look. The scene outside her window became clearer.

It was no reflection.

The abbey was on fire.

"Clear the village!"

Magnus's voice broke as he roared the command at the nearest soldiers. They scrambled to comply, dashing off to round up the villagers. Shouts mingled with the sounds of sorcerers chanting, and white-violet sigils glowed through the haze.

Flames consumed the town. Orange light reflected off Malediction's surface and danced in the eyes of women and children fleeing their homes in terror. Magnus's grip tightened on the sword. Sweat beaded his brow, and a gust seared his face. The fresh scarring around his eye socket burned.

He staggered to a halt at the sensation. Bile coated Magnus's tongue as panic threatened to smother all rational thought. The shrieks that tore through the night sent him back to that torture chamber with its dank walls, gleaming brazier, and endless pain. Cries echoed off stone and pierced his mind like Cheralach's screams as Nicolas dismembered him piece by tiny piece.

His heart thundered against his ribs, and his hands started to shake, but neither the sounds nor the memories crippled him as he might have expected. Instead they refocused him, sharpening his fury like a whetstone. The sorcerers had tortured and murdered the only father Magnus had ever known. He'd been helpless to stop them then.

He was not helpless now.

A man ran toward him through the smoke. His hair smoldered and the right half of his face burned. Magnus remembered the familiar, nauseating smell; he steeled his spine against it and refused to recoil.

The man fell to his knees, lips pulled back as he clutched at Magnus's waistcoat. "Help me!"

Magnus shrugged off his coat and flung it over the man's head, smothering the flames. The man crumpled to the street, sobbing his gratitude. He let the coat fall to the cobblestone, tendrils of smoke curling from his scalp.

Magnus hauled him back up. "Grab a weapon and help others get to the forest if you can."

The man nodded dutifully. "Yes, *Amaa.*"

His injuries would make fighting difficult, but he stumbled into the hazy gloom without complaint. Magnus returned to the road ahead. He brandished his sword and stalked toward the glow of mage sigils, bristling with purpose. It was not long before the remnants of his troop joined him, dressed in leathers and ready for battle. Rylan and Jessie flanked him. Sam took point at Magnus's right hand.

Her eyes flashed with rage. "Orders, *Amaa*?"

Sam was not an arcanist. There was little she could do against a line of sorcerers, but she was a capable fighter. She would be invaluable to the villagers.

"Find Kendi." Magnus looked aside to her. "Clear a path out of the village. The eastern edge, if possible. Save as many as you can."

She nodded once. "Yes, *Amaa*."

As she dashed off into the smoke, Magnus glanced over his shoulder. Rylan and Jessie stared back at him, unblinking.

"What would you have of us, *Amaa*?" Jessie asked.

Kill them.

The voice was a caress of cool air against his neck. Magnus narrowed his eyes. The Guild had them vastly outnumbered, even with the lines of other arcanists forming up behind him.

As averse to violence as Cheralach had been before his death, even he had understood it was sometimes necessary. He would not have hesitated in defending a town full of innocents.

Magnus didn't either. He raised his voice, despite the stabbing pain in his throat, to be heard by all the men and women who followed him to their deaths. "The sorcerers threaten your people. The Alliaansi fight with you. Defend your village!"

War cries rose in a thunderous cacophony. Arcanists screamed, pumping their fists. Villagers willing to defend their town thrust rakes, spades, and forks into the sky. Most followed in Magnus's wake, but others sprinted ahead, eager to die for their families. Remorse pulled at his heart as the first wave of villagers dropped beneath a hail of fireballs and static spheres. Smoke and the sounds of the dying filled the air.

It was just as Kendi had feared. The fall of the School had provoked them.

The Guild had just declared war.

Smoke choked the still, northern air. Warmth still lingered in piles of wood, and ash settled over the cobbled street like a funeral shroud. Char marks blackened once pristine stone walls, and bodies lay at awkward angles all over the town square.

Crabby's bird didn't follow them into the town. Typical. That bastard Paelic had followed them for weeks as they made their way north, dodging Light Paladins and skirting around patrols of mages. Alar had kept thinking Crabby might make an appearance or offer them aid, but she never had.

Some goddess of nature she'd turned out to be.

His boots scuffed trails into the blanket of ash. He waded through the wreckage, memorizing every face. Here, a man with half his hair burned away. There, a pair of villagers, their genders indiscernible, still clutching shovels beside a door to a home that had been smashed in. Near a wagon, a woman with sunken eyes and hollow cheeks stared unblinking into the sky, a spell burn blackening her chest. Not even the flies dared brave the smoke. Not yet. Each face wore its last moments of terror or pain, frozen forever in death.

Hatred darkened Alar's vision. Fawn's Breath had been a peaceful town. A neutral town. A waypoint for refugees and a haven for families of every race. The Guild had killed them all indiscriminately, butchering some in their own homes.

He turned back to his companions. "Where are your gods now, Ravlok?"

The monk winced. The pain on his bearded face might have softened Alar's rage, if not for the next words that came out of his mouth. "Suffering and healing must exist in balance." He lowered his gaze. "Laangor's methods are not well-understood."

Alar's laughter soured in his mouth. His tongue tasted of ash. "You blame the god of suffering for this? I'll tell you who I blame." He searched the ground and dragged his boot over the shape of a fallen sword. Its hilt bore the Guild crest in gold filigree. He bent to pick it up and tossed it to him. Ravlok caught it, his expression numb.

Jack surveyed the town with deadly calm. He fingered the trigger of his crossbow, right eye twitching. "What now?"

They had been instructed to bring Daeya to Fawn's Breath to await the council's approval of her presence in Starlight. With the town destroyed and the forest crawling with mages, Alar didn't plan to stay here any longer than he had to. He turned his face up toward the rising sun. Its weak light barely sliced through the haze.

Any survivors would likely go north toward Kuma'Kiir or east toward Starlight Plateau. Though Kuma'Kiir was closer, Starlight bore the strongest fortifications of any Alliaansi town, and it was the seat of the Alliaansi council.

"We will go to Starlight," Alar said.

He would have to deliver news to Val's wife sooner or later. His heart ached at the possibility of losing Orowen and Kendi too, but he forced the hurt down. There was no time for that.

He returned his attention to Daeya. She'd been quiet ever since they'd spotted the smoke drifting over the mountains. The sorceress stood apart from them, staring down at a pair of corpses. Both were Syljian—a woman and child, who had died cowering in each other's arms. Their bodies were blackened by spell burns.

Alar could have gloated. He could have pointed out how Fawn's Breath should have never been a target—that by attacking the neutral town, the Guild had broken its own creed. He could have told her how misguided she had been, or how evil her Guild was to have done this, but he didn't have to.

She already knew.

"Daeya."

She turned her head. Tears carved pale streaks through the grime on her face. Her fingers curled into white-knuckled fists that flickered with odd golden light.

Alar reached up to remove the layers of assassin's clay and tape from the sides of his head. The pieces of his human disguise fell to the ash-littered street. His tapered ears unfurled from beneath his hair, and cold nipped at his freshly exposed ear tips. He shook his head to drive the lingering ache from them as they settled into their proper position. Daeya watched his every move, her gaze unwavering as he stepped toward her and offered his hand.

"Are you with us?"

Daeya studied his palm for a long moment. Then she reached for him. Her fingers closed around his. A spark shot through him as their eyes met. The force of it took his breath away.

Rage boiled over behind her steady gaze.

"Yes. I'm with you."

Epilogue

Gregory

Gregory's jaw feathered as Normos writhed on the floor of the command tent. The spell tore through the young sorcerer's body, leaving no visible marks, but still provoking pain.

"Mercy, Councilor," Normos whimpered. He clutched his stomach and curled tighter into his shame, his freshly mended nose and pale left cheek turning into the dirt to hide unbidden tears. "Please, I beg you."

Gregory took a sip of his wine, letting the taste of the fine Aivenosian vintage roll across his tongue. "Your interference has cost me dearly, Sorcerer."

Chest heaving, Normos struggled to speak. "She is a traitor. I was only doing as Guild law demands."

The Councilor frowned. That incessant nerve in his jaw seized. "You dare to lecture me on Guild law?" One finger lifted from his glass, prompting another surge of agony that left Normos fighting for air. "You would do well to remember your place."

Finally, Gregory made a sharp gesture with the blade of his hand. The spell ended. Normos sagged into a puddle of limbs, his silk-lined robe caked with dirt.

Such filth was unbecoming of his jealous young protégé. Gregory clicked his tongue. "Get up."

Ever obedient, Normos dragged himself to his feet in a slow, faltering progression of afflicted expressions and stifled groans. While the sorcerer composed himself, Gregory studied the map on the table between them.

Each blanker city was marked by a wooden figurine—a rendering of the city's last known governor. Aon'In's figurehead was a carved likeness of Koraani Alliaar, the Alliaansi founder. The traitorous Cintoshi Serreth Blackburr led the growing town of Willowmarsh, and Starlight's figurehead was fashioned after the late Cheralach Bevausecc. Once he confirmed his suspicions about the new governor on the Plateau, Gregory would have a new figurine made.

Smaller villages were marked by approximation with piccara chips—fools, of course—and the terrain surrounding them was painted in swatches of blue, brown, and green. He turned the fool beside Fawn's Breath over and advanced the monarch denoting his Guild forces toward the neighboring town of Wolf's Bite, or Kuma'Kiir, as the blankers called it.

Outside his tent, Councilor Tressa Blake barked orders at her senior acolytes in that obnoxiously nasal soprano. She would come barging in at any moment to defend herself from voting on the moronic move that had given Normos his opening. Daeya McVen should never have been granted the rank of mage so soon, much less permitted out of his sight. He would be remiss to ever allow the Council to make such a calamitous decision again.

Truth be told, he couldn't fault the boy. Normos's resourcefulness and ambition were admirable. Gregory had fostered both qualities throughout his life—at least, insofar as it shaped him to be the dutiful servant he was. But the boy's jealousy had caused the greatest weapon the Guild possessed to fall astray, and now it would take scrupulous maneuvering to reclaim her.

Normos cleared his throat and straightened, at last regaining some manner of poise. "Shall I go after her? She may be warded, but I'm certain I can find her."

Ambitious, indeed. Their attempts at scrying both his pupil and the blanker spy had failed, and not even the insufferable Mardis Ulrich could track a person through a ward.

"Absolutely not. You have disgraced yourself enough."

Normos flinched and lowered his gaze. He knew better than to let his shoulders hunch, but his clasped hands tightened as if to throttle an unspoken argument.

Apparently, both of Gregory's prized students were feeling rebellious lately. Like tracking hounds given too much lead, they were bound to entangle themselves, trip over their own feet, and lose sight of their purpose. Perhaps it was time this one was reminded who held his leash.

"If you wish to redeem your usefulness, I have another task for you."

The young man's voice broke in his eagerness. "Anything. My will is yours, Councilor."

Much better.

Gregory reached for a carved wooden soldier chip. "Sarikkian has sent Gwen Mar-Pol to see to our saphyrum stores in Ferid. I suspect she will attempt to undermine our war effort and make a plea for the healers again." He hovered the piccara piece over the Healer's City and the seat of his late wife's estate. "You will secure the mine and its stores. Take over the city if you must, but above all," he shoved Mar-Pol's carved likeness aside and set the soldier down next to it, "muzzle Sarikkian's rabid dog by any means necessary."

Normos bowed his head. "It will be done, Councilor."

Gregory waved his hand. "Take Joss and Toby with you."

Anger once more rippled across fine pale features, but the fight left him. "Your will."

A rasp of heavy cloth and a muttered greeting signaled the entry of Councilor Blake. Normos exited with a swish of his robe and a respectful nod to the sharp-eyed woman. Gregory returned to his wine.

Tressa huffed a breath, watching the sorcerer depart. "I'm surprised you let him off so easily."

"This is as much your fault as it is his." Draining the rest of the vintage into his glass, he set the bottle aside with a force that made Tressa wince.

Deep wrinkles mapped the powdered planes of her face. A full head shorter than he but with a temper to match, Tressa Blake was loud, outspoken, and as equally aggrieved by the blankers as he was. Gregory appreciated her shrewdness and confidence, but she had about as much social grace as a rotten tomato.

She put a crimson-nailed hand on her hip. "You couldn't keep her in Ryost any longer, Lucius."

Embers of rage seared his nerves. "A routine mission to bring in a meddlesome charlatan should not have ended in an incinerated port and charges of execution. I told you she was not ready. And to have her powers awaken away from my influence—"

"It provided the undue stress you failed to manufacture back at home," Tressa broke in. "Besides, the others were starting to notice things. It was only a matter of time before they came snooping around. Sarikkian was already asking questions."

He scowled. "This is the last time that fool and his entourage force my hand. I will see them all removed from Council for this."

"Now that, I'd like to see." She folded her arms and examined the troop placements on the map. "So, what do we do about the girl?"

Gregory sipped his wine as he considered her question. Aethersight would continue to fail to reveal Daeya's location until the ward wore off. It was best to avoid triggering certain runes until he found Draeconis and established her dragonbond. A threat to her father could suffice, but only if word reached her. That would drive the wedge further between them and possibly adhere her to the blanker boy in earnest.

Tressa lifted an eyebrow. "Well?"

Gregory tapped the side of his glass with his index finger.

"Send for Cameron Vika."

Acknowledgements

So many people have helped me make this book a reality. Foremost among them is my partner-in-crime, Tim, who entertains so many of my crazy ideas and politely ignores when he catches me talking to my characters in the mirror. Love you, babe.

Dessos wouldn't exist without my D&D crew: Matteo, Charlie, Trevor, Brian, Liz, and Tim. No amount of thanks are enough for breaking me out of my shell and encouraging me to do something I feared.

Big thanks to all the beta readers who offered feedback, and a special thanks to my critique partners: Alicia Leatherdale, E. Rosemary, M.J. Lindsey, Sarah Emmer, and Tia Cantrell. Support from these ladies has been life-altering. If you need another great book to read, they're all amazing authors in their own right, so be sure to look them up.

Thanks to Emma O'Connell, Ellie Owen, and Erynn Snel for helping me polish off all the toddler smudges.

And finally, thank *you* for giving this newbie author a chance.

If I could ask one (okay, two) thing(s) of you, pretty please leave a review, no matter how brief. Reviews are the lifeblood of indie authors, and our success depends on them. Also, please consider contacting your local library to ask if they'll stock my book to share with others. It's just a few minutes of your time that would mean everything to me.

I hope you'll join me for the sequel, *Embers Rising,* coming in 2025!

Pantheon Guide

Saolanni, Greater Goddess of Life

Mira, lesser goddess of creation and birth
Shavaan, lesser goddess of healing
Caelyn, lesser goddess of nature

Ordeolas, Greater God of Order

Silonas, lesser god of fortune and trade
Tiior, lesser goddess of wisdom and knowledge
Delvin, lesser god of law and justice

Baosanni, Greater God of Death

Laangor, lesser god of suffering
Yasuo, Gatekeeper, lesser god of the afterlife
Anordis, lesser god of chaos

Translations

Ancient Draconic (Draegionic)

draegion (DRAY-jee-on): the original inhabitants of Dessos, once bonded to dragons in an effort by the Greater Gods to preserve draegionic magic in exchange for world dominion. Now believed to be dragon riders or tamers in some cultures.
Nashanett (NAH--shan-ETT): (feminine) leader, mistress
Saonivhatt (say-ON-i-VAHT): (feminine) goddess
vhash (VAHSH): no
vheth (VETH): yes
zhev annivhosh (zev ON-i-VOSH): thank you

Brogrenti

aeyak (eye-YAK): a skirt-like garment comprised of overlapping panels of richly dyed linen
braugh (BRAW): strong, strapping
breigh (BRAI): pretty, beautiful
kinnich (KEN-ich): (slang) know
napher gought (NAFF-er GOUT): (derogatory) boil-faced sow
taenach (tie-NACH): a headdress made to cover the neck, head, and face

Syljian

aaken (AH-ken): to know
ama're (AH-ma-re): beloved
Amaa (ah-MAH): (universal) leader, teacher, master
amaare (ah-MAR-eh): to love
aon (ay-OWN): no
caezo (KAY-zoh): (derogatory) feces
ciir (SEER): yes
enniia (en-NEE-uh): daughter
iithe (EE-thay): to eat
nei (NIE): I, my
ros (ROSS) : we, our
ru (ROO): little
ruh (ROO): a suffix added to verbs to express the imperative mood (e.g. give commands)
taapad tiik (TAHP-ad TEEK): thank you

Pronunciations

Aivenos: (AY-ven-os)
Alar: (ah-LAR)
Anwic: (ON-wick)
Baokryn: (BAY-oh-krin)
Baosanni: (BAY-oh-SAW-nee)
Caelyn: (KAY-lin)
Cheralach: (SHER-uh-LACK)
Daeya: (DIE-ya)
Eidosinia: (EYE-doh-SIN-ee-uh)
Keilliad: (KIE-lee-ad)
Laerin: (LIE-rin)
Mardis Ulrich: (MAR-diss YEWL-rick)
Nerimoria: (NER-i-MOR-ee-uh)
Ordeolas: (or-DAY-o-lus)
Orowen: (OR-oh-wen)
Orthovia: (or-THO-vee-uh)
Paelic: (PAY-lick)
Ravlok: (RAV-lock)
Ryost: (RIE-ost)
Saolanni: (SAY-oh-LAW-nee)
Tiior: (tee-OR)
Valaxes "Val": (val-AX-iss)
Varkendios "Kendi": (var-KEN-di-os)
Vortanis: (vor-TAN-iss)

About the Author

Cindy L. Sell supposedly lives in the Midwestern United States with a home full of furry critters, including her two boys and doting husband, but she really spends most of her time on Dessos battling sorcerers or negotiating trade deals with pirates.

She graduated from Washburn University with a creative writing degree, but didn't bother to do anything with it until COVID when she ran out of excuses. When she's not writing, she enjoys bowling, crochet, and riding her '82 Sportster.

Look for Cindy on Facebook, say hi on Instagram, and visit her website for upcoming events and shenanigans.

Books by Cindy L. Sell

The Last Draegion Saga

Remnants of a Scarlet Flame: September 2024
Embers Rising: Coming 2025
Aether and Ash: Projected 2026
Tides of Immolation: Projected 2027

Tales from Dessos

Tipori: Coming 2025